"THERE ARE TWO THINGS A MAN WILL WAIT FOR FOREVER," HE SAID. "LOVE—AND REVENGE."

Suddenly she was in his arms, molded hard against his body, his dark eyes reaching deep to draw her very soul toward him before his mouth covered hers in a burning kiss.

She didn't expect it, not this compelling passion, this primitive, subterranean whirlpool of emotion that drowned her. Overwhelmed, she fell against him, yielding to the caress that explored and devoured her with consuming ferocity.

Juliette's mind reeled. She must get away, and yet it was impossible. Every inch of her was awakened, tingling with inescapable delight. . . .

"*Desert Hostage* . . . is a magnificent read, with the passion and sweep that true romantics will love."   —Vanessa Royall, author of
Firebrand's Woman

"*Desert Hostage* is one of the most beautifully sensuous novels I've ever read. The descriptions were so vivid I felt as though I could see those hot desert sands. And the love story . . . was so thrilling I could barely wait to turn the pages."
—Barbara Faith, author of
The Sun Dancers

"Diane Dunaway has creative talent—there's no doubt about it. A lusty novel in the tradition of E. M. Hull's *The Sheik*."
—LaVyrle Spencer, author of
The Endearment

DESERT
HOSTAGE

Diane Dunaway

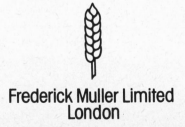

Frederick Muller Limited
London

First published in Great Britain in 1983 by
Frederick Muller Limited, Dataday House,
Alexandra Road, London SW19 7JZ

Published in the USA
by Dell Publishing Co. Inc. 1982

ISBN 0-584-31166-4

Printed by Mohndruck
Graphische Betriebe GmbH, Gütersloh, West Germany

DESERT
HOSTAGE

*To Jonathan, of course, for the inspiration
of his love.*

PART I

ANNA AND THE SHEIK

THE SAHARA—1863

Chapter 1

Every soul is the hostage of its own deeds.
—The Koran

Was it a kiss?

Anna held her breath as the quickened pace of her heart broke the silence of the desert night. Was it a kiss that had awakened her?

Slowly she raised a hand so her white fingers traced the delicate line of her mouth. No, it wasn't a kiss, she told herself. Brandon had gone hours ago to check the men. It must have been something else—a noise perhaps that startled her. Then straining her ears she listened to every sound.

"Allahu akbar," it came again. Yes, that was it—the shouting of voices—and yes, unmistakably the dull thudding of horses approaching at a gallop.

Instantly Anna was upright, thrusting her legs over the edge of her cot and running to the tent flap.

Outside there were Arabs—a pack of them all charging into the circle of tents, reining foaming mounts with one hand and firing rifles with the other. *"Allahu akbar! Allahu akbar!"*

All around, soldiers burst from tents, hauling on their pants and shooting back at the black-robed men who already had tossed torches against the tents and were stampeding their horses.

Her eyes expanding, Anna touched her throat as a scream formed and pressed against the tightening passage. No, it was impossible. She must be dreaming. And where was Brandon?

More gunfire streaked the night sky orange as twenty Arabs rode thundering down the center of camp firing at the half-dressed Englishmen who reloaded, fired, and retreated ever closer to where Anna stood.

One by one the soldiers gripped their bodies, wrenched,

and fell into the sand. Then the dozen remaining were forced tumbling into Anna's tent as they wielded their empty rifles like clubs against the pursuing Arabs who came on with raised daggers.

Stumbling to the back of the tent, Anna stood paralyzed, the blood drained from her face. The canvas surrounding her jerked and tossed and a lantern hanging from the center pole swung back and up and down, flying off its hook and crashing against the tent sides before bursting into flame.

Then suddenly Lieutenant Williams was beside her, the black powder and blood splatters on his face making him seem like a stranger, his eyes those of a man finding himself awakened in Hell.

"Madam . . . Madam Phillips," he said. "They must not take you alive, madam. You would . . . they would. . . ." He raised his pistol to her head. "It is my last bullet, madam."

Anna stared at the soldier, hardly able to credit his words, yet realizing numbly she was about to die. "Brandon?" she heard herself ask as if from a great distance.

"Dead, madam."

The word "dead" echoed inside her, *dead, dead, dead*, and she felt only a strange hollowness. She nodded then. Yes, she would die, they would all die. Did it matter? Everything was impossible, the blood, the screams. Only yesterday Brandon had said there were no hostile tribes within a hundred miles. Was it really just a nightmare? Would she wake up when he pulled the trigger and find herself alone in the tent? But automatically she began, "Hail Mary full of grace, the Lord is with thee. . . ."

The cold metal of the pistol pressed tight against her temple, and somewhere in her mind Anna heard Brandon's voice saying again, "My little Anna, my one true love. Now only death can part us."

Eyes squeezed shut, she held her breath, lips moving fervently. "Holy Mary, mother of God, pray for our sins now. . . ."

There was an explosion. Anna gasped and waited for

death, but terror mingled with relief as she opened her eyes and found herself alive, her ears ringing.

All around, soldiers lay dead and, beside her still, Lieutenant Williams was looking incredulously at his own hand that once had held the gun and now was only a gory stump. Then the lieutenant was knocked to his knees.

For an instant he was dangled by his hair entwined in an Arab's brown fist.

The Warrior's sword flashed and Lieutenant Williams's body crumbled to the floor while his head remained in the warrior's fist.

Anna looked down at what had been a man, hardly aware of her own scream as it released from her throat and was lost in the din.

Panting, she looked up as the tall black-robed Arab perfunctorily tossed the head aside and came to stand hovering so close her vision was filled by his swarthy hawk-nosed face. His curious black eyes seemed to see all of her in a quick appraising glance and his lips drew open in a grin of hard white teeth.

Sheathing his sword, he removed his black burnoose, wrapping her numb limbs swiftly in the rough material. Then abruptly, she was over his shoulder, her head draping down his back as he carried her from the tent.

Outside there was no more gunfire. Smoke stung her eyes and, daring to lift her head, Anna saw the camp was ablaze, the sky and sand reflecting the glowing orange that silhouetted the dark shapes of mounted warriors laden with boots and food and stolen rifles.

The Arab carried her a short distance before she was flung high across a saddle. He mounted behind her in a springing leap and, raising his sword overhead, held it there and shouted, *"Allah! Allahu akbar!"*

His horse plunged forward, throwing her hard against his chest, where an unyielding arm encircled her. Then with the horse's flying mane whipping her face, Anna felt herself swept away through the fire and smoke and enveloping darkness.

Chapter 2

Voices—voices all around. Chanting Arab voices, faces, shapes undulating beyond grayed mists, dimly, like those seen through a distant window. There was a French voice from far away then calling "Mademoiselle, mademoiselle."

Anna rolled her head against softness, trying to speak. But her mouth refused to form the questions that vaguely shaped and surfaced in her reeling mind before floating out of reach.

Twisting, turning, her limbs felt weighted by stones and, because it was too hard to open her eyes, Anna never saw the women of Hamid al-Sharif standing around her divan, watching her with dark curious eyes.

So, *this* was the mysterious white girl who only the day before had been brought to the harem in the master's own arms, they whispered among themselves. She was the palest, slenderest girl they had ever seen, all the color of her skin seeming drawn off by her blazing hair that tumbled around her and onto the carpets in colors of the sun when it glowed on the horizon red and gold and red again. Never had they seen one so rare. Not even the creamy-skinned Berber beauties possessed hair so glorious, and never before had white soldiers dared thrust themselves so far into this land of Mohammed. But seven days before when their presence was discovered and reported to the master, the women of the harem themselves had heard the tribesmen gather before the palace gates and beg the sheik to rid the desert of these infidels.

"They destroy the water holes," complained several tribesmen who had been forced to ride two days without water.

"And their horses eat what little grass there is for our herds," others joined in angrily.

The sheik stroked his smooth chin, leaning down to the imam at his right, and listening most seriously to this holy man who added, "And they believe in three gods, a father, a son, and a ghost, when the prophet Mohammed has said there is only one single god and that is Allah!"

And so it was that, for the greater glory of Allah, the sheik Hamid al-Sharif, fresh from his recent victory over his cousin Yassan Hussar, immediately led a hundred warriors galloping north. But when days later he returned, he brought with him not only rifles and horses, but also this girl more beautiful and more ephemeral than the dawn.

As they stood over her now none of the women could resist glancing at Salsabil, the present favorite, to see her reaction to this white girl's unusual charms. But if they hoped to read the thoughts of the Moorish girl, they were disappointed. The black depths of Salsabil's eyes revealed neither hostility nor surprise and would have seemed disinterested had the women not known better.

Salsabil had been given to the master by her father, the leader of the Ben Sadre tribe to the south. Since that day the entire Ben Sadre tribe had prayed for the girl to conceive the first son of Hamid al-Sharif, thus guaranteeing their recent alliance with this most powerful bedouin lord in all the Sahara.

It was an ambition eagerly shared by Salsabil and, fortunately for her, this white angel who had seemed destined to replace her in the affections of the master now grew paler and paler as she thrashed arms and legs as if in bad dreams, crying out in a strange language only the head eunuch, Omar Zatan, could understand. And even as the eunuch gave her every attention and ladled potions down her throat, the girl's beautiful face still grew more transparent and closer to death until finally the women shrugged fatalistically.

"In sha'Allah," one said. "All is in the hands of Allah."

"By morning it will be over," another whispered.

Then drawing away and salaaming politely to the head eunuch, they returned to the common room of the harem to loll and drink coffee, and to entertain themselves with gossip and speculations.

Hours passed then while Anna hung near death but refused to die, and it was near midnight when the report came, surprising everyone and spreading in whispers, first

among the servants, and then among the women themselves.

Omar Zatan had performed a magical cure, it was said.
With the aid of Allah the girl's fever had passed and she
would live.

Opening her eyes, Anna saw first a blurring blue expanse that slowly focused into a high-domed ceiling inlaid
with dark blue mosaic tiles. She drew a breath inward,
finding the air sweet with the scent of baking pastries, an
aroma that reminded her of the convent kitchens at St.
Genevieve's. From somewhere came the soft haunting
notes of a reed flute, and in the distance came the sound of
water tinkling as if from a small fountain.

She blinked heavily. There was no violence here, and no
sign of the ghoulish Arab warrior who had captured her
sometime before—or had she been captured? It all seemed
like a nightmare now. Could it be that she was dead, and
this heaven? But Anna discarded this notion immediately
as, feeling a sudden breeze, she turned her head and saw a
man, as black and shiny as black jade, standing at the side
of her divan and fanning her with a spray of ostrich feathers.

She rolled her head against the pillows, noticing his face
and bare chest were smooth and hairless, and that his white
pants were full cut down the legs and gathered tight at
midcalf. Coming more awake, she was apparently so preoccupied studying this strange sight that she didn't notice
the approach of a second man until his face was hovering
over her. He was as black and smooth-skinned as the first,
though his jowls were full and sagged like an old woman's
so he seemed both like a man and a woman, and it was
when, unexpectedly, he arched his hairless eyebrows and
spoke in French that Anna was startled out of her stupor.

"You wish a bath, mademoiselle? You are hungry perhaps? It is many days since you are sick."

His eyes were so dark even the whites held a yellowish
tinge, and reaching out a large pudgy hand, he touched her
forehead with the familiarity of having touched her a thousand times.

She swallowed dryly as he continued. "You have no fever. For days you talk crazy. But all that is over now. You
are safe and not to worry."

The fear tightening Anna's stomach began to subside.
She had been sick with fever? Of course! There had been
no attack! It all *had* been only a nightmare, or maybe a
delirious fever. But now she was safe, and Brandon must
be alive!

Relief spread through her stomach and chest and into
her face, so it brightened as the man-woman leaned closer,
his small eyes sparkling with question. "Mademoiselle
speaks French?" he inquired.

Finding her voice then Anna said, *"Oui. Si'l vous plaît.*
I would like something. I feel terribly hungry."

Omar Zatan smiled, not in deference as Anna assumed,
but rather at the unexpected beauty of this girl's melodious
voice. How it would please the master! He clapped his
hands in two brisk sounds to bring servants hurrying.

In minutes, Anna found herself served braised lamb on
skewers, a roasted squab stuffed with rice, and date-filled
pastries spiced with cinnamon that were still warm from
the oven.

Her senses responded ravenously, and though silverware
was not provided, it didn't stop Anna from sampling the
feast and finally eating her fill of what seemed ambrosia
after the simple camp fare. Then when she finally pushed
the plates away and rested back against the cushions, coffee was served, sweet, thick, and boiling hot, in a small
porcelain cup with a geometric design in the glazed surface.

The distinctive aroma of this Arabian brew reminded
Anna of the mornings she had spent with Brandon drinking coffee served just this way by Arab servants. Remembering this now made her wonder again where he was and
when he would come to visit her.

Weakly she lifted a hand to her forehead. How many
days had she lain here? And what trouble she must have
caused, especially after vowing faithfully she would be no
trouble at all.

A servant girl approached, bowing deeply and taking the

coffee tray away as, from beyond the room's arched windows, a bird trilled *pha-La-la, pha-La-la,* over and over. The air was warm, and the stir of fans wafted the floral fragrance of incense past her nose. Blinking against the brightness, Anna noted the sun slowly rising higher, its golden rays illuminating the intricately patterned floor tiles into a kaleidoscope of polished jewels.

Another girl tiptoeing noiselessly on bare feet pulled several filmy layers of drapery closed across the arched windows, shutting out the light and warmth and, looking up at the black man fanning her, Anna stifled a yawn to ask, "Do you know where Captain Phillips is?" But the ebony giant only shook his turbaned head to indicate he didn't understand, while continuing the sweeping movement of the feather fan.

Sighing, Anna turned on her side, aware of the soft comfortableness of the cushions, so different from the hard traveling cot to which she had grown accustomed. Now where was that other fellow? she asked herself, the one who spoke such surprisingly good French. If he were here, he would know about Brandon.

But the black man-woman didn't appear. The sun grew warmer and her full stomach digested contentedly as the mellow tones of a flute surrounded her and echoed in the dome above. She yawned again, feeling suddenly fatigued, her eyelids growing heavy and finally blinking closed.

Only later would she realize she had been drugged. Drugs were common in the city of El Abadan—drugs to awaken, drugs to sleep, aphrodisiacs for sensual delight, and poisons that killed without a trace. But Anna Phillips knew none of this, and only snuggled deeper into the silk pillows and peacefully slept.

Chapter 3

That night Anna dreamed of Brandon, and the next morning awakened with his name on her lips. "Brandon," she whispered with the same devotion as she said her rosaries.

How she adored him, her knight, her hero. And what would have become of her in that cloistered convent into which her loving, but strict, parents had sent her had he not come to the rescue?

Always Anna had considered herself an obedient daughter but her enrollment in St. Genevieve's had come on the heels of a particularly difficult year, one in which her body had undergone a strange and rapid metamorphosis that brought curves where she never had them before, and a series of crying spells. It was a strange and confusing time when it seemed she had changed into someone else who other people now called "lovely," instead of just "pretty," and who held the eyes of gentlemen as never before. But in spite of her protests, and more crying spells that only made her mother nod with a wan smile, she had been sent to the nunnery never dreaming what the future held.

Being an officer in the army of Queen Victoria, Brandon Phillips was an unlikely visitor to the out-of-the-way French convent. And it was even more unlikely that Anna should have met him, since usually the girls were never allowed to see any of the infrequent callers. But it so happened that Sister Cynthia, a senior nun at the convent, had a nephew who had died while serving under Captain Phillips, and he had come to pay his respects on the very day the gatekeeper had taken ill. So when the bell rang, Anna, being nearby, heard it and went to answer.

Later, Anna often thought of that first instant when she saw him, tall, broad-shouldered, hat in hand, his dark eyes looking into hers with gentleness and pleasant surprise.

At once Anna felt herself attracted by a subtle yet compelling force. His manners were flawless, his French accent impeccable, and a warmth emitted from him that touched her even across the narrow path as silently she unlatched the gate and swung it open.

Her face was suddenly hot, and she could barely stammer a *"Oui"* to his request to see Sister Cynthia. He smiled then, a knowing, admiring smile that sent an unfamiliar sensation rushing down her spine. Then, feeling more self-conscious and acutely female than ever before, Anna turned abruptly and guided the way to the visitor's room.

Anna knew then, even before leaving him with the sister, that she would somehow meet the dark stranger again. And months later, during the convent's choir concert in Chartres, she spotted him in the second row, gazing up at her with such a wonderful light in his concentrating black eyes that her heart soared and she could barely remember the words to the music.

"Sinful! Sinful!" a voice inside her kept repeating as, backstage after the performance, Anna struggled with unsteady fingers to tie the bow of her apron so she could join the other girls in serving refreshments to the guests. All males were so thoroughly forbidden. From the curious glances of her classmates, she knew they must have noticed something. But when she entered the large room thronging with people, and Brandon Phillips came to her side, she felt like a child that had spun round and round until the world whirled dizzily in circles and nothing else mattered.

He seemed taller now that he was so close and, unexpectedly, he took her cold hands with firmness that made her shiver as his black eyes searched her face before looking intensely into her blue ones gazing shyly upward.

"Anna," he said, his strong mouth forming the words as she watched. "Come with me now. Be my wife."

That very night they were hastily married by an old priest in a chapel under a canopy of elms. It was a brief ceremony though Anna couldn't concentrate on the words. She wondered if she was dreaming as Brandon slipped a ring on her finger—a solitaire ruby ring, heart-shaped in cut. Then, just before kissing her with infinite gentleness, his deep voice whispered in her ear, "Beloved."

They honeymooned under a rainbow of rapture, and Anna could easily recall the long lazy days and too short nights that took them through the French and, later, the warmer Spanish countryside.

It was endless, a treasured time of awakening, a time of soft words and caresses when Anna discovered just what it meant to become a woman—to be kissed over every inch of her body, to be filled with ecstasy that grew with every touch, and to feel the world explode in a consuming pas-

sion that whirled her heavenward as the prayers at St.
Genevieve's never had.

So the days and nights blended together in a latticework
of love and happiness such as Anna never imagined could
be. And as they rode, or walked, or nestled together in bed,
they shared stories of their past lives and wondered at the
miracle of their meeting that first magical day.

It seemed then as if it would never end. There were moments when Anna's eyes filled with tears from the kind of
special joy that comes when one is aware of perfect happiness at the moment of experiencing it—the kind of joy that
always, however beautiful, is shadowed by a sense of fore-
boding. Then one morning it seemed to Anna that this impending doom had fulfilled itself when Brandon informed
her he had only a short time of "leave" remaining—"Only
three weeks," he said. "Then I'll be departing for duty into
the Sahara."

"Three weeks," Anna repeated, realizing she was to be
alone again and "tucked away in a Spanish cottage," as
Brandon put it, waiting for his return.

"But I've been 'tucked away' all my life until now," she
protested, reaching to encircle his neck with slender arms
and stroking the small diamond-shaped birth mark behind
his ear with gentle imploring strokes. "I can't bear it any
more. You *must* take me with you!"

At first Brandon was firm. "It would be impossible," he
said, shaking his head. "Much too risky. We'll be riding
through unmapped territory—no place for a woman."

His tone was final. But Anna's new-found love gave her
courage to beg. So as the days passed, bringing the time of
departure frighteningly close, Anna risked his anger by
bringing up the subject again and again, and entreating
him with growing desperation.

"But please, Brandon. Don't shut me away when I
have only begun to live." Her fingers clung to the front of
his shirt. "I want nothing but to be with you. I'll do anything—carry water—groom your horse—anything! I won't
be any trouble. I swear! Only please don't leave me!"

Moved by her outburst, worn down by her pleas and by

his own growing love for his child-bride, Brandon looked down at her tear-streaked cheeks, her perfect mouth, her wide entreating eyes. Then with the warmth in his heart extending to his loins, he imagined her beside him during the long desert nights. Would it do any harm to let her go? he asked himself. The recent expeditions into that area had met with no more resistance than an occasional horned viper. It was considered a safer than ordinary assignment, though there was always the possibility of trouble. The region was filled with people whose customs were still strange to civilized ways. But he could get permission through connections at headquarters, he told himself. The old man owed him a favor or two. Precautions could be taken, and if he were careful. . . .

So, just when Anna thought she had failed, Brandon miraculously consented, raining kisses on her face when she threw herself into his arms. Then three weeks later, at the head of fifty men and scores of horses and camels and servants, they rode out from Tripoli into the Sahara.

The journey had been almost dreamlike in its pleasantness until this, Anna thought. And now, propping herself up on one elbow, she tried to remember just what had happened right before the nightmare began.

Clearly she recalled that night when they had camped beside one of the series of muddy, brackish, and almost empty wells that the natives referred to as *mughawwiyat*. She remembered eating dinner, and that four of Brandon's officers had sat around the portable camp table with them entertaining her with tales about the desert. Maybe then it was something in the highly spiced lamb prepared by the Arab cook that made her ill, or something in the water, since everything afterward seemed a blur.

If only Brandon would come and clear up the mystery, she thought glancing down to the heart-shaped ruby ring sparkling fire on her left hand. Then slipping it off, as she had many times, she read again the inscription on the underside of the stone that said simply, *Beloved*.

Certainly he should have come to her by now, she told herself sitting up with sudden resolve. Then swinging her legs out of bed she squared her jaw. If Brandon wouldn't come to her, then she would go to him. But today she was going to find out *what* was going on.

Chapter 4

Hurrying along the palace corridors, Omar Zatan glanced down through arched windows to the tangle of El Abadan's streets that twisted like ancient cypress branches among mud-brick walls, date-laden palms, and towering minarets. From the large royal courtyard directly below he could hear the excited voices of the crowd gathering there, and also the moans of the victims rising together like that of a single wounded beast. But to this Omar gave little attention other than to curse that he was late and the executions were ready to begin. Instead, he was most concerned by the disappearance of the white girl whom he had intended to present to the sheik tonight as the final glory in his day of triumph over his enemy Hussar.

Where was she? Hadn't he left orders she was to be watched? But only a moment ago he had found her room vacant, and now emitting a groan directly from the bottom of his rounded belly, Omar Zatan rolled his eyes heavenward. By Allah! If she had tried to escape the penalty was sure—a slow painful death by torture would be her fate, and nothing, not even her beauty, could save her.

Immediately Omar Zatan hurried on, puffing up the palace steps to the top floor, his white robes outlining his squat body as finally he turned the corner into the harem's large common room. Then leaning against a pillar to pant, he felt a sweep of relief as he saw the white girl with the others, curiously following them to the windows where they, too, would view the executions. Allah be praised she was taking an interest at last, the eunuch breathed with a twinkle coming into his yellowish eyes. But what woman could resist the sight of blood?

In her search for Brandon, feeling for the first time a prisoner, Anna had wandered down a long hallway which terminated in a wide luxurious room. Along one side of it the sun flowed in through arched windows and across the rest were scattered richly patterned carpets, low couches, pillows, and tall brass candleholders. It smelled lightly of incense and tinkled with the sound of the small tiled fountain splashing in its center. But none of this seemed nearly as surprising to Anna as the half dozen gold-bespangled girls whose breasts were only hazed beneath colorful dresses. They turned their gazes from the high windows and stared curiously at her.

Could they be prisoners too? Anna wondered. They didn't seem unhappy, though. They looked rather like a flock of butterflies. Coming forward, Anna asked, *"Parlez-vous français?"* And when no one responded, "Do you speak English?"

Consulting each other in whispers, the girls giggled before shaking their heads while one of them with midnight-black hair came closer, pointing to herself and saying, "Salsabil."

In return, Anna pointed to herself and pronounced her own name. But then none of them was looking at her anymore as a strange noise rose from beyond the windows like chanting or moaning and all the girls turned back to see.

Oh, something was wrong, terribly wrong, Anna told herself pressing her temples with massaging fingers. Everything seemed wrong, yet the heat and this headache made it impossible to think. So she followed the others to the windows, hoping to find a clue of understanding, though she somehow knew what she would see even before she reached the arched opening and looked down in the courtyard below.

Anna gripped the tiled wall for support.

She had never seen an execution before, let alone of two hundred shackled men, ragged and whimpering like animals beside a pit of burning coals and glowing hot instruments. They didn't even look like men anymore—some were buried up to their necks in the sand while others lay shackled and filthy under the eyes of pitiless half-naked guards. A throng of white-robed men circled them, triumphantly chanting words she could translate as "Death to

Hussar, death to Hussar!" And then she could only blanch, moisture beading her forehead and dizziness overcoming her as she recognized the hawk-nosed Arab who stood on a raised platform just beneath her window, his black robes billowing in the gusting winds—the devil himself presiding over the pits of Hell.

The sun overhead was a molten ball of white fire, its intensity making even the guards move from one foot to the other as they waited and watched their master for the signal to begin. But Sheik Hamid al-Sharif seemed in no hurry, his booted legs standing wide, his arms crossed, his gaze roaming over the vanquished army as grim lines grew deeper around his mouth.

Normally he thought of mass tortures and executions as tedious but essential spectacles designed to demonstrate his uncompromising mercilessness to his enemies and to inspire his following. But today was an exception. His triumph over his cousin Yassan Rafir Zabol Hussar was the culmination of a bitter rivalry between them, a rivalry which began as boys when Hamid's father had captured Yassan Hussar, heir to the Hussar leader, and taken him hostage.

It was customary for one tribe to take hostages of another to guarantee peace between the two and to treat hostages with respect befitting their station. So it came to pass that Yassan Hussar and Hamid Sharif, only a year different in age, had grown up like brothers, terrorizing the palace servants, shooting darts out the palace windows at the merchants below. But then, when Yassan reached the age of fifteen, everything changed. Yassan Rafir Zabol Hussar was ransomed by his father and taken back to his desert stronghold, and when next Hamid had seen him, they had become what fate of birth had always decreed they would be, rivals and the deadliest of enemies.

Earlier in the day, recalling their childhood, the sheik had considered sparing Yassan Hussar in an act of mercy. Yet open treason had been committed and the blood of loyal subjects had been spilled. Mercy now would be considered weakness and the cruelty of the desert had long ago taught the sheik that weakness was a luxury reserved only for women. Now it would surely invite other challenges to his power. Knowing this made him imperceptibly straighten his shoulders as he faced the prostrate form of Yassan Hussar.

Yassan Hussar quavered. The elders of the Hussar tribe had advised him against challenging Hamid al-Sharif, but he had ignored their warnings.

How could Hamid al-Sharif, the son of an Algerian concubine, be capable of outmaneuvering his own clever strategies? He, Yassan Hussar, was the product of a Sudanese princess, a woman from the same noble line that in generations past once controlled El Abadan and the rich trade routes to the south. This fact alone made his claim to the throne a legitimate one that Allah himself would uphold—or so he had thought.

Now Hussar raised bitter eyes to the wide-standing boots of Sharif. Once he had planned his own moment of victory when the warriors of Hamid al-Sharif would suffer under the tortures he would inflict. But it was not to be. Today Sharif triumphed, and he must submit. But the sands of the desert were endlessly changing, were they not? Even now, his own infant son, Abu Hussar, was safe in the Tibesti Mountains. Only a few years and he would be eager for Sharif's blood and the blood of his offspring. He would be avenged.

Above his head now Hussar heard Sharif's clipped command, "Begin."

Silently Hussar's lips moved in prayer. "Praise be to Allah, Lord of creation, the compassionate, the merciful, king of judgment day. When the sky is rent asunder, when the stars scatter and the oceans roll together, when the graves are hurled about, each soul shall know what it has done and what it has failed to do."

And thus committing his soul to Allah, Yassan Rafir Zabol Hussar dropped his forehead into the dust.

Chapter 5

In the misty predawn light, Anna lay on the rumpled pillows where she had flung herself, tangled hair tumbling in a red-gold mass around her limp shoulders. Hours ago she had expended every tear, and now was too numb to feel the pain of her spasming chest and her burning eyes or to move her lifeless limbs. Fixedly she stared at the high ceiling, not in reflection, but rather in suspension of intelligent thought. Aware only of a deep and black emptiness, fathomless and hopeless, she didn't even protest when she felt herself lifted into the flabby-skinned arms that she recognized instinctively as Omar Zatan's.

She clung to him then like a child, laying her head against his chest and ignoring the soft heaviness there that suggested breasts. He rocked her gently, silently. But he gave her little solace, his presence only awakening her tortured mind so the stunned voice within her repeated again, "*Brandon is dead! Dead!*"

The eunuch's pudgy hands stroked the rumpled red-gold head, comforting this slave girl as he so often had the others during their fits of depression or hysteria concerning those vital matters of the master's favor, pregnancy, birth, death, and miscarriage. He spoke now in a low, almost cooing voice, "But, Mademoiselle, why are you so sad? Do you not find the master young and strong? Is he not bold? a prince among princes?" Looking down at this fragile girl in his arms, Omar felt her begin to sob again and bury her face in his robes.

His hand moved to her forehead. "You are not feverish," he said. "Are you still so frightened? Come, come, you will make yourself sick with all this weeping. Eat now, little one, and you will feel better."

Anna sat up, weakly brushing back the damp hair that stuck to her cheeks. "I won't eat anything," she said in a cold voice.

Omar's yellowish eyes smiled at her indulgently as a salaaming servant removed her sodden pillow and replaced it with a dry one. "Change is often as difficult as it is inevitable," he said. "There are those who come here grateful for the honor. But there are also those who do not. They always say, 'I won't this,' and 'I won't that.' But in the end, it is always changed. You will see. In three days time, things will be different."

Omar's voice was calm and so completely confident that Anna said, "But I won't change! *I* will be different!" with a firmness that told Omar she meant it.

"Mademoiselle is spirited," he remarked, his expression unchanged. "It is a trait which pleases the master."

"But I will *not* please him!" she burst out, exasperated at the failure of her words or anything she did to affect him.

"It is better to please than to displease the master." He eyed her seriously. "The mademoiselle must understand that in the desert there are many who have little to eat, and not even a tent to sleep in. There are many then who come to El Abadan—many eager to serve the master where there is plenty to eat and gardens and pleasant entertainments. You are honored, mademoiselle, having been chosen by the master himself. But one cannot be foolish and forget that those who anger the master must die."

The black eunuch continued his advice. "All of us must please the master. When the master is pleased, the servants are pleased. But when the master is angry, the servants are afraid and unhappy. One follows the other, you see? And it becomes only intelligent to please rather than displease."

Anna was staring at him and asking herself for a last time if this could actually be possible—that she, a civilized Frenchwoman, was to become the slave of her husband's murderer. Then, refusing to show how frightened she was, Anna lifted her chin and turned her back, refusing to speak again or even look at the food which was already being brought forward on trays. She would not eat! What more could she lose now, and what reason to go on living?

Two more days passed, and then another night, and rumors circulated through the harem and were told and retold concerning the new girl.

"She is a royal princess from a tribe to the north," one

said, and the others nodded. Of course, what else but the indulgence of a royal upbringing could explain this one's bold ways?

The white girl's wild behavior and refusal to eat lasted nearly a week and they watched her grow pale and even thinner than before. But it all ended one day when the head eunuch, in his wisdom, strangled a worthless female infant and threatened to do the same every day as long as the white girl's rebellion continued. The hot-eyed girl had screamed then until she fainted and had to be revived. But after this she became obedient, and as the days continued, the harem settled once again into a peaceful, if less eventful, routine.

Indeed, Anna found herself outmaneuvered by Omar Zatan, who had so quickly discovered how to use her sensibilities against her. So now, afraid to rebel for the sake of the squalling babies so readily sacrificed, Anna had no recourse but to submit to whatever they wanted. This turned out to be what seemed an endless series of baths and grooming, and worst of all, meals of rich food which she had to force down her throat that still was constantly tight with unshed tears.

Omar Zatan praised her then. "This was necessary," he told her in his cooing voice. "Life can be so pleasant, you must try to enjoy it." And in spite of her determination not to change, the lazy, seductive atmosphere of the harem began weakening her resistance as days became weeks. Just the fact the sheik had not appeared relaxed her sense of impending horror. Perhaps he would never come, she told herself. And finally, having learned to speak more Arabic, Anna unbent enough to talk to the other women.

To her surprise, they told her they were not prisoners. Most of them had come to El Abadan as gifts from their fathers to the sheik. Far from being distressed at their situation, they considered it a great honor—though not so great an honor as becoming first wife. And when the women mentioned this they often rolled their eyes in her direction.

From them Anna learned about the harem, about Salsabil and the rivalries of the past, about the sheik, his feats of strength and bravery, and of his temper, which they told

Anna could be fierce. He was to be feared most when he was angry, they told her with hands raised in gestures of wonder. He had been known even to personally execute the one daring to offend him without waiting for a guard. "Even my father and brothers fear him as do all men," said Zaier, a girl Anna knew to be the daughter of the headman of one of the tribes allied with the sheik. "Ah, he is magnificent," she finished, sighing. But then, seeing Anna's reaction, Zaier took one of the white girl's chilled hands into her own as she added, "But you must not worry. *You* are certain to please him."

As always at these times, Anna looked away and said nothing.

The routine of the harem never varied, so when Anna entered the main room of the harem one evening to find the whole indolent atmosphere changed, the women chirping and preening before the burnished brass disks that served as mirrors, her heart seemed to stop with a thud.

Activity like this could only mean that a visit from the sheik was imminent, and she was just calculating a hiding place when Omar entered with a dozen servants in his wake, directing them in rapid Arabic and waves of his fat cocoa hands.

Immediately Anna found herself in the care of four women who would hear no protest as they led her into an oval tub whose steaming rosewater eddied up in dream-like mists.

Since her capture, Anna had been bathed twice each day. But now was different and they scrubbed her skin and then her private parts with extra care before washing and rinsing her hair with something that made it soft and radiant.

She was taken out then, and dried and perfumed, and draped in filmy veils the same blue of her eyes and so light they revealed her slender limbs in alluring shadow even as they covered them.

The women made small admiring noises as they put tiny embroidered slippers on her feet and slipped three thin gold bands along her upper arms. Then, using a soft brush,

Omar Zatan himself blackened her eyelids with kohl and
stained her lips and suddenly pale cheeks with carmine.

When it was all done he smiled and gave her a satisfied
pat on her wide-eyed face. Then the servants took her near
the fountain like a fragile ornament and placed her on a
cushion there before leaving to help the other girls ready
themselves.

Self-consciously, Anna tucked her legs tightly under her
gossamer skirt. But the material was too short and too
transparent and her shapely calves were still exposed.

She tried to control herself, knowing that she flushed
and whitened by turns, her breaths coming short. But she
couldn't control any of these reactions that raged through
her.

When would he come? she asked herself. And when he
came, what would he do? Did he mate with his women like
a rutting stag? Did he take each one away separately, or
was it done with the rest watching? And what would he do
with her? Anna's imagination flew and she jumped when
she heard Omar Zatan's voice behind her.

"Mademoiselle must try to be calm," he said. Glancing
up at the eunuch's pleased expression, Anna fought back
an impulse to run.

There is nowhere I can go, she told herself again. It
would gain nothing but more humiliation. She stiffened her
spine and raised her head, and Omar, seeing this, thought
she seemed suddenly regal in a way that pleased him more
than he could have hoped.

"Your union with Hamid al-Sharif is written in the stars
with favorable signs," he said. "We all must bow before
what has been fated."

Anna turned her face away. She had learned that, according to Islam, each soul was ascribed a fate on the fortieth day after conception which was indelibly written in
Allah's book and could never be altered. But Anna didn't
believe this. This was not *her* fate. No never! There must
be some way to escape—to hide.

Her cheek was touched and it seemed the head eunuch
understood her thoughts when he said, "Do not worry, little

one. The master may not choose you. You are but one of many beautiful women, no?" He indicated the others with a gesture of his hand. "And all will be eager for his favors. With so many flowers near the hive, the bee does not wander far. Perhaps tonight you will only observe and learn what pleases this man who is your master. But do not forget you are *his*. And when the time comes that he chooses you, there can be no thought of refusal. No woman refuses the master just as no man disobeys him. To do so means certain death."

He stopped speaking and when Anna remained silent, her eyes downcast, Omar didn't say more and it was an abrupt welcoming cry that broke the silence and echoed in the dome above her.

Everyone paused, all turning at once to a tall, hawk-nosed figure coming silently down the steps, a black and gold cheetah padding softly in his wake. Then, in a flurry of veils and lip rouge and the tinkling of ankle bracelets, the girls were running to meet him.

Chapter 6

Radiating a sense of unquestionable power, the sheik Hamid al-Sharif strode across the carpets and sat down easily on a large square cushion. The cheetah lay beside him, panting, its ocher eyes rolling toward the gathering girls.

Halfway across the room, Anna slid behind the raised portion of the fountain, blocking herself from his view and peeping around its edge.

How well his harsh features were etched in her memory. Just those eyes had the power to make her stomach churn as she watched the girls, all bright with joy, kiss their master's hands and look up at him with devotion on their lovely faces.

The sheik spoke to each girl in turn, sometimes fondling this one or that one familiarly, as one might fondle a dog. Then he waved a hand, and in response, a single flute from somewhere beyond a drawn curtain began a haunting melody that echoed alone in the domed ceiling before being joined by the brisk sounds of hand drums.

A tall angular man entered then, wearing a black robe that accentuated his gauntness and a pointed hat displaying all the signs of the zodiac embroidered around its sides.

His face was a mysterious intricacy of tanned leather lines, and flourishing a silver wand in wide airy strokes, he produced puffs of blue smoke that made the girls cry out in wonder.

The smoke floated to the ceiling, disintegrating in the blue dome. But when Anna looked back again, the wand had disappeared, and in his bony fingers had materialized an egg. He closed his fist once before unclasping it again. A green parrot was suddenly there, completely alive and squawking loudly. The girls giggled in the happy notes of children as the bird flapped its wings, and the magician took two steps to put it on the outstretched arm of Salsabil.

Salsabil's dark eyes were sparkling, and she looked to be the essence of earthy sensuality in her coffee-colored veils as she held the bird out, first to the sheik, and then for the others to admire. The magician continued performing one trick after another, producing red light, then lightning, and finally rain from the end of his wand before disappearing himself in a puff of blue smoke.

An awed hush came over the room. Then the girls clapped their hands in another tinkling of gold bracelets and cried out with delight. But the magician didn't reappear, and now the flute grew mellow with sensuality, and with a word from the sheik, Katin and Fatima rose from their places at his feet, lifting their arms gracefully overhead and moving around the tiled floor.

Their hips swayed sinuously, first thrusting, then undulating in perfect rhythm to the drum beats. Then spinning round and round, agile as cats and feather light, their veils twirled high to reveal their thighs and waists and bared jiggling breasts so a new light came into the sheik's half-closed eyes.

Anna shuddered, pulling back closer behind the fountain. If only it would be over and she could escape his attention. At least at the moment he seemed well enough entertained and had not glanced in her direction. Perhaps Omar Zatan was right. With so many willing mates, why search further?

It was then that the parrot noticed the tray of orange slices resting on the tiles near her. With a wild flapping of wings, the bird flew off Salsabil's wrist and soared in a short arc before landing beside the tray of fruit just inches from Anna, drawing everyone's attention toward her.

Instantly Anna dropped her eyes to her lap. A knot drew tight in her stomach as the girls chattered and laughed at the bird as it picked up an orange slice in one claw, and ate it so quickly the pulp remained sticking to its hooked beak.

Had he noticed, Anna wondered, her mind racing wildly. Would he suddenly call her?

She waited for his voice, her fingers whitening as they clung together. But he said nothing and at last, mercifully, the music began again and dancers dressed in bright purple costumes swept into the harem in a series of dramatic leaps that fascinated everyone.

Still Anna kept her head down, seeing the dancers only from the ankles down and hearing tambourines spicing the music with lusty energy over the sound of her own pulsing heart. Had he noticed her? Of course! But what was in his face? boredom? interest? dislike? Did he plan to kill her as he had Brandon? And when she could bear the suspense no longer, she let her eyes hesitantly move across the tiled floor and slowly upward to the sheik's face.

He was looking directly at her, and her bounding heart jerked to a halt as his charcoal eyes filled with a deep glow so compelling she found herself unable to turn away while a blush heated her cheeks and neck and even her arms.

She could not know that he had always been aware of her, that he had noticed her from the first moment he had walked down the steps, catching her unaware, a frightened angelic child.

Certainly *this* was a houri from paradise, he told himself with the conviction of a man presented with hundreds of women and able to judge. How easily he could imagine her wreathed in flowers of heaven and offering nectar to the

martyrs as they entered the kingdom of Allah. But not
wishing to frighten this most alluring of females, he had
ignored her as first, even as his curiosity asked if white
women could possibly be made differently from Arab
women. He rubbed his cheek and smiled. It was a matter
bearing investigation.

It was this smile that broke the spell, enabling Anna to
pull her eyes away and pretend an interest in the dancers
who performed for several more agonizing minutes before
they ended in a finale of drums. Next, the storyteller came
and sat before them, opening a large gilt-edged book.

Anna couldn't understand the story, but she dared not
look away from the old man who told it. She was woman
enough to know that look in a man's eyes—that look of
approval, of curiosity, of desire. So when the end of the
performance finally came, Anna's gaze again dropped to
the floor.

She waited for what would happen next—for him to
speak, to come to her. But to her surprise, the sheik ignored her again, not even turning his proud head in her
direction when he finally rose and walked up the alabaster
steps.

Both Fatima and Katin had been chosen and were flanking his sides, their lusty giggles floating back to those left
behind as they disappeared down the hall.

There was a sigh from some of the women that hung in
the air as relief washed over Anna in a flood and it seemed
she could suddenly breathe again. She had been spared. He
had chosen others! But in spite of this, Anna didn't feel
truly safe until she had hurried to her private chamber.
Then after being helped out of her filmy veils and jewelry
by servants, who gossiped in whispers about those the master had chosen, Anna slipped into bed, too exhausted to
question the miracle of being spared, or to consider what
tomorrow, or tomorrow night might bring. And laying her
head on the silk pillow, she was quickly asleep.

Chapter 7

Exhausted, Anna slept deeply for hours before the lights of dreaming flashed on, and she was aware of herself standing on a wide, open plain, limitless from horizon to horizon. In front of her a funnel of mists were rising and a figure within the mists moved ever closer. She stared, trying to see who it was when abruptly the mists were caught and blown apart in a puff of wind and Anna felt herself totter in giddiness before she was running, her arms wide open like wings, and she was calling, "Brandon! Brandon! Oh praise God you are here and alive!"

But Brandon didn't move or return her cries of joy. He remained as solemn as a statue and looked at her accusingly as he pointed to a pile of bloody bodies—those of the English soldiers killed that day. Yes, she should have died then, too, she thought. And looking back at Brandon she saw him suddenly fading, his shape becoming distorted—transparent.

Oh God! He must not leave her—not now—not just when she had found him again!

She ran harder, shouting louder, "Brandon! Brandon! Don't leave me. Please!" And then he was there, and she in his arms, weeping and laughing at once, his lips on hers hot and insistent, his hand lustfully wrenching open her blouse to fondle her breasts.

It was not a usual caress. Usually he was so gentle. But now Anna didn't care. He was alive! Alive! And she welcomed his rough hands, pressing even closer as she answered his kiss with eager parted lips.

It was only after that—when she suddenly knew a hand between her legs—that the fog surrounding her began to clear and recede, that with a rush of terror she realized she was no longer dreaming, and yet there was still a persistent mouth over hers, and an exploring hand searching the secrets of her body. She was awake! Really awake, and this was real, the sheik, surrounding her, pressing her harder, drowning her in his hateful grasp. But when she screamed against his driving mouth she was surprised to feel him pull away.

Horrible! Repulsive! And she had returned his touch, his kisses! Struggling then with all her strength, Anna crawled from beneath him, off the bed and onto her feet in a desperate scramble which, to her further surprise, he did nothing to prevent.

There was a single candle burning, and in its light she saw both wonder and amusement on his dark face as she kept moving backward, now unable to look away from the bulge that reared hard and ready beneath his loose trousers.

The sheik followed her frightened gaze and laughed with dancing eyes before speaking softly in Arabic, a question in his tone as he came forward, the candlelight playing on the muscles and white jagged scars of his bared chest.

Anna shook her head, backing away and dragging a silken coverlet to her breasts.

The sheik paused, frowning and issuing what sounded like a sharp order. But all the Arabic Anna had learned abruptly flew from her, and she could only stare uncomprehendingly, her lips quivering.

The sheik's frown deepened and there was a pounding rush in her ears as she retreated still further, stepping on the hem of her gown and stumbling as she said, "Please . . . Oh God don't, please," unable to recognize the husky sound of her faltering voice. "Don't do this to me. In the name of your God and mine. . . ."

The sheik tilted his head slightly to one side, and there was a glimmer of understanding in the gaze that watched her. He stepped closer, a smile curving his lips, his eyelids half closing as he spoke, his brutal voice now seeming to vibrate with an underlying tenderness, as if speaking to a skittish horse.

Were not all women frightened until they properly knew their master? the sheik was asking himself as he said, "Little flower, sweet rose of Sharon," watching her azure eyes grow even more brilliant. He came closer. "You need only obey and I shall not hurt you—pale little flower, priceless jewel. Do you not know our meeting was planned in the great book of Allah and is written in the stars?"

The sheik moved his other foot closer. He had not intended to take this slave girl before she had recovered, particularly since Omar Zatan had warned him of her fragility. But tonight, when he saw her in the harem, peeping from behind the fountain, looking as enchanting as an unexpected oasis, an arrow of desire had pierced his loins. All that white skin—that hair as rich as the ruby on her finger, she was irresistible—different from any woman he had ever known. But at the end of the evening, when she had still shown neither curiosity nor the smallest desire in her frightened looks, he had remembered Omar's warning and had attempted to satisfy his lusts with two of his other women. But when he had taken them to his large fur-scattered bed, and caressed their limbs, and breasts, and sex, his thoughts had known only this mystical houri of paradise. And later, when he had dismissed them, he had found himself still unable to sleep. Rising, he had wandered aimlessly in the narrow hallways before finally finding himself here, parting the curtains to the bedchamber of this newest, most fascinating, of his female possessions.

How charming she was now, he thought, with her large eyes the color of morning sky looking at him as if he were a genie suddenly appeared out of magicians' smoke. And how fearfully she had fled to stand with her back pressed against the curtained wall of her chamber. The flaming pink hue of her cheeks had spread to color her throat and slender arms, and through the silk gown he could see her high pointed breasts so rosy, so delicate, so milky white, that the hot stirring of his desire grew stronger. His eyes returned to search those blue pools, and again a slow smile spread across his lips as he came closer still.

He was an animal, a filthy, grinning panther, Anna thought, with cold terror making her legs shake. She was cornered. If she could only die before he touched her. If the carpet beneath her feet would only open and swallow her up like the whale had Jonah. But time ran out. His hands slid around her waist, and in a quick bending movement, he had picked her up like a child and laid her on the thick rug before kneeling over her, pinning her between his knees.

Anna gasped as his brown fist seized the jeweled dagger sheathed at his waist and drew it out. A musk-scented hand closed the scream in her mouth. There was a ripping sound as her gown was sliced open, exposing her heaving breasts. Then her wrists were captured and pressed to the carpet overhead, his furred chest rippling with every movement.

He came close, speaking in Arabic against her breasts as he kissed and sucked and fondled them. Her legs were opened and held apart, his knee bracing them, and Anna felt his hand wander lower, past her navel and beyond, to explore the softness between her legs.

She cried out, arching, twisting, jerking, pulling against his hold. But her movements made no difference. She was out of breath, pinned like a butterfly to a mat as his weight shifted and the thick knob of his manhood drew across her abdomen and pressed between her widespread legs and her own flesh gave way to his thrust that molded them so tightly that they were one.

Panting, Anna dropped her head back against the carpet and stopped struggling. She was beaten. He could have his way now, and he knew it. The lock on her wrists was released, and she felt his hands slide along her waist, her belly, and to one breast before his thumb was teasing the erect nipple of the other, and she knew a thrusting rhythm within her.

Looking up, she saw that his partially lidded eyes were focused inward, lost in enjoyment as he rode her with building momentum.

Ugly, brutal, ghastly! A beast, a beast! Frantically she flung out an arm to the side, knocking as she did something cold and rounded, and twisting her neck, she saw it was the hilt of the dagger he had so carelessly tossed aside after ripping her gown.

Stretching every tendon, her fingers reached for it, hooking it at last with the tip of a fingernail, and pulling it closer until her hand closed around its thick handle. Then, clenching her teeth, mindless of the consequences, she raised the weapon and drove it into him, feeling his flesh yield beneath the tapering point.

A tingling horror rushed through her followed by unreasoning elation. She'd killed him! Yes, murdered him! But then her arm was violently jolted, sending the knife skidding across the floor to the foot of a large brass incense burner.

Abruptly the sheik was on his feet, staring incredulously, first at his slashed upper arm, where blood gushed and dripped off his elbow, and then back to her, as if seeing her for the first time.

The cheetah was suddenly there, too, looming over her, smelling blood. It growled, fangs bared, whiskers stiff in the golden candlelight. It crouched to leap and Anna screamed. The sheik grabbed the animal's jeweled collar with his good arm and pulled it back.

At his master's touch, the cheetah stopped growling, though it never took its ocher eyes from her as it sat back on gaunt haunches, flipping the end of its tail from side to side.

Cowering on the floor, Anna clasped her blood-stained gown to her breasts as the sheik struck a bell whose deep tones seemed to echo in her head as well as down the hall. What had she done? She must have been insane!

That she would die was certain, and now, remembering the horrible executions she'd seen, Anna shivered as perspiration trickled down her underarm.

A servant running in stopped short and bowed, as his gaze passed from his master's slashed arm back to her with disbelief.

The sheik's voice was calm and clipped, as he spoke in the same tone he might have used to order a meal.

The servant bowed again and salaamed, rolling his eyes toward the ceiling and then in her direction before hastening out again in a rush of sandal slaps that disappeared down the hall.

Anna bit her lip, the muscles around her mouth tightening and jumping out of control. Any moment a number of guards would return and seize her. She would be whipped, her eyes pierced out, her bones broken with steel hammers before red-hot irons were applied to her flesh. Then just as she was about to die anyway, she would be executed by strangling. Oh, she remembered it all! The groans of the victims she had seen him murder seemed to fill her ears as she raised her eyes to find the sheik still staring at her.

Sheik Hamid al-Sharif was amazed. Was it possible? he asked himself. Could this fragile childlike girl, whose neck he could snap with one hand, have considered, have truly dared to stab him—and with his own dagger! Who would have suspected that this woman, pale and alluring as the poisonous blossoms of the oleander, was also as deadly?

Anna pressed herself further back against the wall as the royal surgeon dashed in with the royal executioners only two steps behind, their swords already drawn, coiled whips in their fists. Immediately they moved toward her, their broad meaty shoulders hunched, their faces immobile. But an order from the sheik made them stop short and eye her with a mixture of astonishment and merciless savagery.

A little black boy, apparently the surgeon's assistant, was hauling in his medical bag as the surgeon quickly examined the wound. Then turning to the executioners, the surgeon spoke orders sending both his assistant and the two executioners dashing from the room.

So, she wasn't to be killed immediately, she thought, wishing she would faint rather than have to sit here so frightened her throat and heart gave separate hammering sounds. The sheik was going to prolong her agony. Maybe he would want her execution to be a public spectacle.

The executioners and the assistant of the royal surgeon returned carrying bowls of water, strips of cloth, and yet another small bag that the surgeon opened to reveal a number of shiny metal instruments.

Apparently the alarm had been sounded outside, and Anna could hear the harem stirring and the screams of women as the news was passed from hallway to hallway.

She stayed cringing on the floor, watching the surgeon examine the gash, which was very deep and ran the full length of the sheik's upper arm. He pressed on the cut and the bleeding subsided. Then drawing a flask from his bag, he poured its clear substance over the wound.

One side of the sheik's mouth twitched. But it was his only gesture as his unreadable charcoal eyes continued to study her while the surgeon took up a curved needle and began to sew the wound closed. The needle pierced his flesh and created new small wounds as it was done.

The cheetah wouldn't lie on the rug, but kept pacing relentlessly. It flared its lips in a curling snarl as it padded back and forth, rolling its eyes in her direction and growling in a low rumble. Anna expected the animal to pounce and tear her throat to shreds, but the seconds ticked away and he didn't strike.

When the sheik's arm was finally closed, he did not order her dragged from the room as she expected, but instead motioned the surgeon out with a nod and dismissed the executioners with an impatient wave of his hand.

Still his eyes never left her, and when the other men were gone, he walked to stand looking down at her along the bridge of his hawked nose.

Anna couldn't control her trembling. She had bitten her lip through some time ago, and vaguely tasted the blood as she looked at this man's lean brown hands, and pulled further back to cling to the wall.

His good arm grabbed her shoulder and brutally forced her face down on the carpet. Fear overcame any resistance left in her. Numb, breathless she didn't struggle. Yes, he would kill her himself, with his bare hands, just as the women told her. Well, thank God it would be quick. But while she steeled herself, still he didn't end her life. Instead he threw a leg across her as if she were a horse, spreading her legs. Then, from behind her ear, she heard him say in broken French, "Give me a son from your belly, fierce little tigress," before his hardened shaft roughly entered her and thrust swift and deep until his pleasure was spent.

Anna could only lie beneath him gasping, her fingernails biting into the carpet. But even then he hadn't finished with her. In moments he was large and ready, his body churning in and out. Then once more he emptied himself in one last burrowing movement before pulling free and rolling up onto his feet.

She lay before him, naked, sprawling, and faint. Weakly,

she drew her bruised thighs together and watched as he walked to the arched doorway that led to the hall.

Pausing there, the sheik spoke to the cheetah who came walking low-slung and easy, a conspiring grin about its black-striped jaw as the sheik's quiet words seemed to join the two in a mutual pact. Anna watched as he stroked the cheetah's lowering body which dropped across the threshold, blocking any hope she might have of escape. And as its master turned and disappeared down the hall, the great cat shifted its glowing eyes onto her and methodically began licking its large claw-tipped paws.

Chapter 8

No, it seemed impossible that she, Anna Phillips, could have become the favorite, the plaything of a desert sheik who called her to him every night and used her for his pleasure in varying ways in which she had never before imagined a man might take a woman. Impossible, she told herself. But as a month became two, she lost all hope of being rescued, and worst of all began to suspect she was pregnant—though she refused to really consider this completely ghastly possibility. Finally when her servants began examining her abdomen with a judging eye and she could no longer deny the unspeakable truth, she had lain on her bed and cried until her distressed servants called for Omar Zatan.

"It is the will of Allah, who is also your God," Omar Zatan said, his round face unable to conceal the delight he felt at knowing this favorite of favorites had conceived.

"Your God is not the same as mine," Anna said, raising her head and sniffing back still more tears. "If he were, he never would have permitted this. Never!" Stifling her sobs, she dropped her face in her hands with a horror and weariness that moved Omar Zatan to stroke her shoulder with utmost tenderness as he said, "But is not your God the God of Adam and of Abraham, the God of Jesus who Mohammed himself called a prophet of Allah? Yes, you see I have read your Christian writings," he said as she raised her streaming eyes. "And is your God not the God of the sky, the moon, and all the stars and the governor of all life in the world, the God who sees all events? And can you not believe that this is His will and surrender yourself to what has been written? Why must you struggle and rebel when life could be so simple and full of pleasure?

"Yet in this, too, the will of Allah can be seen. Ironic is it not that it has been your resistance against the master that has made him favor you so. 'The fiercer the woman, the fiercer her son.' It is an old saying. And as any man, the master wishes for a son brave as a tiger and proud as the finest stallion. You are the only woman who has ever dared risk torture and death to defy him. In you he sees the virtues of power so lacking in most women. So it is *you* he has chosen to bear his heir. And in the stars the wise men have already seen this destiny to be yours.

"Through you will come a great leader who will not only strengthen the existing alliance between the five tribes, but will join all the tribes between Morocco and Masr, which you call Egypt, so we all speak as one voice. It is a dream long held by the master's father, and his father before him, who was the first Grand Sanusi to rule El Abadan."

With thick fingers then, the eunuch took five oranges from a silver bowl and arranged them around the edges of a low circular table.

"These five oranges are the tribes of the desert." And taking a bronze incense burner and placing it in the center of the circle of oranges he continued. "Here is our master in El Abadan in the middle of the tribes, while here to the south in the Tibesti Mountains"—Omar took a small ivory hyena and placed it on the table to one side—"here is the tribe of Hussar who, in spite of the death of Yassan Hussar, are still powerful and numerous and only waiting with greedy eyes as they watch the rich caravans which pass under the protection of the five tribes to Benghazi in the north and back to Wadai in the south."

Anna shook her head with irritation. "But I can't see why I—"

Omar's hand gestured for her silence. "But of course

you cannot see when you think only of yourself and what *you* want and cannot listen!" the eunuch snapped before rolling his eyes heavenward, and in throaty Arabic entreating Allah to deliver him from the ignorance and stubbornness of women.

Abashed, Anna sat back again, and in her silence, Omar continued, taking a blue silk scarf and draping it river-like through the middle of the oranges and beside the incense burner indicating El Abadan. "This is the Wadai-Benghazi trade route, and the life and blood of my people. It provides not only tribute to the master for his protection, but today it carries necessities such as dates, cotton cloth, and palm oil for cooking, as well as pleasantries like coffee and cloves and cocoa, and riches like diamonds and ivory and gold. But for many years it was not so. Many years ago, before the master himself was born, these five tribes were not united as one but constantly at war, foolishly feuding among themselves and allowing free rein to the powerful Hussar tribe to plunder the caravans that brought these necessities. So even as there was war, there was hunger also, thus weakening the tribes still further. And so it remained for years until Allah, showing his displeasure against the tribes, withheld the rain so all the grass died and there was no pasture for the goats and camels. So they starved in great numbers and this brought even greater death and suffering to the people until finally the leaders of the five tribes were forced to journey to El Abadan, where the wells have not dried in a thousand years, to ask the Sheik of El Abadan for permission to fill their waterskins at the city's well."

Anna cocked her head, interested though her voice held a note of annoyance as she asked, "Well? Did he give them the water?"

Omar was pleased to see the disdain leave the favorite's rebellious blue eyes and he continued. "The old sheik was very wise, and told them they might fill their waterskins only if they each clasped the others in brotherhood. Of course this they were unwilling to do, so the old sheik made them go away and not return until they could settle their quarrels and do as he bid them.

"So the leaders of the tribes returned to their tents, but at the end of seven days came again and bowed before the sheik. 'Highness,' one of them said, 'we five tribes of the great desert have too many quarrels to allow us to embrace the others as brothers. But though we are enemies, we cannot let our people perish. Therefore we have agreed to embrace you as our leader and peacemaker. From this day forward all past disputes will be put aside, and we will vow to follow the wisdom of your counsel when future quarrels arise, and the wisdom of the sons that come after you, so that no more blood will be spilled and our people will be spared.'

"So the master's grandfather agreed to keep the peace as Grand Sanusi and peacemaker, and in a few years, the tribes had become stronger, and fewer were hungry, and the Hussar were forced back to the mountains to plunder only the unwary who traveled there, and the bells of caravans were often heard as they came from the north and returned from the south.

"The Grand Sanusi then produced a son to rule in his place, and this leader in turn produced a son who is our master, Hamid al-Sharif. And now you see, you must give him a son to rule when one day he, too, passes to the kingdom of Allah, so a leader will be left to rule not only these five tribes, but unite all the tribes of the desert into one nation. Many men of vision and wisdom pray it will be so. But if the master dies without an heir, then once again the tribes will fall into their old quarrels and feuds and grow weak until the Hussar will become bold and sweep out of the mountains, ravaging the caravans and causing the people to starve again, and the French and English, who now come nearer and nearer, will be free to feed on our weakness like vultures on dead camels."

Omar's cocoa hands patted her bronzed hair, thankful that the favorite was listening at last, as he finished by saying, "So it is that the birth of an heir is all-important. You must give up all thoughts of escape and think only of the child that grows within you. And do not be afraid of the nights to come. Now that the master's seed lies in your

womb, he will not risk disturbing it and will take his pleasure elsewhere."

So Anna had to be satisfied with that. What choice was
there? At least she would not see the sheik again until after
the child's birth. She must use all her strength to plan her
escape. Surely with all the gold the sheik had given her she
could find someone to help her. She must, somehow. She
must believe there was a chance or how could she continue
to live, particularly when it would only mean someday returning again to the sheik's bed and having him use her as
before. And how long could she fight the easy life of the
harem? How easy it would be to accept, to even look forward to these luxuries—the rich food, the baths. She
thought of the sheik and shuddered. Oh God, if she didn't
escape soon what else might she come to accept . . . or
even enjoy? The opportunity must come! She must make it.
Surely the Lord wouldn't forsake her, she told herself. And
then, months later, as if her prayers were finally heard, help
came from a source she least expected.

"How proud you must be now that the mark of the master's favor is upon you," Salsabil had exclaimed one morning, indicating Anna's rounding belly with a careless wave.
"Surely now you are not so unhappy as you once were."

Anna, who had been sitting alone and serving herself
tea, glanced up to find the girl standing several yards
away, bare feet firm on the floor.

During the past, Anna had always been too distraught to
notice anything except her own suffering. But now, assured she would no longer be called to the sheik's bed, she
was in a better frame of mind to notice how unhappy Salsabil's lovely face had become—the darkening under her
eyes, the fullness of her lower lip.

The beginnings of an idea stirred as Anna set her cup
down with a small click against the tiny ivory inlaid table
and said, "You hate me, don't you, Salsabil? Admit it to me
and at least then we will be honest."

Salsabil started, surprise crossing her expression before a
glint of hatred showed in her eyes. "Yes," she said lowering
her voice to a harsh whisper, "I do hate you and all whites
that destroy the water and the grass of my people and take

what is not theirs." Coming closer Salsabil leaned over her like a large menacing bird. "When the master was mine it was my body he slept beside, he spoke gently to me and made me happy as never I was before. But then you with your pale skin and eyes came to the harem and now it is you he sees—you who carries his child. Yes, I do hate you!"

There was a warning note of hysteria in her desperate cry that softened Anna's voice as she asked, "Now what will become of you?"

Salsabil lowered her eyes, waving her hand toward a gray-robed woman bending in a shapeless lump to scrub the fountain tiles with meticulous care. "I will grow old as all women grow old," she said. "And I will work like that one. I will grow so old no man will desire me, and I will be without even the comfort of children. But what does it matter now? Without the master's favor, or a son, I am nothing. I have failed my father's desire, and I will be forgotten just as that old woman is forgotten. But why is what will happen to me any concern of yours? Why do you ask me these questions?"

Anna lifted a cup from a tray and poured a cup of the jasmine tea, a column of steaming fragrance billowing up between them. Anna measured her words as she spoke. "I ask you because I have a plan that can help both of us."

"A plan? What do you mean a plan? Why would you help me?"

"Because by helping you, I help myself."

"What do you mean?" The Arab girl had sidled closer.

"I mean, if you are so anxious to be rid of me, why don't you help me escape," she said easily. "If I were gone, wouldn't the master's favor return to you?"

Salsabil's face, which only a moment before had held a glimmer of interest, now turned to one of disgust as she snarled in a way that reminded Anna of the sheik's cheetah. "You are as round as an elephant and just as clumsy. Even if it could be arranged, you couldn't ride a horse. And if you couldn't ride, you could not hope to escape! You are a fool," she finished flatly.

She started to walk on then before Anna stopped her by

saying, "But I don't propose escaping now, but after I am delivered of this child. Then I can ride a horse again. I could escape if someone could arrange it. And whoever did could have all the jewels and gold the sheik has given me," Anna finished, pouring a second cup of tea in a way to reflect cool finality.

"You are still a fool," Salsabil said waving her rouged palms to dismiss her. "If you have a son no one would dare help you and the heir of all El Abadan escape. And even if you did escape, the master would follow to the end of the world and would not stop until the heir was returned. Anyway, if the master did not catch you, the child would most certainly die in the desert."

"But this child may not be a boy and heir. It could be a girl. And either way, I would not ask to escape with it. I will leave the child here in El Abadan." Anna's voice displayed the emotionless fashion in which she had reached this decision.

Salsabil had come a step closer, disbelief in her voice as she asked, "You would abandon this child—the master's child, and the bones and blood of your own body?"

Now it was Anna who tossed her head and squared her jaw rebelliously as she took sugar from a tiny wooden bowl and stirred it round in her teacup before saying, "What is this child to me? It is a child of hate, not of love. Do you know that your master killed fifty of my people, murdered them before my eyes. Would you, Salsabil, as an Arab, ever forget that? Would you ever forgive?"

Salsabil's eyes tapered narrowly. Revenge was something she could understand. "I would *never* forgive! The whites, too, have killed and never will I forgive them."

Anna nodded. "You see, we understand each other better than you think. I have not forgotten or forgiven. I want nothing of this child that is of his making."

Salsabil gave her rival a long considering look, really seeing for the first time that this girl, even younger than herself, looked much older. How strange that their common purpose might bridge this chasm between them. Then in a sudden rush, an idea occurred to her, and leaning closer she said, "Yes, perhaps it is possible for you to escape if you are willing to give up the child. A cousin of mine works for a camel trader in El Abadan. He will know when the caravans are expected to come and to go, and I could send word to him. He is a fool who has always wanted me to run away and marry him." Salsabil wrinkled her nose. "As if I would become the wife of a camel driver. But I could tell him I was coming, and then you could go in my place. You would be on a caravan to the coast before he could discover the truth, and then you can wave the diamond that the master gave you beneath his large nose, and he will do as you say."

Anna felt herself smile, and sighed long and hard with pure relief, as if a weight laid on her shoulders was suddenly lightened. How easy Salsabil's plan sounded. Give her only a week or two after this child's birth, and she would be ready. She would be gone from El Abadan before the sheik even realized it, leaving him his heir so he would have little reason to pursue her. Yes, if she could just endure her captivity a little longer and have this child, she would see France again—suddenly she was quite sure of it. And nodding to Salsabil, who came to kneel on the pillow across from her, Anna held out a cup of tea that she accepted, the two women sharing a smile across its rim.

Chapter 9

The months passed and winter came, cooling the desert's burning expanse, bringing sandstorms that halted all activity while it tossed the dunes into hard-driven pelting streams that left everything blanketed in a smooth layer of perfect white.

The rains followed, coming in a sudden torrent that made rivers of the streets, and poured through roof cracks and in windows, and turned the sand blanket to mud. It could last for an hour, or a day, but afterward the sun always came out and burned everything dry again, as if the water had never been.

Then spring came in a sweeping burst of color that covered the desert in a blaze of tiny flowers that pushed their blossoms just above the sand and bloomed and died as swift and ephemeral as a passing mirage. It was a time of year when Allah was said to touch the earth, a time of festivities in El Abadan, and as fate would have it, precisely the time when Anna's baby clamored for exit from the swollen womb.

"Escape, escape," Anna whispered over and over, thinking of the simple but masterful plan she had arranged and trying to renew her strength as the hours dragged by and she writhed with pain.

She grimaced as another contraction bore down on her, and swimming within the pain, her mind drifted to the sheik and a few nights before, when he had taken his evening meal with her.

"You grow fat and lick your fingers like a greedy cat," he had said smiling as he watched her consuming portions of saffron rice and cakes and lamb. "It pleases me to see you eat so."

He looked down at her distended belly, and with complete possession, laid a hand just below her navel.

Anna no longer bothered to pull away. What was the use? And in a moment when the baby kicked, as it had been doing since morning, his harsh face took on a gentle light before he smiled with pride and a little awe. Then retreating, he carefully selected an orange from a silver bowl, peeled the skin, and separated the slices before holding it toward her on a small plate.

Anna took it. To refuse was unthinkable, and popping a slice in her mouth, Anna glanced down at her roundness, wondering if ever she would regain her once slim figure.

He seemed to know her mind. His women, Anna had learned, had few secrets from him, and he said, "You are large now, but that is natural and good. But when the child is sprung from you, then once again you will be as graceful as a wild flower." He smiled then, taking a pinch of rice in his fingers Arab fashion and putting it in his mouth.

"And will that please you?" Anna asked with a hint of sarcasm.

He chewed the rice and swallowed before commenting

factually, "You pleased me before when you were slender. But with a son in your belly, you please me even more."

Another delicacy arrived in the long succession of dishes that formed the royal dinner, and inspecting the concoction of glazed and baked fowl, the sheik selected the choicest portions and served them to her.

"And what if it is not a son but a daughter instead?" Anna asked.

The sheik seemed unmoved by this possibility as he ate a drumstick held between beringed fingers. "But it *will* be a son—the wise men have already assured me."

"But what if it is not? What if it is a girl?" Anna continued. "Are the wise men always correct about such things?"

The sheik frowned and set the drumstick down. He seemed even larger than usual as he leaned toward her. "She-devil!" he spat. "You should not carry such thoughts in your heart. Would you have a girl-child just to taunt me?"

Anna shrugged against his reaction, though inwardly she was pleased at his displeasure and for the time being, at least, she knew he would not punish her for impertinence. "I don't care what I have," she said popping another orange slice into her mouth. "A boy, a girl, it makes no difference."

The sheik was on his feet, a scowl ridging his wide forehead and his face darkening as he pointed a lean finger at her. "It would be best that it is a boy, Ann-Ah," he said ominously, pronouncing her name with his characteristic emphasis on the end. "And understand, woman, if you do not give me a son this time you will not cheat me. I will have the son I want and I will have him from *your* body!" He leveled a finger at her in the way he did to his subjects when his words were to be carried out perfectly, a gesture that frightened everyone and one he had never used with her.

"If this child is a girl," he continued, "then again you will lie beneath me until you are round with child. And if that child is also a girl, then you will have another, and another. . . . And it will continue until you give me a son!"

Anna cringed, now recalling those words. Then reminding herself once again of her escape plan, she thought
of France and silently began to pray for strength.

But now, thrashing in her bed, Anna felt weaker than
ever. Since dawn her pains had worsened, though the baby
seemed lodged like a stone.

Opening her eyes to narrow slits, Anna noticed the faces
of her attendants had lost their earlier excitement and had
grown round-eyed with anxiety as nervously they fluttered
in and out of her view in a flapping of robes.

Twisting in her misery, Anna tried once again to picture
her husband. "Brandon—Brandon," she whispered aloud,
trying to bring that beloved face into focus. But strangely,
the passing months had faded his image and it seemed
Brandon, like everything of her life before was disappearing—lost somewhere beyond the endless stretch of sand
that marooned her here.

"Escape, escape," she whispered trying to rally herself,
though even these words had lost their meaning. Perhaps it
was better to die as surely she soon would. After this, she
would never feel really free again. The sheik had taken
her, had marked her his, and now she could hardly remember the face of the man she loved. Then as another pain
came she moaned, "Brandon, Brandon, I'm coming to
you."

Out of the blackening waves of semiconsciousness, a
voice spoke "Ann-Ah."

Narrowly opening her eyes, she found the sheik's brown
face blurring above her as a servant helped him off with a
travel-stained burnoose.

Vaguely Anna realized he must have returned from the
tribal council at Galia. Had he returned because of her?
she wondered, feeling oddly revived by his presence and
the coolness of his hand on her forehead.

How gentle he can be, she thought as he spoke to her
softly in Arabic. "Strength, my beauty, my treasure," he
said in a deep resonating voice. "Come—show me the tigress again." Then his arm had slipped behind her, and she
felt herself lifted to a half-sitting position, and he was holding a cup to her lips.

The liquid had a sharp taste as it slipped down her throat, but she drank, his firm arm reassuring. Yes, he would save her. He wouldn't let her die like this.

When the cup was empty he gently gathered her tighter in his arms and, lifting her, placed her on an oblong stool while still supporting her from behind so she was half sitting.

"Breathe," he commanded. And she obeyed, breathing deeply, filling her lungs, though she felt too weak even for this, and when another cup of the bitter liquid was put to her lips, she drank again.

Somehow her energy felt renewed, her vision sharpened, though the pain was potent as ever and she began twisting against his hold as another spasm gripped her. What a weakling he must think her. No doubt his Arab women were more efficient when it came to natural functions. And looking up at the sheik, she saw in his face an expression of pity that sparked what remained of her pride. Did he think she was going to die from this child he had so easily planted within her? No! She wouldn't let *this* kill her. And writhing again, she moaned before straining with renewed grit. She would show him what she could do! And this time she felt the baby move.

Again pain faded the hurrying figures that moved in and out of her vision while during the last few semiconscious moments, Anna was aware of the sheik carefully wiping her face with a soft cloth as he spoke in a mixture of his language and hers.

The vise came again, violently crushing her in its jaws, harder, harder. A fiery, searing pain was cutting between her thighs, tearing her apart. Oh God, if only she could die! And then in a mad burst of agony that brought a scream from the pit of her stomach, it was over.

"A son! A son! I have a son!" The sheik's voice turned the tension above her into shouts of happiness.

Anna looked up. The light grew dimmer, the walls and people receding. The last thing she remembered before slipping into a deep sleep was the sheik's exalted expression as he held the red squalling infant high in outstretched arms.

* * *

Years later, looking back, Anna sometimes wondered what life might have been like after that if everything had gone differently. Perhaps in time she might have forgotten her husband and the world she had known before and come only to recall her luxurious life as "favorite," mother of the heir, and first wife to the sheik of El Abadan. But what might have been was shattered in a single moment the following day when a pendulous-breasted wet-nurse with a wide smile presented Anna her son, and the gurgling baby looked up.

Anna's breath rasped inward in the sharp cry of one who is cut to the bone and waiting for the blood to appear. Merciful God, this wasn't the sheik's child, but Brandon's! If the shape of his tiny face left any doubt, it was erased by the diamond-shaped birthmark behind his ear, identical to Brandon's.

Inwardly she shivered, clutching the baby to her in a protective, loving gesture that made her attendants smile and a voice from over her shoulder say, "So you love the son if not the father, Ann-Ah?"

It was the sheik. And holding tiny Brandon to her breast, Anna shrank from him, her eyes turning cold as glass. As the sheik's dark face leaned over her child, his sharp features seemed more sinister than ever before, though his smile was gentle. Repulsion tingled up her spine and she flushed scarlet. Did he know? Did he even suspect? Not only was there a birthmark, but the child's skin, though still reddish, was fair like hers.

Anna tried to discern any question in his expression. But she could read nothing but paternal pride. Her thoughts raced. Surely he must realize she had been no virgin that first time. But of course when she had stabbed him, there had been so much blood and confusion, he could have drawn whatever conclusion he pleased. And men were so vain—they would believe whatever was most flattering.

Looking at him now, she longed to throw the truth into his arrogant face. But she didn't dare. Surely then her son would be murdered just as his father had been. No! No one must know . . . never even suspect!

Rocking her baby, Anna cooed softly to him. It seemed as if Brandon had come back to her in the form of this tiny child, hers to love and protect. Tears sprang to her eyes. And now there could be no escape. A baby could never survive the trip across the desert, and she could never abandon him. Brushing her own tears off the baby's white arm, Anna glanced bitterly up at the sheik's triumphant expression. He had won, though he would never know why. For all her struggles and rebellion and plans of escape, she was held here by ties that were as old as time and as unbreakable. The jaws of the trap had closed with finality. Then quite suddenly, with a sweeping chill that made her shiver, Anna Phillips realized that she would never see home again.

PART II

KARIM AL-SHARIF

THE PALACE OF EL ABADAN—1884

Chapter 10

The sun was just lifting itself above the city walls of El Abadan as Karim al-Sharif strode down the stone steps and into the palace gardens, long robes fluttering at his booted heels.

Dawn was Karim's favorite time, an hour which sometimes found him waking up among his love-sated women or, more often, galloping across the desert at the head of his father's security patrols. This morning, however, was to be spent differently. In less than an hour Karim would be guarding his father during a journey to the Assar oasis, a hundred kilometers to the south. They would be gone several days and now he was hurrying to join his mother and pay his respects before leaving.

As he entered the garden Karim adjusted the neckline of his outer robes. This morning he had made certain his robes were spotless, and that the smell of women and of pleasure had been washed from his body. He had long known how shocked his mother could be by the sexual side of his life, no matter how natural, even commendable, his father considered it to be. He wouldn't want her to know how he had spent the previous night and, recalling it himself, pictured the new sultry-eyed beauty he had brought to his harem only the night before. Then, smiling, Karim continued down the cobblestone walk, passing between acacias and oleanders whose coral blossoms reminded him of the girl's lips.

A slight breeze swayed palm fronds overhead, disturbing the cluster of bees darting ravenously around its pollen clusters. Then rounding a curve in the path, Karim came upon his mother sitting alone on a carved stone bench.

She was very erect, her profile still young and clean-lined, though something about the thinness of her shoulders made her seem fragile and somehow old. And it was only now as she turned slowly and saw him that her perpetually sad eyes glimmered with light.

Lifting his mother's hand, Karim brushed the back of it with his lips in the French greeting she preferred to the more traditional salaam where one touched the forehead, lips, and breast in a flowing motion.

"Brandon, my son," Anna whispered with an almost passionate ring.

"Mother," Karim answered simply with a loving smile before seating himself close beside her. That she called him Brandon Phillips instead of Karim al-Sharif as everyone else did seemed to Karim perfectly natural. She had always done so and it was, he supposed, her own pet name for him. So it was not her address that brought concern to his eyes, but rather how much thinner she had become, accentuating the ephemeral quality that had always clung to her. With extra gentleness he held her thin veined hand as she smiled up at him.

He is so tall, Anna was thinking, even taller than his father. How proud Brandon would be if he could see his son now. He had proven himself a champion at the spring festival last year, defeating all the tribal champions in accuracy with a rifle and in knife throwing. Then only a month ago he had won the yearly *palo* contest, a brutal game played on horseback in which the men competed for possession of a beheaded goat which, after it was tossed high in the air by an elder, became the property of any man tough and skilled enough to successfully fight off the others.

The object of the contest was simply to get the goat any way possible and keep it long enough to carry it across the goal line at the distant end of a sandy flat below the cliffs of El Abadan. There were no rules to the game. All means were used except actual weapons. Tripping an opponent's horse, or several opponents uniting to unhorse a single one were all permitted and encouraged by the crowd that lined the sides of the field to cheer their favorites.

Seated in a private pavilion behind a screen so she could see but not be seen, Anna had felt unable to look, though she couldn't possibly have looked away. So putting her hands to her eyes and spreading her fingers to peep be-

tween them, she had watched the men gallop fiercely up
and down the field. But in the end of it was Karim, bloody
and bruised but smiling, who rode his black foaming stallion across the goal and onto the raised platform where the
most revered elder, Ali Ben Zadi, awarded him the prize of
a gold medallion.

After that day the respect shown him by the men was no
longer simply that due his status as crown prince but because he had shown himself a leader. Even the older ones
began asking his advice on various matters and inviting
him to their houses and tents to dine and to eye their dis-
cretely displayed daughters.

Almost shyly now Anna's eyes studied her son as she
thanked heaven for the thousandth time that the desert sun
had bronzed his skin as his heredity had not. For all ap-
pearances this young man before her was as Arab as the long
head scarf that twisted round and round his head to form a
turban, the very end being left to drape rakishly to one
side. No one had ever suspected his real parentage, or if
suspicious, had not dared to speak. And now as Anna
watched him she wondered if it was the time to tell him the
truth or if she should wait. How could she begin a fantastic
tale? What would he say? She had always intended to tell
him someday but, in her mother's eyes, Anna still saw in
his grown-up face what remained of the child that he had
been. For all his strength and handsomeness and twenty
years, Brandon was still her baby and, despite his maturity,
he still possessed a fiery temper. Who could tell how he
would react to learning his real father had been murdered
by the man he now so proudly called by that name? It
could so easily end in disaster. It was this fear that kept her
silent on the matter now, reaching instead to touch the long
bronzed fingers that so resembled his father's, as she asked.
"Why are you leaving El Abadan, my son?"

A servant appeared with tea which was served with cups
and saucers instead of a single demitasse used by Arabs.
Karim took his cup and sipped from its edge rather than
downing it in a single gulp as he did when among the men.

"Englishmen have camped in the ruins of the old fortress at Sevit," he explained. "There has been trouble concerning the well water there, and the Assar tribe has complained and called a tribal council. I go with my father to hear the words of the Assar. Then the council of elders will decide what is to be done."

Anna's wan face was startled into animation. "Englishmen? Here?" she said, her thoughts suddenly racing. From time to time she had heard of parties of Europeans, but never as near as the fortress of Sevit. Oh, if she could only go to them and take Brandon with her. Perhaps she could explain their circumstances and be given protection. A kind of elation expanded within her for a moment as she thought of seeing familiar white faces, of speaking her own language, and of hearing news of England and France.

Glancing at her son, Anna burned to tell him her secret but, fighting down the impulse, she compressed her lips. No doubt the English force was small, she told herself, and would be no match for the sheik's pursuing forces even if they did agree to protect her. Anyway she could never risk being the reason for another slaughter. And thinking of this made the hope she felt diminish and pass away, fear suddenly taking its place as she asked her son, "What will the sheik do to the Englishmen?"

Karim didn't miss the hesitation in his mother's voice. He had always known she didn't accept the people of El Abadan, or her position as first and most honored wife of his father. Instead she clung to her white ways, even insisting he be educated in English, French, and geography in addition to the lessons his father gave him in trade, medicine, horsebreeding, war strategies, and the Holy Koran. And during the time he spent with her she would often remind him, "You are half-white, Brandon, you must always remember that."

Now he squeezed her small hand and kissed it. "Do not worry, Mother. There should be no need for bloodshed. The complaint from the Assar chief was unspecific, probably only a minor matter. The English will certainly not challenge a force larger than their own and, if they go in peace, there will be no need for trouble."

Looking up into his dark, smiling eyes Anna listened to the deep tones of his voice that reminded her of that brief happy time twenty-one years ago when it had been her husband's voice. How well her son understood her, just as his father had, and like him, tried to be reassuring. Still her forehead creased with worry as she said, "But, Brandon, you must be careful. You must remember you are half-white. You must not let the sheik raid the fort or commit murder!"

"There is no need to commit 'murder,'" he said calmly. "We will only turn the white men away." But he could see his words had little effect on his mother's fearful expression.

She didn't speak for several minutes, her eyes looking at him with a sad longing. She reached within her robes and withdrew a ring threaded on a long gold chain. She held the object in her closed palm for a moment, shutting her eyes briefly as if in prayer before unclasping her fingers and slipping the chain and the ring over his head.

Karim had seen it many times, a heart-shaped ruby ring inscribed simply *Beloved* on the underside of the stone. His mother had once told him it was an heirloom from her family. He always had wondered if perhaps there was more that she did not say, but he did know she valued it more than any of the magnificent treasures given her by the sheik.

"I want you to have this," she whispered. "This ring has been dearer to me than you can understand now. I want you to take it with you and wear it always as a symbol of my love."

Karim felt his insides shift with a soft emotion. Then, as gently he embraced his mother, he noticed tears in her eyes. He held her closer then, as if she were his child. "I will wear it always," he said solemnly.

"Yes," she said. "And I love you. Promise you will always remember how I love you."

He nodded. "I promise."

"And promise me," she continued, her eyes opening wider. "Promise me there will be no bloodshed, that the English will be spared."

For a moment then Karim paused and studied his mother. It was not an easy promise to make. While he was his father's heir, his powers were severely limited until he actually assumed the throne. And if the white soldiers should become hostile. . . .

"Promise me," she repeated, her thin hands now clinging to his sleeve. "Promise the English will not be harmed."

How pale she is, Karim thought, and how fragile. The weight of her sorrow and love pulled upon something deep within him. Could he deny her anything? Then pressing the ring to his lips, he dropped it down the neckline of his robe to rest against his heart before saying, "I promise."

Chapter 11

It took only a day to reach the camp of Ben Sadi Assar, leader of the Assar tribe, and once there, Karim could easily see, as could everyone, that the Assar's well had caved in.

Silently, the sheik led the way down the short hill and scraped his boot in the dry sand where once water had been. Nearby palm trees were still flourishing, but while there was underground water for their needs, it obviously was out of reach of the tribesmen and, therefore, of the goats that gathered around the collapsed opening, hanging their heads and bleating plaintively.

Still the sheik was silent, his face impassive, and no one else spoke as he led the way back up the hill and into a large tent.

When Karim, following directly behind his father, bent to step under the tent flap, he was surprised to find the council of the five tribes already assembled there and waiting.

Karim touched his forehead to show proper respect for his elders before seating himself in the hassock next to but lower than his father's and arranged in a circle with the other cushions and hassocks.

Karim hadn't expected them to meet so soon. He had expected an opportunity to fill his stomach and to quench his thirst. But seeing there would be no delay for such luxuries, Karim removed his thoughts from his clawing hunger and, with a developed self-discipline focused his attention instead on the meeting at hand.

The Sheik of El Abadan, Grand Sanusi, and leader of the council was the first to speak in a quiet serious voice.

"We have come, and we have seen the damage to the well of this oasis that is the proper domain of the tribe of Assar. And now we ask the leader of the Assar, Ben Sadi Assar, to speak of those who have dared commit this unholy act of desecrating this well and source of life."

All heads turned to Ben Sadi Assar, whose cold countenance fixed them all with a look of greatest gravity.

"The English soldiers," he began from between clenched teeth. "They have proven themselves once again more treacherous than hyenas. All men know this oasis has been but a small watering hole yielding only ten skins of water between dawn and dusk. Always the sides of this well have been fragile so they must be treated respectfully and drawn with great care. But the white men are greedy. They are not satisfied with the slowness of the water, though it has served my people thus for a thousand years. The whites came with tools of a type we have not seen before, great metal scoops operated by ropes, and with these they dug the well, though it was not our wish, and only promises not to raise arms against the whites without taking counsel kept our sons from raising their swords against them. Instead we only asked the white men to stop—begged them." Assar's black eyes snapped. "But to our pleas they only responded with foolish promises, saying they could make the well yield more water than could ever be remembered, enough to double our numbers of goats. But the whites have always lied, and so it was proven again. But this time Allah himself punished those who dared interfere with his plan. For their impudence the well collapsed, burying those men who dared defile it."

Assar paused, looking to each elder, his voice cold as he spoke again. "Now the white men have gone to the abandoned fort at Sevit. But they go leaving behind a well destroyed and useless. And though we have dug until our backs are broken, still the water hides from those who have abused it, providing drink only for these noble palms while our herds drop into the sand and perish."

Hashad Babir Rasoun, sitting at the left hand of Assar, nodded in agreement, his own eyes narrowing with anger as he added, "But the English have not only desecrated our well, they also have brought us their infidel sickness that marks the faces of the young and weak with red spots before they die of a wasting fever. Enough I say! The English take our lands, our water, and even our women as their own." His hand gripped the hilt of his dagger. "Now they must be shown this land is not theirs, but ours, and that we are not men who would cower beneath the stamp of their boots. I say we attack the fort at Sevit and burn it and the soldiers to dust!"

Karim shifted on his hassock, glancing about the room and feeling even more uneasy as four other elders nodded in agreement. Though he would one day inherit the title of Grand Sanusi and leader of the council from his father, it was considered improper for him to speak when the elders were gathered. Instead it was his place to be silent and to listen and learn from them. Such was the custom of his people, but while he did not speak, a dark look of concern came into his alert eyes.

It was an expression not missed by Sadi Assar, who did not show the disapproval he felt. He had hoped to convince the Grand Sanusi immediately of his plan, thus demonstrating to the rest of the council his influence. But now he could see that Karim would object although each man here knew the heir himself to be half-white, and therefore his opinions untrustworthy. Already some here feared the succession of Karim al-Sharif, particularly during a time when the whites were their greatest threat. Could one of white blood be expected to act strongly against those of his own kin? they had asked.

Now Assar stared coldly at Karim al-Sharif before turning to the Grand Sanusi. "Perhaps the son of Hamid al-Sharif wishes to speak?" he asked sarcastically. "In his youth perhaps he thinks his wisdom greater than those who have lived longer."

All eyes turned to Karim who suddenly felt more acutely half-white than ever before. He knew that because of his blood his judgments would be questionable in this matter. Yet remembering again his promise to his mother, Karim cleared his throat, and looked directly at Assar.

"The honorable Assar will please forgive my intrusion into the council and accept my gratitude for an opportunity to speak. I put a simple suggestion before my elders. Since it is the English who have destroyed the well, let them be the ones who rebuild it."

Assar looked startled as Karim continued. "If we kill the English, we still have no water. It has already been said that the whites have tools of which we have no knowledge. With these tools perhaps the well can be repaired. Do not the white men need water as much as we?"

The eyes of both Hashad Babir Rasoun and Ben Sadi Assar were piercing as Assar spoke. "And what of honor? You want to negotiate with these white dogs? The son of Hamid al-Sharif would let this unholy desecration of the well, an act forbidden by Allah, go unanswered? And if honor is of no concern, then what do you say about their diseases?" Assar finished glowering.

Keeping his face politely masked, Karim wondered at the unreasoning of these elders. Perhaps it was his "white side" that made him hesitate to kill the English—and of course his promise. But couldn't they see that a slaughter of these men would gain nothing but a transient satisfaction—a pointless revenge? He faced Assar squarely.

"Since this disease has already spread among our people it will continue to spread whether or not we kill the English. But isn't it known that the white men who bring disease also often bring the means to cure it? Let the white men repair the waterhole with the tools that we have not. And when this is done, let them give us medicine to cure the red spots. Then they will be made to go in peace from our land."

Outraged, the chiefs Assar and Rasoun seemed to rise as one toward the younger man. "By Allah!" Rasoun began before a gesture from the chief Ali Ben Zadi silenced him and made him sit back on his hassock.

Ali Ben Zadi shook his head so his gray beard wagged at them. His heavily lined eyes squinted to sharp points as slowly he gazed round the circle of men. Then with the dignity befitting the eldest member of the council, Ali Ben Zadi said, "The son of Hamid al-Sharif has wisdom in his words. Do none of you believe it is better to drink than to kill? The white infidels have wronged the tribe of Assar as they have many others. But when a camel yields milk, one does not slaughter it for its meat. How is it wise to kill the English when it is they who can best repair the damage? How is it wise to kill the English when it is they who can cure our sons of this treacherous disease? I give my support to the plan of Karim al-Sharif."

Karim felt a constriction in his chest relax. To have the support of the most revered of the council was a good sign. But it was when he saw a look on his father's face that told him he had won that his breath came easier. His promise would be fulfilled.

There was little more debate, Assar and Rasoun being unwilling to publicly side against both the son of their leader and Ali Ben Zadi. So a decision was made to negotiate with the whites first for medicine and repair of the well before any further measures were taken. The following morning, the sheik, Assar, Karim, and a complement of warriors all rode directly to Sevit where they entered the white men's fort, their faces expressionless, their silver-decorated rifles unslung and flashing in the intense sunlight.

They were greeted in faltering Arabic by one soldier while others looked on, then Karim addressed the Englishman in his language, asking to see his captain.

A few onlookers murmured with surprise at this Arab's unaccented command of their language. The soldier nodded curtly and asked, "Who should I tell him is here?"

"My name is Karim al-Sharif. I speak for my father, Hamid al-Sharif."

"I'll inform Captain Clayton," the soldier replied. And turning to face around in a neat spin, he marched in the opposite direction, shouldering aside a heavy rug that hung suspended over a doorway in the crumbling mud brick wall.

As they waited, Karim noticed the suspicious way the English soldiers eyed them, and the equally suspicious way his own warriors had their rifles plainly visible, the butt ends resting on the pommels of their saddles, the muzzles pointing upward, their fingers only a fraction of a second from the trigger.

Minutes ticked by as they waited. The sun beat down unmercifully, and the horses had begun pawing the soft earth before finally footsteps were heard approaching from behind the rug.

The soldier appeared again with another, heavier, man in his wake—apparently Captain Clayton, hair grayed at the temples and gold patches decorating the shoulders of his tight-fitting white shirt. His eyes were most striking of all, large and deeply blue so they seemed almost violet. But besides being more beautiful than any man's eyes Karim had ever seen, it pleased him that they were clear and straightforward, the eyes of an honest man.

The first soldier indicated Karim, saying, "That one, sir."

Captain Clayton walked to Karim's horse and paused. "I'm told you asked to speak to me, young man," Captain Clayton said in a polite tone. But Karim's equally polite reply was stopped just as it was begun when an Englishman with smaller gold patches on his shoulder pointed to one of Assar's warriors and shouted, "It's him, by God—the one who led the raid on the supplies. Thieving nigger!" And waving his hand to another soldier he shouted, "Sergeant Danover, arrest this man!"

Somehow the shooting started. It happened so quickly Karim never knew exactly who began it, but suddenly the warrior beside him was blasted off his horse, and Karim found the Englishmen's rifles lowering to point at him.

All hope for negotiation vanished, and governed by his instinct to survive, Karim raised his own rifle, quickly took aim, and fired before whirling his horse and shouting to the others to take cover.

They were immediately pinned down by English fire.

For several minutes it seemed hopeless. But then Karim heard the battle cry of the Assar tribe, which had been waiting beyond the dunes, and now he silently praised Allah as he watched his Arab brothers charge toward the fortress wall in a wave of flying robes and dust and plunging horses, firing as they yelled *"Allahu akbar,* God is great!"

Looking from behind the wagon, Karim blessed the attacking warriors even as he cursed his own stupidity for trusting the whites. What a fool he had been, even instructing his men not to wear their normal amounts of ammunition lest they alarm these English.

Bending over his rifle, Karim fired carefully, making sure each bullet found its mark. One soldier fell, then another, and a third plummeted from the wall overhead before a shout made Karim turn round to see his father, who, having apparently run out of ammunition, was engaged in hand-to-hand combat with two soldiers.

Scrambling to the sheik's assistance, Karim had just thrust his dagger into the back of one soldier when a new sound of rapid rifle fire dominated the din, and raising his eyes to the top corner of the fortress wall, he paused, astonished to see a gun such as he had never seen before, a gun mounted on three legs that could swivel to point in any direction while firing continuously.

The sheik and all the men were staring at this ominous machine, watching as it pointed over the fortress wall and down onto the charging Assar warriors who were instantly mown down like dry grass in the wind—men and horses suddenly squirming on the sand like smashed beetles.

Then the gun was turning again, and this time pointing down upon them, its bullets shattering their wagon barrier to splinters and hitting anything in its path as its rain of bullets moved toward the sheik.

Looking for a way of escape, Karim's eyes turned to the fortress gates and, seeing them closed and latched, he realized they must be opened or they were trapped. He shouted to his father. Then flinging himself on a horse, he charged for it, bullets splattering around him.

Reaching the barrier then, he leaned down to unfasten it. A bullet careened past his ear, burning a hole in the wooden gate. Another struck beside it, and another before his horse suddenly spun and heaved and, jerking forward, collapsed.

In a desperate leap, Karim jumped clear of the horse. Then lightning flashed in a shower of hot fire and all was dark.

Chapter 12

Where was he? Karim's head throbbed as he opened his eyes, momentarily blinded by the dusty streamers of light that pierced through the niches in the rock wall surrounding him.

He was in a cell—taken prisoner. That much at least was clear, and clenching his jaw against the pain that soared up his neck to hammer his forehead, Karim rose until he could peer through one of the largest cracks between the rocks. He found himself looking directly into the open area in the center of the fort where, only that morning, he had ridden in, so naive and full of optimism.

What had happened to the others—and his father? . . .

Rumbling sounds seemed to come from within his skull. But as consciousness emerged, rising slowly from a deep chasm, he realized it was the sharp beat of a drum and the stamping of boots as soldiers began marching past his cell in flashes of leather and rifles and uniforms.

Jumbled thoughts chased about in his brain, and looking toward a figure at the far end of the open space, Karim's brain finally focused on a single question.

Was it possible *that* figure was his father—hands tied behind his back, face streaked with blood, standing alone facing the soldiers who made a sharp mechanical turn to form a line opposite him?

Yes, his father—impossible as it was, his lips making a taut line as he refused a blindfold with a jerk of his imperial head, his eyes straight forward, his expression unmoved.

At one side of the line of soldiers, Captain Clayton

stood, violet eyes hard as he raised a sword in salute and the drum began a continuous roll like the pelt of heavy rain against the roofs of El Abadan.

"Ready!" Captain Clayton's voice was clipped.

In a snappy motion the soldiers all brought their rifles chest high and paused.

"Aim!'

Together the rifle barrels were leveled at the sheik, who remained motionless, his feet wide astride.

Then Clayton's raised sword fell. "Fire!"

The rifles blasted with a deafening roar, throwing the sheik backward, and drowning out a strangled "No!" that cracked in Karim's throat as he clawed his way up the rock wall until he stood looking out the barred cell window.

His father lay sprawled in the dirt, in a pool of spreading crimson, his chest a gaping hole. An iron fist shackled Karim's soul with guilt as he blankly realized it was *he* who was responsible, *he* who had trusted the whites, who had led his father, scantily armed, into their camp. And they had killed him—the Sheik of El Abadan, the richest, most powerful leader in all the desert—murdered him!

The soldiers lowered their rifles, and placing a toe of one boot at the heel of the other, together they spun neatly round, marching off to the count of "Hut! . . . Hut! . . . Hut!"

Then two additional men came into view drawing a cart already half filled with manure. They stopped beside the sheik's form, one man reaching for his feet, and the other his arms, to sling his body onto the top of the manure pile. Then brushing their hands free of dust, they hauled the cart beyond the fortress gates.

Impotent rage filled Karim's chest until it hurt to breathe. Curses came to mind, but none terrible enough to match his fury. As long as he lived, he would remember, and he would hate—and by Allah, he would have his *revenge!*

The sun shone fierce and blinding so the agony in Karim's head made him reel as hot tears poured out of his eyes and down his neck. Then letting himself fall face down on the dirty floor, he pounded his fist into the dust and cried.

*   *   *

Had Karim but known it, his father's execution had not
been an action lightly taken, but rather one carefully carried out with calculated risk.

Captain George Clayton wasn't a man given to rash actions of any kind, but he had a job to do and he was a man
who prided himself on accomplishing the task before him.

Months ago he had been sent to the Sahara by order of
Queen Victoria herself, to explore, to map, to maintain an
outpost, and most of all, to dominate those rich trade routes
considered ripe for English investments.

So far his task had not been an easy one. The journey
had been arduous, the previous maps largely inaccurate,
those sheiks with whom he was to bargain for dominance
of the trade routes elusive. And now his patience had been
tried to the limit by the constant thievery of their already
short supplies, by a lack of grass and water for his horses
and food for his men. Also, to make matters worse, Captain Clayton had seen his soldiers, one by one, stricken by a
fever resembling measles that he could only imagine was
some kind of native pox, whose debilitating effects had
spread through the ranks, further weakening his tenuous
hold on the small fort.

It was an intolerable position, one that had to be recti-
fied. Neither their food nor their medical supplies could
stand any more thievery, while these Arabs were getting
more daring every day. Yes, Clayton had told himself, the
situation was steadily worsening. He must make some show
of strength now. These Arabs had to be given a lesson.

So Captain Clayton had done his duty. He had executed
the leader of what he had been assured were bandits (one
of whom having been positively identified by his own lieutenant). And it was only afterward that he thought again
of the young English-speaking Arab, and hearing he had
been taken prisoner, went to see him.

Captain Clayton found the young Arab sitting on the
floor of his cell, the look in his dark impenetrable eyes as
dangerous as a viper's. He couldn't have been more than
twenty, yet his face had the hard glittering coldness of a

much older man. Yes, and there was something else curious about him, too, something that stood out beyond his fiercesome looks and flexing jaw. Indeed, Clayton thought, he was as light-skinned as many of his own men, and his features seemed, well, almost white. And where did he learn his excellent English?

But Captain Clayton's questions were to remain unanswered since he had not time to speak, only time to regret entering the young Arab's cell alone when the lad leaped upon him like a giant cat, knocking him to the floor and sliding a knife expertly between his ribs.

In the gathering clouds of unconsciousness, the last Clayton knew was the sound of his own inadequate thrashing, of the cell door clanging open, and of the guard's voice saying, "My God! He's killin' the captain!"

Karim cried out with frustration as two frantic guards pulled him off his prey. The makeshift knife fashioned from a metal plate had slipped and the English captain was left alive. Karim continued to struggle, but then a white hot pain shot through his head, his legs crumbled, his cheek hit the floor, and everything vanished.

When Karim came to, it was the following day. He didn't know how long he had been unconscious, but sniffing the wind, he knew a storm was brewing. And that night, when it came, bringing a blinding swirl of sand that shrouded the desert and forced the English to take shelter, he saw his chance for escape.

Like the mourning cries of desert spirits, the wind howled and, under the cover of this eerie wail, the English never heard the lock of Karim's cell burst under the impact of a loose stone from his cell wall or the guard's call for help before being rendered unconscious. Under cover of the flying sand Karim secured a mount from the stables and disappeared into the open desert, where only a native would dare venture and only a fool would follow. The next morning even the hoof prints of his stolen horse had been obliterated.

* * *

It took Karim five days to reach El Abadan, his skin almost black from sun, his heart filled with a new bitter hatred.

He was taken directly to his harem, where he was revived and where he remained recovering for several more days, still unaware of the final, horrible truth. And it was only when he was strong again, that haltingly, salaaming until their faces touched the floor, his ministers told him his mother had died, abruptly, ten days before from the ravages of the white man's red-spotted fever.

At first the young sheik had said nothing, though every muscle of his face tensed. Then he demanded to see the body, and, when he had seen it—bloated, ghastly as it was, he shut himself in his most private room and spoke to no one.

His ministers took up a vigil at his door then, and for three days nervously drank coffee and ate nothing as they conferred in low voices. It was two more days before the young sheik appeared again, and there seemed nothing left of youth in the hard warrior's eyes that looked back at them.

"Is this not the leader we have prayed for?" the ministers whispered. And one by one, they fell to their knees before the new Sheik of El Abadan.

Later, Karim cursed the days of ceremonies necessary by tradition for the inheritance of his father's titles. If he had attacked the fort at Sevit immediately, he might have had the opportunity to capture Clayton. But as it was, Clayton was gone when his warriors overran the fort a fortnight later, taking the soldiers by such surprise they were killed without resistance. Karim supposed he had gone back to England, but no one knew for sure, and no prisoners were taken who could tell. So when the fort had been burned to the ground, Karim al-Sharif stood in the rubble circled by the elders of the five tribes, his face carved of stone as he raised his father's sword and spoke clearly to the heavens.

"I, Karim al-Sharif, swear to avenge the wrongs committed against my people, to free them from the greed and power of the whites, to kill the Englishman Clayton, and to sell his women and children as slaves. Before Allah, this I swear!"

Chapter 13

As heir to the throne of El Abadan, Karim had been carefully trained by his father in matters of strategy, trade, warfare, and the Holy Koran, and this education was enlarged by his mother's knowledge of the outer world and the languages of the whites. But Karim's enemies wasted little time in testing the young sheik's skills. He had hardly come to power before an ambitious cousin raised a rebellion against him, the Hussar began a series of raids on his caravans, and crop failures which, in the past, had signaled a year of famine, were reported in the south.

But the sheik of El Abadan, undaunted and with skill beyond his years, rallied his loyal forces and put down the rebellion in a single swift, bloody purge, then defeated the Hussar in a stealthy ambush, chasing them back to their mountain stronghold. And in the early spring that came to the south that year, the sheik ordered new crops planted and opened the city's granaries and rationed the grain so the people would not starve.

Yet this was only the beginning. Next the sheik met with the leaders of other tribes beyond the five of his existing alliance, and persuaded many to join with him. Though some still refused, fearing retribution from the Hussar, he strengthened his forces to twelve tribes, making him more powerful than any lord had ever been in the great desert. In the south he purchased more land for crops and a gold mine. To the east, he enlarged his circle of spies, placing them in the Hussar camp. And with the new, most modern weapons made, including the rapid-fire Gatling gun, he defended the trade routes even more mercilessly than his father had.

So prosperous years followed, and El Abadan grew to be

the capital of African trade, a distant outpost known only remotely by outsiders, a conduit of riches from the Mediterranean to the African interior and source of those plumes, wine, diamonds, gold, and ivory so treasured by Europeans. And on those traders who used his trade routes, the sheik levied a tariff so his coffers grew. But the English soldiers came ever more often, and the French and Italian were more numerous than before.

With their gold they corrupted the governments in the cities, so they dominated not only business there, but politics as well. Finally then, saying they were invited, they established a military presence, an army that Arabs could join only as servants and grooms. And with this army they entered the interior, this time more well equipped than ever, and marched along the trade routes to guard goods bound for European traders. Often they left small detachments behind, slowly spreading their influence even into the desert. And when the time came that they could no longer be ignored, it took all Karim's will power to bargain with his hated enemy now that they were too well armed, too organized simply to attack as before. And even as he sat across the table from the English captain and his two lieutenants, hatred burned in Karim's heart. But while he knew they would stop at nothing to have access to the trade routes, the sheik had a bargaining chip of his own.

"Why not pay for the use of these trade routes as Arabs have paid tariffs for centuries to those who protected them?" he suggested, sipping tea in the English fashion. "Already my men guard these routes. They know the land, and its dangers, and protect the goods I myself buy and sell. Would this not be less costly than to deploy English troops to protect English goods? So much simpler for me to punish these bandits when they dare attack than it is for you. And there are many bandits in the desert. Have you not already discovered this?" His strong teeth showed in a smile. "And many of these bandits particularly prefer to attack whites, whom they consider their enemies."

The veiled threat in the sheik's words did not escape the three English soldiers. But aside from the chill they all felt whenever this young man fixed his black eyes directly into

theirs, the English officers were impressed by the civilized
way in which he conducted business—like a gentleman
seated at a table instead of like most of these savages,
squatting on cushions.

They had heard he was ruler of a desert city, and leader
of a powerful alliance far to the south, but he had avoided
all questions concerning this. And while his manner was
intimidating, he inspired confidence, and strangely, while
they feared him, they believed the promises he made. Anyway, they told themselves, they were grateful to him for
keeping them from equipping yet another vulnerable outpost far into the desert. And who wanted another disaster
like Khartoum?

So it was agreed, and hands were shaken all around.
And in the months after, the English didn't regret their
decision as the sheik faithfully carried out his part of the
bargain, protecting the English goods with the same care,
and swift retribution, as he protected his own. For their
part, the English paid the tariff, pulled their troops back
to the cities and occupied themselves with struggling with
the French and Italians over control of the riches they were
able to extract from those they could. Karim quickly took
advantage of this, making similar trade arrangements with
the French and Italians as well, taking their gold for protecting their shipments while he used their payments to buy
coffee and tobacco fields in east Africa, diamond mines in
the west, and land producing black oil, a substance with a
growing market in Europe.

But even as he kept his promises to the whites, Karim
spoke to his ministers of uniting all the tribes in the desert
into a true nation free of English or French or Italians—an
independent nation where all men would be free. And
when it was so, he told them with gritted teeth, their voices
would speak as one and they would be heard throughout
the world. And to this his ministers nodded their heads.
Indeed, they thought, this young sheik was even more cunning than the old one.

So the reputation of Karim al-Sharif grew along with his
riches, and by the time Karim reached twenty-six, all
twelve tribes were prospering beyond all the times before,

and a time of peace came when the need to take arms
against bandit or rebel came less often, and then not at all.
The whites became occupied with their own squabbles and
ventured into the desert less often.

The time had finally come when Karim could safely
leave the governing of El Abadan in the hands of his ministers and embark on his mission of vengeance. Though
years had passed since his father's death, Karim's memory
of that cursed day had not dimmed. He would kill Clayton
and destroy everything the Englishman held dear. Now, at
last, he could begin.

The first thing he must do, Karim told himself, is learn
to move comfortably in the Englishman's world. Hadn't his
father always warned him to know his enemies well?

"Keep your enemy close to your heart," the old sheik
had tutored him. "Then how can he draw his sword without bringing your attention?"

As he thought and planned, Karim grew more and more
curious about the lands of the whites beyond the Mediterranean. What might France, the country of his mother's
birth, be like? he asked himself during the nights when he
could not sleep. And what riches could the white lands hold
for his Arab brothers? After all, Karim reasoned, if the
French, English, and Italians could purchase the goods of
Africa, pay tariffs, and transport them across the Mediterranean, couldn't he do the same? And wouldn't that give
him more gold, more power for the eventual uprising
against them? So, in the spring of the year 1890, Karim
al-Sharif set out alone for Paris.

"An Arab," one middle-aged woman remarked to her
friend as together they leaned out a window high above rue
des Martyrs and pointed to the white-robed figure below.

Her friend's head turned to look. "Humph!" she exclaimed, pausing to nibble a small pastry. "Certainly is a
haughty one if you ask me. Just look at the way he carries
himself—proud as Lucifer, and just like the whole quarter
is here for his personal benefit."

The first woman nodded, cocking her curly head as she

continued to squint at the young man continuing down the street. "Funny how a man can still look so manly when he's wearing those robes instead of pants. Just take him for example. Now you'd always know *he* was a man."

The friend nodded, and both women continued to watch as the Arab strode down the cobblestoned street and turned at the corner of rue des Abbesses, disappearing from view.

Now Karim found himself on a more crowded street lined with small cafés whose tables and chairs spilled out into the street.

A crowd of people were sitting at the tables sipping wine and chatting, and Karim had walked only a short distance past them when a girl suddenly fell into step behind him.

This was not the first time Karim had been solicited in the two days since his arrival in Paris. Each time before he had impatiently waved the woman away. But now he allowed this one to stay, and when he didn't rebuff her, she quickly increased her stride to walk beside him.

She was not beautiful, though passingly pretty, and the skintight blue dress, which branded her for exactly what she was, was made of spotless poplin, revealing the tops of breasts tanned *café au lait,* and glowing with health.

In Islam, such women were considered to be without souls. But this one seemed different than others, as if a spot of light still glimmered beneath the surface where she was, as yet, undefiled. And watching her smile up at him, Karim noticed her expression was not forced and lacked the brittle quality typical of her kind.

What would she bring in the slave market of El Abadan, he wondered idly, a thousand dinars? Two thousand, perhaps?

Maria, too, from behind her smile, watched with an evaluating eye. He was obviously an Arab, and a devilishly handsome one, and the confidence in his stride was not the way of a poor man. How did he like his women? she wondered, sucking her lower lip, and already feeling him between her legs in her lusty imagination.

Even if he wasn't rich, Maria decided, he would be someone more interesting than my regulars, and besides, I might have something interesting to tell the girls at Quintet's tomorrow.

Her mind made up then, Maria ignored any further misgivings, and acting as if they had already been introduced, pointed an arm up the street and said, "Look! There's the Café de la Vache Bleue. Let's go in!"

The Arab's eyes penetrated hers for a moment, sending a shiver of unfamiliar excitement and a little fear up her spine before he nodded. Then together, they moved off.

The fortyish, thick-bellied Italian who owned the çafé, acknowledged Maria with a curt nod as she came in. Earlier in the week she had arranged with him to receive a tenth of everything her "customers" spent. He was glad for the business that Maria and a number of other "working girls" brought in, but, as he told the cook, he had no respect for her kind, and he didn't bother to personally seat them now, but rather indicated an available table with a jerk of his double chin.

Maria led on. She had hoped that the café would have the intimate atmosphere it sometimes did in the late afternoon. But unfortunately, it was crowded with a boisterous group of habitués that made it louder than usual.

One member of this group was particularly drunk, and foul language and cigar smoke drifted from the corner where he sat leaning his chair back against the wall and gesturing widely to his cronies.

Some things can't be helped, Maria thought with an imperceptible sigh. And in spite of the men, she resolutely walked the young Arab between tables of laughing couples to finally seat herself at the only vacant one, unluckily, near the unpleasant men.

A *garçon* appeared in a crisp white waistcoat, nodding perfunctorily and scribbling down Maria's order of an expensive wine, and sharing her look of disappointment when her "patron" ordered only coffee. Then, flourishing his round tray overhead, he was gone again through the swinging kitchen doors.

While they waited, Maria chatted affably, moving from one topic to another with hardly a pause, trying to find a subject to interest the young man. But his expression remained serious and tinged with boredom, and running out of things to say, Maria felt awkward by the time their drinks arrived. The *garçon* indifferently set their order before them, then straightened up, his eyes glancing to the ceiling as he rolled on the balls of his feet with an air of expectation.

It took a moment for Karim to realize what was expected, and when he did, he reached inside his robes, producing a heavy gold coin that he set on the waiter's tray with a dull tap.

Maria's red mouth formed a soft "O" before spreading into a smile.

The waiter looked from the coin to the young Arab and back again before he took it and left, returning several minutes later with a large stack of paper francs as change.

The transaction was apparently noticed by one of the men at the next table, and taking his cigar from his mouth, he spoke loudly out one side of it to no one in particular.

"No wonder these bloody *niggers* are so thieving poor. Even when they get a little money they spend it all showing off for a whore."

Coarse laughter followed along with several other comments too low to be heard.

Maria looked from the Arab to the men, forcing a laugh at their words and startled to see a deadly flame leap into the Arab's black eyes.

"How can you be insulted and laugh?" he asked, ominously quiet, reaching into his robes and rising from his chair.

Maria grabbed his arm, frightened words suddenly spilling from her so rapidly that Karim had difficulty understanding. Only the words "jail" and "foreigner" were clear, but they were enough to make him pause and remember suddenly he was not in El Abadan where *he* ruled, but in Paris. And this wasn't the first lesson he'd learned about the way the whites preferred to treat Arabs.

Don't be a fool, he told himself, staring murderously at the man who now turned away, choosing to ignore him.

Now it would draw too much attention to himself and destroy his plans. So sitting down again in his own chair, Karim expelled his breath slowly.

"Have some coffee," he heard Maria's voice through the receding waves of fury. "Don't pay any attention to them. They're drunk."

She was shaken by the incident and, at the moment, was asking herself why she had solicited this barbarous young man in the first place. This is a lesson for me, she thought. If I get out of this I'll be more careful.

"Who are those men?" Karim asked coldly, still looking at the back of the one who had insulted him.

"They seem English to me," Maria answered, relieved to see the explosive look ebbing from his face so now he seemed only very angry. "*A vôtre santé,*" Maria toasted him with her wine before sipping it. But Karim still ignored her, the fury of years redoubling within him now—a canker bursting with poison. English! How he hated this particular breed of white. Now he could do nothing—but one day . . . one day!

Turning back to the girl then, he regarded her silently, a plan forming in his mind before he said, "Take me to where you live," in the tone of a command rather than a request.

Maria, who had been thinking about bringing up this topic, bounced up from her chair, all her gaiety returning. Walking so the cheeks of her buttocks jiggled against her tight skirt, she led the young Arab back between the crowded tables and out into the street.

"This way," she said motioning. And together they started up the old cobblestones the way they had come.

Home for Maria was a small basement flat beneath a sweets shop, which, upon entering, Karim found clean and tidy, and decorated simply but with a warm comfortable quality that he found appealing. He walked its length, looking with interest at the number of small pictures, the little couch with needlepoint cushions, and the kitchen with its wooden spoons and gadgets so common to a French home, but totally unfamiliar to him.

* * *

"That's a nutcracker," Maria explained as Karim lifted a carved wooden man with a wide painted grin down from a sideboard. Then taking the wooden man from him, she placed a walnut in its jaw and squeezed the handle. A sharp snap followed and a piece of shell fired out and ricocheted off the table top.

The man seemed interested, so removing the walnut from the nutcracker, Maria peeled away the rest of the shell and shiny brown skin, and handed the nutmeat to him.

Curiously, Karim took it, and placed it in his mouth, slowly chewing, and finally swallowing the tidbit. Then, for the first time, he smiled, and a magnetic warmth entered his eyes that touched Maria so that she knew at once she would do anything short of murder to make him look at her that way again.

"I have a lot to learn," he commented more to himself than to her as he moved about her apartment. He seemed thoughtful for a moment while examining everything with his eyes. Then casually he drew her to him and kissed her. Without saying another word, Maria took his hand and led him to her bed.

It was getting dark, and his chest seemed only a dark outline against the sheets. Her fingers caressed his chest hair, letting the fine, though abundant, mass trail between her fingers. She was aware of his sweaty smell that was not pungent, nor sour, but a fresh musk. There were ridges beneath her hands, and she wondered if they could be scars. Once, two years before, she had bedded a criminal (though she hadn't known he was one at the time). And another time she had sold herself to a Spanish Gypsy (on a dare). Both of those men had scars, and bringing the single candle closer and setting it on the round bedside table, Maria was surprised to find one so young with so many similar marks.

Pulling his robe off his shoulders, she touched each one of them, first with her fingertips, and then, bending close, with her tongue, working from his neck downward over the hard swell of his pectorals and onto his belly, feeling the thicker hair and the skin that had not reached the sun, which seemed nearly as light as her own.

She was reaching for the hard head of his penis, already stabbing high against his robes, when she paused, thinking suddenly that some men didn't want a woman to take the lead, and concerned about making any *faux pas,* she sat back on her haunches beside him and whispered huskily, "Is there something particular you would like? I'd love to do anything you wanted me to. *Ton plaisir est mon plaisir.*"

He smiled with that same touch of magnetic warmth that enchanted her. "Do as you usually do," he said. "What do men of your country prefer? I want to learn everything about Europeans."

He was completely at his ease, so unlike many men, and particularly young ones. He seemed as if women made love to him often, and it was something he accepted, as the master accepts the adulation of a slave.

Maria smiled her most seductive smile. She knew how to drive a man wild, how to do all the things "good" wives would never dream of doing. And this man she wanted to please more than any she had encountered. And so she began, gently, taking everything slowly, kissing his body with lips and a flickering tongue and running her fingers gently along his inner thighs, and then higher, to brush the curling hair at his most sensitive of parts, and knowing as she did that he was hard and ready, even before she took him in her mouth with practiced skill, slowly, moving over every bit of that engorged member to the very top where her tongue made swift circular motions before returning down the shaft and then repeating.

She knew what extreme pleasure this gave a man, that soon, when she came to the top he would strain against her mouth. She had even had them beg her for more when, sometimes, at that pinnacle of intense desire, she would pause to feel her full power. But when she did this now, eager most of all to have *this* man beg for what she gave, he neither begged or even spoke. Instead, as if he already knew this game, she found herself quickly on her back and entered with firm, if not brutal force.

So! He could be impatient after all, she thought as swiftly he spent himself deep and grew hard a second time. And now he did the work, in long sure strokes, seeming to know already how to bring her to stunning satisfaction such as she had never known. And afterward, as they reclined together among the sheets and pillows that Maria had herself embroidered with pink poppies, he surprised her by saying, "You have a very clever and pretty little body, Maria," as idly he touched her thigh with a long finger. "But I am interested in more from you."

"More?" Maria asked, her imagination somersaulting. What could he mean? "Of course I'll do anything. But what is it you want me to do?"

"It is my wish that you teach me the customs of your people so well I can be mistaken for one of them. Then when you have taught me all you can, you will forget the Arab I am now. And in return, I will start you in any business you choose."

Maria's head spun, remembering the gold coin he'd handled so casually. The proposition was like something out of a dream. He wanted to stay, not just tonight, but for many more. And later . . . well, later she would see.

He had spoken as if her refusal were out of the question, and she affirmed his attitude with an eager nod.

"Yes, of course, you already speak French well." Maria's eyes perused him appraisingly, cocking her head before she continued. "Yes—in European clothes you could easily pass for a Frenchman or even a Spaniard, couldn't you?"

"It is agreed, then," he stated. "Tomorrow we begin."

Again Maria nodded, a new excitement brightening her features. "But what shall I call you?" she asked as an afterthought. "You will need a European name."

The man smiled then, a slow inward smile. "Call me Brandon Phillips," he said. "Monsieur Brandon Phillips."

Chapter 14

Six months later only a trace of Brandon's former wildness was left, just enough to give him a certain air of excitement which caused women's heads to turn whenever he walked down the street. And now it was no longer an uncivilized Arab who sat across the table from Maria in their new stylish apartment but a suave, polished European dressed as a man of the world. But, staring into her salad bowl one night, and picking at its contents without appetite, Maria had to admit to herself that, just as his progress had been marvelous, her usefulness to him was quickly diminishing. She had exhausted her repertory of information and now the silent meals they passed together gave her little cause for hope.

You are a fool, Maria, she told herself. He will leave you and you have always known it but still you have let yourself fall in love with him.

She sighed heavily, remembering her aunt, who had always said her luck would never be good, and glancing up at Brandon, she told herself that he had never pretended to love her, although he had provided exactly what he had promised. In the bank in her name was a generous sum with which to open a business of her own once they parted ways. A group of girls would be profitable, she thought. Or she had always dreamed of owning a florist shop. She sighed then, leaning forward and ringing a small bell to signal for the next course to be served.

The young maid appeared, hired by Brandon when they had first moved to the larger house. And now Maria realized that once he left, the maid would be a luxury she couldn't afford, at least until her business became profitable, and this pained her. The girl's presence had made Maria feel more like a lady than any of the other things her patron had provided. Now the realization of soon losing the girl increased Maria's sense of melancholy.

Another half hour ticked by on the large wall clock be-

hind him. Still he didn't speak. Maria added more coffee
to her cup and sipped it before pushing it away, her hand
enclosing again the half-full glass of white wine that remained. Suddenly then she found herself unable to post-
pone the inevitable for even one more agonizing minute.

"I will miss you, monsieur," she said sadly. "But perhaps
you will think of me, sometimes, and remember little
Maria who turned you into a Frenchman?"

M. Phillips looked up from his coffee and studied her a
moment with a certain friendly warmth. "I'm grateful for
all your help, Maria."

His tone was polite but the distance in it cut her more
than hostility would have. Tears gathered in her eyes, and
she pulled herself up sharply. He is only being honest, she
told herself. He had never made love to her as men had
sometimes done, making reckless promises, and compli-
menting her beauty. He had always been distant and busi-
nesslike, although kind, and after the months they had
spent together, she knew little more about him than on the
day he had first come to her little flat on the other side of
Paris.

Her lips quivered. The sense of finality in his posture
brought a pain stabbing her heart. She pictured the apartment bare of him, his cravat no longer tossed carelessly
across the bed; his elegant ivory toilet appointments gone;
the masculine smells of leather and shaving soap disappeared.

Suddenly Maria felt desperate—reckless, and burst into
tears.

"Monsieur Phillips . . . Brandon!" she wailed, her
arms parting in entreaty. "Please don't leave. I will do anything if you stay. I love you—only you—I didn't know how
much! You have become my life!"

Gaining control of herself, she paused, already regretting
her undignified and useless outburst. She bit her lip tentatively and glanced at him, wiping her eyes with a napkin.

He was looking at her kindly, but made no move to take
her in his arms or to silence her tears with gentle kisses of
reassurance as she prayed he would. There was only a long
silence which stretched out between them.

At last he spoke, calmly, as if trying to quiet a child.

"You have done a great service for me, Maria, and for this you have been paid as we agreed." When she didn't look up his big hand came to cover hers. "Love doesn't come to a man as easily as it does to a woman," he finished.

Maria dabbed at her tears. There was no point in debasing herself further, she told herself firmly, although she had little dignity left to preserve. You have always known this day would come. And trying to square her sagging shoulders, she comforted herself with the thought that at least she would never have to sell herself again.

At ten o'clock the following morning, a group of men arrived who silently carried M. Phillips's personal belongings out to the waiting phaeton while Maria, standing on the steps outside, pressed her mother's handkerchief to her lips, trying to contain her sobs.

A half hour later, with silk hat in hand and dressed elegantly, Brandon came down the steps. Lightly he kissed both Maria's tear-streaked cheeks in the French manner before stepping into the rear seat of the carriage. With a crack of a whip, it lurched away, clattering down the cobblestone street.

Maria pressed the handkerchief tighter to her mouth, watching it turn the corner. Then as abruptly as he had appeared that first day on rue des Abbesses, he was gone, as surely and finally as if he had never been.

PART III

JULIETTE CLAYTON

Chapter 15

"Blood!"

"Yes, of course 'blood,' Lady Pottersbee! It *does* make a difference. And Juliette Clayton has some of the best. It would be a disgrace to the school, and to all of us, if she were expelled for lack of funds."

Mrs. Welwright confronted the director of Miss Fayton's Girls' School, Lady Pottersbee, who, at the moment, was seated at her impressive desk, haloed by a portrait of her late husband on the paneled wall behind her.

"At eighteen, Juliette Clayton is one of the most promising of all the girls," Mrs. Welwright continued, curly head held high as befitted her own aristocratic bloodlines, impoverished as they were. "Juliette Clayton is not only intelligent, she is a beautiful child as well. She could benefit greatly from the help this school can give her in gaining a place in society, particularly since her mother is not here to help her, and her father is gone, too, dying a hero in the Queen's service."

Lady Pottersbee inspected Mrs. Welwright through her lorgnette, a little finger curled ever so slightly. "Perhaps Juliette's mother should have thought of what would become of her children when she married a soldier rather than making one of the brilliant matches that were offered. She was even considered as a bride for Prince Edward, I'm told," she commented in an icy tone. "Why should I have to make compromises now, when Juliette's own mother was too foolishly romantic to think about the future. Tuition is the source of reimbursement for your teaching services here, Mrs. Welwright. Or hadn't you considered that?"

Mrs. Welwright looked Lady Pottersbee directly in her steel-gray eyes. "I have thought of that, Lady Pottersbee. But surely Miss Fayton's could do without more tuition from Juliette Clayton. She is such a bright girl, thoughtful of others and with a curious, probing mind. And there is so little remaining in the funds her father left her. It is not right to turn out a fine student when—"

"Yes!" Lady Pottersbee interrupted, rising to her feet in a rustling of her taffeta umbrella skirt. "And that is precisely the point, is it not, Mrs. Welwright? There is *very* little left in her father's funds, barely enough, and already she is working in the kitchen. Just how much leniency do you expect Miss Fayton's to allow?

"This school has been in my care since Lord Pottersbee died, God rest his soul, and I don't intend to see it mismanaged now. Miss Fayton's needs higher tuition from all the girls and Juliette Clayton is the only one who cannot pay it. Already concessions have been made. Not only was she given a room in the attic when she couldn't pay for a better one, but she was given the opportunity to work in the kitchen. Truly I feel we have been generous enough!"

"It is not Christian to throw the girl out!" Mrs. Welwright said in the tone her students referred to as her battle cry.

"But it is not practical to keep her!" Lady Pottersbee's voice was just as firm.

The two women glared at each other, and both of them would have been shocked had they realized that the subject of their disagreement, Juliette Clayton, was at the moment three floors below in the pantry being pawed by the footman, Stewart Drake.

Cruelly Drake pressed his fingers against her wrist bone, noting Juliette didn't shrink with fear and pain as the other housemaids had always done. But he already knew this one was different—fancied herself a lady she did, in spite of her position at Miss Fayton's. For weeks now he had been awaiting an opportunity to show her exactly who was in charge here, but now, just when he expected her to cower she turned on him furiously.

"Take your hands off me, Mr. Drake! And if you must persist in this forward and rude behavior, I will report you to the butler!"

"The butler, you say?" Drake laughed a throaty bellow. "That old drunk? Do you think he would interfere with anything I do when it's me who does his work for him the

times he's too full o' the bottle to do it himself?" He
squeezed her wrist tighter, glad to see a flicker of pain
come into her magnificent eyes—eyes that haunted a man.
"And anyway, I'll just tell him that you lured me in here.
It'll be your word against mine, and it's *you* who has the
reputation to keep, isn't it?" He laughed. "We men are expected to have a little fun you know. But you girls—" He
wagged a thin white finger at her. "You know what people
say about girls like that. And already old Lady Pottersbee
is looking to throw you out on your fancy little arse."

Juliette's face dropped, and seeing her hesitation,
Drake's voice became wheedling. "Now Miss Clayton—
Juliette," he continued, his other white hand reaching for
her other wrist. "I don't want to hurt you. Give me a kiss
or two, and a little touch of those sweet tits of yours, and
I'll let you go. It's not often I come across such a pretty girl
all alone."

"No! You will let me go now and leave me alone," Juliette countered, realizing she was cornered and there was
little to stop him from taking any liberty he chose. "You
followed me here, it's not by accident, that we're alone.
You planned this like you did with the other girls. Now let
me go before I go straight to Lady Pottersbee about you. If
I'm to be thrown out anyway, at least I can get you dismissed as well. Now let me go! And next time save your
attentions for someone who doesn't find you as repulsive as
I do!"

Drake's eyes crawled over the girl. She was wearing a
serving gown with gray puffed sleeves, high white starched
collar, and white scalloped cap. But even in this plain garb,
Juliette Clayton was astonishingly desirable.

A suggestive smile played on Drake's lips. Such women
are sent by the devil to torment men such as me, he
thought, a sneer crossing his face. And what fun to tear off
that demure dress and fondle her flesh. He had imagined
over and over how the young firmness of her breasts would
feel, and had wondered if the triangle of hair where her
thighs met was as golden and pale as that on her head.
Now he would see!

In a swift swing of his arm meant to terrify her, Drake

swept off her cap with his arm, unleashing her torrent of blond curls tumbling down her back. He expected her to scream, to retreat, and was astonished when she came at him like a fury, slapping him soundly across the jaw, and kicking him on the shin bone.

Stewart Drake howled like a wounded dog. "Bitch!" he screamed, grasping his leg and drawing it up as he hopped on the other. "Who do you fancy yourself?" He rubbed his leg vigorously, an evil glint in his eye. "You may think you are better than me, but you have to work for a living just like the rest of us downstairs and that puts us all on the same level, whether *you* like it or not."

Juliette raised her chin, brushing her hair back from her face. "I don't mind working," she retorted. "But I am not like the maids who are afraid of you."

Drake let his leg down and winced before his mouth twisted sarcastically. "Still Miss High-and-mighty, are you? Well, let me tell ye, my smart little lassie. You may have had noble ancestors on your mother's side, but they abandoned her when she married the likes of your father. Now that he's dead you haven't seen any of your relatives rushing to pay your tuition to this fancy school. So what's to become of you now that your father's money is nearly run out, huh? Do you think one of those high steppin' lords is going to want to marry a penniless waif like you?" He hooked a thumb to his chest. "When you realize a few things you'll be happy ol' Stewart Drake gives you the time o' day. Pretty house maids of your sort are common fare, ye know."

The footman's disdain didn't alter Juliette's dignified pose.

"You are coarse and vile, Mr. Drake, and no decent woman would have you—not if you were the only man in all England. Now, if you'll excuse me . . ."

Juliette started past him, but quickly he grabbed her shoulder and pressed it painfully with his fingers.

This was too much! Long ago Juliette had learned to take care of herself, and now she flew at him with doubled fists, striking him soundly on the chest before she was thrust back against the wall shelves so jars clanged one

against the other before tumbling to the floor and shattering. Then the candle was abruptly out.

In the dark there were curses before Drake said, "Now
you can just stay in here and think about what I said. And
when the cook gets back, you can explain this mess that
you've made." Then the door opened and slammed shut
and the click of a key in the latch told her she was locked
in.

Running to the door, Juliette fell hard against it, though
it didn't budge, and she withheld from beating on it with
her fists. *That's* just what he wants me to do, she told herself. How it would delight him to hear me screaming for
help when the staff isn't even expected back till afternoon.

Fumbling about in the dark, Juliette found the candle
and relit it from a match in her apron.

An orange glow revealed the broken jars and fallen supplies spilled on the pantry floor. Indeed, how was she going
to explain this? And retrieving her cap, she stuffed her
thick hair back under it before sitting on a large tin and
resting her chin in her hands. Damn the man! He isn't
satisfied that he has all the other serving women helpless
before his lusts—he expects to intimidate me, too, Juliette
thought. But worst of all, most of what he had said was
true. She was a student here though still a maid. And while
she did have to scrub floors and serve meals to the other
girls and sleep in the attic, it wasn't this that she minded so
much as being an outcast among her classmates and knowing that after graduation it would be just the same. Instead
of leading the kind of life the others would, she would be
condemned to the mundane existence of a governess or
working in a shop, never having a chance to live.

No, it was impossible even to hope she might somehow
regain the happiness she had once felt before her father
had died. While he was still alive, her life had been so different. She had been sad, of course, when he had to leave
their stone cottage in the country for his duties in various
parts of the world. But always she could look forward to
his return, and the times they shared, the light in his eyes
when he held her on his knee, and the small gifts he inevitably brought in his large pockets. But then, when she was

only eleven he had returned one final time after being wounded by an Arab he had taken prisoner during a raid on his fort in the Sahara. He had seen a series of doctors then but the injury done to his lungs couldn't be repaired, and she watched him grow weaker and weaker, until he had to stay in bed all the time, and finally one morning, she wasn't allowed to see him, and instead, numbers of people came who talked in hushed voices, and the house-keeper, Matilda, cried.

The next day there was a funeral where everyone cried more. She remembered them carrying her father out of the house in a long wooden box with a flag over it, and she knew he was never coming back again.

After that she had been sent to Miss Fayton's, where her father had specifically written in his will that she should be educated as a lady, and to this end, he had also willed all his assets.

When Juliette had first come to Miss Fayton's, she had thought this renovated castle the loveliest place on earth. But she soon discovered she was considered quite different by the other girls there who rejected her with thinly veiled contempt.

Sometimes the girls were admonished by the teachers for not treating their "inferiors" kindly as all "true" ladies were expected. But this became more embarrassing than if nothing had been said. And in the classes which lasted most of the day, Juliette learned about a world she knew she would never be a part of, and cultivated tastes that she would never afford, and manners she would never use. And afterward, she would work until late into the night in the kitchen before doing her class assignments by a single candle in her attic room, often until the early morning hours. If only Papa hadn't said in his will that I be educated here, I would take the little money left and run away, Juliette thought. And it was exactly this she told Millie when, nearly an hour later, her friend discovered her locked in the pantry and let her out.

"I hate this place," she said vehemently. "I hate its gray walls and those old portraits in the hall with their dour faces. You can't do anything that's fun without being reprimanded. And what good is it for me to attend a school like this when I'll just have to get a position as a governess or a lady's companion anyway? These girls get meaner every day, and lately they've been worse than ever!" Juliette finished, her hands resting on slender hips, her eyes flashing rebelliously.

Millie was another student, and Juliette's only friend at Miss Fayton's besides her favorite teacher, Mrs. Welwright. She was tall, slightly gangly, had a head of glorious red hair, and was also considered an outcast by the other girls, not because she was poor, but because she was an American, and therefore considered somewhat "crude" by definition.

"It has gotten worse, hasn't it?" Millie said, shaking her red curls that were cropped stylishly short in the front. "It's simply that you are far too pretty and so much smarter than they are. I'm sure they are all secretly grateful that they won't have to compete with you for husbands now that we're all eighteen and expected to spend at least our first 'season' in London."

"Well, I won't be competing," Juliette stated flatly.

"Precisely," Millie said. "If you were they would be much worse. Then you would be a real threat. But don't consider yourself too unlucky for that. At least you don't have parents who'll give you away to some potbellied old man simply because he's the highest bidder. The rest of us will be expected to go to London and march around at lots of stupid *bals blancs* and receptions where we'll be ogled by numbers of lecherous men twice our age who, if enticed by our youth and virginity, will press their suit with our parents. Then, if they are properly titled and wealthy enough, we will be given away into their beds like so much property. Count your blessings, Juliette," she finished. "At least you can marry the man you want and there'll be love between you instead of simply sharing a butler."

In spite of Millie's light tone, Juliette could hear the pain in her voice and grew pale imagining her friend sacrificed in marriage to such a man. "Oh, Millie," Juliette began suddenly full of sympathy. "I never thought of it that way. I had no idea that you . . . that all the girls . . . that

. . . what was expected—not really, although I suppose I should have."

"Never mind," Millie said with a wave of her hand meant to dismiss the matter. "It's never put in such blunt terms as that, I don't want to upset you. I just didn't want you to be too unhappy down here." She smiled. "What are you wearing to the Easter Ball?" she asked changing the subject.

Juliette colored suddenly, her eyes dropping. "I . . . I'm not going."

Millie reared back, her expression faltering. "Not going? Don't be a goose. Of course you're going! It will be a chance for some fun after all this drudgery."

Juliette's eyes remained downcast. No one else had ever asked her for an excuse—they all knew that she was much too poor to afford a proper gown. She had hoped simply to be absent from this ball as usual, but now. . . . "You see I . . . well, I don't have anything suitable to wear. Everything is unpresentable except for the skirts and blouses I wear to class, and even they are nearly out of fashion. I never have attended a ball before and if you'd been at Miss Fayton's last year you would already know that. I can't go, Millie, I simply can't."

"Oh, but you must! This ball won't be any fun for me if you're not there, too. You simply must come. I know! You'll wear one of my gowns. It's true I'm bigger. But clothes are easy to alter. I've watched my maid do it lots of times. Please!"

Millie's face was eager and sincere and Juliette paused, torn between her desire to at last actually attend a ball, and the humiliation of having to borrow clothes. Then she smiled and hugged her friend before saying, "I think you are the most generous person in the world, Millie."

"It's not that I'm so generous," Millie replied. "It's that the other girls are so jealous, and after this ball, they're going to have more of a right to be, because you're going to be the most beautiful girl there. I'll see to that." And putting her long arm around Juliette's neck, Millie hugged her in return.

Chapter 16

True to her word, that night Millie gave Juliette a gown, in fact, her choice of many lovely gowns which she arrayed on the bed and around the room in a dream of colorful silks and velvets and ribbons.

Dazzled by the display, Juliette tried on several, turning round and round in front of the long mirror until her choice came down to three.

One was a princess gown of white satin trimmed by black velvet ribbon, with sleeves of black lace over white satin, and white embroidery on the skirt. There was a second gown of brocade with a silver lace stand-up collar and satin folds of *bluet*, a new deep shade of blue. But as last Juliette chose a simple satin gown in a deep violet blue that heightened that shading in her eyes—a Worth's design of elegant simplicity, its wide neck line dipping low with large puffed sleeves, edged with ribbon, dropping just slightly off her shoulders. She tried it on a final time and, whirled before the mirror, noticing just how enticing she looked with the tops of her creamy breasts peeping above the neckline to fill out the upper part of the hourglass ideal, while a petticoat with ruffling filled out her girlish hips to fashionable fullness. Yes, she really was prettier than she had thought. Two weeks later, when Juliette entered the ballroom, her costume completed by long suede gloves and heeled slippers, she knew she was truly beautiful for the first time in her life and felt a little like a princess in one of the romantic fairy tales she had read as a child.

"My word! Look over there," said a portly distinguished-looking man with a gray-flecked beard and a monocle pinched between brow and cheek. "I thought I had seen all the Fayton girls. But I've never seen *her* before."

"It would be difficult to overlook that one," the other replied. "Such a rare loveliness in her face and graceful as a willow. Striking I'd say. No doubt she'll be snapped up before the end of the season."

The other man raised his eyebrows in agreement. "Yes. She seems quite different from the rest—actually human. The others seem cold fish beside a girl like that."

Across the shiny circular floor, other eyes observed Juliette's entrance. "Who is she?" Rodney Keiths's voice was hardly above a whisper as he inquired to the majordomo.

"Her name is Juliette Clayton, sir. One of the Fayton girls, though, unfortunately, she is an orphan and without connections beyond her attendance at Miss Fayton's."

Rodney Keiths's clear gray eyes had not moved off her. "She's beautiful!" he said.

"Yes, sir. A lovely child. Such a pity she had no dowry."

The young man looked startled and slightly insulted. "But she *is* beautiful. And what difference would a dowry make to me?" He adjusted his cravat and pulled straight the lapels of his jacket. "Champagne, Stephens."

"As you say, sir," Stephens said. It would have been above his station to make further comment. Anyway, the chit was of the nobility on her mother's side, at least. So, rolling back and forth on the soles of his mirror-polished boots, he signaled the footman for champagne, noticing that Drake wore a particularly sour expression tonight. Still, the footman came at once, holding a full tray of champagne glasses poised chest high.

The young Lord Keiths was quick to take one in each hand then, and in a moment had moved to Miss Clayton's side.

Juliette jumped as his voice came from behind her, and turning round, she lifted her eyes to a face she had never seen before, a well-scrubbed, friendly face.

"Sir?"

"I asked you if you would care for some champagne," Rodney repeated.

Juliette felt her cheeks suddenly burn. "Well, no, I don't . . . I mean . . . I don't drink champagne, or never have at least."

Rodney smiled. She had blushed and seemed genuinely flustered. Was she really so unsophisticated? It was not a trait for which the polished Fayton girls were noted. Most of them were more experienced than their years, and in spite of their white dresses and smooth hair, not altogether innocent. By now he thought he had met all of them at some time or another when his sister brought her classmates home during the holidays. Most had a brisk, haughty way about them that offended him. No, he had never met *this* girl before, yet here she was, looking up at him as bright as an angel, her neck and shoulders glowing smooth in the candlelight, and those eyes. Certainly she would be this season's sensation.

Rodney held the champagne glass toward her. "You really can't decide firmly against anything until you've given it a fair chance. Why don't you have a bit and see. You might find you like it."

Juliette watched him, trying not to fidget with her hands or to say anything that would be boring or would reveal her for exactly what she was—a girl "out of her element." And suddenly confronted by this smartly dressed fellow with such curious gray eyes and carefully kept blond hair, Juliette felt like one of the servants all dressed up and making a fool of herself. Stewart Drake had been staring at her all evening with that awful look on his face. And then, to make matters worse, this man was offering her champagne.

Juliette smiled then, her Miss Fayton's training coming to the rescue. And she managed to say, "Thank you. How kind. I suppose it would be only fair to give it a chance," as she took the glass and brought it to her lips.

She sipped carefully to cover the tightness in her throat which refused to relax as the champagne bubbled on her tongue. Then, raising her eyes to look again into the young man's face, she noticed it contained none of the insincerity she had grown accustomed to seeing in the expressions of the people of his level of society. "Well, it is quite good," she said finally. "Really wonderful, in fact. I had no idea. But then that was silly of me. Everyone always told me champagne was divine."

"You don't attend many parties, then?"

"No."

"Really? But let me introduce myself. I am Rodney

Keiths," he said bowing easily. And in a gesture that was
smooth as it was impossible to refuse, he offered his arm.

"And I am Juliette—Juliette Clayton," she said, curtsy-
ing and taking his arm.

Immediately they were promenading around the edge of
the dance floor. Juliette took another, longer, sip of champagne that was easier to swallow than the first, though
everything became complicated when Rodney Keiths
asked, "Have you been a Fayton girl long? I haven't ever
met you before."

"Well, no—or rather, yes. . . . That is, I don't attend
many parties. Anyway, you wouldn't have remembered
me."

Rodney's eyes sparkled. "I would have remembered, I'm
certain. You have—well, unusual color hair, don't you
think? I've never seen any quite so pale."

Remembering not to fidget, Juliette kept her hands from
reaching to her hair, which was not elegantly dressed in
combs or with aigrettes like the other girls', but was one
length and fell down to the middle of her back.

"Well, I suppose so. Though many of the other girls are
blond, too. Mostly, my hair is overly long. But I like it this
way."

"Yes, it is lovely. Long hair seems fitting for you. Wearing it loose is so much more attractive than stuck to your
head in that formal way most girls do their hair."

Juliette smiled. *He really seems to like me,* she thought,
and he's so easy to talk to. Suddenly the whole ordeal became easier, so that she didn't even think of refusing when
he took her hand and asked, "Would you care to dance?"

It was a waltz. And, as in a dream, Juliette felt herself
being twirled round and round under the glittering candles
poised high over the large ballroom in hanging crystal
chandeliers that reflected pale rainbows around the room.

Occasionally Rodney asked her questions about herself,
and when she was evasive he didn't pry, but continued to
gaze at her appreciatively. Under the glow of his attention,
Juliette blossomed, finding herself amazingly vivacious and
with suddenly more to say than usual. It became easy to

laugh, and she found herself thinking, but *this* is not so difficult, after all.

It was only during their seventh waltz, when the ball was nearly over, that Juliette touched earth enough to notice Lady Pottersbee and Lady Boroughs deep in conversation, their scrutinizing glances flickering up at her before their heads dipped together again as they commented further.

Juliette's lips compressed and her legs felt suddenly stiff as the dreamlike quality of the evening evaporated.

With sudden forwardness, she pulled Rodney from the dance floor to the opposite end of the ballroom where she became abruptly conscious of more curious glances in their direction. Around the edge of the dance floor, hushed conversations were hidden behind feather fans that opened and closed and swished like so many birds.

With a jolt, Juliette realized they were gossiping about her, criticizing her, no doubt, for appearing, and for dancing with a man she hardly knew for an entire evening. She felt as if they had turned a spotlight on her, and cut with embarrassment and wanting to escape, she said to Rodney, "Let's not stand here. It's very hot. Walk me out into the garden."

Rodney's eyebrows raised subtly in question. Was she actually flirting with him? Was she even aware of the indiscretion she was inviting by going into the moonlit garden alone?

He studied her wide eyes, finding them guileless, but strained.

He took one of her hands closely in his then, and Juliette walked at his side through the wide-flung doors into the carefully manicured gardens and down a path until they were beyond the illumination of the ballroom. They paused there, and raising her hand, he kissed it.

"Juliette," he said, caressing each syllable. "I've always liked the name. But you are more lovely than any name could fully describe."

Automatically, Juliette's eyes darted back to the doors, expecting Lady Pottersbee's condemning countenance to appear. Taking what Rodney said as a gallantry, she replied politely, "You are so nice to think so."

Rodney squeezed her hand again, an impetuous emotion captivating him. Usually he found girls lacking any quali- ties to attract him. Blondes in particular had always seemed too washed out, too pale for his taste. But Juliette was as brilliant as a jewel—her complexion glowed with the warmth of ripe peaches . . . and her eyes, touched by violet in the deep blue pansy-soft centers, seemed enor- mous, and full of a certain innocence that made him feel manly and more protective than ever before. He leaned nearer.

"You must let me kiss you," he whispered.

The word "kiss" brought Juliette sharply to earth, mak- ing her worries concerning Lady Pottersbee and the others dissolve before a wave of apprehension.

She stepped backward. Tonight had been a fairy tale, a dream, but suddenly she felt like Cinderella, and the clock had just struck twelve.

I never should have come, she thought silently shaking her head and backing away—never should have borrowed Millie's dress. I don't belong here, I've never belonged here! Suddenly, she imagined everyone laughing at her and suppressed an urge to pick up her dress and run out the garden gates and so far away she would *never* have to face any of them again. But of course that was impossible. She had come and must somehow endure what remained of the evening and do nothing to disgrace herself further.

"I didn't mean to frighten you with my boldness, Miss Clayton," Rodney said noticing her agitation.

"I don't feel frightened of you. It's that. . . . Look!" she began in Millie's forthright way. "I'm not what you think I am. I'm a Fayton girl, but only because my father, who was a soldier, wrote in his will that I should attend here. He left everything he owned to pay for it. But it's not enough, and now I work in the kitchen to make up for what I can't pay. If I weren't wearing these gloves," she waved a hand in his face, "you could see for yourself I'm not a lady. I have absolutely no business being at this party. It's for girls with lots of money whose families want them to marry men with titles, and not for girls like me!"

Juliette dropped her head, reminding Rodney of a

flower beaten down by rain. "Now I'm sure you're sorry
you asked if I liked champagne in the first place." Her
hands fidgeted uncontrollably. And when he didn't answer,
she turned to flee.

Immediately his hand enclosed her arm. "Don't go!"

"No! Don't you see!" she said. But Rodney's hand was
insistent as he pulled her back.

So it was true! he thought. She was just as unspoiled as
she seemed. Impossible to think of her in a kitchen. No,
her hands were never made for scouring pans and serving
meals. It couldn't be. No one, not even the infamous Lady
Pottersbee, could be so heartless. Yet Juliette's eyes, like
clear stars, told him it was exactly as she said.

She raised her chin. "And don't you dare feel sorry for
me," she commanded. "I can see that you do, and I loathe
pity. My father may not have been titled, but he was a
wonderful man. I only wish he were alive and I could be
with him rather than in this horrible place. Now, please! I
must go!"

Rodney's hand did not give way. "But I *don't* pity you.
In fact I think you are, well . . . rather marvelous, so different from those stiff-necked girls. I could never abide
any of them, no matter how much I'm supposed to marry
for the family." He looked hard into her rare and wonderful face. "Juliette," he said aloud. And feeling suddenly
overcome by the nearness of her, by the sculptured line of
her throat, her warm sweet smell, the high rounded curve
of her breasts, and squeezing her small hand again, he
whispered, "Marry me!"

Chapter 17

"Marry you!" Juliette repeated incredulously. "But that's
impossible. You must listen to me!" Her voice trailed off in
a whisper as another couple, arm in arm, strolled past. The
dancing had stopped and the garden filled with chatting,
laughing couples. "I have no parents," Juliette continued

low and urgent. "In fact, no one at all. I'm an orphan without a dowry . . . without anything! If you married me
your parents would disinherit you."

"I don't care." Rodney's voice was determined. "We
would be together and you would be my wife! I know eventually they would accept you. Anyway, they can't disinherit
me. Let's go tonight—right now. We can run away."

Juliette's violet eyes filled with a snapping light. "You're
making fun of me," she said, trying to pull her hand out of
his too-tight grasp. "One of the other girls told you to do
this!"

He stared at her, letting a moment pass. "No! Can't you
see I'm serious? Are you so naive that you don't realize
how beautiful, how completely desirable you are? Would I
be more convincing if I dropped to one knee? I believe it is
traditional." He smiled, starting to lower himself. "Of
course everyone will see me, and it will cause a scandal,
and then you will *have* to marry me."

"No, please!" Juliette dipped to pull him up to his feet as
she glanced warily behind her. "It's impossible. Can't you
understand? I don't want to get married, not to anyone.
You've been very kind, but if you mention it again I'll
. . . I'll be forced to leave the ball."

Rodney could see by the steadiness of her eyes and the
firm set of her delicate jaw that she meant it. His face lost
its enthusiasm. He bowed gracefully as before. "Then
please accept my apologies, Miss Clayton," he said in a
solemn voice. "I'm sorry to upset you with my impetuosity.
I won't be so bold again. If you could forgive me perhaps,
you could accept me as your friend."

Rodney's politeness was winning, and Juliette couldn't
help but be charmed. She nodded then with a laugh.

"It's a bargain, then?" Rodney asked.

"Of course. Truly I'm in need of friends and I think you
are very kind to want to be mine."

He smiled. "Then it's settled." And taking her hand, he
kissed her slender gloved fingers again before taking her
arm and leading her back to the glitter and light of the
ballroom.

* * *

"Well, all I can tell you is that I wish it had been me," said Millie the next morning after Juliette confided the events of the previous night. "I'd be Lady Rodney Keiths this morning, and let the devil take his mother. She is said to be a terror. But if her son was already married, what could she do? He was right when he told you he wouldn't be disinherited. He's her only son. And married to him, everything would be settled and I wouldn't have the prospect of meeting the Duke of Hutchen next week, who everyone says is rotund, over forty, and drinks."

Juliette frowned, and turning back to the large copper kettle, began stirring the vegetable soup, the fragrant steam rising around her. "I thought of all people, Millie, *you* would understand. You have always been so independent. Don't you see? I couldn't bear to cause such a scandal." She looked down into the cauldron, at the vortex of the swirling broth. "Anyway, I don't love him."

Millie looked stunned. "*Love?* Love is a luxury! Haven't I been telling you? He is young, handsome, and titled, and he doesn't have any oddities—at least that people gossip about. Doesn't that satisfy you?"

"No! I simply won't be a source of humiliation for anyone. I won't marry at all. No, never! I'll get a position in a shop, and when I earn enough money, then . . . well, then perhaps I'll leave London!"

"Well, maybe there's no sense in discussing it now," Millie said, seeing it was useless to argue with Juliette, but determined to make her friend see reason before it was too late. "Just think about what I've said, and later we'll talk again."

As it turned out, Rodney Keiths was determined, too. Every week he came to see Juliette Clayton, and Juliette was relieved that after the first burst of gossip following the ball, everyone seemed to accept her relationship with the young lord, and Lady Pottersbee even unbent to whisper to her the advantages of such a match and no longer complained about her "lack of funds" and instead hinted that when she was a rich matron, she should not forget Miss Fayton's and all that had been done for her and how "in need" the school was of "support."

Although she always enjoyed Rodney's company, as the weeks went by, Juliette was aware of a subtle uncomfortableness growing between them. Her time was running out. Soon he would demand a decision, and she didn't know what to say. Certainly she was fond of him, but shouldn't she feel something else? And as the weeks passed, she still felt confused, often tossing in her bed at night and wondering if she really was in love with Rodney, and if, perhaps, she should simply do as Millie kept insisting, and marry him.

"What are you going to do?" her friend would sometimes ask. "Do you really think you'll like working for a pittance in a ladies shop? And what matron would hire you to watch her children and have all your prettiness under her husband's nose? Nonsense! Of course it's impossible! Why won't you see you have no choice?"

To this Juliette turned a silent shoulder. Somehow it would work out, she just knew it. But every day graduation grew nearer, and Rodney became more persistent, his heart written on his face as he swore to love her forever and do anything to make her happy. And then one day he kissed her.

It had happened so quickly, so spontaneously, that it took them both by surprise. They were riding together one afternoon when Rodney told her in the tone of a national calamity that he would be going away for a few days to his family's estate at Elderwood. His mother was celebrating her birthday, and it would be several days before he could gracefully return.

They halted their horses and sat side by side. Then he reached and took both her hands in his, and abruptly, Juliette realized her time had run out even before he said, "And while I'm gone, Juliette, I want you to think about my proposal and see if . . . if you can find it in your heart to love me, even if just a little. I don't ask for more. They say first comes marriage and then love follows. I know we would be so happy."

Of its own violition his horse sidestepped, and suddenly Rodney found himself beside her, her riding skirt brushing his breeches, her fathomless eyes wide and innocent and looking into his. Her lips were close . . . so close . . . it seemed the most natural . . . the easiest thing to do, and he kissed her.

Juliette didn't know what to expect. As an orphan she had been given little affection, and had learned to do without it. Still, she let his lips touch hers, curious to find out what *it* was like. But the caress matched none of the wild, heart-throbbing sensations described by the other girls, and instead, *it* was a vague, overly wet, and somehow coldly stiff gesture that left her feeling embarrassed as she pulled away, hardly aware of his stammered apology.

There was a silence then that grew horribly long. She didn't know what to say and, apparently, he didn't either, since after that their eyes never met again as, in a strange state of agony, they rode wordlessly back to Miss Fayton's.

It was all so flat and disappointing, Juliette thought later. And she knew now that since she had allowed this intimacy, he would become even bolder and more persistent. Oh! If only she could make up her mind!

But then one day—less than a week afterward, and only hours before she was to see Rodney again, a letter was delivered for her.

At first she thought it must be some mistake. But the long official-looking envelope was clearly addressed *Miss Juliette Clayton*, and so, with curious hands, she opened it and read.

May 2, 1891

Dear Miss Clayton:
I am writing to inform you of the death of your uncle, Sir Henry Thorpe, your mother's eldest brother.
    It was Sir Henry's wish that you should inherit his full estate in the mount of £160,000 annually on the condition you change your surname from Clayton to Thorpe, your mother's maiden name.

I am prepared to effect this change for you legally upon receiving your permission. You may contact me at my office, 12 Dorchester Way, London, England.

Your servant,

M. William Bond
Solicitor

Chapter 18

The offices of Mr. William Bond were located near the Bank of London and Throgmorton Street on the third floor of a gray stone building built in the fifteenth century by Henry VII. It was a gloomy building, but in spite of its exterior, Mr. Bond's office was warm and tastefully paneled with oak and dotted by brown-toned carpets on shiny wooden floors.

Juliette had worn her best shirtwaist blouse with cuffed sleeves, and an ivory skirt that was belted at the waist, and she noticed that when Mr. Bond greeted her with a smile, his eyes made no secret of their scrutiny.

She exchanged formal pleasantries with him before allowing herself to be seated in one of the heavy leather chairs. From under the brim of her simple hat, she frankly studied him while he tapped a pencil against the wide oak desk several times before speaking.

"So! You are the fortunate Miss Clayton—or perhaps I should be addressing you now as Miss Thorpe. I must admit I've been somewhat curious about you. Sir Henry spoke at length about your mother. You are her image, it would seem—except for the eyes, of course. Hers were green. You have your father's eyes, and my word, they are an unusual color, really a very deep blue, and yet, yes, decidedly violet shaded." Mr. Bond paused and smiled slightly. "You'll forgive me. I had to take an exact description so when we met I could be sure no one was attempting an impersonation. You must realize there are many who would want to be in your position."

Mr. Bond's round face became concentrated as he joined his hands to make a triangle with his forefingers. Even from the few words of greeting he had exchanged with this young woman he could discern she had learned her lessons at Miss Fayton's well and would not disgrace the name and fortune she was to inherit. But there was something else, too, a natural innate grace about her that was born rather than taught—a certain regal way her head set upon her slender neck, and the manner she moved her hands. It was there, too, in her walk, and how she sat firmly upright in the chair that convinced him more than anything that she was indeed the daughter of Amelia Thorpe and the granddaughter of an earl.

"Tell me about your father, Miss Thorpe," he said at last. "My client told me very little about Captain Clayton."

Juliette cleared her throat lightly, her gaze looking directly into his. "I was quite young when my father died."

"Yes, and how did it happen? Did anyone ever tell you?"

Juliette's face became grave. "When he returned from his duty in the Sahara he was wounded and he often would tell me about his fort being attacked. It was one of the Arabs that wounded him, a man who had been captured during the raid. He once told me his name, but now I no longer remember. The wound was serious and. . . ." Juliette paused, looking down at her hands that already were less red since she had been excused from her kitchen duties. How well she remembered her father, how thin and white he had gradually become, as if a huge leech was slowly sucking his life's blood from his veins. His description of the Arab had been so vivid she was still plagued by nightmares on occasion—horrible visions of a devilish creature, a cape falling from his shoulders, a black turban around his head. In her dreams he would thrust her father with his dagger again and again before galloping away, his mocking laughter echoing behind as he disappeared into starless black.

Juliette's fingers locked together in her lap as slowly she raised her eyes. "After that my father died," she continued. "He was the only one I had in the world other than our housekeeper, Matilda. I was sent to Miss Fayton's, in accordance with my father's wishes."

"And you have been there ever since?"

"Yes."

"So you have learned to be a lady."

"Like the other girls, I've learned to act like one."

"And you hope to become a real one, no doubt. It is normal for Fayton girls to marry titled men, isn't it?"

Juliette's serious expression didn't change. "Usually they do, although I have no plans for marriage."

Mr. Bond thoughtfully nodded his head. "But you are still young. No doubt you will marry. But let it be perfectly understood now." Bond's eyebrows drew heavily together and dropped lower over his nose. "Until that time when you reach twenty-one or are married, your fortune will remain legally under my control." He leaned back. "Then control reverts to you, or, no doubt, your husband. And if you ask my advice," he continued, and Juliette noticed a curling black hair growing out the end of his nose, "you'd better choose a man competent at managing money." He raised a prophetic finger. "It's not uncommon for a spendthrift husband to ruin a woman's fortune."

Bond paused, and if he had not been—despite his fifty-seven years—so captivated by Juliette's full red mouth as she spoke, he might have noticed the firmness of her delicate jaw, and the faint straightening of her shoulders. Days ago she had decided to fight for her independence. Her voice did not change, but Mr. Bond found himself being pierced by those truly magnificent eyes. "I would like to ask a few questions," she said.

Mr. Bond nodded.

"This income I am to inherit, is it based on property or stocks? I must be frank. I never met my uncle so I have no idea what he might have left me, or for that matter why he should will his fortune to me now when I haven't heard from him in all these years."

Mr. Bond cleared his throat. "Yes, you would wonder that of course. The reason is simple. Your uncle was a man who kept to himself most of the time. He had little use for anyone but he did feel a responsibility to carry on the family line. Unfortunately, his only son was killed in the same fire that took his life. He had no other children and Lady Thorpe was dead years before. Therefore it became necessary to activate a particular clause of his will that gave his fortune to his nearest relative, providing he or she was willing to carry the Thorpe name."

Mr. Bond leaned forward in his chair. "As to the exact extent of your good fortune," he said, opening his top drawer and pulling out an official-looking document at which he glanced as he spoke, "first there is a house in London on Windbury Street, a fashionable part of town near Hyde Park and not far from Buckingham Palace. Your uncle had not lived in it for some time though, so it is in need of some redecorating.

"Now, let's see," he returned to the document. "Yes, and seven polo ponies, which I doubt you'll be using although they are all fine stock and shouldn't be difficult to sell. And there is a yacht called *Whimsy* that is a small but lovely craft, and, of course, one hundred sixty thousand pounds a year as income from your properties and investments."

He handed her the document containing an itemized list of the contents of her house. Her eyes ran down the page, seeing in a blur the words *twelve rose bushes, one hundred cases of wine*, before she reached a series of company names.

Only a few of the companies were familiar to her; *Clark Oil* was an American company which Millie had mentioned. Then there was *Rolls-Royce, Simon Aeronautics, Caledonian Railway,* and many others before there were listings like *Two acres—Passons County,* or, *12 Rinley St.—Warehouse.*

Juliette looked up. "And who would you contact if you wanted to buy or sell any of these assets?" she asked.

Mr. Bond untented his fingers. "I am the manager of all funds and properties until, as I explained, you are married or you reach twenty-one."

"I see. And who decides how this money should be invested. I mean, I don't have any choice about this, or do I?"

"No, not until you assume control."

"I see," Juliette said. "I assure you, I have every confidence in your cleverness. But for so fine a 'guardian' as you, there must be some fee."

"Indeed, I consider the amount stipulated in your uncle's will adequate."

"And that amount is?" Juliette asked, her voice factual as when she began, though now Mr. Bond showed a squint of uneasiness about his eyes.

"Fifteen percent is what is standard." He retrieved the document from her and began rolling it up.

"And for you, is it fifteen percent?"

Mr. Bond's cheek twitched uneasily. "Your uncle was a generous man, and under my direction his investments prospered. I receive twenty percent."

"I see. Twenty percent of one hundred sixty thousand pounds a year is . . . thirty-two thousand annually. What a large sum."

Again his cheek twitched. "You have learned your lessons at Miss Fayton's exceedingly well," he said tightly.

Juliette raised her chin to look the solicitor steadily in his eyes. "And I imagine these investments are in companies rendering the most profit for . . . shall we say, all concerned?"

Mr. Bond sat back in his chair, his neck settling down between his shoulders like a wary bird. Suddenly he was seeing this slender girl in a new light.

"It would do no good to misrepresent myself, Miss Thorpe. It would be easy for you to find out that your money is invested in firms where I hold an interest. But I assure you they are all sound investments that will insure your future and the future of your children. You will profit by them greatly."

"I'm sure both of us will, Mr. Bond. It seems we both stand to gain—or perhaps lose. That is, *you* stand to lose should I decide to remove my money from these firms which are also profiting you."

William Bond frowned. He leaned forward again, his palms pressing on the desk top, his eyes narrowing as his body shifted uneasily. "Perhaps you didn't understand,

Miss Thorpe. The law states quite clearly that *I*, the guardian of the estate, have full authority over the Thorpe fortune until you marry or come of age. It is not possible for you to have control over these funds." He leaned back once more, bringing his fingers into a triangle beneath his chin as it doubled disapprovingly. "Not a shilling of these funds can be spent without my approval, and since you are an obviously rebellious young woman, we may as well understand one another at the onset. Bluntly put, Miss Thorpe, I control *you!*"

Juliette licked her dry lips. It took all her strength to face this formidable man, but the thought of her dreamed-of freedom hanging in the balance forced her on. "As I said, I'm sure you are an excellent financial administrator, Mr. Bond. And, after all, why should I concern myself with how my money is invested as long as I have £160,000 a year. But don't you say that you 'control me' only *before* I am twenty-one?" Her eyes fixed on Bond's which were now growing wider with concern and he didn't look so awesome as he had a moment before. Juliette smiled slightly. "Well then, Mr. Bond. Since that is the case, I propose that you allow me complete freedom to do as I please now, *before* I am twenty-one, and in return, I will promise to allow you to invest—and to profit from—my money *after* I am twenty-one."

Mr. Bond's eyebrows flew up and he let his breath out in a single rush. "I will have you know, Miss Thorpe, *this* is a reputable firm." He cleared his throat and coughed. "We will *not* be bribed!"

Juliette's gaze did not falter. "Certainly you couldn't consider what I suggest as bribery, Mr. Bond. I am simply offering you unlimited years of investing millions for a small favor, less than three short years of your indulgence."

Mr. Bond stared, amazed to find so clever and astute a brain in the head of a female, and a young female at that. His was a reputable firm, but he was also a practical man. He was not invulnerable to financial ruin, and to pull the Thorpe millions out of his companies would be no less than a crisis of major proportion. On the other hand, to be assured of these millions to invest in the future would provide tremendous security—and profit. There was only one obvious course of action. He coughed again and cleared his throat. "I see. So if you are to be your own mistress then what do you plan to do?"

"To travel. I don't know where yet. I've always wanted to see the world."

Mr. Bond's face was stern and he paused so that the pendulum of the big grandfather clock behind him made the only sound in the room as it clicked from side to side. "Very well then," he said at last. "I agree on one condition."

"And that is?" Juliette asked, trying not to let the triumph she felt creep into her voice.

Mr. Bond fixed her with another stare. "You ask for freedom to make your own decisions, Miss Thorpe, but we cannot forget that I am still legally responsible for your actions, and will be seen as such by everyone. My reputation is of upmost concern to me, as I trust yours is to you. So while I grant you the freedom to conduct your own life without interference from me, I must demand that you conduct yourself so that you draw no scandal to yourself, and thereby to my good name. I can agree to your proposal only if you agree to mine, and if the time comes when there is even a breath of scandal, then understand, our bargain no longer is valid, no matter what you plan to do with your money later. In other words, Miss Thorpe," Mr. Bond said as he leaned forward again, "I am willing to give you all the rope you wish. But don't make the mistake of taking so much that you hang yourself."

Chapter 19

April 10, 1892

Dear Millie,

I'm writing you from Las Flores del Mar, a resort on an island off the Spanish coast, which a certain Madame Gascon (a lady I met while in Paris) recommended as the highlight of the spring season.

So far, I'm not disappointed. The hotel itself, an old mansion built a hundred and fifty years ago by a Spanish nobleman, is a dream that sits elegantly on the beach with dozens of gardens I can see from my balcony on the second floor.

At the moment, not too many people have arrived and it is generally deserted, though there is Lady Linley and her son, Bosley, and Roberto, who gives me a tennis lesson occasionally. I'm told, however, that in a week or so the hotel will be quite full in expectation of the horse race, the Spanish Cup, to be run in the middle of May. It's an event I've heard about, but never expected to see. Truly, Millie, I wish I could live forever frozen in time. And now every morning I wake up with a wonderful remembering that everything isn't a dream, but a reality, and there are no more nasty girls and no Lady Pottersbee to bother about.

Well, I will stop for now. It is nearly two in the morning, and though I'm not tired at all, I'm still planning a long ride on High Times early tomorrow so I should at least try to sleep. Please write when you can.

Love, Juliette

Rereading the letter, Juliette folded it and slipped it in a long narrow envelope before her pen scratched the address on its surface. Then rising, she walked to her balcony, idly tapping the edge of the envelope against her open palm.

Leaning against the wrought-iron railing bordering the plaster and wood overhang, Juliette breathed deeply the warm breezes and looked down at the churning and splashing water below. For a stretch up the beach, the moonlight revealed waves of azure and jade gliding up the shore in shallow fans. In the opposite direction, the far wing of the hotel was visible with other balconies and tiled roofs emerging out of a thick of greenery.

An hour before, the moon had broken the sharp white line dividing sea and sky. It began as thin crescent but then grew slowly larger to sit full on the horizon, a long silvered arm stretching across the sea toward her. Taking another deep breath, Juliette leaned forward to pluck a flower from the gnarled vine growing against the wall. It was then she noticed with surprise the figure of a man directly below, trotting along the beach with vigorous ease as he gazed out to sea.

Though he was only a dark shape, Juliette could tell he had a large build and, while her eyes followed him, he never glanced up in her direction as he moved silently along the shore before turning into the rolling waves.

With powerful overhand strokes he propelled himself away from shore until his dark head was only a tiny dot in the glowing moonlight. Beyond the breakers he seemed very much at home, and turning again, he swam parallel to shore.

Juliette studied the far-off dot with puzzled eyes. What sort of a man would plunge into the tumbling sea alone, and at this hour? she wondered absently. Did she know him? It seemed she should, with so few people staying at the hotel. Yet she recognized nothing about him.

She shivered as the breeze blew harder and cooler and her arms bumped with goose flesh. Still she hesitated to go inside, aware of a sense of expectation in the air, even in the tempestuous toss of the waves. Then she laughed at her own foolishness. How silly, she told herself. It must be she was worried about Rodney. After almost a year, guilt still gnawed at her every time she recalled the look on his face when she told him good-bye.

How she had hated giving him pain after all his kindness. But after a sleepless night pacing her attic room she had decided that to become his wife out of pity, when she wanted no husband at all, was too much to ask. "You must try to understand," she had told him the next day. "I just don't feel . . . well, anything . . . at least what it seems I *should* feel. I never agreed to marry you before, and I can't agree to it now. I don't want to disappoint you, and maybe someday, yes . . . possibly someday I *will* marry, and if I do, I can't imagine whom I would want more for a husband than someone as kind and generous as you. But for now, it is impossible. Please . . . if you could only understand."

Rodney laughed, trying to seem good-natured, though the sound stuck awkwardly in his throat. "Yes, of course, Juliette, if that's your decision. I can even understand your desire not to marry, especially with the kind of opportunity you have now. I think it's only natural that you would want to be independent for a time, particularly after being under old Lady Pottersbee's thumb all these years. But all girls eventually marry, and I'll be patient, although I'm not used to having to wait for anything that I want as much as having you for my wife."

His voice held no bitterness, and his face seemed boyishly handsome and understanding, so much so that Juliette felt selfish as she never had before. "Only promise me," he continued, "that if you should decide to take a husband that it shall be me." He finished with a look that touched Juliette in the same way as the eager gaze of a collie puppy.

His request was an easy one to fulfill, Juliette thought, jumping at some way to relieve her sense of responsibility for his unhappiness. Who else would be a more considerate husband than Rodney? And feeling sure she would never marry anyway, she had nodded.

"Yes, of course," she had said then. It was such an easy promise to make, she told herself. And if it made him happy. . . .

So they had parted friends, just as Juliette hoped they would, and in a week she set sail aboard the *Whimsy*.

She traveled first to France, and then to Germany, Austria, and to Italy, attending balls and parties, and meeting dozens of new people who treated her with curiosity but with acceptance, too, and even warmth on occasion.

Often she saw the other graduates of Miss Fayton's, who surprised her by greeting her like an old beloved schoolmate and introducing her to their families and particularly to their brothers.

She had been nervous at first, still feeling somehow out of place, but that faded quickly. She learned to dance and to make polite conversation with those same people who had snubbed her less than a year before.

So her circle of acquaintances grew. She was invited

everywhere and some even whispered she was "debutante of the year." But all this Juliette took with diminishing interest, finding her status in society much less important to her than being able to go wherever she wanted, and at any time, to do exactly what she pleased, and to have the luxury of everything being done for her.

There were men, of course. She never attended a ball without receiving a flurry of flowers and invitations the next day. Her interest in men, however, was limited to their use as dancing partners, or riding companions, and sometimes she did accept a yachting invitation. Generally though, they interested her very little and she learned to keep them at arm's length, turning down their proposals as regularly and dependably as Big Ben, and always mindful of Mr. Bond's warnings that a "scandal" would result in an end to her freedom.

So now, nearly a year later, here she was in Las Flores del Mar, an island paradise where every "season" the wealthy of Europe gathered. And from here . . . ? Well, she had purposely made no plans. She wanted everything to remain as spontaneous as possible so she could go as her mood moved her in this long, unhurried and unhindered, investigation of life.

Looking from her balcony now, Juliette scanned the band of water beyond the breakers to find the man reversing his course and retracing his way back toward the beach.

I wonder if I've met him before, or perhaps ridden or played tennis with him, Juliette mused.

She was still watching when the smooth motion of his arms wavered abruptly. Then pausing midstroke some fifty yards from shore, his head disappeared.

Squinting against the chilled darkness, Juliette came suddenly alert. What was he doing?—not a dive surely. And now the man's head appeared again, bobbing uncertainly before once more his arms were thrown in the air and he disappeared underwater.

Juliette's fingers reached to her lips as the man's head remained invisible for what seemed an endless period. No, he wasn't diving, not like that! And when his head broke the surface again, she realized he was trying to float as a level-headed swimmer does when seized by cramps.

Juliette's heart thudded madly. She tried to remember everything she had ever learned about swimming and rescue during the brief course at Miss Fayton's, designed less for the ocean than for possible pleasure-boating accidents. Then she was dashing from her room, bounding down the steps and out of the hotel, and racing along the beach toward the stricken man.

Hopelessly far from shore, Brandon Phillips fought for his life. Every few moments the cramps lessened, releasing him from their iron grip long enough to catch a breath. But then his arms and legs were seized again by spasms, and what seemed like invisible hands pulled him underwater to writhe uncontrollably until once more the cramp eased and he rose breathless to the surface.

Each time the cramping lasted longer before release came. And each time he thought his lungs would burst before his head topped the surface again.

This time he glanced toward shore, which only moments before had appeared so close and now seemed like an endless chasm, impossible to cross.

In a short time, perhaps only moments, he would drown, and again now the spasms gripped him like a sea monster's tentacles, wrapping around his body and pulling him under.

Holding a hastily gasped breath, Brandon fought to unbend the numb curling of his legs while, for what seemed an eternity, they remained knotted and useless.

His chest burned, ready to burst, and a dizziness crept over him so everything darkened and plunged about.

Then he felt a chilling calm, a sudden, inexplicable peace and an acceptance of fate.

From somewhere came the sound of his own mocking laughter and for a brief instant it seemed he understood everything more clearly, more completely, than ever before. Then he was falling, down . . . down . . . into an unknown depth of no return.

PART IV

IN THE BEGINNING

Chapter 20

How much time passed, Brandon couldn't tell. But then, as if by a miracle, light appeared through blackness. His staggering senses registered that he was above water—breathing—and his heart pounded. The fresh sea air had never seemed so clean, so wonderful. He drank it in, each gulping breath bringing greater consciousness.

To Juliette, it seemed that she struggled forever, swimming with all her strength, her muscles shaking from fatigue and threatening to fail as she held the man's head above water and dragged him slowly toward shore.

Ahead, the breakers foamed in white lines that raised and tumbled onto the beach, and coming near them, Juliette paddled to catch a rising swell to carry them closer.

The splashing water rose and pulled them forward before settling again. Juliette's lungs ached out of breath as her strength faded. Then, just when she thought she couldn't swim any further, her toes touched a sandy shelf.

Brandon Phillips touched down, too, planting his feet on solid ground with indescribable relief before standing up on legs that no longer writhed out of control.

The moon had ducked behind thick clouds, darkening the figure of his rescuer to only a slender outline clothed in pajamas, a boy of about fifteen, he thought, who struggled with haphazard splashes toward shore, obviously exhausted from the effort of saving him.

Brandon stepped back into the deeper water, putting an arm around his rescuer and helping "him" as they stumbled together onto the shore before falling into the sand on hands and knees and panting loudly.

Heedless of the man beside her, Juliette gasped. It was perhaps three minutes before her heart's wild beating subsided and the air began to pass in and out of her lungs with less effort and pain. Then, finally glancing up, she found the man hunckering down on his heels in the sand. Apparently he had recovered and was now watching her.

He was the first to speak, in fluent French that held a cultured note. "If you had been with Napoleon against the Russians, the outcome might have been different, I think," he said. "You are a remarkably brave young man. I might easily have dragged you under."

Juliette's eyes sparkled in spite of her exhaustion. In the dimness, she must indeed look like a boy, with her hair braided and wrapped close to her head. Mischievously, she said, "It was nothing," in a voice that sounded hoarse and strange even to herself. "I saw you from my hotel room. It's very late, and there was no one to call. I couldn't just let you drown."

He seemed to smile, although she couldn't see clearly. "I'm grateful you didn't. And I certainly would have if not for you. But now you're exhausted. Perhaps a drink of brandy would help revive you. I'll take you back to your room, and we'll ring for some," he finished, getting up and taking her forearm to pull her up also.

"Ring for some?" she questioned, coming to stand tottering in front of this man who was even larger than he first seemed. "At this hour?"

His arm outstretched to steady her shoulder. "Well, of course."

"But I wouldn't dream of disturbing the servants in the middle of the night."

He laughed shortly. "But I would," he said pulling her along as he started toward the hotel. "What are menials for?"

Juliette flushed with anger as she recalled herself, not so long ago, as one such "menial." "Well, they're certainly not to be rousted out of bed at three in the morning for anything so trivial as a glass of brandy."

She felt more than saw his amusement. "You are obviously more considerate of servants than I am. But, very well. I'll bring you some from my own stock. Say in twenty minutes?"

He was walking beside her with the direct tread of a man who knows what he is about. His profile was as cleanly etched as a Roman coin, and as handsome, though he was too arrogant, and no gentleman could ever seem completely "gentle" with shoulders broad as his.

So he thinks I'm a boy, Juliette mused. He seems so sure of himself, his manner suggests he doesn't err often—or expect to. The corners of Juliette's mouth curved slowly upward as a plan occurred to her.

"Good," he said, apparently able to read her change in mood. "I'm glad you're feeling better. Now tell me your room number and I'll bring you the brandy."

"All right," she rasped. "My room is number twelve on the second floor. Don't knock, I'll leave the door open."

The man nodded. "I'll be there in twenty minutes."

They parted company, Juliette going up the hotel steps, and Brandon disappearing among the garden foliage in the opposite direction.

It was just a minute short of twenty when he appeared again, his swimming clothes changed to a simple white shirt casually buttoned, dark pants, and mirror-polished boots that shone in the starlight as did the jeweled flask in his hand.

Taking the hotel steps two at a time in easy stride, he entered the heavy double doors and proceeded upstairs to the second floor hallway, which was dark except for a narrow width of light extending from a door at the end.

Out of habit, Brandon scanned the hall corners, his eyes probing the door alcoves before noiselessly making his way to the lighted one. As requested then, he pushed the door open wider without a knock.

Brandon Phillips was not often taken by surprise, but now his face perceptibly changed as he stared.

The only evidence of the youth he was expecting to see was the pajamas deposited in a sodden heap on the floor. In "his" place was a lovely girl, her hair loose about her face, sitting up in the postered, Spanish-style bed where a light quilt covered her up to the impish grin on her face.

Teasing laughter floated toward him as she saw his features register the anticipated surprise. Then Brandon closed the door behind him and locked it, pausing to allow his eyes to adjust to the bright light.

It took only a moment for him to recognize the same girl

he had noticed several days before. Then she had been riding a horse with accomplished skill and at breakneck speed along the shore, easily outdistancing a dandified English gentleman pursuing her in vain. Yes, he remembered her quite well, and now his dark eyes perused her laughing ones, which seemed oddly familiar though he couldn't remember from where—deep blue eyes, and was that a touch of violet?

"I see," he said, "and if I'm not further mistaken," he continued with a slight bow, "you are Miss Juliette Thorpe."

He set the jeweled flask on a nearby table beside a large arrangement of roses. Juliette was aware of a slight scar grazing his forehead, and the firm prominence of his slanting cheekbones as he walked to the edge of her bed and stood, arms crossed, and looked down at her. "But how do *you* know my name?" she demanded. "We've never been introduced. And what's yours?"

His large black eyes with absurdly long lashes assessed her frank gaze before smiling in amusement. He gave her another bow, and clicking his heels said, "Most people refer to me as Monsieur Phillips, but I would be pleased if you would call me Brandon."

Juliette cocked her head. M. Phillips—it was a name often bandied about these resorts of the rich and famous, and was mentioned as one of the wealthiest men in Europe, and a most sought-after bachelor.

Certainly he was handsome. But there was a certain wildness about him, too, which made all his good manners seem only a veneer. "Ohhh," she said knowingly. "So *you* are the French millionaire I've heard about, the one that all the mamas want their daughters to marry."

One side of M. Phillips's mouth turned down, and his eyebrows raised in a quizzical expression. "You surprise me, Miss Thorpe. Are you always so direct? I didn't think it was considered proper for a lady."

Juliette laughed. "No. Sometimes I can be evasive and not direct at all. How about you?"

"Usually I say what I think. But I'm beginning to imagine not nearly as often as you do."

Juliette's rosy lips smiled. "I've learned there are circumstances where you can say what you think. One of them is when you are independent enough not to concern yourself with the opinions of most people, and another is when you run across someone you are doubtful of seeing again. It seems both circumstances prevail at the moment. Now, tell me how you know my name?"

M. Phillips's hands moved to rest on his hips in an interplay of the muscles on his bronzed forearms. "I'm not sure I want to tell you now," he said.

"No?" Juliette's blond eyebrows went up. "But I'm interested. I didn't think anyone here in Las Flores del Mar was aware of me particularly, or who I was."

Now he laughed warmly. "A girl like you? I'm certain the staff, and probably every male under eighty, has made a point of knowing who *you* are. When I saw you riding one day on the beach, I asked. A steward told me your name."

He paused then, his gaze dropping deeply into hers and cutting through that barrier that exists between individuals meeting for the first time. It was a look more intimate than if he had touched her, and Juliette's face heated as he said, "Do you know you are the most exquisitely lovely woman I've ever seen?"

"You are . . . I . . . well . . . you are very kind," she said, knowing she must be red as a lobster and wondering for the first time if her plan to trick *him* had backfired. What would Millie do now? she asked herself—or Mrs. Welwright?

Brandon smiled to himself. How easily she blushed. So enchanting—and so impetuous. He frowned at her then in mock disapproval as he asked, "Do you often invite strange men to your bedroom?"

Juliette swallowed. The teasing note in his voice told her that the dangerous moment had vanished, and her blushes receded as she said, "As I recall, you insisted on coming."

"And now that I'm here," he spread his arms in question, "what am I supposed to do?"

Juliette smiled. "To be *very* surprised, to give me a drink as you promised, and then to go quietly with a little less confidence in your ability to predict genders," she finished with a giggle.

"I am *very* surprised," he said. "I always thought I could distinguish a woman anywhere. I suppose I'm not used to seeing them wear pajamas. Why do you?"

Juliette shrugged. "They are more comfortable. But I should tell you that at first the idea shocked my seamstress, too. I never thought I would have occasion to be seen in them in public. But just think how much more difficult it would have been to rescue you wearing a nightgown."

Brandon recalled the wet pants clinging to her gently curving hips when she had knelt on hands and knees in the sand, and wondering now how he hadn't realized before that *this* creature could only be female. He said, "Indeed pants do have certain advantages, I suppose. But feminine things would suit you better."

"Oh?" Juliette said, indignation in her teasing tone. "You seem to have a lot of opinions, Monsieur Phillips . . ."

"Brandon," he corrected her.

"Indeed, Brandon," she yielded. "Do people always do as you say?"

"Usually."

"And if they don't?" Juliette demanded, her chin rising a half inch.

"I have found methods to deal with resistance." His dark eyes sparkled. "Truthfully I can say I never go without something I want."

There was another pause as they faced each other and Juliette wondered suddenly why she was fencing with this man over such matters when she was really exhausted from saving him and should be asleep.

The doors to the balcony were still open and the sea breeze blew through the room, moving the draperies and bringing the fruity fragrance of the blooming vine toward them.

"You must tell me what I can do to repay you for rescuing me," Brandon said after a time.

"It was nothing. Please don't mention it again. You certainly would have done the same for me."

"Yes, but I would ask you for something in return."

"Well, if you insist then, you can give me some brandy and consider your debt paid." She took a glass from the table at her bedside and held it toward him.

"All right," he said after a moment's hesitation. Then taking the glass he strode across the room to another table where a pitcher of water sat beside the vase of red roses. He filled the glass half full with the water and then added a dose of brandy from the flask. As he poured, the facets of crystal caught the light in a refracting play. Then setting the flask down, he whirled a silver spoon in the center of the drink as he nodded toward the roses. "From an admirer?"

"Not an admirer exactly, a friend really."

He brought the glass back and handed it to her before sitting down on her bed as casually as if it had been his own, and watching as she drank the pale brownish liquid. "Tell me, Juliette, are you American or English?"

Juliette opened wide eyes to look over the rim of the glass. "Why can't I be French or Austrian or Dutch?"

"Because only an American or English girl would play a trick like this. I'd like to hear that you were American," he added.

"Really? Why? Don't you like the English?"

"Usually I detest them," he said, a cold note creeping into his voice.

"Then you'll have to detest me," she said frankly, "because I'm one of them."

Brandon studied her. "In that case it seems I'll have to make an exception," he said and smiled. "It wouldn't be right to detest the person who has saved your life."

Tipping the glass upward, Juliette finished the last of the brandy. Already a warm numbness was traveling over her, and setting the glass back on the table, she pulled the light quilt higher and snuggled deep into the pillows. "Thank you again for the brandy, Monsieur . . . er, Brandon. I don't mean to be rude, but I am very tired. I'm not used to

swimming, you see, and you are quite heavy. I really want
to go to sleep now."

There was a sense of acute exhaustion about her, and
Brandon realized she was not being coquettish, but sincerely wanted him to leave.

"Then I will go," he said rising from her bed. "We will
see each other again." He gave her cheek a gentle caress.
"Goodnight—for now," he finished and bowed again.

"Goodnight," Juliette returned with a yawn in her voice
as he turned and quietly went out, pulling the door shut
behind him.

It took Phillips only a few minutes to reach his villa
where Rashid hovered at the entrance, silent and watchful
for his master's return.

"*As-salaam alaykum, Sayyid,*" the servant greeted him.
"*Wu alaykum as-salaam, Rashid.*"

Then Karim al-Sharif climbed the stairway and passed
down the hall, not even glancing at the door next to his left
invitingly ajar. Instead he went directly into his own suite,
waving out the Arab manservant who silently appeared.

Pulling off his own clothes, he lay down on his back in
bed, an arm crossed behind his head, the other hand absently toying with the heart-shaped ruby ring dangling
from the gold chain around his neck. For a long time then
he stared at the ceiling, his thoughts making him smile
slightly to himself.

Chapter 21

Lucille Madeaux was not a prostitute. Rather, she considered herself an actress, and a good one, and most people
agreed.

It was on a spring night in Paris that Lucille had met
M. Brandon Phillips. She had just given the opening performance of a new theatrical in which she played the princi-
pal part of Loella, a peasant girl of loose morals, a role that
suited her voluptuous figure and flaming red hair. At the

party afterward, Lucille felt like a goddess, receiving compliment after compliment from gentlemen who kissed her hand with special meaning, often leaning closer to whisper bolder praises in her ear. And so on triumphant wings, Lucille's evening sailed past, and was already more than half over when she was introduced to a latecomer—a M. Phillips—and confronted suddenly with this darkly alluring stranger, Lucille felt as if both the music and the laughing, gossiping crowd had disappeared into oblivion.

Lucille had heard his name before. A "debonair savage," one friend had described him. Yet it wasn't until later when Lucille had returned to her room and was able to once again think clearly that she realized it was not just his looks, or even his imperious manner that had put her in such a whirl. It had been something else indefinable, something almost, yes, almost primitive that made him, from that first moment, irresistible.

He did not flatter her as the others had; his lips only brushed her hand. And he was only polite as they exchanged amenities, though she could feel his eyes examining her with the detailed care of a connoisseur. He wanted her, yes, she knew he did—and she was stabbed with disappointment and surprise when he made no attempt to make her his mistress, either that night, or when they met twice more at subsequent parties.

Just this fact made him a source of tantalizing frustration, which made her pace her room afterward, reviewing his every look and gesture, wondering if she still attracted him, or if she had been mistaken all along. So, at a dinner party several nights later, when he discreetly gave her a set of emerald earrings, obviously originals from Fabergé, and invited her to accompany him to his villa in Las Flores del Mar, she didn't even think of refusing. No, refusal would have been impossible. She accepted immediately, for the first time in her life not thinking of the future or any boring practicalities. The fascinating possibility of being with him had eclipsed everything else, and leaving Paris and her part as Loella, she packed her suitcases and traveled to Marseille.

* * *

Once aboard his private yacht, Brandon had conducted her through its many rooms decorated with the finest wood and the finest draperies and chandeliers in subtle, flawless taste that seemed so much a part of him. Then he touched a bell that brought a silent woman who conducted Lucille to another gorgeously appointed compartment with a rich forest green couch and thick carpets and three shyly smiling maids.

She was bathed then in a tub of foaming pink bubbles, and her feet were massaged, then she passed the subsequent hours until dinner sipping spiced tea. But, unable to think of anything but him, she was trembling with excitement as the dinner hour approached and, discarding her chemise and corset, she dressed in nothing except her most daring gown of gold lamé. It was a French creation which clung to her luscious hips and revealed much of her large breasts. Joining Brandon in the salon for cocktails, she placed herself so close their knees touched, and occasionally his arm brushed her erect nipples.

He was silent while they ate their sumptuous French meal, observing her with serious opaque eyes that made the moment all the more intoxicatingly mysterious. And after dinner—afterward had been unique even for Lucille, who considered herself a woman of the world. Once he had touched her, all her wiles, all her self-control, and attempts to seduce him failed, and she found 'herself out of her depth and suddenly at the mercy of an unleashed passion she had not known she possessed.

He was masterful—commanding, and she obeyed, giving herself as never before, and receiving as she never dreamed possible. She was swept away, forgetting everything under the onslaught of his wickedly primitive desires, until at last, exhausted by a final swoon of ecstasy, she had fallen asleep.

But, of course, *that* had been just over two weeks ago, Lucille told herself. And this morning it all seemed dimly and unhappily distant as she lounged at the breakfast table, stirring sugar into her coffee, and not failing to notice that the sparkle in Brandon's eyes disappeared as he rounded the corner and saw her. A man growing bored was easy to recognize.

Who was he really? she wondered again as he silently took his place at the table. She knew almost nothing about him except that he was extremely rich, and gossip said he owned a large merchandising empire stretching from England to Africa. But just exactly what Brandon did remained unknown. He was a mystery of incongruent parts. Even the ruby ring he wore on the chain around his neck seemed strange. It was not an extremely large or valuable stone—yet he always wore it. She wondered who might have given it to him, but had never presumed to ask him anything of a personal nature. At first she thought there was time enough for confidences later. But as it turned out, those intimate details she had waited to hear whispered in the dark were never forthcoming.

Again Lucille sighed, her eyes staring down into her coffee before covertly glancing at him again. He ignored her silent signals, reaching instead for a letter which sat before him on a silver tray.

Taking a small knife, he slit open the seals with an agile movement that Lucille imagined could just as easily have slit someone's throat. Then putting the opener back on the tray he dismissed the servant with a barely perceptible nod, removed the paper from the envelope, unfolded it, and read.

In guarded looks, Lucille watched as his eyes moved back and forth across the lines, and curiously now, his face did alter, the civilized air melting as his eyes darkened to a fierce murderous look that made Lucille's flesh crawl.

So! It was settled, Brandon said to himself, reading the letter again.

April 1, 1892

M. Phillips:
  As instructed, have investigated whereabouts of one Captain George Clayton.
  Investigations show he died eight years ago from wounds received in the Sahara on a mission in Her Majesty Victoria's service.

*Only living family, one daughter. Indications she
once attended school in London.*

*Upon your request will ascertain present where-
abouts. Awaiting your instructions.*

William Sleth

Brandon's teeth clenched and his jaw twitched. It had
been two years since he had first inquired about the man
who had killed his father. Initially he had assumed it would
be easy to find George Clayton and take him to El Abadan. But the chances of locating him grew slimmer if not
nonexistent when the building containing the military rec-
ords Brandon needed burned to the ground.

It was then Brandon had hired a private investigator and
turned the search over to Sleth, a man with a reputation
for reliability. And now, finally, Brandon knew Clayton
was dead, apparently from the wounds he himself had inflicted. For all these years his father had been avenged, his
oath fulfilled.

Clutching the paper, Brandon stared unseeing at the
words, recalling that day in the fort at Sevit, still able to
hear the drums and Clayton's clipped, "Ready!—Aim!—
Fire!

Even now his guts churned with the memory that could
never be wiped out. Clayton! The name had become synon-
ymous with infamy. Just seeing it in the written word was
enough to recall his hatred for this man and all his arrogant race.

A surge of rage swept over him. He had sworn not only
to kill Clayton, but to sell his daughter as a slave and,
wanting the sweet satisfaction that only carrying out his
sworn vengeance could bring, his back teeth clenched as he
spoke over his shoulder to Rashid, who was always near.

"Rashid, a quill and paper." And when it came he
dashed off his reply in a quick hand.

Sleth:
  Find the girl.

   B. Phillips

Chapter 22

Juliette Clayton Thorpe slept much later than usual that morning, not awakening until the sun flooded in through her balcony doors and across her bed in a shaft of golden light.

As she came awake, the black-eyed visage who had played such a prominent role in her dreams the night before receded so she caught only a brief glimmer of him before he slipped back into the darkest recesses of her mind.

Yawning like a sleepy kitten, Juliette opened her eyes, remembering as she did a luncheon date with Mrs. Welwright. And sitting up with a lazy stretch, she swung her long legs off the bed, blindly reaching over her shoulder to pull the cord that summoned her maid.

Mrs. Winston was only that moment hurrying in on her small feet carrying in both hands a large bouquet of red roses still wet with dew and tied with a wide velvet ribbon to match. She curtsied in a short dip. "Good morning, miss. A steward just came with these flowers. I imagine they're from Lord Keiths." She smiled a small approving smile. "Such a gentleman he is to send you flowers every day. And, see, miss—this morning there's a special note with them."

"Yes, of course," Juliette replied, coming more awake and thinking that indeed Rodney was an absolute darling and so understanding about everything.

She plucked the small envelope from the ribbon attached to the bouquet and turned it over in her hands.

From somewhere Mrs. Winston produced a tall blue urn. "Will this vase be suitable to you, miss?"

"Yes, that's fine. Thank you, Mrs. Winston. But now please lay out my knickers and a blouse. I'm meeting Mrs. Welwright in half an hour on the terrace and going riding afterward."

"Yes, miss," Mrs. Winston bobbed another curtsy before disappearing into the large closet. Then breaking the seals of the note Juliette withdrew it and read:

April 2, 1892

Dearest Juliette,
London has become so dreadfully boring without you that I've decided to join you in Las Flores del Mar. The Spanish Cup will be run on the twenty-first of this month, and I've decided to race my stallion, Titian Regency.
Unless there is difficulty with the voyage, I'm expecting to dock soon after the third of May. Do try to meet me if you can. I miss you terribly, and I'm not the only one. Half of London has been asking me what you are doing so far away when all of us are here.
I saw Millie at a ball recently. She sends her love—as do I.

Rodney

On the hotel terrace of Las Flores del Mar, lunch was being served amid the tinkling of silverware and china and the busy bustling of black-uniformed waiters as they moved between the umbrella-shaded tables and catered to the needs of the wealthy looking clientele seated there.

Juliette stood only a moment at the wrought-iron gateway before the *maître d'hôtel* came to her side.

"Miss Thorpe!" he said rolling the "r." "How good to see you this morning."

"Thank you," Juliette said, smiling also and looking beyond him to the patrons already seated. "Perhaps you could tell me if my companion, Mrs. Welwright, has arrived yet?"

"Indeed she has, Miss Thorpe. Perhaps ten minutes ago. Would you care to join her?"

"Please."

The man nodded, and still smiling, moved off with a flourish, leading Juliette through the maze of chatting clusters of friends and potted palms to where Mrs. Welwright was sitting at the end of the terrace nearest the tennis courts.

Juliette owed the idea of Mrs. Welwright becoming her traveling companion to Millie. Juliette now regarded it as her friend's most ingenious suggestion.

"You simply must hire a companion," Millie had told her before leaving London. "People are already starting to talk. Your circumstances are most unusual. There just aren't any independent women who are single and young as you are. Traveling alone is out of the question. It won't matter that you actually *do* nothing wrong. The gossips will make sure that it *seems* you do. Your reputation will be ruined. And what will Mr. Bond do then? He sounds the type to carry out his threats."

"But I won't have some old woman running my affairs for me and telling me what I can and cannot do," Juliette protested. "I've had quite enough of *that* from Lady Pottersbee!"

"But of course you won't," Millie said cajolingly, knowing her friend's determination. "But companions are hired as servants of a sort and can be dismissed if they don't please you. It isn't like Miss Fayton's, you know. What you need is a nice lady with whom you get along and who won't mind what you do but will protect you from gossips and not ask questions."

Juliette nodded. "Well, yes. But can such a person be found?"

Millie laughed. "Now that you have so much money, love, it will be quite easy. Just tell them from the outset you won't tolerate any meddling in your affairs. Do you think that those highborn ladies who travel without their husbands are actually faithful to them? Pooh! Of course not. But they are discreet enough to take a companion so no one can talk about them. It's sort of a game, you see. No one really expects you to *be* good—only to *appear* good." Seeing Juliette hesitate, Millie continued. "And why not Mrs. Welwright? You always were her favorite student. She is a lovely woman, the only real human being at Miss Fayton's. I bet she wants to escape from it as badly as you."

Juliette was struck by the idea. And, as it turned out, Millie was right. Mrs. Welwright agreed at once and, in less than a week, Juliette found that the older woman had become not only her companion, but her confidante as well. Already she had helped her with countless details of travel engagements and accommodations and small emergencies and had become once and for all indispensable. And now, as Juliette neared her table, delight brightened the lady's features. "Good morning," Mrs. Welwright said as the *maitre d'hôtel* pulled out a chair and held it as Juliette sat down. "You slept late this morning. You're feeling fit, I hope. You certainly look it."

"Indeed I am," Juliette replied smiling. "I was up late, so I slept in."

A waiter appeared at Juliette's side and she ordered a pastry as Mrs. Welwright poured her a cup of tea.

"Oh really, did you meet someone interesting last night?"

"No!" Juliette answered too quickly, wondering even as she did why she had bothered to lie. She had found it possible to tell her friend anything. But somehow the occurrences of the previous night seemed a private matter she found herself unwilling to share with anyone. "How are you enjoying Las Flores del Mar?" Juliette asked, changing the subject.

"It's beautiful—more so than I ever imagined. I never thought I would have a chance to do more than talk about the Spanish islands to an audience of bored girls who would only be interested if it was a place included on their grand tours. And yet, here I am! I can never repay your kindness, Juliette," she finished with warm affection.

"It's not a 'kindness,'" Juliette corrected. "It is a bargain—an exchange of services. I take you with me, yes, but I couldn't go respectably without you. And speaking of that, what do you think of going to Switzerland in a week or two? I hear it's wonderful in summer. Rodney is going to race his stallion here in a week and we can leave after that."

"Switzerland! Yes, of course!" Mrs. Welwright agreed. "Summer in the Alps—cozy chateaux—fields of wild flowers."

"Truly, it doesn't matter to me where we go," Mrs. Welwright continued. "Switzerland, Germany, or even back to France. I'm finding that all this travel makes me feel as good as I used to when I was young. Go wherever makes you happiest, Juliette, and go now while you can. Before long a gentleman, if not Rodney Keiths, then another, is certain to woo you in precisely the right fashion, and soon enough, you'll be married and settled in one place."

Juliette laughed as if Mrs. Welwright were teasing. Mrs. Welwright smiled, too, raising her teacup to sip. This morning Juliette had an extra flush to her cheeks, she thought, and tendrils of pale hair had escaped to blow about her face and neck so she looked sunny as the morning and twice as irresistible. "You laugh now, Juliette, but I'm quite serious. You are much too warm and tender-hearted not to fall in love. Your beauty and gaiety have already attracted dozens of men."

Juliette wrinkled her nose. "And my money, Mrs. Welwright. Don't forget that. I don't think their interest is prompted entirely by my 'beauty' or my 'tender heart.'"

"So cynical and so young!" Mrs. Welwright protested with a laugh before cocking her head in acceptance as she continued. "Well, you are right. It is common enough to marry conveniently. But there will be the *right* man for you. Someone who will appreciate you both inside and out. I will be sorry to give up traveling, though I'll gladly become, instead, your children's governess."

Juliette no longer laughed, but looked at the older woman wonderingly. "You sound so sure!"

"Certain things are unavoidable. You have other needs besides this one for independence. Sooner or later you will discover them."

A small frown pinched Juliette's brow. "Well, I don't suppose it really matters if you don't think I'm serious. I imagine after I have been single for say . . . ten years? Then you will be convinced. I actually thought that since you have been cooped up in Miss Fayton's, too, you'd be the one person to understand. Would you want to be imprisoned like that again for the rest of your life, being told

what to do and when?" Juliette grimaced. "Let those
women marry who must in order to eat. I'm going to stay
single and independent, probably forever, or at least for a
very long time."

A waiter approached, holding a large tray high on the
ends of his fingers. Then lowering it to waist level, he
placed before the two ladies several plates and cups of fine
china, a basket of pastries, and another steaming pot of tea.
"Will that be all?" he asked. And seeing the ladies nod, he
moved off again at a brisk pace.

Mrs. Welwright touched the intricate scrolling on the
edge of her saucer. She would have spoken again, but looking up, found Juliette's attention fixed upon the two men
playing tennis on a court adjacent to the patio, and turning,
she watched them too.

The man facing her, Mrs. Welwright recognized as Roberto Francisco de Alvarez, at the moment considered one
of the finest tennis players in England and France, a fact
that made him something of a celebrity here in Las Flores
del Mar. Often in the last few days she had seen him on
the court giving instruction to eager pupils. But today it
appeared Roberto was not giving instruction, but rather
was an earnest contender in an arduous match against a
large man with wide athletic shoulders and a crop of black
hair.

Haughty at first, Roberto had walked onto the court and
waved his arms in circles before assuming the classic
crouched-down, racket-up position.

The serve came, a lightning stroke that sent the ball
spinning past before he could return it, and the second
point was the same.

The third serve he did return, but then the ball was shot
past him again, and after several disastrous volleys following that one, Roberto lost his cocksureness. Then, when he
was two games behind, he began desperately pouring energy into his play, perspiring freely as again and again he
was forced on the defensive, running from sideline to sideline and back to intercept a long drive, only to have his
scrambling return played back to him just over the net.

It was altogether a formidable display of strategy and skill by the large man, and interested by this show of expertise, a small crowd of curious observers gathered on the sidelines.

"Look at that big fellow over there," observed Lord Howard Linley, leaning on his silver-tipped cane, and pinching a monocle between cheek and brow. "I dare say he is running that young Spaniard Roberto into the ground."

"It isn't surprising to me," said another man. "His opponent is quite an unusual man."

Lord Linley raised a bushy eyebrow. "Really, Sir William? You seem to know something. Tell me about him."

"Well, I've heard the gossip, of course. Can't help but be exposed to it when one stays in these seasonal hotels. It seems people speak well of him, although little is really known of his origins—only that he is some sort of merchant prince—a multimillionaire. And he has a reputation with women that makes even our naughty King Edward seem like a schoolboy." Sir William laughed softly with enjoyment until, noting Lord Linley's serious expression, he coughed and cleared his throat.

"Yes, I'm familiar with his sort," the Lord replied, his monocle pinched needlessly tight. "The raw ambitious type—the type to jostle in the marketplace instead of having his future secured in land as do true gentlefolk. No doubt this chap is here hoping to marry into a titled family," Lord Linley finished, tapping his cane's silver tip against the low rock wall surrounding the court.

"Perhaps," Sir William replied. "It's more common now, these *new* marriages. Can't say that I fault anyone, however. These are changing times and the 'old money' is trying to infuse itself with some new blood." Sir William looked narrowly at Phillips as the large man blasted a shot past Roberto and the play stopped as a lanky ball boy ran to retrieve the ball.

"But even if he could have any one of the daughters of the starving gentry, Monsieur Phillips doesn't appear interested in marriage. I've often wondered why he hasn't taken advantage of one of the prestigious matches he's been offered. The rumor I heard yesterday might explain his reluctance to make a proper liaison."

Lord Linley gave his head a slight forward tilt. "Oh? What rumor?"

Sir William scanned over his shoulder and came closer before speaking in a lowered voice. "I've just heard it said that Monsieur Phillips has Arab blood in his veins, a halfbreed actually. It's possible Monsieur Phillips has never taken a wife out of a desire not to embarrass himself."

At the word Arab, Lord Linley's monocle dropped with a tinkling against his waistcoat button. "Arab blood you say! What a scandal if that's true! Even those money-grabbing mamas will think twice about such an alliance," he said, poking his cane hard against the stone walk. "To marry one's daughter to someone like that would be irresponsible, to say the least. One has to think of the future and of grandchildren."

"Yes, perhaps," agreed Sir William. "But one also has to think of the family coffers. Anyway it is only a rumor. There may be nothing to it. And no one has had the nerve to ask him directly."

"Certainly he doesn't have the appearance of a halfbreed. But what you've said intrigues me, Sir William. I think I'll make inquiries on my own. There must be someone who knows. Perhaps even his servants could be enticed—"

Sir William interrupted, laughing shortly and waving a hand. "Oh, quite impossible, I'm afraid. The reason people think he has Arab blood is due partly at least to the band of nigger cutthroats he keeps as servants. They treat him like a bloody king. They won't even speak to you, let alone gossip about their master. Take my advice and be careful."

"Ah! And there it is!—the last point!" Lord Linley said as the match ended.

Obviously exhausted, Roberto took the towel offered by his valet and mopped his head before walking to the net to shake Phillip's outstretched hand.

M. Phillips bowed slightly from the waist before jumping the net and putting his arm across the young man's shoulders. Together they walked toward the hotel terrace.

Chapter 23

"Someone you know?" Mrs. Welwright asked, making Juliette aware that she had been staring at the tennis match.

Blushing, Juliette turned back to face her. "No, not exactly, just someone I met briefly."

"A handsome gentleman," Mrs. Welwright observed.

Juliette turned again watching Phillips walk away. "Yes, he is nice looking if one finds large men attractive. But he is too overbearing to be a real gentleman."

"Oh?" Mrs. Welwright said, pausing to study his receding back. "Yes, I imagine he does have a certain domineering quality." She glanced to consult a small watch attached by a fine filigree chain around her waist. "Oh! I hadn't realized it was so late. I'm to play whist at two, and it is almost that time now. I'll be on the upper balcony if you need me. Will I see you for dinner?"

Juliette nodded, accepting the older woman's motherly kiss on her upturned cheek, and watching her make her way up the wrought-iron stairway that curved upward along the whitewashed wall to terminate at the second floor.

Looking around the patio, Juliette noticed that the crowd had dispersed, leaving it deserted except for a nearby table where Lady Linley sat with several other ladies.

Absently twisting a blond curl around one finger, she gazed at the sea which sparkled in the sun like diamonds against sapphires, thinking again of Switzerland and high peaks and quaint villages and all the places she would explore.

"I see you're still here," a deep melodious voice said, drawing her abruptly back to the present. "I hoped you wouldn't be gone before I could come back to see you."

"Oh, hello," Juliette said, knowing who had spoken before glancing up. "It seems you are not any worse for wear this morning. You certainly gave poor Roberto a beating."

He had changed from his tennis clothes and now looked as fresh as ever in pants and shirt. He leaned down, bracing one hand on the back of her chair and the other on the table. His mouth curved as he watched her. "It is fortunate that cramps are not a hazard in tennis," he replied. "May I sit down?"

Juliette laughed and nodded, and Brandon took the chair Mrs. Welwright had just vacated, pulling it closer before sitting down.

A waiter, seeing the identity of the additional patron, rushed to his side, becoming even more solicitous as he inquired, "Would you care for something, Monsieur Phillips?"

Brandon ordered a tomato juice and lime, and the waiter, seeming almost honored by the request, bowed lower than usual before turning and disappearing in the direction of the kitchen.

There was a silence that followed as Brandon pointedly surveyed Juliette's riding knickers. They were the newest cut, beginning tight around her tiny waist, and becoming fuller so they were modest as a skirt before narrowing down to slip into the tops of her boots which buttoned from the sole to just below her knee. He shook his head with disappointment. "I was prepared to think quite a lot of you, Miss Thorpe," he said. "But now I'm beginning to question my decision. I find a woman who cannot accept herself as a woman rather tragic."

At first Juliette thought she hadn't heard correctly. She knew that none of the men she was acquainted with actually liked her knickers, but none of them had been so . . . well, so forward to say so. Still Juliette's face remained composed and she even smiled slightly as she said, "I'm sorry you don't like my knickers, but they are very comfortable, much more so than a riding skirt, even if they seem less attractive to you." Her regard met his. "I assure you I accept myself as a woman."

"You really don't care what I think do you?"

"Not particularly." Juliette's tone was matter-of-fact. She glanced past Brandon to another tennis game in progress.

"But you shouldn't take it personally. I don't usually care what anyone thinks—at least about what I wear."

"No? So you don't care whether men find you attractive?"

"No, I guess I wouldn't want anyone to think I was ugly. But I let the women who really need a man to be the ones to please them. Fortunately I'm not in that position."

Brandon studied the girl's composed features, imagining how she might look swooning with passion, her defiant eyes limpid, her flesh yielding, her lips parting beneath his.

From the first moment he had seen her sitting in bed, wide-eyed, her cheeks flushed, her breasts softly curving beneath the white pajamas, he had made up his mind to have her.

Of course there was the matter of Lucille, and thinking of his current mistress caused a line to draw itself between his brows.

He found the European method of changing mistresses both uncivilized and overly complicated. There was always the inevitable tears and scene, the ugly words, threats, and more often pleas.

How much better were the customs of his country where, if a man desired a woman, he simply purchased her, or stole her, and added her to his harem. Still, in spite of the complications, his mind was made up. He would make the necessary arrangements. Indeed there was something unusual about this girl that made the trouble of having her negligible when weighed against the obvious reward.

"But what if a man should need *you*," he asked. "What should he do then?"

Juliette shrugged. "Sometimes a man says he 'needs' me—or more often that he wants to marry me. But then I always ask myself, what does he actually know about me except that I'm pretty enough to satisfy his vanity, and wealthy enough to make him overlook the fact I'm pedigreed only on my mother's side? I can't imagine basing a lifelong relationship on something like that—can you?"

"No," Brandon said honestly, never having considered a "lifelong" relationship with any woman based on anything.

"You see, you even agree," Juliette said looking past him again to the other men playing tennis as she sipped her tea.

A bud vase stood in the center of the table containing a rose bud just beginning to unfold its petals to the sun's warmth. Reaching forward, Brandon cupped the blossom in his hand, bringing it to his nose and drawing in its fragrance.

"How old are you?" he asked. "Seventeen, perhaps?"

"Nineteen," she corrected.

"You look even younger—barely a woman."

His gaze was steady as he looked at her over the top of the flower. "When you have grown up you may find it pleasant to evoke a man's desire."

The waiter arrived and set a drink before Phillips before leaving again.

A flash of irritation showed in Juliette's eyes and then vanished. She leaned forward. "And what would you have me wear, monsieur? You seem to have a lot of opinions. I'm sure you must have one about that!"

Brandon smiled slightly and looked her over slowly, with a sense of having evaluated many women. Knowing clearly what appealed to him and what did not, he said, "To begin with, you should throw away those horrible pajamas and find a nightgown to suit you—something to compliment your figure instead of detracting from it."

Juliette felt her temper rising at his calm impertinence. "Such as?"

"Something soft and flowing—something deep blue and touched with violet like your eyes, something light enough to cling to your thighs and breasts when you walk."

Abruptly Juliette's cheeks were flushed and burning. She lowered her voice. "Yes. I'm sure it would suit you, too. But *I* don't need to suit anyone except myself, monsieur. So it doesn't really matter what *you* would prefer."

There was a bite in her voice, and she felt her heart pumping furiously. What a rogue he was! And twice now his dark eyes had sunk into hers, probing her most secret

thoughts and making her acutely, and somehow dangerously, aware of her own femaleness.

Before she knew how she had gotten there, she was on
her feet. "You will excuse me, won't you," she managed to
say in a normal tone. "I'm really on my way to the stables."

Brandon was not accustomed to being dismissed when
he would have stayed. He rose to his feet, towering over
her. "If you don't mind," he said, 'I'll accompany you. I
have a small, private matter to discuss."

Aware they had already caught the attention of Lady
Linley's table, Juliette was unwilling to argue and only nodded, starting out of the patio. Brandon followed and, when
they were well out of sight of the tables, he paused under a
wide fanleaf palm tree, where the sunlight slanted between
the pointed leaf shafts, dividing the ground under their
boots into wedges of light.

"I have something for you," Brandon said, reaching into
his jacket. "A small memento in thanks for saving my
life." He withdrew a narrow box and held it toward her.

A curious butterfly dipped and fluttered between them
as Juliette glanced up at his face and took the covered velvet box, unhooking the small gold clasp before lifting the
lid.

Juliette had seen pearls before—most often adorning ladies at balls and receptions. She had even purchased a set
of earrings for herself several months ago when a London
storekeeper had entranced her with tales of their origins—
of how the pearls grew and were taken out of oysters of
exotic islands and passed from one primitive to another,
guarded, treasured, fought over, until finally reaching London and the ears and throats of those rich enough to afford
them.

Juliette couldn't resist holding these up to catch the sunlight, marveling at such purity and iridescence that seemed
to emit from an inner illumination. There were two dozen
or so, the center pearl being the largest, and alone worth a
small fortune, and the rest arranged in graduated size from
the catch, which was a tropical flower intricately carved
out of gold.

Expectantly, Brandon watched the girl as she admired the gift, but none of the surprised coos of delight, or kisses, or tears that were normal on such occasions were forthcoming. Instead, after several moments she closed the case and held it back toward him. "I'm very flattered," she said seriously. "They're the most beautiful pearls I've ever seen. But we both know, Monsieur Phillips, that I cannot accept such a gift."

Brandon stared, thinking at first he hadn't understood correctly. Then he frowned. Just this morning he had carefully selected these particular pearls from his private collection, imagining what she would look like wearing them and nothing else. Now to have his gift thrust back at him was the last thing he expected or wanted.

"But you must accept them! Surely such stuffy conventions don't matter when the circumstances include the fact that you saved my life?"

Juliette continued holding the box toward him. He was correct about the latter, but she wasn't being "stuffy." Instead, she sensed that encouraging this man would be a mistake. "Perhaps then you will have to consider me stuffy," she said noticing how the tiny scar on his jaw twitched at her words. Then thinking she might have hurt his feelings, she added, "I really think it is a beautiful necklace—truly magnificent. I just couldn't keep it." She laughed. "Anyway, just think how terrible pearls would look with my riding knickers."

There was a silence as he appraised her with a puzzled expression. Then finally he laughed, too, reluctantly taking back the case and tucking it inside his jacket. "Very well, then. Another time maybe you will honor me by accepting it. Will I see you tomorrow?"

Juliette felt uneasy beneath his compelling black eyes. As before he seemed to see within her, probing into her thoughts before his look softened.

Just as the night before, she felt as if he had touched her. Who was this man? she asked herself? And why did he make her feel like an inexperienced rider mounted on too-spirited a horse. There was something about him, a feeling—a fear he instilled that she didn't understand.

Now he leaned closer, his voice lowering. "There is no need to be frightened, mademoiselle," he commented as if indeed he had read her thoughts.

"I'm not frightened!" Juliette declared. "But it is perfectly plain you don't approve of me, so why do you want to see me tomorrow—or any day?"

Both his eyebrows arched. "Why does any man want to call upon a woman? I find you charming, mademoiselle," and with a slight bow and a smile, he reached to kiss her hand.

Surprising even herself, Juliette pulled away as if he were a snake. Her back was stiff though she didn't retreat.

"I see," he said withdrawing, a touch of amusement in his voice. "Perhaps we will not make any plans now. But we will meet another time. Possibly then I can convince you, but for now, *au revoir*." And before Juliette could speak, he bowed again in a way that seemed to Juliette somehow sinister. Then turning, he was heading away from her, back down the path.

Chapter 24

In his villa Brandon stood on a high balcony overlooking the sea and a wide stretch of sandy shoreline a hundred meters below.

Dawn was unfolding in a glow of pink that washed across the sky and, leaning against the railing, Brandon was aware of the high-pitched calls of birds echoing against the cliff as they swept open-winged above the rolling waves, disappearing and reappearing in and out of fog pockets that hung in the still air.

Sunrise was Brandon's solitary hour, a time he typically spent reviewing, considering, and planning matters of importance and, this morning, he was particularly thoughtful as with one hand he unbuttoned his waistcoat and loosened his cravat.

During the course of the previous evening he had arranged to be introduced to a M. Jean Bouleseur, a man he knew to be arranging for a shipment of arms to the French—arms his spies had informed him were destined for French forts in the Sahara. Then once he was conversing with the man, it had been a simple matter to engage him in a game of cards.

Pulling a cheroot out of a box to his left, Brandon bit it between his teeth before striking a match along the railing with a hiss and a flash of sulphur.

How childish these Europeans were, he thought. Give them enough to drink and let them win at foolish games, and they were willing to tell you anything.

It had been easier to find out the names of those responsible for guarding the shipment and the details of their route than it was to lose the first series of play. And it became easier yet to then recoup his losses and, having learned all he wished to know, relieve the easily flustered Frenchman of five thousand francs.

Then, playing his quarry like an exhausted fish, Brandon let him gain a little before making him lose it all again, and finally, near four this morning, M. Bouleseur had given up and ended the game.

"Of course you must not tell any Englishmen what I have told you, Monsieur Phillips," he warned, with a short nervous laugh. "That would be disastrous. But of course *you* are a Frenchman too, no? And Frenchmen understand such things."

Brandon nodded. "You have my word—I assure you I would never consider telling the English."

So the naive monsieur had gone his way. And now Brandon's eyes narrowed as he took a long puff of the cheroot before opening the first three buttons of his shirt.

Of course it would be easiest to destroy the shipment before it reached the Tripoli coast. But if that wasn't possible, then he would simply have to confiscate the rifles himself. Clearly he had no choice. Those guns must not reach their destination.

Leaning against the railing, Brandon meditatively puffed his cheroot as he planned each step—whom he must contact, the men he would need, the strategy he would employ.

Minutes ticked past as the sky turned a deeper pink. Then, of its own accord, Brandon's inner eye focused on quite another image—on the face of Juliette Thorpe as he had last seen her, eyes wide and indignant, her cheeks flushed.

He scowled, and continued scowling. Normally he never gave more than polite attention to any woman unless he wanted to make her his mistress, and even then he gave the project no more time than necessary. He could never remember any female distracting his thoughts like this one. Furthermore, it was now clear her conquest would require more attention than he normally considered warranted by any woman.

He shook his head, forcing those deep blue eyes—were her irises actually striped violet?—and that full red mouth out of his mind. Women were typically his last priority—a form of recreation. The French must be his concern at the moment, and those rifles. And he couldn't forget the Hussar either, since his spies had told him they were venturing further and more often out of their territory. It was rumored a large force was gathering. And their cleverness could not be underestimated. Already some of the Hussar warriors had diabolically disguised themselves as members of the Assar tribe and, in a sudden night raid, stolen some of the younger and prettier women from the neighboring Babir tribe. It was days later that the true identity of the villains became known as Hussar, but in the meantime, the Babir had nearly entered a war with the Assar, an action that would have ended an alliance of eighty years.

The muscles of Brandon's jaw tightened as he considered the incident. How easily all the strides toward Arab unity could be lost, and he was so far away. Any day the Hussar might attempt a similar tactic and succeed.

Raising his head, he looked out across the sky as it turned from pink to shades of gold. Then leaning over the railing, he tried to get a better look at the mounted figure splashing in the shallow waves.

Was his desire playing tricks on him? Was it an apparition? Or was it indeed Juliette Thorpe, disappearing into a thicket of fog before emerging out the other side.

He had seen only glimpses of her the last several days, but there was no mistaking her coming closer, riding a large chestnut, her legs swinging free of the stirrups, her long, unbound, hair flying in the breeze and catching the sunlight as it topped the horizon and poured over.

The waves traveled up the shore, turning to mercury and reflecting gold and red as Brandon's eyes followed her as if held by a magnet.

Since the day she had refused the necklace, he had tried to forget her. She was a different type to him, a "respectable" woman, and the sort which usually interested him not at all. But while she had decidedly taken a dislike to him, he found her coming to mind more and more often.

How brash she could be, like the desert wind in summer, while, paradoxically, she had most recently been avoiding him with the shyness of a gazelle. It had amused him to watch her enter a room only to leave when she detected his presence. She had even altered her direction several times when their paths would have crossed.

Women never avoided him. Why did she?

Purposely he had never been forward, never taken her into his arms or caressed her as he would have liked. He had imagined her reserve would have vanished by now. Yet she still avoided his company, while certainly she was not so standoffish with others. And there were many others— men who spoke to her whenever they met, taking her hand and sometimes kissing it. On the contrary, she didn't seem to mind how many of *them* flocked around her.

Her hair was blowing out behind her now in a sparkling golden veil as her horse came out of the water and broke into a brisk trot that took her up the beach.

Brandon's frown deepened. In fact, Juliette Thorpe seemed on quite friendly terms with several of these other men, he thought, recalling how only yesterday she had been laughing and talking with one of them in particular. His jaw tightened. Then turning, he spoke over his shoulder. "Rashid!—bring my horse."

PART V

THE CHASE

Chapter 25

The glory of sunrise had turned into bright daylight as Juliette rode up a narrow sandy path that ascended a cliff and then leveled out to a gradual incline.

Thinking her own thoughts, she glanced back over her shoulder at the wide vista of the sea receding further and further below, and then around her at the abundant donkey grass as she breathed in its subtle, earthy fragrance.

Reaching the crest of a rise, Juliette pulled the stallion to a halt, aware of the steady hum of insects and tiny brown butterflies flitting in busy profusion. Ahead was a stand of trees and bushes that appeared to grow more dense further inland. For some time there had been no path to guide her, and now she impulsively gave her horse his head, and watched to see where he would go on his own.

Feeling his mistress's hands relax against his bit, High Times responded first by stretching and breaking into a purposeful trot in the direction of the trees.

Dropping the reins, Juliette playfully spread her arms out like wings, the wind lifting her hair and sweeping it back from her face as she posted up and down to the steady pace and hummed a song her father used to sing.

> *The desert sand, the desert sky*
> *we march along as days go by*
> *Don't try, my dear, to hold me fast,*
> *my kisses and my love won't last. . . .*

She would have continued, but her concentration on the song was interrupted as High Times snuffed loudly and pulled to one side.

Still Juliette let him go, wondering what he had smelled, ducking her head as they entered a grove of trees, and sitting his smooth trot as he wended his way in and out among them, leaping over a fallen log before nudging his way through a stand of thick ferns.

Between the parted branches a pool emerged and, walking to finally stop at its edge, High Times dropped his muzzle into the cool water and drank, tiny rings expanding outward with every swallow.

The pool was perhaps twenty feet across and dappled with sunlight through the leafy canopy of trees overhead. Water lilies dotted its surface, and boulders, like giant steps, emerged out of the water on the far side.

"So this is what you smelled," Juliette said dismounting and giving the chestnut's shiny neck a pat as he raised his water-streaming lips.

Enchanted by the idyllic scene, Juliette walked along the pond's edge, carefully keeping her boots out of the mud as she bent and trailed slender fingers in the water.

It was cool, but not chilling, and very clear. Moving to the side where a tiny stream ran into it, Juliette made a scoop of her hands and drank deeply.

It was sweet in her dry throat, and she drank another scoopful before standing up again and tentatively looking from side to side.

This was such an isolated, out-of-the-way place, she thought. There weren't even trails leading here to suggest it was frequented by anyone.

The midday Spanish sun, directly overhead now, had grown intensely warm and the clear pond seemed so beautiful, so inviting. Wouldn't it feel lovely to have its fresh coolness all over her too-warm flesh?

Again her eyes darted around, but there was not a sign of human presence now, or even recently. So, unable to resist the temptation, she sat herself down on a low rock and pulled off her long buttoned boots and all her clothes, draping them over the ferns before wading into the welcoming freshness.

It was even deeper than she anticipated, and walking until she couldn't touch bottom, Juliette swam with wide-reaching strokes to where the sun, coming through the branches above the pond, dappled a clump of water lilies.

She plucked one, tucking it behind one ear, and treading water, examined the blooms, noticing there were three distinct shades, lavender, deep purple, and a pink one with a purple throat.

Their spicy scent brightened the air, bringing several bees flitting delicately onto their petals and plunging into their recesses in search of the goodness within.

Moving away, Juliette swam to the far side of the pond to the boulders. Then with a little leap and kick, she propelled herself up onto the surface of the lowest rock, settling herself comfortably in the shade before leaning her head back against a higher rock.

Contentedly, she listened to the stream gurgling a few yards away and to the haunting coos of doves overhead, as she watched a pair of dragonflies dance about in the air.

Dreamlike, the moments slipped past, until suddenly she was startled by a movement among the trees on the opposite bank.

Her head jerked up to scan the stand of ferns on the opposite side. And now, unmistakably, she heard the sound of hooves muffled against the damp ground.

A pang of fear gripped her. Noiselessly, she slipped back into the pond, taking a breath before dropping into the water so only her wide eyes and forehead were visible. Then squeezing herself against the rock, she held perfectly still.

Possibly it was only a passerby—someone who would not notice her—or even a lost cow. But when the footsteps came closer, and the branches of a large fern parted, her startled gaze found none other than Brandon Phillips, guiding his horse into the clearing like a stalking animal.

Juliette clung tighter to the rock, praying he would realize his intrusion and go, even as she cursed her own foolishness. But instead he dismounted and walked to the pond's edge. Black boots in a wide stance, hands on hips, he glanced only briefly at the ferns drooping under the weight of her clothes before his mocking gaze scanned the pond and came to rest directly on her.

Juliette's heart charged frantically as his eyebrows arched. There could be no more attempts to hide and, with a splash, she turned away, shielding her breasts with her arms and looking back over her shoulder.

"Why have you followed me?" she flared, blushes coloring her cheeks. "What right have you to intrude on my privacy?"

The large man's eyes sparkled and his smile broadened in a show of white teeth. "It's true I followed you. But I never expected to find so charming a scene. Believe me, I am surprised as you, although I imagine more pleasantly. You make a lovely wood nymph. It suits you better than being a boy."

Juliette glowered, blinking back tears of humiliation in her reddening eyes. He was so completely unabashed! Any other man would have retreated at once with a profusion of apologies. He was mad!—yes, mad!

"I am not a boy!" she said in a tight voice.

"Yes. That is much more apparent now."

"And not a nymph either! And . . . Oh! I don't care what I look like to you and I—"

"I'm sure you don't. You want me to go, don't you?" he interrupted as he sat down on a nearby rock, stretching his booted legs before him as casually as if meeting her at a garden party instead of here, in this ridiculous situation with only the thin shield of her hair floating around her in a spreading fan.

"And I do intend to go," he was saying. "But first, I want to know why you have been avoiding me."

Juliette's color deepened. "If you had any decency, monsieur, you wouldn't be asking me such a rude question."

"Rude?" he repeated. "I'm surprised you bring up the topic of rudeness when you have been so completely rude to me. Or is it customary for you English to avoid someone as obviously as you have been avoiding me? Am I really so repulsive?"

"Of course not, and I haven't been exactly avoiding you, not . . . not really."

"No?" His eyes grew serious and accusing. "Then why did you leave yesterday from the terrace when I came to luncheon, or the tennis courts the day before. And why did you avoid my path in the garden afterward? Don't you think you have been quite rude? It seems if I want to speak to you I have to resort to—alternative means." He smiled and spread his arms palms up in a patently French gesture, "*Et voilà!*"

The fact that all he said was true only served to infuriate Juliette more as she felt herself trapped. She hadn't realized he had seen her those times in the garden or at luncheon. Certainly he had not appeared to notice. Yet how could she deny the truth?

She drew back deeper into the shadows of the rocks though she lifted her chin as she said, "You have no right to be here, no right to question me! This is an outrage! I demand you go immediately!"

She was horrified when she heard him suddenly laugh. "Demand?" And more softly, "Demand?" he repeated in mock dismay. "My poor Juliette. In your present circumstance it is impossible to 'demand' anything from me. But I will offer you a bargain."

"What do you mean 'bargain'?" she snapped.

"I mean, since you seem to want to get rid of me, I will promise to go on the condition that you do me the honor of dancing with me at the French ambassador's ball tomorrow night."

"You have gone mad, monsieur!" she burst out. "You expect me to dance with you after . . . after this! You are . . . I find myself disliking you intensely and . . ."

"Of course you're angry with me now," he interrupted. "But I'm trying to make amends. Anyway, isn't it clear you have no choice?"

Juliette's mouth compressed to a narrow line. "No?" she said braving him with a steady look. "What if I refuse?"

Phillips's black eyes shone as if he found the alternative preferable. "Then I will wait here until you get cold enough, or tired enough to come out. I don't think you can stay in there very long. I can be a patient man—although it is possible that I might become impatient and come in after you. The decision is yours. But either way, we are certain to know each other better."

Juliette wanted to scream, to spit in his face. But what difference did her anger make now? She was undone and they both knew it. Would he really come in and drag her out—naked? No, impossible. He was bluffing—or was he?

And even if he didn't do that, he could easily let it be
known that he had discovered her swimming naked in a
woodland pond. It was the sort of sensational talk that
quickly passed from one to another, creating a storm of
scandal. A juicy tidbit such as that wouldn't damage M.
Phillips's reputation, while it would tear hers to shreds. She
could never forget that her freedom depended on the absence
of such talk.

Her eyes appeared twice their normal size when she finally spoke.

"It seems I have no choice but to accept your 'bargain,'
Monsieur Phillips. But I'm surprised you have to resort to
such means to persuade a woman to keep your company,"
she finished caustically.

He continued looking at her, seemingly unaffected by
her rancor. "Usually they come quite freely," he said factually before adding with another smile, "as you will soon."

"Never!"

The word shot out violently, but his smile didn't fade.
"But you *will* be there tomorrow night." It was more a
statement than a question.

Juliette nodded. She could feel herself shaking and no
longer trusted her voice.

"Good," he said. "Then I will go. I keep my promises,
you see. And I *do* beg your pardon for my interruption."

He rose leisurely from the rock, his eyes admiring the
shimmering image of her back in the clear water and the
mantle of hair—so much longer than he had imagined it
would be. "Until tomorrow, then," he said bowing gracefully and comically blowing her a kiss. Then turning, he
mounted his horse and rode back toward the trees, his
broad shoulders disappearing into the thick greenery.

Chapter 26

The following evening, Juliette could hear the hotel orchestra playing a waltz in the ballroom as she stood in front of
her mirror. She was dressed only in a lace-trimmed che-

mise, garters, stockings, and a long petticoat ruffled down
the back like the trailing tail of an elegant bird.

Her hair was already coiffed, brushed back from her
face into a riot of soft curls pinned at the back of her head.
The style accentuated the delicate perfection of her features and, at the moment, the puckering of her brow.

In her agitation, she had already dismissed Mrs. Winston, who had, for the previous hour, been tense and wordless under her mistress's ill temper. And now, on top of
everything else, Juliette couldn't decide which of her gowns
to wear.

Since seven o'clock, she had tried on one gown after another—gowns from the finest couturiers in Paris. But she
had rejected every one of them.

It was insufferable to be ensnared by anyone, let alone
this unspeakably rude Monsieur Phillips! Ever since she
had safely retrieved her clothes the day before she had
been trying to think of some plausible excuse—some way
to escape this rendezvous. But she knew eluding him was
hopeless. Already the man had demonstrated he would not
be thwarted. So with another frown, Juliette held up a long
pale green gown in front of her, turning sideways to see its
effect.

It was an original by Amelie, a light airy confection of
chiffon that floated around her like a sea of mist. The
large puffed sleeves were of dotted *mousseline de soie* under a ruffle of beaded satin, and the hem and neckline
were also beaded so they winked and flashed in the light. It
was a lovely dress, she thought, turning side to side again.
But the neckline was decidedly too low for this instance.
Already this Phillips man had seen quite enough of her. So
pulling it off, she tossed the dress on top of her bed where
dozens of other gowns already lay in a colorful disarray of
crepon and florentine and rich lutestring, and turned back
to the gowns remaining.

Her mouth twisted in a grimace. She simply had to decide on something. If she didn't appear soon, he might
come for her—forcibly, if necessary. She wouldn't put anything past him, and wasn't a scandal just exactly what she
was trying to avoid?

Glancing in the mirror, Juliette tried to compose her face. "I won't give him the satisfaction of knowing how upset I really am," she told her reflection. "Certainly, I've endured worse humiliations at Miss Fayton's, and I can endure this. It will be simple. After one dance my promise will be fulfilled. After that I'll never need to speak to this vulgar Frenchman again. And from now on, I'll be sure never to go riding so far out alone!"

Her resolve renewed, Juliette reached into her wardrobe and pulled out her violet gown of fine Persian silk. It was simply cut with a narrow tapering skirt that was fitted in front and full in back, with large off-the-shoulder sleeves that puffed to the elbow. Its line enhanced her slender waist perfectly and its scoop neck was only moderately low, showing just the first swell of her breasts.

Her mind made up, she slipped into it, turned before the mirror, and decided she was satisfied. Taking a large painted silk fan and opening it wide with a snap, she set out to join the glittering throng.

A receiving line stretched out into the marble foyer that was dominated by several large flower arrangements and a majordomo announcing guests.

The French ambassador and his wife, with whom Juliette had first become acquainted in London, greeted her warmly, admiring her dress and calling her "quite the loveliest of all the young girls'."

Then she was inside the ballroom and immediately surrounded by a group of young men and women who all at once admired her gown and told her how much they had missed her in London.

Juliette smiled a stiff, absent smile, making comments mechanically as her eyes roamed the room. The music stopped and a new dance began. A voice asked her to dance, and she accepted, not knowing who it was until she turned and saw Bosley Linley, Lord Linley's eldest son.

He was only slightly taller than herself and, unfortunately, forced to wear spectacles. They were thick and unbecoming, and Juliette knew he would have discarded them if he could have done so and still recognized anyone.

Usually Juliette took a sisterly interest in Bosley, inquiring about his schooling at Cambridge, and his mother's health. But tonight she was preoccupied, and as they made their way around the floor, she answered his remarks in clipped syllables.

It was only when Juliette caught Bosley glancing at her strangely that she realized how odd she must seem. But then, before she could change her behavior, she caught a glimpse of M. Phillips, and instantly, all other thoughts vanished like a blackboard being suddenly erased so only a puff of powdered chalk remained.

He was leaning unconcernedly against a pillar near the windows, talking casually to two older men who listened to him and nodded with apparent interest and agreement.

As she watched a new anger rose within her. What could he be saying that so absorbed these men's attention? she asked herself. And when Bosley, always the gentleman, inquired diffidently whether she was perhaps not feeling well, she snapped a harsh, "No!" that surprised even herself.

Stricken, Bosley continued to lead her timidly around the room in silence until, at last, the music stopped. He guided Juliette into a chair, stammered an excuse, and made his way back to his mother's side.

The orchestra began the first notes of a lively polka and Juliette, standing on the sidelines, felt her stomach fluttering. Had M. Phillips noticed her? Yes, of course. If he had seen her those other times she was trying so hard not to be seen then certainly he must have noticed her now.

She gripped her fan tightly, waving it until her curls blew and wondering if any moment she would see his imposing frame coming through the crowd to claim her.

Well, let him, she thought. Better to dance now and get it over with. But another part quavered at the thought of his touch. And when another voice asked her to dance, again she accepted immediately relieved that her dance with *him* might be postponed.

It was Roberto, the man Phillips had beaten so soundly at tennis the morning after she had rescued him, and fortunately, Juliette didn't have to worry about making polite conversation. Roberto kept up a continual stream of chatter, mostly about himself and the latest tennis matches he had won.

As they turned round the floor, Juliette peered guardedly over Roberto's shoulders to see Brandon still in the same place, the two men still listening intently. And after that, she couldn't help but glance at him each time they went by.

What a striking figure he made in evening clothes. His perfectly tailored jacket flattered his triangular frame, and underneath his coat he wore a waistcoat and a narrowly ruffled white shirt with black pearl studs. He seemed quite at home, calmly smoking a foreign-looking cigarette and occasionally gesturing with a long narrow hand. The gentlemen remained attentive as ever, and another joined them to add his thoughtful nods to those of the others.

Again the dance ended, and when Roberto escorted her to the edge of the floor and offered to bring her champagne, she smiled her assent.

Already her mouth was dry, and her head was throbbing, too, by the time he returned, two glasses in hand. Then moving to the other side of the room they joined a group of acquaintances.

Purposely Juliette had turned so she couldn't see Phillips. Of course, with a glass of champagne in her hand, she was not eligible to dance anyway, and her unapproachability gave her confidence.

When she finished the first glass, she allowed one of the waiters to give her another, and consuming the second as quickly as the first, she felt much better and began joining the conversation, a fact which pleased Roberto, who waved again to the waiter for more champagne.

The lights glowed, and the music seemed gayer than ever, and Juliette felt her apprehensions melting away.

What did it matter about the pompous Phillips? It was only a dance, something that could be done and over with. How silly of her to make such a fuss.

She laughed heartily at one of Roberto's jokes, and when he asked her to dance again, she smiled brightly in acceptance.

As they made a turn round the floor toward where Phillips had been lounging with the other gentlemen, Juliette tossed her head and laughed, hoping he would notice what a good time she was having. But then, glancing out of the corner of her eye, her heart skipped as she saw he was no longer talking with the two men, but rather with a woman instead, a beautiful woman who reminded Juliette of Botticelli's Venus, though this woman was more buxom and her hair was a honey blond.

Oh, what a fool I've made of myself, she thought savagely. He probably isn't even interested in dancing with me. He has just made the bargain to amuse himself at my expense, to make me come to this ball and then to guess when he will ask me to dance. All evening he has been dangling me like a toy, yes, a toy, while he shows his attention to others. And all the time he's known I would be afraid to leave. Oh, how he must be laughing! Just the thought was infuriating. And when the dance ended, she took another glass of champagne and drank it.

How dare he humiliate me in this manner, she told herself, trying to get another glimpse of him through the crowd. As far as I am concerned, my promise is fulfilled. If he thinks not . . . well, just let him tell everyone. I no longer care!

When the next dance ended and all the younger set were gathered on the sidelines, Juliette smiled warmly at the group, bidding them good night before flashing a particular smile in Roberto's direction and turning to leave.

As she anticipated, the young Spaniard came immediately to her side. "Perhaps I could have the honor of walking you back, Miss Thorpe?"

Juliette's pleasant look turned up to meet his eager one. "Of course," she agreed, hoping Phillips would witness her departure. "How kind you are."

Both surprised and delighted, Roberto offered his arm. And smiling, Juliette was about to take it when a voice interrupted them, seeming to exclude any argument in advance.

"I believe Miss Thorpe promised this dance to me."

In one motion they both turned to see Brandon Phillips,

who nodded in greeting first to Juliette and then to Roberto.

"Monsieur Phillips!" Roberto said, admiration lighting up his brown eyes. "It is good to see you, sir!"

Phillips smiled, too, clapping Roberto on the shoulder. "Roberto, old man! How have you been?"

"Quite well, sir. I was actually wondering if you would care to play another game of tennis sometime?"

As they conversed, Juliette's thoughts flew in a flurry, all her resolutions faltering. Then to make matters worse, as Brandon spoke, he was taking her hand into his and drawing her toward him with a possessiveness that made her want to scream.

To make a scene was unthinkable, and well he knew it, too, as a slightly raised eyebrow seemed to tell her. What could she do but submit, her lips compressed as she went to him, lifting her other hand between them to press against his broad chest.

He seemed so tall this close, so tall she was unable to see over his shoulder.

"Perhaps you could teach me your serve," Roberto was saying. "It's quite the most devastating I've ever encountered."

"Yes, of course. On Friday. Shall we say ten o'clock."

Eagerly Roberto agreed, and with a bow and a nod to her, moved off. Then Brandon's arm was slipping around her waist in a firm but gentle grip, and the music began.

Chapter 27

It was a waltz, and Juliette found herself suddenly among the other dancers and being turned round and round with long confident strides that made her dizzy.

She tried to remember all the barbed things she had planned to say. But, at the moment, when he was silent, and outwardly observing every courtesy, nothing she planned seemed exactly right. So, confused and self-conscious, Juliette kept her eyes downcast and turned away, refusing even to look at him.

As for Brandon, he found himself surprised at the unusual arousal he felt holding this girl in his arms. He had always known that Juliette Thorpe would be stunning in feminine clothing. But now, as his eyes roved slowly over her ripe, full mouth and peach-tinted neck and shoulders, he had to resist a raging urge to press his lips against the vee where her throat pulsed in tiny waves.

She was so slender, so light in his arms—the very essence of youth, of glowing life and, at the moment, of ill humor.

"You have nothing to fear from looking at me," he said after they finished a second turn round the dance floor in silence. "I won't turn to stone from just a look and neither will you and I would prefer looking at your face instead of the top of your head."

Juliette jerked her face up, wrathful eyes sparkling forcefully into his. Indeed her irises were striped with a darker shade, he thought. Perhaps *that* was what made them seem a deep violet, the color of royal velvet.

"I'm not afraid to look at you," she snapped. "If looks could be fatal, Monsieur Phillips, then *you* would already be dead!"

It was horrible when Brandon's laughter rolled out deep and throaty, and Juliette felt even more agitated to realize Lady Linley and the Countess Milshire were craning their necks to glimpse her among the dancing couples as they passed.

"Shh," Juliette said. "You laugh too loudly and too impertinently! You'll have everyone gossiping about us!"

"What gossips say doesn't trouble me. Besides, you amuse me. What a hotheaded vixen you are. Hasn't anyone ever taught you any manners?"

"Manners?" Juliette hissed between clenched teeth, glancing again at the two ladies who now had their heads together whispering. "I warn you, monsieur," she continued in her most devastating tone, "Keep your distance or you will find I have claws."

He lifted her hand from his shoulder and brought it to

his lips, kissing the backs of her fingers. "Who would have guessed such soft hands could be so dangerous. But I'm not concerned." His eyes played with light as he smiled broadly. "I have a way with wild creatures."

Juliette jerked her hand away. "I should have left you to drown. You are the rudest and most egotistical man I've ever been unfortunate enough to meet. And . . ."

" . . . And you, Miss Thorpe, are a most beautiful young woman," he interrupted smiling again. "Come, dance with me," he continued. "If you wish to argue, I promise there will be time later."

Juliette faltered. The champagne had released her temper but now muddled her words so she couldn't think of exactly what to say. So still keeping her head high she nodded a formal little nod, but a nod just the same. She had no choice anyway, that much was clear. And suddenly she was being swept round the floor in an embrace that pressed her breasts into his chest, and when she turned her face away, as if to ignore him, Phillips indulged in several sets of complicated steps that forced her to pay attention to his lead, while silently she wondered, with a touch of alarm, when the dance would end.

But it didn't end. And he continued holding her tightly as they swung with winged agility round the floor in a rustle of silk, his arm pressed possessively against her back.

The champagne bubbled inside her, and the thousand candles seemed to blur into one golden warmth. A soft buzzing was in her head, and when the music stopped, Phillips propelled her out a nearby doorway onto a balcony before she could think of saying no.

There was an iron trellis where a vine grew twisting high overhead, and Juliette leaned against it, breathing deeply in an attempt to clear her head, and not wanting even to look at Phillips until she decided whether to stay here in the coolness with this unpleasant man, or return to the overly warm ballroom where she would undoubtedly begin to perspire.

Phillips had moved closer, putting his back against a carved wooden column that supported the overhanging roof. He didn't try to touch her, he merely drew a gold

cigarette case from inside his coat and placed one of the
dark cigars between his lips. He lit it, puffing until a
cloud of the sweet aroma rose around his head. He was
quiet—even contemplative and as moments passed without
words, Juliette listened to the distant lap of the waves.

I've fulfilled my promise, Juliette told herself, and now
I'm free to leave. But the air, so fragrant, felt wonderful.
It was such a beautiful night, and shifting her weight from
one foot to the other she remained where she was, con-
tented to watch the stars, which were like far-off lanterns,
and to feel the refreshing breeze.

His eyes on Juliette's profile, Brandon drew deeply on
his cheroot, exhaling long and slowly. She was an unusual
girl, intelligent, beautiful, and maddeningly aloof. Yet before, when he held her in his arms, he could sense the
woman in her, too—the dormant desire that would so easily blossom into ripeness. Now he realized he wanted her
with a primitive need to possess, a need never experienced
in the past. Always before he had felt unaffected by the
typical fierce jealousy that characterized his Arab countrymen. But suddenly he understood why brother might murder brother, and a man might kill his best friend. It would
be easy, even natural, to kill any other man who would
dare touch this woman.

The champagne still bubbling in her head made Juliette
dizzy. She grasped the iron balcony railing and took another deep breath. Suddenly in the midst of the garden's
loveliness and the stars and the strains of music drifting
from the open doorway, she felt in some far-reaching way
that everything was as it should be.

From somewhere in the darkness, Brandon's hand was
taking hers. His clasp was firm, though gentle, and once
again he brought the back of her hand to his lips, kissing
the soft flesh on her slender fingers.

Juliette started to pull away, but he held her fast until
she stopped pulling and let her hand remain in his.

"It seems, Miss Thorpe, that we are having what you
English term 'a bad start,'" she heard him say matter-of-
factly. "I'm sorry because I think we could become such

good friends. Please accept my apologies if I have offended you."

Juliette glanced up at him, surprised to see that he looked sincere. How changeable and how charming he could be. And somehow, at the moment, she no longer cared that he had been egotistical and overbearing before.

A smile appeared and grew at the corners of her mouth. Then she laughed lightly. "I think, Monsieur, that you are quite stubborn and probably so used to having your own way that you take it for granted."

A look of pleasure came to his features. "Flexibility has never been an attribute of mine," he commented. "Perhaps the lack of it has grown to a fault."

Still his energizing hand held hers, making her fingertips tingle. She looked toward the sea again, glad the shadow of the trellis covered her face from his searching eyes.

He squeezed her hand. "Don't run away, little one. I will not harm you," he whispered in a teasing tone.

All at once Juliette felt foolish and horribly transparent. Usually she could easily control the gentlemen who courted her, turning them into willing slaves. But *this* man seemed like none of the others. His code of behavior was entirely his own. She wasn't certain what to expect—he hadn't even tried to kiss her. And glancing up briefly, Juliette couldn't keep herself from wondering just what his mouth would feel like pressed against hers.

She laughed then, suddenly nervous he might once again discern her thoughts. "I'm not afraid of you, Monsieur Phillips. Are there women who are?"

"That doesn't matter as long as I don't frighten you."

Juliette couldn't look at him. She turned toward the garden and, to her surprise, saw something moving in the shadows—a figure.

Brandon must have seen a change in her face since, without turning around, he said, "It is Rashid, one of my servants," before she could ask. "He is usually close to me. Don't let his presence upset you."

Juliette looked back at Brandon, and then to the figure again who already had melted into a darker corner. On the contrary, it seemed better not to be completely alone with this man.

"He is a bodyguard?" she asked.

Brandon nodded. "He is that and other things. He's been at my side for twenty years."

"If it's a bodyguard you keep so close, perhaps it is *you* who is frightened, monsieur," she said with the hint of a challenge.

He shrugged. "Often a man who has many interests and a certain amount of wealth has enemies. My father before me had bodyguards, and so do I."

"He wasn't with you the other night swimming."

Brandon smiled. "A nearly fatal error—except for you. You have my gratitude—forever, if it would please you."

"I wouldn't ask for so much—at least not 'forever.' "

"No, but you have it anyway. And since you wouldn't take the pearls, I'll have to find another way to thank you."

Juliette looked at him sidelong, wanting to circumvent this dangerous ground. "I think, monsieur, you give this matter more attention than it deserves."

"Indeed?"

"Indeed." And to change the subject, Juliette asked, "Why did you go swimming the other night when it was so late and so lonely? I've wondered about it ever since I saw you dive in."

Brandon braced an elbow against the column and looked out beyond the lawns and fibrous trunks of palm trees to where the sea crashed in a hypnotic rhythm of white surf.

"I wanted to be alone. I was looking."

"Looking? What were you looking for?"

Suddenly he seemed to drift very far away, and following the direction of his gaze, Juliette waited for him to speak.

"There are times when the world closes in," he began, "When there is neither space nor peace and everything seems tarnished. Once life was fresh and full of meaning. When I left home to seek a fortune, I was full of dreams and ideals. I thought reaching my goals would bring everything I wanted. But now that I have within my grasp all that I thought would satisfy me, I find it does not. Somewhere the essence of my dreams has vanished in the face of reality. Looking back I see how far I've traveled. Yet occasionally now I ask myself why."

There was a pause inside the ballroom as the music stopped and, for a time, there was only the sound of the sea rushing in and out.

"But perhaps you can find your dream again," Juliette said feeling that a tiny crack in the door of this mysterious man's character had been opened to her. "It is a person's dreams that get him over the rough spots in life."

"You are so young, Juliette. What do you know of life's troubles?"

"I know a little, more than I let on. Tell me what troubles you most now?"

Brandon drew again on the cheroot before dropping it off the ends of his fingers and crushing it under his heel. Mists blew across the moon, forming a pale rainbow against the light as it passed. Then the full brightness shone again on Brandon's face, so Juliette could see the mood of reverie had already left him.

Now his eyes were bright as quicksilver and teasing as before. "At the moment," he said, "my 'troubles' are even worse than usual. Usually I find my life tolerable, that is until recently, when I've found myself wanting something that continues to elude me."

"Really! And what is that?"

"A treasure," he whispered coming closer as his gaze traveled from her hair to her eyes to her lips. "One fit for a king—a combination of gold and amethysts and rubies, so rich it hasn't been fully assessed."

Juliette stepped backward. "Oh?" she said light and bantering, though she noticed again that no one had joined them on the balcony. "And now what will you do?"

"Very little, at least now. I've found the treasure is well guarded by a tigress whose mood changes in the blink of an eye. She is unpredictable and has claws."

Juliette laughed. "How frustrating for you. But didn't you say you have a way with wild things? Maybe you'll be able to convince this tigress."

"I've tried cajoling," he said. "And that has brought me nearer. But this creature is wilder than imagined and I'm afraid I have a long wait until I can so much as touch the treasure let alone call it mine."

"So what will you do?"

"At the moment I have in mind to be patient and persuasive. But if there is no alternative, I will be forced to use power."

"Ohhhh, power!" Juliette said, her eyes dancing, her heart beating much too fast. "I thought power was the prerogative of kings. Are you really so powerful, monsieur?"

Brandon only smiled. It had occurred to him the day before when he had found her alone at the pond to simply kidnap her, and it occurred to him now. His yacht was waiting in the harbor, and arrangements could be made to make it seem she was elsewhere until it would be too late for any rescue.

Were he in his own country, there would be no question. A prince simply took what he desired. But here, even he had to adhere to European customs, a fact which now annoyed him.

"I imagine the extent of my power will be tested only if persuasion fails. That will be soon enough to judge."

Juliette raised her eyes, sensing something beneath his light tone that made her shiver.

A part of her mind urged her to make some excuse, to leave this unusual man. Yet, at the same time, a certain fascination made her stay. She did not answer, and noticed him looking toward the ballroom where the music had begun again and couples were beginning to dance. On his neck, just behind his ear, she noticed a diamond-shaped birthmark.

"Shall we dance?" he said. And not waiting for her acceptance or rejection, he was already taking her in his arms and whirling her back through the door and onto the dance floor.

In his arms, Juliette was swept away again by the same excitement as before. He was silent then, his dark eyes seeming even darker, and he didn't smile.

It seemed her feet barely touched down as they glided

round and round. Juliette also found herself somehow lacking in words. And aware only of the violins and the sweep of rustling silk, and most of all, his arms holding her, time took on a new dimension, and she no longer noticed its passing.

They moved from a waltz to a polka, Brandon carrying her through those lively steps so it became easy. It seemed then only a moment had passed when suddenly it was over and the music had stopped.

On Brandon's arm, she bid her farewells and thanked the host and hostess. Then they were crossing the garden toward her room, his arm encircling her shoulders.

A golden glow covered everything, and when they stood together outside her doorway, Juliette no longer thought of consequences or future as, with a tingle of warmth, she wondered if he would kiss her.

Still he was silent, his expression serious, compelling, as he brushed a stray blond curl from her temple. And when he bent down Juliette couldn't keep herself from raising her own mouth.

A pang of disappointment registered as she felt his lips press her brow instead. Then he was holding her away from him.

"I look forward to our friendship, mademoiselle—and to the days to come." Then he bowed, formally, as gracefully as a prince. *"Au revoir,"* he said, and turning, left her, disappearing down the darkened hallway.

Juliette stepped inside her room and shut the door softly behind her.

Walking aimlessly around her bedroom she undressed, leaving her gown and stockings and chemise where she dropped them. Then in a hazy radiance, she slipped into bed, recalling with a smile how they had danced and how he had held her before she fell deeply asleep.

Chapter 28

The morning following the ball, Juliette Thorpe awakened early, full of a strange new excitement that wouldn't let her remain in bed.

Immediately she dressed, choosing forest brown knickers, and quickly fastened the last pearl buttons of her shirtwaist blouse as she headed for the stables.

When she arrived, she wasn't surprised to find Brandon Phillips there, already mounted and waiting to join her on her morning ride.

She had thought of him several times this morning, concluding that he wasn't at all the monster she had once considered him to be. He had been a perfect gentleman last night, she thought. And maybe—yes, what harm would it do to see him again? In a few more days I'll be leaving for Switzerland anyway, and probably will never see him again after that, she told herself. So while Juliette would normally have given any male intruding on her morning solitude an icy reception, she now smiled a greeting, mounted her own horse and shouted, "Race you to the farmhouse!" before urging her chestnut into a flying gallop across a field patchworked with clumps of wildflowers.

High Times leapt forward, seeming to sprout wings so that his hooves skimmed the grass as Brandon's black horse dashed after.

They had galloped up a long gradual incline and then down again before Juliette looked back, expecting to pull up her horse to wait for Brandon. But turning, she was surprised to find him directly behind, riding easily in the saddle as his mount kept the pace.

Juliette leaned lower so High Times body extended like an enormous greyhound as he scooped up the ground in long leaping strides. But after galloping up a second hill and down again, Juliette could still hear the black at her heels.

They went on, the wind rushing against Juliette's face so

tears came to her eyes. She wiped them away with the back of her glove and leaned lower over the chestnut's straining neck.

Again High Times lengthened his strides, pulling away from the black. But as they continued the big horse began quickly losing speed again while Brandon still remained just behind High Times's churning flanks.

Panting, Juliette reined her mount to a halt, twisting to face Brandon.

He was chuckling, white teeth bold against his tanned complexion. "You didn't get away quite so easily," he observed, bringing his horse so close the suede knee of his knickers briefly brushed hers.

"Usually High Times outruns everything!" she said, edging her chestnut two steps away.

Brandon reached forward, running his hand under the black's mane and flipped the long mass of hair back and forth with fond familiarity as he said, "This horse has won several races in Paris. He has a son winning races as well. But you challenged me, Juliette."

The breeze tossed Juliette's blond hair which had come unbound so it fell down in a shiny torrent. She brushed it out of her face to look closely at Brandon's stallion. Certainly he had lines for speed, and his small intelligent head suggested Arabian blood. It was hard to know what to say. He had surprised her again. She felt foolish, but any protest would make her seem a poor loser, so silently she turned away, this time urging High Times into a trot and reining him on the narrow path that continued uphill.

Brandon took a place beside her and neither spoke as they rode stirrup to stirrup, climbing ever higher, finally reaching an orange grove. Eight or so swarthy looking men in flowing robes were in the clearing at the summit, apparently making some kind of preparations.

Arabs! Juliette had seen few of them, but whenever she did, it was impossible to repress a shiver of revulsion and a pang of fury as she recalled all the bitterness of her father's death. Even so their presence made her curious and, guiding her horse in their direction, she paused to observe them as she came closer.

In the center of the clearing, surrounded by blossoming trees, was erected a large circular canopy with black tassels and a black and brown striped dome. A table beneath it was set for dining and was circled by large black and brown cushions. The occasional clang of a pot, and the fragrances of food from beyond her view told Juliette they were cooking.

As she sat watching, several of the white robed men turned and salaamed obsequiously. Their attention made her feel conspicuous. She was reining her horse away when Brandon's hand suddenly closed around her arm.

"Come," he said simply, "our breakfast is nearly ready."

He's joking, Juliette thought, but her eyes filled with surprise as she saw he was already swinging a lean muscular leg off his horse.

"Our breakfast?" she questioned.

He nodded. "Come," he repeated.

She couldn't refuse, she was here. Apparently he had prepared all of this for her. So she let him help her off her horse, and handed the reins to an Arab who came forward, bowing low before leading the horses away. Then Brandon drew her under the canopy, clasping her hand so naturally Juliette didn't think of rebuking him.

"Make yourself comfortable here," he said indicating the grouping of elaborate cushions. And when she positioned herself, making an attempt to sit rather than recline, he lowered himself easily beside her.

Before them the green hills dotted with orange trees stretched below to the ocean. The fragrant air was filled with small insects that buzzed around their heads until, at a signal from an attendant, a small Arab boy, also dressed in spotless white, took up his station behind them waving a large woven straw fan back and forth in a smooth regular motion that discouraged the pests and cooled the air.

Sniffing the sweetness, Juliette looked pensively at the view. It was a long time before she turned back to Brandon and found him watching her.

"You're very sure of yourself, Monsieur Phillips," she said then. "What if I had decided to refuse your invitation this morning?"

He shrugged. "I would have breakfasted alone." A sweep of his arm indicated the hills and trees. "It is pleasant here, although more pleasant with you. I'm honored you came."

An Arab servant approached, the breeze billowing his robes as he bowed and offered Brandon a tray of silver that held two long-stemmed goblets.

Taking them, Brandon dismissed the servant with a nod before offering Juliette one of them.

She took it, sipping from its gilded edge. She was not surprised to discover it contained champagne, sparkling and very dry.

"Tell me," she said then, looking at the receding back of the servant. "Why do you have Arab servants?"

Brandon tilted back against the cushions sipping his own champagne. "I suppose because I'm an eccentric—and because they are excellent servants." He cocked his head looking at her thoughtfully. "They aren't exactly devils, you know. Their 'Allah,' for instance, is the same God as the Christian one. Does it bother you they are Arab?"

He didn't move, but Juliette felt his interest focusing intensely on her answer. She considered telling him the truth, but somehow it seemed too personal, and some of the reserve she had learned at Miss Fayton's prevented her. She shook her head. "Not bothered at all, only curious. You must know how curious we English are." She smiled. "Do you always picnic in such elegant style?"

"Not always. Sometimes elegance is superfluous." He swirled the champagne around in his glass with a slow rotation of his hand before toasting her. "To English girls and their 'curiosity,' " he said teasingly and drank before continuing. "But today I've made a special occasion. Do expensive things impress you?"

"Sometimes when they are very beautiful or very old. Truthfully I prefer the view to anything else. Nature is the greatest magnificence."

He nodded, then waved a hand toward the horses being watered a short distance from the camp. "Tell me about your horse. He's an unusual type to see a girl riding."

Juliette followed his regard to the chestnut where she could discern the many scars that marred High Times's shiny coat, making him appear a brutish sort that were not often ladies' mounts.

Juliette leaned back among the cushions, but unexpectedly the movement on the slippery silk brought her sliding to sit right beside him, and once there, it seemed awkward and foolish to spring up again. So acutely aware of his leg next to hers, his hand on the cushion near her breast, his lips only a breath from hers, she swallowed hard and said:

"It was over a year ago. I happened to be in a poor section of London when, walking past an old shed, I saw High Times tied up in a corner and being teased and beaten by a bunch of street toughs. I didn't know how else to stop them other than by offering to buy the horse. They agreed, but somehow during the exchange I must have gotten too close to poor frenzied High Times, who knocked me down and broke my arm. Later though, we were able to make friends. He's quite gentle now and I take him everywhere I go."

Brandon seemed thoughtful as he said, "So you took him into your favor even after he hurt you."

"Yes, of course," she said. "I couldn't blame the poor horse for what others had made him be. Anyway, he had speed in every line. It was so obvious he was meant for better things than dragging a London coal vender's cart."

"You are generous," he stated simply. "I don't have your forgiveness."

Juliette glanced at him curiously. "Have you a lot to forgive, monsieur? Is that why you so detest the English?"

Brandon's gaze focused on Juliette with a new alertness. Why did she ask? he found himself wondering. Could she possibly know something? "I don't detest you," he said.

"No? Are there those you do? A special English enemy list?"

Juliette had meant to be playful. But suddenly she realized his eyes were deadly serious and shone like silvered mirrors probing her mind.

A chill slid down her spine so she wished suddenly she hadn't pried. She was relieved then when another servant came with a larger tray and, bowing, offered it to Brandon.

His eyes slid away from her as he lifted the lid from the covered platter and the savory aroma drifted toward her. Then he sampled the contents, apparently approving, since he used his long golden fork to feed her one of the tiny rounded hors d'oeuvres. Now his eyes had softened again. Or maybe she had only imagined that deadly look.

"Excellent," she exclaimed, rolling the tidbit in her mouth. "What is it?"

"Dove hearts rolled in spices and sesame seeds and cooked in wine."

Juliette wrinkled her nose. "Not dove hearts really?"

He smiled. "In the Sahara, it's a delicacy."

"Tell me about the Sahara," she said, glad to see the cold light had not returned to his face.

"Perhaps one day soon you will honor me with a visit and see for yourself. The main focus of my business is in Africa and I frequent it often. You would enjoy the adventure of a caravan."

Juliette shrugged noncommittally. "I do plan to travel a great deal. I'm certain to visit that part of the world sometime. I've heard it's beautiful and very exotic."

"You will learn to like it, I think," he said with strange emphasis.

The servants interrupted them again, bringing more trays gracefully held over their turbaned heads. Silver plates were placed before them on the low table and these were followed by a series of jewel-encrusted platters full of more aromatic preparations that were presented first to Brandon who, after sampling and approving each dish, served her the choicest portions.

It was a long, leisurely meal which Juliette enjoyed with appetite, praising each dish for its deliciousness, although never again asking the contents. And as they ate, Brandon entertained her with stories of the Sahara, its beauty and the sport it offered. She urged him on, finding herself absorbed by his descriptions of sunsets, of a game the Arabs played called *palo* and by anecdotes concerning hunts for a rare mountain sheep called mouflon.

What sort of man is this? Juliette asked herself as he spoke. At times he seemed cold, impenetrable as a stone, and yet he could talk of a sunset in details full of sensitive inspiration. When he paused to sip champagne, she sat thoughtfully tugging on a curl.

He asked about her life then, and she spoke of her travels so far, of what she had seen and where she wanted to go in the future. As it turned out, they had many experiences in common. He had traveled everywhere she had, and they had even gotten lost in the same way the first time each had visited Rome.

It was afternoon before Juliette realized that she had lingered far longer than she had ever intended. What was it about him? Hours had passed as minutes in a way that seemed queer, and a little disturbing and all at once she thought she must escape.

Getting abruptly to her feet, she almost knocked over the low table. "I'm ready to go back now," she blurted. I should have left sooner. It's just . . . I didn't realize how late it was."

Frowning, Brandon stood up also. "Of course, I'll take you back whenever you wish. But have I offended you? Only a moment ago you seemed content to stay."

"I . . . I was. But now I realize I must go. Please understand. You haven't offended me. On the contrary, it has been a wonderful morning. It's just that it has gotten much later than I . . . intended . . . than I thought."

She felt foolish now standing here awkwardly, flushing. Why had she been so abrupt? Certainly she could have extricated herself without making a scene.

Finally his gaze softened and registered a flicker of understanding. Turning, he waved a hand.

Instantly a servant was there. Brandon spoke several words in what sounded to Juliette like fluent Arabic and the servant trotted in the direction of the horses.

Coming a step closer he took both of her white hands into his bronzed ones. "Tomorrow then," he said. It was not a question.

Juliette realized she must say yes or risk being delayed.

The warm tingling of his touch increased her urgency to get away.

"Yes . . . yes, of course. Tomorrow," she said.

"Good." He released her hands as the horses arrived, and taking her around the waist, lifted her effortlessly onto the saddle. Then mounting his own horse they rode side by side back toward the blue expanse sparkling far below.

Chapter 29

A series of days followed the ambassador's ball filled with such a blur of activity and emotions that, later, Juliette could remember them only as a jumble of days spent beside Brandon—mornings spent galloping across the island's grassy slopes, and afternoons lunching or swimming along the craggy shoreline. The nights they danced to the hotel orchestra at the frequent parties to which they both were inevitably invited, and during these, Juliette did notice there were a growing number of "looks" which they received—curious, uncertain looks from the older women, and patently envious looks from the younger ones.

She knew they were gossiping about her, but somehow none of it mattered. What difference did it make what *they* thought? she asked herself. She was doing nothing wrong by seeing this man—nothing at all! He had been a perfect gentleman, never even mentioning again that day at the pond—an incident she was determined to forget, and never even trying to kiss her. Sometimes she would wonder about this. Every other man in her acquaintance had tried to kiss her. But whenever this occurred to her she was always quick to remind herself that it was much better that he wasn't more forward. In such a short time she would leave and never see him again.

There had been a play one night, a festive production filled with the romance and tragedy that seemed such a part of Spain, in a setting of frolicking abundance and vibrant songs and dances and costumes of red and black and silver.

Then, one day, as suddenly and unexpectedly as always, Brandon appeared on the terrace just as Mrs. Welwright entered the wrought-iron gates to his left.

The two greeted one another. Then together they approached her table where she was already breakfasting opposite Bosley Linley.

Mrs. Welwright looked more serious than usual. There was a slight strain in her "Good morning," Juliette noticed. But this was quickly overshadowed by Brandon himself, who, having already greeted a pouting Bosley, offered his arm to her.

"This morning I'm taking you aboard the *Black Hawk*," he said with a smile before turning to the older woman with a polite bow. "You will forgive us, Mrs. Welwright?"

Juliette was hardly aware of Mrs. Welwright's deferential words, feeling instead swept away by the delight of the spontaneous outing with this man. So saying polite goodbyes to everyone, she took his arm and headed for the docks.

This was Juliette's first glimpse of the *Black Hawk*. The yacht was anchored at the end of the pier, its sails ready to be hoisted as bobbing with the swells it stretched its ropes and pulled against them like a mighty steed eager for a run.

Bringing her aboard, Brandon took command, giving orders that resulted in the craft moving around and then slowly out of the harbor as the sails were hoisted.

Leaning over the rail, Juliette joined hands behind her back as she watched the prow slice through the gray billow and the spume foaming back. A sharp screech overhead drew attention to a pair of pelicans flying wing tip to wing tip as they skimmed the white caps, their heads cocked to one side as they waited to sight their prey. Then abruptly one of them folded its wings, diving arrowlike and, with a cry of triumph, pulling out a silvered fish that reflected the sunlight as it was carried wriggling away.

At a leisurely pace, they sailed slowly along the shore, high cliffs rising a hundred feet in the air between wide sandy beaches where groups of fishermen were hauling in their catch of lobsters in hopsack bags.

They continued south until the sun had reached its peak

and began to slope toward the west. Then the crew brought
the craft about and anchored it in a small natural bay surrounded by even higher crags where birds were building
their nests in eroded hollows and shelves.

A gateleg table was set up on the wooden deck at the
widest part of the stern where Brandon seated her opposite
himself. Then handing her a crystal goblet of wine, he
raised his own in a toast. "To our friendship," he said.

Juliette smiled as their goblets touched in a distinctive
ring. "Yes. And to today, for itself and nothing more," she
added, and drank.

From that point on the conversation, as usual, flowed
easily, and after their glasses were filled a second time, an
Arab servant approached, and, bowing, announced lunch.

This time the meal was a decidedly English one of mari-
nated beef, Yorkshire pudding, and vegetables expertly seasoned in the English style. Again Juliette marveled at
Brandon's versatility. He spoke no fewer than five languages and could seem French, Spanish, Arabic, or even
English, as he did now in his white sailing clothes.

"You are like a chameleon, constantly changing from
one identity to another," she said. "You make me dizzy the
way you constantly turn into different people. Are you
ever the same?"

"I travel all over the world, and entertain varying people. My chef is trained to suit a variety of tastes and I have
an equal variety in my wardrobe. I may appear to change,
but I am really only one person with many sides." He
paused, looking at her fondly. "But tell me—what do I
seem like to you?"

Juliette tilted her head, and after several evaluating minutes said, "You seem to me very proud—abnormally
strong—undoubtedly quite clever—and possibly cruel."

Brandon leaned back in his chair. "And does such a
combination appeal to you?"

Juliette smiled. "Proud is all right as long as you aren't
so proud you forget everyone else but yourself."

"And strong?"

"Strong is good. Being strong suits a man."

"What about cleverness then?"

"A good trait, certainly a handy one."

"And cruelty?"

"I hate it."

Brandon frowned, and, seeming unaccustomed to finding excuses for himself said, "Sometimes life combines to make a person what he would not be under different circumstances."

Juliette nodded. "Yes," she said. "Possibly that's why I'm so independent now. If life had been different maybe I would feel differently. But in times past, I experienced things which made me realize that if I could somehow escape my circumstances, I would be independent and never give it up."

"It means so much to you?"

"More than I can tell you. It is a rare thing for a woman to be still young and her own mistress. Usually she must wait be widowed and by then she is often too old to enjoy herself. I intend to make the most of what I have. I'm happy now, and I desire nothing different."

"You're very fortunate. Most people can never say that. But you are young. You may find life has more to offer than what you fill your days with now. You may even discover that there are nights connecting the days which can be even more pleasurable."

Juliette looked up to find his eyes smiling directly into hers. A sense of self-consciousness swept her. But then, to her relief, a servant interrupted them with a tray of pastries that he held forward for her selection.

Immediately delighted, Juliette looked over her choices. As a child she had never been allowed such treats, and Miss Fayton's had been too strict for such extravagance.

It was only since she had been set free that she had the opportunity to sample such delicacies. And now her eyes wandered over the array of desserts, of chocolate, raspberry, and lemon mousse, of rice pudding, apple tarts, poached fruit in port, and *mille-feuille aux fraises,* before she finally chose an éclair covered with whipped cream and shaved chocolate. And when it was set before her with a cup of tea, she began devouring it without preliminaries.

From beyond her view, someone strummed a guitar, filling the air with soft strains, and Juliette, occupied with the combined taste of Dutch chocolate topping, pastry, and custard in her mouth, did not notice until after she was finished that Brandon had not said a word, though his attention was still on her, seemingly pondering a question. So as the servant removed her plate, she said, "You seem quiet all at once. What are you thinking?"

"About ways and means."

"Ways and means?" she questioned with a teasing note. "I thought you much too rich to be concerned about such trivialities."

"Unfortunately, in this case, my wealth is not helping me."

"No? What an uncomfortable position for a millionaire. Still," Juliette said, putting an elbow casually on the table, "it seems to me, Monsieur Phillips, it would do you no harm to go without something you want now and then."

Brandon smiled lazily with half-closed eyes. "I dislike 'going without' intensely," he said. He leaned forward. "And I haven't decided yet if I will have to go without. You've evaded me so far, my little tigress, but I haven't given up."

Juliette's slender eyebrows arched. "Oh?" she said, refusing to take him seriously. "But I think you've come quite a long way. I find you *very* persuasive."

He took her hand, his warmth infusing her. "But that's not true," he said suddenly serious. "You have consistently kept me at arm's length."

Juliette pulled against his grasp. He was right, of course, and she knew it, and when she continued to pull, he did let her go.

"Closer than 'arm's length' is impossible, I'm afraid," she said stirring her tea. "In a few days we will be even further apart. After the Spanish Cup is run, I'll be leaving for Switzerland."

Brandon's brows shot together. "Leaving? You can't *leave!*"

His voice contained an imperious note that made Juliette stiffen and, deliberately, she lifted the spoon out of her teacup and laid it on the saucer with a click before saying,

"I'm afraid I must. I only stayed this long because a friend of mine, Lord Keiths, will be running his horse in the race. I was always intending to leave. Maybe I should have made it clear sooner."

His face was like granite. "I'm sorry," she said placing her hand over his. "Please, let's not quarrel, Brandon. The time left is short, and I'm still willing to make the most of it."

He brooded a moment more, but her touch combined with his name spoken so sweetly moved him. His lips curved upward and his face lost some of its hardness. Then raising his glass in a toast he said, "To the time we have left, then."

Juliette heard herself laugh nervously as she touched his brandy snifter with her teacup. They drank together. Then Brandon lowered his glass and continued. "And who can tell. Plans often change. It's possible we have more time than you think."

His eyes never left her as he sipped again from the edge of his glass.

Juliette felt the whispered rush of danger in his words but, choosing to ignore it, she immediately changed the subject. "Tell me—this is the loveliest yacht I've ever seen. How did you acquire the *Black Hawk*?"

She was grateful when he didn't balk, but changed direction with her, briefly telling her the circumstances. And afterward, the atmosphere between them returned to one of friendliness, though, even as they talked, Brandon's thoughts seemed distracted.

It was late afternoon when the *Black Hawk* docked at Las Flores del Mar, and the crew secured her to the landing. Then Juliette disembarked down the gangway on Brandon's arm, and, ironically, it was at that moment that Rodney Keiths rounded the corner of the yacht house and came into view.

As the young Englishman caught sight of Juliette and the large bronzed man, he stopped abruptly, a startled expression crossing his face, followed by irritation.

Imperceptibly, Juliette winced, cursing her luck. Still,

there was nothing she could do but introduce the two men, which she did, watching them shake hands.

Seen next to M. Phillips, Rodney Keiths grew younger before her eyes, seeming suddenly only a light-haired boy whose countenance shifted nervously beneath Phillips's poised calm.

"I'm pleased to meet you," Rodney said insincerely as he looked up into the other man's face. A steward had told him Miss Thorpe had gone sailing on the *Black Hawk,* but he had made no mention of this tall, dangerous-looking fellow, whose band of native servants were now swarming over the dock nearby.

It was Juliette who finally broke the constrained silence. "But when did you get in, Rod?" she asked, taking his arm and trying to ease his tenseness. "We weren't expecting you until tomorrow."

"Only a few hours ago. Titian was very nervous on board, and threatened to kick his way out of his stall. We thought it best to make the crossing as fast as possible. Did you wish I hadn't come?"

"No—no, of course not. It's simply a surprise to see you. You're looking well."

Rodney's eyes grew suddenly soft. "And you are looking more beautiful than ever."

"So you own race horses," Brandon asked politely.

Rodney turned to Phillips, another show of irritation crossing his face. Couldn't this man see he was not wanted? Why didn't he go away and leave them alone? How he had missed Juliette. And how he had hurried to see her, bidding the captain to make all haste. Titian had actually been calm as a rock on board, though the horse had been a valuable excuse for arriving early.

"Yes, I do," Rodney replied shortly.

"And they are all fine horses, I imagine," Brandon said, smiling slightly at the Englishman's discomfort.

Rodney turned back to the tall man with a frown forming between his blond brows. "The finest horses the pound can procure," he answered with a sense of hauteur. "You see, monsieur, my father was none other than Lord William Edward Keiths."

Now it was Juliette who frowned. Normally Rodney never threw his family title into the face of others. It embarrassed her, and doubly so now, considering the discretion with which Monsieur Phillips conducted his own affairs. "Rodney is very fond of his family," she said trying to smooth over his brashness.

Brandon nodded, and Juliette could see his smile was one of indulgence for the waywardness of a child. She felt Rodney tug on her arm. "Please, Juliette! There is a very important . . . personal matter I must discuss with you . . . alone." Rodney turned to the tall man, his dislike barely concealed. "If you will excuse us, Monsieur Phillips?"

"Of course," Brandon replied, without another choice. The two men exchanged polite amenities before Rodney, triumphant, turned his full attention to Juliette, grasping intimately the hand she placed through his arm, and leading her away toward the hotel.

Looking after them, Brandon's jaw grew fixed in a hard line. What kind of woman was this? he asked himself. And why did the smile she gave that young Englishman tear at him with claws of jealousy? Or was that what she intended? Surely, she must know his affection for her was more than casual, though he had never taken her into his arms and made his every intention clear. Perhaps *that* was his mistake. Yet she was different from all the others, too shy, too uninitiated, too independent to approach so unabashedly. Somehow she had become important to him. How charming she was . . . those eyes that could look so fiercely into his, that heartbreaking loveliness that was her jawline, and that subtle pout of her lower lip that almost begged to be kissed. How essential had become the light, fresh way she laughed, and how easily she made him forget, for a brief time, not only that he was the Sheik of El Abadan, with the weight of a destiny on his shoulders—but also that he hated all English.

Long ago she began infiltrating his dreams, if not actually disturbing his sleep, and for two days now he had delayed his departure for Africa, though he had been informed the rifles and ammunition were at the docks of Marseille and due to be loaded.

It was the kind of recklessness that could lose everything, and yet he had stayed, sensing in her a kindling of the same fire that burned in him. Yet, today, with all the forthright audacity so typical of the English, she had announced her plans to leave, stating the fact with complete ease, as she might have spoken of the weather.

Did she think he was one of the fools who danced attendance on her?—that he could be shunned as she inevitably shunned them, one after another.

Brandon pulled out a cheroot, lit it, and drew in deeply. The tobacco tasted bitter and, jerking it out of his mouth, he hurled the cheroot into the water where it hissed like a snake.

By Allah! Juliette Thorpe *was* leaving—but not the way she imagined!

Chapter 30

The flames of a thousand candles set the Las Flores del Mar ballroom ablaze with light as voices and laughter rose above the lively strains of the hotel orchestra.

It was yet another party, the celebration of Lady Linley's birthday, and a gala affair with all the notables in attendance, dancing and enjoying the lavish food and drink.

At the stroke of midnight, Bosley Linley walked onto the stage, flushed with champagne and stammering only slightly as he called for the crowd's attention.

The roar of voices subsided and, amid a rustle of gowns, everyone turned to face Bosley, and also Lady Linley who was seated behind him at the largest table.

Bosley raised his glass. "To my mother," he declared in a loud voice that carried to every corner, "the dearest and finest lady in the land. May she enjoy continued health, happiness, and all the finest things of life, which she so richly deserves."

The glittering guests raised their glasses in turn, joining in the toast, and from around the room came shouts of "Hear—hear!" and, "Happy Birthday!" before everyone drank together.

As the glasses were lowered, the orchestra burst into a flowing melody. Lord Linley escorted his wife to the center of the large burnished floor, and together they danced a single turn around it alone before other couples joined them.

It was the apex of the festivities and yet, to Brandon Phillips, standing a full head above the crowd, it appeared that at least one of the guests was absent.

Twice already he had circled the edge of the ballroom, glancing from face to face, occasionally nodding to gentlemen he knew, and noticing that Rodney Keiths, who seemed to be feeling his liquor, was lecturing a group his own age with broad hand gestures. But still he didn't see Juliette. So now, Brandon moved to the wide-flung double doors that opened into the garden and stepped outside.

It was a balmy night, a light breeze carrying the fragrances of rose and jasmine as silently he scanned the broad lawns and low shrubbery and empty marble benches. Then moving down a path leading to the center of the garden, Brandon suddenly stopped short as above the sounds of a fountain splashing he heard angry voices.

"How can you say I led you on?" came the high-pitched, indignant voice he recognized as Juliette's. "I never have or would! I find you despicable!"

There was a low guttural sound. "Whether you despise me or not, I intend to have a kiss," said a man's voice. "I didn't take so much trouble to be turned down."

"I won't! Now let me go or I'll yell your name at the top of my voice. And don't think I won't dare because I will!"

The man's reply was cut short then as, in a few long-legged strides, Brandon burst on the scene with a suddenness so startling the small stout man holding Juliette let her go and fled.

Juliette had been pulling with all her might, so the abrupt release of her wrist sent her careening backward. Stumbling, she tried to catch her balance before, inexplicably, she found herself fallen against a man's chest, his arms closing around her.

Squaring her jaw, she flung her head around to look into her assailant's face. But seeing then it was Brandon, she laughed tremulously.

"So it is you! I wondered who else might have followed me."

Brandon did not speak at once. Instead, having safely, and so easily, captured his quarry, he slowly scanned her, the cascade of silvery hair fallen loose down her back, the high flush in her cheeks, the heaving tops of her impudently high breasts, the white chiffon gown that swirled around her as light as a fairy's veil.

As always she was enchanting, he thought. But tonight there was something different. The childlike quality that usually characterized her had taken on a certain new flavor—a womanliness that had not been there before. Could it be, he wondered with an unfamiliar sense of exhilaration, that at last his patient wooing was having results?

Juliette had stopped struggling, expecting Brandon to release her, and wondering suddenly if it was his lips that brushed the back of her neck, she looked down nervously at the tanned hands clasping her waist as he spoke from behind her.

"You should be more careful. It's dangerous for you to be wandering in these gardens alone."

"I thought I was safe," she explained. "The party was stifling and I came out here. It is so lovely tonight. I never imagined that drunken man would follow me."

A silent moment passed as she stood pressed against him, and when still Brandon didn't release her, Juliette realized she had escaped one altercation only to find herself in another—possibly far worse one.

"You are careless. A beautiful girl alone is a temptation to any man."

His hands moved to her shoulders, and before she could resist, he turned her to face him, pulling her so close she could feel the strong thumping of his heart against her throat.

Rivers of delight pulsated over her flesh, but there was no time to think as his fingers cupped her chin, tilting her face to meet his black eyes glowing fondly fierce.

"Even I can be tempted," he was saying. And taking a long tress that curled in his fingers, he brushed it back from her temple.

A languid desire poured into Juliette's blood. He was so close that she wanted to melt into him, losing herself in that broad expanse of chest as every sense urged her to do. How easy to let this happen, she thought even as another inner voice whispered, "You must not—must not lose control."

She straightened then, pulling back against his hold, her eyes darting about, furtively seeking some means to put him off. But the garden was empty. They were completely, dangerously, alone.

"You are alarmed," she heard him say. "But I will not harm you. Haven't I proven that I'm not a beast? You are precious to me—a treasure I long to possess. But among my Arab friends there is a saying that everything shall be in its own time. And so it shall be with us. There is nothing to fear."

"It's not that I'm afraid," she said. "It's that . . . it's that . . ." She couldn't think clearly, and her lowered eyes fixed involuntarily on his mouth—now perilously close to hers.

"Juliette, Juliette," his lips were saying. "Haven't you ever known the arms of a man or understood the desires you evoke?" He gathered her closer, her breasts pressing hard against his chest. "Do you know how beautiful you are?"

Juliette raised a hand so she touched the broad width of his shoulders. He was like a magnet, encircling her, overpowering her—stimulating every fiber of her being even as the inner voice repeated, "Escape! Escape!"

Yes, escape, she thought. But her pushing hands felt weak. And when she heard herself say, "Brandon . . . Brandon . . . please don't . . . Brandon," it was more a sigh than a command.

His eyes bored into hers, seeming to see her more

deeply—more completely than anyone ever had, a look that touched her soul. Then, lowering his proud head, his lips drew closer . . . closer. "Come," she heard him whisper, "kiss me."

Transfixed, Juliette stood motionless. Then, just as his mouth would have claimed hers, Juliette clutched at what remained of sanity and turned her face away.

Still undaunted, he came, pressing his burning lips beneath her ear, his breath scorching her as he continued down her throat in a fiery brand.

She buried her neck in his chest, attempting to foil his advance. But his lips passed down onto her white shoulders before dropping to kiss the curving flesh above her breasts.

Beneath the caress Juliette's resistance melted like a frozen pool in the first spring thaw. A rush of emotion exalted her senses as weakening waves of desire pulsed through her body.

She wanted . . . yes . . . wanted him . . . as she had never wanted before, wanted him in this strange compelling way that damned her resistance and drove her on.

Then suddenly, from somewhere beyond a hedge came the laughter of a group of passersby.

The thought of being discovered immediately broke the spell, pulling her back from the brink of she knew not what, and pushing her fists against Brandon's chest, Juliette's lips trembled as she spoke in a ragged whisper, "Oh, Brandon . . . please . . . please stop . . . you . . . you . . ." and then, because she didn't know what else to say, "You're crushing my dress."

He straightened at her pleas, relaxing the arm that molded her against him, though still he didn't set her free.

Desperately, Juliette's thoughts stumbled one over another as she tried to think, to consider anything besides the burning patches on her skin where his lips had touched. He was like champagne—like poison. If he kissed her again she would be lost. If only those people would come closer, and he was forced to release her. But when she heard their laughter again, it was from further away.

"It is only a dress, a piece of cloth, although a very lovely one," he was saying softly in her ear. "Someday I will give you many others. Stay here with me now—or have I hurt you?"

"No! No, not hurt, only . . . I . . . I." Then suddenly a desperate ploy occurred to her. "It's just that I want to wash my arm in the fountain where that odious man touched me," she said guilelessly as possible.

Brandon raised a dubious brow as he appeared to consider her words. Then apparently approving, he relaxed his arm, and pulling a large linen handkerchief from an inner pocket, offered it.

Relieved, Juliette moved away, dipping the handkerchief into the fountain and pulling it out again to swish, first over one arm, and then over the other, all the time keeping a nervous eye on him as he watched—waiting, dark and striking in his formal clothes, his arms crossed as he observed her with appreciative possession.

Juliette couldn't have known that all morning Brandon had been thinking of her and of the homes he would build for her—two in France if she wished, one on the Riviera, and another in Paris. Then, after he had taken care of this business in El Abadan, he would take her to his chalet in Switzerland, or Russia, or Germany—wherever she wished.

In the moonlight now, she seemed a silver-haired spirit of grace and light, and noticing how her eyes looked at him so huge and shining, Brandon imagined their first night together. As he pictured Juliette's slender body reclining naked and aroused in his arms, Brandon noted that she had finished her task and had screwed the handkerchief into a loose ball that dripped a narrow stream of water as she appeared to weigh it in her palm.

He was waiting for her to drop it before taking her into his arms again, when, with violent suddenness, there was a blinding flash and a scattering of lightning against blackness as a stinging force hit his eyes, and, in the same second, with utter disbelief, Brandon realized it was his own handkerchief flung from Juliette's hand.

Stunned, he was a moment wiping the moisture out of his eyes. Then looking for Juliette, he saw she was racing down the starlit path toward the hotel, looking a creature of mist and dew in her pale clinging gown as she disappeared beyond the hibiscus trees like a dream into the void.

Gasping for breath, Juliette ran as fast as she could, slowing only when she neared the hotel steps and realized he wasn't following. Then dropping her pace to a walk, she tried to regain some composure.

It would never do to appear before everyone in her present wild-eyed state. Putting her hands to her cheeks, she found them burning even as her fingers trembled.

How can he affect me so? she asked herself realizing what a startling menace he had become. It's just that he's so . . . so different from all the others, and so . . . well, really so primitive. For a while he had been so polite and almost distant, but now. . . .

A frown puckered her brow as she walked across the lawn. No—after tonight she must *never* see him again. Not even for a moment, and particularly not alone. And composing her features in as placid a line as she could manage, Juliette walked up the hotel steps and entered the laughing gaiety.

Chapter 31

Brandon did not follow Juliette but the following morning, feeling an urgency he had never before experienced concerning a woman, he went to the stables expecting to meet her for her regular ride. When she didn't appear after a half hour had passed he went back to the hotel and inquired her whereabouts from the steward.

"With Lord Keiths, I'm quite sure, sir. I saw her with him only a few moments ago. Playing tennis they were."

Brandon tipped the lad and moved onto the tennis courts where he found Juliette, slim and lovely in her white tennis dress. She pretended not to notice his arrival and played with first one partner and then another, never giving him a moment to speak to her. At first, relieved she hadn't left the island, Brandon found her evasive ploys amusing. But after an hour, his good humor turned to frustration and he

approached Rodney Keiths who was standing on the sidelines, having just lost a game to Roberto.

As Rodney saw M. Phillips striding toward him, he tried
to conceal some of his displeasure. Gossip had informed
him of this Frenchman's constant attentions to Juliette before his arrival. Today Juliette had been marvelously attentive to him while ignoring this fellow and he felt his
confidence returning.

Perhaps, Rodney mused, Phillips was rankled at finding
himself rejected. Certainly there was something sinister,
even dangerous in his deliberate manner—the man was as
balanced and calculating as a cat preparing to spring. Rodney cleared his throat. For the present, he decided, it was
best to be civil. So swinging his racket boyishly over his
shoulder, he said, "Good afternoon, Monsieur Phillips. I
see you have an interest in tennis this morning," knowing
full well it wasn't tennis that brought him.

Phillips appeared to take the comment good-naturedly.
"Yes, I'm interested. But it appears I have no luck today."

"What a pity," Rodney retorted. "Still possibly another
time. Tennis is not usually my game, but Miss Thorpe
wanted especially to play this morning. Horse racing is my
sport. Are you planning to attend the Spanish Cup tomorrow?"

Brandon's expression was opaque. "I wouldn't miss it.
I'm also interested in racing."

"Yes, so I've heard. Miss Thorpe did mention you had a
stud farm nearby," said Rodney, a touch of boredom entering his tone. "But I don't think I've ever heard of it."

Brandon smiled as if indulging the other man's ignorance. "It is a private stud, so I doubt you would be acquainted with the name. The stallion is not available to outsiders. He is pure Arabian, and I don't taint his blood with
lesser quality mares."

"Oh?" Rodney lifted his eyebrows disdainfully. "I've
never thought highly of Arabian blood," he replied. "Our
English stock is the finest in the world!"

"You think so? But I disagree," Brandon countered. "I
think the purer the Arabian blood, the finer the horse. Un-

fortunately, you English have diluted the Arabian blood in your stock to such a degree that you've taken the strength from their legs and the fire from their blood. Now your English thoroughbreds are constantly lame and can't travel a fraction of the distance an Arabian can."

Rodney flushed. What a fool this Frenchman was. Everyone knew English horses to be superior to anything in the world. And more irritating was the factual manner in which he spoke, as if what he said was merely the truth, nothing more or less.

"Well then, I think we should test this theory of yours," Rodney sneered. "Titian Regency is the finest example of English stock ever foaled. If you have a horse you think is finer, enter him in the Spanish Cup tomorrow. We'll match their speed and see which of us has the better horse."

Phillips's grin was disconcerting—like that of a hungry animal confronted with a hearty meal. "Done, then," he said thrusting out a sinewy hand to seal the bargain with a shake. "And to make it more interesting, shall we make a side wager of say . . . twelve thousand pounds . . . even odds?"

Rodney's swaggering air slipped momentarily. He was short of cash. He would not actually receive his inheritance until next year, and he couldn't borrow any more. But of course, Rodney quickly assured himself, he couldn't possibly lose. By tomorrow night he would have the last word— and the twelve thousand pounds. He shook Phillips's hand. "Done," he said.

The day of the Spanish Cup dawned sunny and hot. By ten o'clock, the large open area around the oval track was filled with milling spectators. Some wandered idly about while others arranged last-minute wagers, constantly scanning and rescanning programs before stuffing them into pockets with perspiring hands.

By half past ten, the lords and ladies and the governor of Las Flores del Mar had arrived and secured boxes and were now relaxing under white umbrellas with other important personages, while those less fortunate sweltered in the standing room between the track's railing and the front row of seating. From within her own box, Juliette Thorpe raised field glasses to observe the barns on the far side of the track where she knew Rodney would still be nervously overseeing every detail.

Moving to her left to the front row of boxes, Juliette spotted Lady Linley chattering vivaciously with Countess Landry seated next to her. Bosley was there too, sitting with several friends and looking cheerful, slightly drunk, and out of place holding a large cigar.

Still scanning to her left, Juliette noted Sir William's box was empty and, turning her glasses onto the third box, she was startled to find herself looking directly into the bioptic stare of another pair of field glasses.

Her lips pursed in a smirk as she jerked the glasses downward. Juliette didn't have to see the raven black hair and the white smile to know it was Brandon Phillips and, embarrassed and confused, she turned away.

Finally the bugle sounded and the horses were parading past.

There were six in the field, and Rodney's Titian Regency was third from the rail. The very essence of thoroughbred nobility, he trotted with agile grace, his ears pricked forward, his large dark eyes looking at the crowd.

Titian's jockey, nicknamed "Domino" for the two black moles on his left cheek, was suited up in white and gold silks that set off the horse's chestnut coat and held the Keiths's family crest. As they passed the stands, Domino leaned forward, standing up in his stirrups as Titian broke into a canter, his mane sweeping back against Domino like licking red flames.

There was a silver-gray horse entered by Kaiser Wilhelm of Germany, King Edward's own nephew, and a dun-colored horse, but few took notice of him, their attention being drawn instead to the horse bringing up the rear of the field, a black horse who danced on slender springy legs, his muscles rippling with every movement as the sunlight played off his burnished coat in flashes of blue-black.

As the black passed, Juliette chanced a glance in Brandon's direction. Finding him watching his horse, she took the opportunity to study his well-etched profile, his firm jaw, and long straight nose that so resembled those of Roman coins. Her limbs tingled with the memory of her head pressing against his broad chest, the fascinating light in his black eyes, and his lips traveling over her heated flesh. Once in his arms she had wanted to stay. He had a way of making her forget everything but herself. And yet she couldn't shake the intuitive sense of danger he aroused in her.

A movement behind her then made her turn to find Rodney entering the box, his coattails rumpled, his ascot limp from the heat as, sliding into the seat beside her, he began his usual retelling of all the frustrating mishaps in the barn.

Poor Rodney. He was always like this when Titian was racing, Juliette thought, and put a quieting hand on his arm.

Rodney paused, finding himself enchanted by the fathomless orbs smiling at him from beneath her white cartwheel hat. He smiled in return, squeezing her gloved hand. Was ever a girl more perfect? Rodney asked himself. And with her blond hair drawn back in a thick chignon at the back of her long neck, she seemed as cool and fresh as a flower despite the heat.

Did she know of his recent difficulties? he wondered, swallowing nervously as he considered her reaction. If only his luck would change—she need never find out.

"I missed you," he whispered. "I can't tell you how much."

Rodney's devotion was written on his face and Juliette touched his arm fondly. How very dear he was.

"I've missed you, too," she said. "I've often recalled those days we used to spend in London and how you made me feel . . . well, rather special as no one ever had since before my father died. I'm very grateful."

Rodney's eyes flickered with a touch of pain. "I only wish you could find something more than gratitude in your heart. Maybe you were an outcast then. But now, you seem to vanquish every man who sees you. I've seen how they all ogle you and jump to your service at the slightest notice. And then there's that French frog Phillips. It makes me think that. . . ." His lips couldn't bear to form the words. For so long he had wanted her, time making him only more determined than ever. During the previous year, his mother had cast all the likeliest debutantes before him. But always he found himself thinking that none compared to Juliette. If he couldn't have her, then he would have no one. And if she insisted on her present track of avoiding marriage, then he wouldn't marry either. Sooner or later she would come to her senses—and he would be waiting.

Juliette placed a silencing finger on his mouth. "Rodney! How can you even think of such a thing? There is nothing between me and any of these men, even Monsieur Phillips. We are simply friends." But as she mouthed these words, Juliette knew Brandon had awakened feelings in her beyond mere friendship.

Rodney nodded, bringing her hand to his lips in a worshipful gesture. He was somewhat relieved by her assurances. But a persistent uneasiness still gnawed at him as he watched three buglers in red livery march onto the field and blow the call to the post. There was something different about Juliette, a new femininity, particularly in her dress, and he couldn't help wondering if the change was not somehow linked to that detestable Frenchman.

The horses were well past the stands now, and at the bugler's call, the horses turned and moved briskly back down the track.

The steward, a stout middle-aged man, governor of the island, stood at the starting line, flushed and sweltering, his face nearly matching the burgundy color of his elegant velvet coat as he held high the ceremonial pistol that he would fire to start the race.

Wrestling their excited mounts, the jockeys moved them into a line, one next to the other. As if in protest, the black pawed and stamped flinty hooves, digging at the thick turf and tossing his refined head. Then, in a burst of energy, he reared high, his forelegs stamping the air.

Two attendants in white dusters came to the jockey's aid, firmly taking the black's bridle and leading him into line with the others where he still danced beside them as the tension grew.

The governor raised his pistol a notch higher. Then the gun sounded, echoing against the stands. A roar rose from the crowd as, in an inferno of straining muscles and heaving lungs, the horses thrust forward, Titian Regency, with his extreme length of stride, getting a slight edge over the rest so at the end of a furlong he led by a length.

Hooves thundered in a dull booming, mighty legs pounding against the turf as the horses rounded the first turn and then the next, Titian still staying in place, not gaining or losing against the pack that streamed behind. The black was in last place as he jerked his head fiercely against the rigid hold of his jockey.

In a blur the glistening horses blended with the bright silks as bodies surged down the far rail, the gray gaining ground on Titian until they were nose to nose.

The crowd went wild as the two horses charged on, rounding the last turn still matching strides while neither jockey used his whip, each saving his horse's remaining strength for the finish.

Again the crowd roared, and at first Juliette didn't see the cause. But then, looking back in the pack, she saw the black stallion's jockey had released his check on the black's bridle and now was leaning low in the saddle.

Clumps of turf flew from beneath the black's heels as he shot along the outside, past the pack and began bearing down on the lead horses.

Domino raised his elbow to look back under his arm as he heard the crowd's roar. His face registered surprise. He had never considered the black as serious competition, yet the horse was coming on, his teeth bared, his eyes rolling as he charged boldly faster.

Now it seemed to Domino that the sun was suddenly hotter, and the distance to the finish line even further as he brought down his whip on his horse's chestnut flanks. The gray had already fallen behind and suddenly the black and the chestnut were all alone.

Domino gritted his teeth as the black's nose reached Titian's laboring shoulder. Then raising his whip high, and making it appear an accident, Domino swung it hard against the black as the smaller horse started to pass.

He was astonished when the black did not veer away. Instead, the horse's eyes rolled wickedly in his triangular head until they showed red at the corners. Then he lunged, teeth bared, not at Titian, but at Domino!

Surprised and thrown off balance, Domino jerked his big chestnut in a sudden unconscious movement that pulled the two horses together. It was an accident. But he had no time to recover. With a sickening crash, the heaving bodies collided.

Already, the crowd was on its feet, screaming as chestnut legs entangled with black for a horrifying moment before glistening flanks flung downward onto the scarred turf.

The black tumbled over himself, his head tucking down like a gymnast as he rolled forward, the rest of his body following in a flailing ball. The Arab jockey, wide-eyed and openmouthed, looked to the side before leaping off, avoiding by inches the large-boned bay as it thundered past like a heaving steam engine.

Domino was not so lucky. Titian fell on his side, pinning the jockey's leg beneath his full thirteen hundred fifty-seven pounds, and with white-hot shards of blinding pain, Domino heard his own leg snap like a dried branch.

The big horse thrashed, trying to get up, but losing his balance, he slipped and rolled onto his back, trapping Domino beneath him so that the jockey could only wait as the chestnut rolled over and crushed the life from him.

The crowd screamed and some women fainted. Juliette was out of her box, Rodney close behind. And in spite of her flouncing Persian silk dress, she ran to the railing, ducked under, and dashed toward the swarm of people already pressed around Domino.

Ahead of her a woman screamed and someone called for a doctor. Then, as the man directly in front of her stepped aside, Juliette brought a hand to cover her mouth as she saw Domino, or rather, what had been Domino.

Juliette felt dizzy, and, swaying, she reached for Rodney. But she looked about only to find Brandon at her side, his dark eyes concerned but calm as he assessed her with a frown.

Wondering if she would faint, and silently damning the

tightness of her stays, Juliette clasped Brandon's arm and leaned gratefully on its solid reassurance as she watched the horror.

To their left, the Arab jockey was getting to his feet slowly, his black and white silks streaked with dirt and blood from an ugly cut across his forehead and abrasions on his chin and arms.

Together they walked toward him and the jockey salaamed as Brandon approached and laid a hand on his shoulder, speaking low Arabic words, full of warm concern.

The jockey bowed again and smiled. He had apparently escaped serious injury and seemed humbled by Brandon's attention. Then Brandon waved to two other men who came and helped the jockey off the field.

He turned back to her then, searching her face and giving her a reassuring squeeze with the arm placed around her waist. "Let me take you from here. I'm afraid the other jockey is beyond any help," he said, indicating where the crowd was bending over Domino.

Still feeling sick and fearing she would faint, Juliette only nodded. If only she weren't laced so tight. If only she could get one clean breath of air clear to the bottom of her lungs. Oh, no wonder men thought women were weak when they had to be laced into something so tightly that they couldn't even get enough oxygen. So tottering in her high heels, Juliette let Brandon escort her back under the white rail and through the pressing throng toward the carriages parked under an avenue of trees behind the stands.

At the front of the line a shiny black carriage stood, its door held open by a servant who bowed as they approached. Then, helping Juliette inside, and seeing her sink into the velvety comfort of the seat, Brandon called something to the driver. Then he was stepping in beside her. There was a crack of a whip, and immediately the carriage pulled away as the driver turned the four matched grays around and headed them off at a trot.

Chapter 32

With a subtle curve to his lips, Brandon watched Juliette leaning against brown velvet cushions, beads of perspiration glistening at her temples, all the color gone from her face.

A moment before she had seemed ready to faint, and with an involuntary tightening in his loins that he chose to ignore, he had undone the constricting neckline of her dress down to the tops of her breast. Now, warily, he turned to look out the back window.

It was essential they weren't seen on this road or followed. So far events had played into his hand, but still, he had known Juliette long enough to realize he could not be completely certain of anything until it was done, and he wouldn't feel absolutely confident until she was aboard the *Black Hawk,* and they had put out to sea.

He glanced back to Juliette, his eyes traveling over her face. And what would she do then? he asked himself. What would she say when she realized he had abducted her? Already he had sampled her temper. His insides filled with a kind of laughter. She would be furious, of course—a regular termagant. But that would pass and he would teach her to love him. How long could any woman resist her own desires? And he knew this woman wanted him with all the power of first passion. He had seen approaching surrender in the way her lips parted as he held her in his arms and in the soft molding of her body against his. Once they were alone—once she could no longer avoid him the outcome was inevitable. After a week or two in his bed, she would change, and when she came to her senses and consented to marry him, they would already be on their way to El Abadan.

Everything would be different then, her love for him would help her understand why this kidnapping had been necessary. He would tell her everything, and she would realize he couldn't have waited any longer. The French rifles and ammunition were sailing to Tripoli for transport into the desert. It was absolutely necessary that he intercept them, particularly now when recent cables had informed him the Hussar was moving suspiciously in the direction of Tripoli. Was it possible his enemy also knew of the shipment?

At the thought Brandon's face hardened. It was a chance he couldn't take, not for Juliette, not for anything. She would have to understand.

Looking behind them again, Brandon noted there was still no one following, and his eyes returned to Juliette who seemed even more pale. If he had not wanted to alarm her, he would have undone her dress and unlaced her corset. English dresses were not without charm, but those stays allowed only shallow breathing. And imagining Juliette wearing the clingy thin silk garments he would order sewn for her, he opened the windows so a breeze blew through the coach.

Grateful for the cool air against her damp face, Juliette leaned closer to the opening, all her thoughts concentrated on trying not to be sick.

She swallowed against the sting of bile in her throat and took long slow breaths for several minutes while the Spanish hills rushed past in a flash of wispy grass and orange trees. Finally then, her stomach began to settle and when she could fill her lungs again, she began to collect herself, glancing up at Brandon, who sat wordless and unreadable beside her, and then down to her own gaping dress.

Automatically she gathered the opening together in one hand. Though she realized that unbuttoning it had been the sensible thing to do, she flushed as she said, "I guess I was quite shaken. It seems you came just at the right moment. I feel better now." Looking out the window she asked, "Is this the direction to the hotel?"

Brandon looked down, his expression inscrutable as he said, "I'm glad you're feeling better but I'm surprised you decided to come with me. The last time we met you weren't so inclined. Dare I hope this indicates a change of attitude?" he finished on a teasing note.

Juliette's blush deepened. "The 'last time' we met, Monsieur Phillips," she said firmly sitting up straight, "you were extremely overbearing. As I've told you before, I wish to avoid all entanglements."

"And you find me—how shall I say then . . . entangling?"

Juliette's lips drew a tight line as she looked away. Why had he brought all this up now? She was just feeling better and now it seemed he was making things difficult all over again. "Entangling is the wrong word. Complicating would be better. Anyway you must know what I mean. I don't want to jeopardize my . . . my future."

She felt him take her hand, his touch making that same tingling lightness flutter up her arm.

"Your future?" he questioned. "Is that what made you run away?"

"No! . . . I mean yes! . . . I mean, if I stayed with you it was certain that I . . . that you . . . that we would have. . . ." Juliette paused, flustered and annoyed at her own reactions and dishabille, and by the returning memory of her resolution never, never to see this man again. And when she looked up to find his eyes dancing with amusement, she gathered her neckline tighter with the other hand as she said, "Oh, why are you making me explain? You know perfectly well what I'm talking about. I didn't want you to kiss me, that's all, and you know it!"

The hooded expression didn't change. "Yes. But I'm curious why. Do you find me distasteful?"

Juliette looked back toward the window. "You know I don't." Her voice was low. "You know I find you . . . well . . . attractive."

Brandon laughed shortly. "I suppose I should be flattered, even if I'm still not attractive enough to kiss. Or do you even know about kissing? You seemed in need of some experienced instruction."

"Oh!" Her head jerked around. "That's not true!" she flamed, inching away. "I've been kissed before."

"Really? And did you like it?"

Juliette glared. "No, I didn't, in fact, and I can assure you I wouldn't like your kisses any better!" Her eyes dropped to his mouth as she swallowed convulsively. "You see, I'm not the kind of girl who likes affection. I never did as a child, and I don't like it now. I'm sure there are other women—aren't there, monsieur?—who would be glad to favor you. Why be concerned whether I do or not?"

His hands moved to clasp her shoulders, a mysterious, pleased expression just behind his features. "You don't fool me, Juliette. You aren't as frozen as you would like to appear." He took her hand and kissed the backs of her fingers before turning it over, pausing to deftly unbutton her sleeve and expose her inner wrist, before pressing his mouth there, too.

Juliette felt her pulse jumping beneath his lips and abruptly tried to jerk her hand free. "Stop that! Why are you being so forward and such a . . . such a rogue?"

"Rogue," he repeated raising his eyebrows. "Rogue?" He laughed still holding her hand. "I think you haven't had *enough* 'rogues' in your life. I think you like *me* because I *am* a 'rogue.' "

Frightened yet strangely fascinated, Juliette stopped struggling as he drew her closer. "And I'll tell you a secret, my little one," he said softly a new luster shining in his dark eyes, "Today—right now, you are coming with me onboard the *Bla*—"

A sudden noise interrupted him and made both their heads turn to look out the rear window.

Juliette heard him curse under his breath as he recognized Rodney's coach approaching at breakneck speed, swaying and jostling on its springs and seeming ready to overturn, while Rodney himself hung out the window, ascot undone and blowing past his ear, his face purple, his arms flailing as his mouth moved with words drowned out by the din and clatter of the horses' hooves.

Frowning, Brandon turned to her. "I'll make short work of him."

Juliette grasped Brandon's forearm. "No!" she said, alarmed. "Please. Rodney is foolish, but for my sake, don't . . . don't hurt him."

"So you wish to protect him?"

"We are old friends. He does only what seems best to him. I owe him more than I can ever repay."

Juliette's eyes pleaded and Brandon hesitated. "I see. And if I agree, what will you give me in return?" His gaze rested pointedly on her mouth.

Juliette lifted her chin. "You are not a gentleman, Monsieur Phillips, to bargain with me like this."

Brandon raised one mocking brow. "But it is you who asks this favor, mademoiselle," he chided. "It is *your* 'old friend' who comes, no doubt, to challenge my honor. It seems if I am to let the insult pass I should be given some compensation."

"And what would you have?" she asked, fearing the worst.

"For you to meet me tonight, at midnight, in the hotel gardens by the fountain."

Rodney's coach was beside them now and Brandon called to his driver to stop. The carriage jerked abruptly as the horses slowed and finally came to a dancing halt.

Rodney's coach stopped too, and without waiting for a footman, he threw open his own door and emerged to stalk toward them.

"Your time has run out, *ma petite*," Brandon said. "What shall it be? Do you meet me tonight, or do I deal with this young man in my own way?"

Juliette's overbright eyes darted from Brandon to Rodney and back again. She had no alternative. If they should fight a duel of some sort, or even if someone should witness an argument, everyone would find out. It would be a scandal and her reputation would be ruined. William Bond would probably not even listen to her explanation before cutting off her funds and thereby her independence. And what if Brandon should actually hurt Rodney? No, she couldn't allow it. So with a fleeting frown, Juliette compressed her lips and nodded. "Obviously I have no choice, as usual, Monsieur Phillips. I will be there, but not because I want to."

Brandon nodded also and his face grew suddenly serious. "Poor Juliette," he said as he stepped from the carriage. He reached his long fingers to caress her chin with a gentle stroke. "Your kind heart makes you very vulnerable." Then turning, he walked out to face Rodney.

Chapter 33

Juliette doubled her fist and plunged it into a satin pillow on her narrow bed.

Oh, how could she have promised? And yet, how could she have done anything else? As usual, it had been Brandon's game and he who commanded the situation.

With chilled fingers Juliette swept her long unbound hair out of her face. Just the thought of him roaming outside in the gardens made her shiver. How long would he wait? Already she knew patience was not one of his virtues. And what would he do when she didn't come?

Certainly she couldn't deny he had kept his part of the bargain. Indeed, his self-control had been admirable as he silently waited while the younger man raged and insulted him. Long, horrible, moments had passed before Rodney controlled himself. Then Brandon had spoken to him in a voice so low Juliette couldn't make out his words. But whatever he said, it appeared to settle the matter. Slowly brightening, Rodney had finally shaken Brandon's outstretched hand.

Just then, Lady Linley's coach appeared round a bend in the road, carrying the lady solitarily back from the race.

The coach rolled past, then stopped, turned around, and pulled up close to Brandon's carriage.

Lady Linley's face peered sharp-eyed out the window, taking in the two men in a single curious glance before looking directly at her.

"Is everything all right, dear?" she questioned in a high-pitched voice. "Would you care to ride the rest of the way with me?"

In spite of this woman's obvious curiosity and her reputation for prying, Juliette was eager to escape the pending awkwardness of deciding which man she should ride back with. So smiling brightly now, as if she hadn't a care in the world, she called back, "How kind of you to invite me." Then as Brandon's footman reluctantly opened the door,

Juliette picked up her long skirt in her left hand and stepped out, not giving a backward glance to the two men, as Lady Linley's footman carefully helped her in.

"Poor dear! Did both carriages break down?" Lady Linley inquired when Juliette was seated.

Juliette opened her fan and casually began fanning herself as she answered matter-of-factly.

"No, not broken down actually. It was only that Monsieur Phillips so kindly offered to ride me away from that terrible accident. He had some business with Rodney . . . ah . . . Lord Keiths, and when Lord Keiths caught up with us, Monsieur Phillips stopped so they could have a word together. Gentlemen's conversation always bores me," she continued, smiling her sweetest smile and stifling a small yawn. "It was so nice of you to stop and bother about me."

Juliette watched Lady Linley closely. As she wondered if this sharp-eyed lady could possibly believe such a story, she suddenly felt the older woman put a thin wrinkled hand over her own. "Now don't worry yourself, dear," she was saying in a motherly tone. "Men will do what they do, and there isn't anything we women can do about it. The sooner you understand that, the easier life will be."

Juliette smiled weakly as the older woman continued. "But never mind them, it's an hour back to the hotel, and you and I can have a nice chat."

It was a trying hour filled with Lady Linley's endless gossip. But finally they reached the hotel and Juliette alighted with the help of the footman.

She waved Lady Linley off then, and holding her composure long enough to climb the stairs to the privacy of her room, she threw herself full-length on her bed.

What a day! And it wasn't over yet! What about her bargain with Brandon? She couldn't break it—dared not. Again she sank her fist into the pillow. Oh, what a mess!

For an hour her thoughts raced in endless circles until a gnawing pain in her stomach reminded her she hadn't eaten since morning. She rang for her maid, who unlaced her and helped her out of her dress before going to the kitchen and returning with a tray full of food, which Juliette could only nibble at and swirl around her plate as the carved ivory hands of the clock moved continuously forward.

At eleven o'clock, Juliette forced herself to go to bed, and feeling utterly exhausted, managed to sleep for an hour before awakening to a sudden tingling sensation that rushed over her with a new urgency.

In her half-waking, half-sleeping state, she imagined Brandon's lips again pressed against her throat and traveling down to caress the flesh above her breasts. She trembled beneath the cold sheets, a sensation manifesting itself in her abdomen and spreading with liquid warmth.

Her eyes opened with a snap then, and uttering a soft cry she sat up, throwing back the covers and turning on a light.

What had he done to her? Why couldn't she escape him even in sleep? Juliette squinted against the brightness of her lamp, suddenly aware then of a noise coming from her balcony.

Catching her breath she held it, listening intently.

Again the noise came, and yes, it was from her balcony.

Quickly she grabbed her dressing gown and slipped it on, running to the balcony doors on tiptoe. Her heart pounded as she pictured Brandon's mocking smile. She would put nothing past him. He was not a man to be thwarted, and she *had* made a bargain with him.

Twisting the brass handle of one of the doors, she silently opened it and stood in the opening looking over the rail to the empty beach and back to the gnarled vine entangling itself around her balcony. The whole vine was shaking now with a movement that was not the wind.

Wide-eyed, Juliette stepped back, pulling the long curtain in front of her. Was he there? Had he come for her?

Somewhere in the distance a bird cried as the sea rushed in and out below. A breeze blew softly against her face. Again the vine trembled, but it was not Brandon who then abruptly appeared over the edge of the balcony, but rather a tiny cream-colored kitten who pulled itself up onto the railing, ears pricked toward her as it mewed plaintively.

"So it was you," Juliette said walking forward and taking the kitten in her arms. Then leaning out over the railing, she gazed out to sea and then in the direction of the garden as, inside, the clock chimed three small bells indicating the hour.

She had not gone to him, and he had not come. It was better this way, she told herself. So soon she would be leaving him behind, and seeing him tonight would have made everything more difficult.

Juliette petted the kitten, making small coos of comfort until it began purring. Then clutching it to her heart, she walked back into her room, the sounds of the sea diminishing behind her.

So much has happened to me in such a short time, she thought, and somehow, indefinably, everything seems different, as if something has changed forever. Her lips compressed. When had it happened and how? she asked herself, knowing the answer without thought.

It was Brandon Phillips who was responsible, and well he knew it too. If only she didn't respond to him, but he was so intense, so wonderfully exciting. Whenever she was with him she felt mesmerized, fascinated. And his touch . . . how did it affect her so?

Abruptly, Juliette paused again as a sudden emptiness ranged within her. The kitten nestled against her, purring loudly and, as she stroked it, she suddenly felt a wild compulsion to go down into the garden. She did care about him, yes, of course she cared. How could she deny that? He was the most . . . she searched for a word . . . yes, the most provocative man she had ever met. He wouldn't be in the garden by now, and she wanted to go there, to be where he had been, to walk where he had walked—she couldn't sleep anyway.

Traversing the length of the room and back again, she paused beside the tall poster bed. No, he wouldn't be there now. No one would wait so long for anyone, unless they were in love, and Brandon didn't love her, not really. He wasn't the type of man to care deeply about any woman. With men like him it was just the conquest that was important, and no doubt he had many. But of course she didn't love him either, she was far too sensible. Yet it would be lovely in the garden, she thought, and it is my last night here.

For a moment more she wavered. But then, her mind fixed on the obsession. She *must* go, if only for a short time. And not letting herself think further, she quickly donned a simple batiste gown with wide sleeves before twirling a light cloak around her shoulders. Then turning out her light, she ran silently from the room.

Chapter 34

In the garden a full moon reflected in shimmering silver off the rustling hibiscus and palm leaves as a breeze tossed them lightly.

Pausing on the narrow path, Juliette tilted back her head to stare up at the moon. No, not even the moon looked the same, she thought. All at once it seemed more golden and perfect than ever before, its soft light seeming to reach within her and radiate a warm glow.

Soon, yes, day after tomorrow, she would be leaving for Switzerland. But she would never forget Las Flores del Mar, or the last few days. Nor could she deny that a part of her heart would remain here long after she had gone.

She walked on toward the center of the garden, the fountain's splashing growing louder as she approached. Then walking to its edge, she leaned so close tiny cold splatters hit her face and bare arms.

A gust of wind swayed the tops of the palm trees, tossing their fronds about for a brief moment before it grew still again. Then turning her back to the fountain Juliette scanned the garden surrounding her.

It was deserted, and she sighed, her heart thudding painfully as unbidden tears filled her eyes until two droplets hung suspended on the sweep of her lashes. She reached a hand to brush them away, then pressed her lips in an effort to hold down a rush of emotion that threatened to consume her.

But what if he *had* been here? Somehow that would

have been so much worse, since, if he had come, how could she . . . could she have denied. . . .

She paused, not wanting to think further, and stiffened her spine. Well! Thank heaven she *was* leaving! In time she would forget him—certainly she would. Soon she would be exploring the Alps and meeting new people and Brandon Phillips would become only a pleasant memory instead of . . . well, instead of what he seemed now. She did care for him, yes, with the sort of fascination that schoolgirls had, but nothing more. What else could it be in so short a time? She shouldn't . . . she wouldn't take it seriously!

Again she sighed and looked up into the sky. The moon was diminished now by a mist across its face so it no longer smiled and was only a strange white light.

Pulling her cloak closer then, she stepped away from the fountain and started back toward the hotel. But she had only walked a few steps when a movement in the shadows startled her.

Immediately she was poised for flight as a very tall shadow slid across the path and a figure emerged from the trees.

"So, you do keep bargains," he was saying, the deep timber of his voice sending a tingling dart up her spine. He strode forward, high polished boots flashing like mirrors in the moonlight. "You seem surprised. Did you hope I wouldn't wait? Now tell me the truth, Juliette. Aren't you even a little glad I did?"

Juliette knew her face looked incredulous, and feeling an urge to run but knowing she couldn't possibly, she blurted out, "I haven't kept the bargain . . . I mean, I didn't think you would be here," as her feet backed away. "I didn't mean to come, really . . . not to meet you. I never thought you would wait. I. . . ."

He was beside her. "There are two things a man will wait for if they are cut deeply enough, *chérie;* revenge and love. And since you are here. . . ."

Suddenly she was in his arms, molded hard against his body, his dark eyes reaching deep to draw her very soul toward him before his mouth covered hers in a burning kiss.

She didn't expect it, not this compelling passion, this primitive, this subterranean whirlpool of emotion that threatened to drown her now. Her arms felt weak as she pushed against his thin silk shirt before, finally overwhelmed, she fell against him, yielding to the caress that explored and devoured her with consuming fierceness.

Juliette's mind reeled. She must get away, and yet it was impossible. Every inch of her was awakened, tingling with an inescapable delight.

Over their heads a bird burst into brief song that echoed sweetly in the night.

"So now you are silent." He smiled. "Sometimes words are superfluous, but I would hear you say yes, Juliette—yes to becoming my wife, and you will make me a happy man." A hand brushed a curl from her face. "We'll marry tomorrow. I've already made the arrangements."

At the word "marry" Juliette was startled out of her stupor. Her mouth rounded in astonishment. Again she pushed weakly against the hard curve of his chest.

"No . . . no, Brandon . . . you must be mad, or joking. Marriage is impossible. Let me go! And don't look at me like . . . like that."

"Like what, *chérie*?" He laughed softly. "Do I have stars in my eyes? I feel as if I do. No. Now that you're here, I don't intend letting you escape. Tomorrow you will be my wife—will that be so horrible? Your heart beats with a strength that suggests you might enjoy more than my arms around you and a few kisses."

Aware that indeed her pulse was flying like the beat of wings, Juliette rallied her forces, straightening against his arm as she said, "Brandon, you know it is impossible. I don't want to marry anyone . . . even you . . . I. . . ."

The force of his tightening arm interrupted her. "All this talk is foolishness, Juliette! I swear I love you as I have no other woman. Can you deny you care—that you want me?"

"No, but . . ." she faltered.

"Then why must you make difficult what is so simple? Marry me! Be my wife!"

His voice, his strength, his very presence compelled her surrender while her thoughts were confused as the scattered pieces of a difficult puzzle. Within his embrace nothing else mattered. How she wanted to say yes. But something kept her from that fatal word, and instead she repeated, "Brandon, I can't. Please. Haven't I told you before? Why must you be so . . . so . . ."

"Entangling?" he chided, "or complicating? Juliette, Juliette." His black brows drew together in a frown. "Was ever a woman more stubborn? What must a man do to win you?"

His arms shifted in a swift movement and she found herself lifted like a child and again his mouth took possession of hers.

He was gentle, encouraging her response, which she gave in spite of herself as his lips explored her and sensations raced beneath her flesh, gathering in fiery circles in her breasts and between her thighs in a wonderful frightening ache. And when he finally pulled away, his mouth remaining only an inch above hers, Juliette was dimly aware that her lips were trembling.

"Say yes, *chérie*," he whispered. "I will make you happy—happier than you are now, though you are too innocent to know it."

Juliette felt out of breath, engulfed by the commanding strength of his arms, the hardness of his chest, the overpowering command of his will. Everything had narrowed down to him. There was no escape as his look penetrated her again, "Say yes, *chérie*—now, before I am driven mad!"

The note of desperation in his impassioned voice broke Juliette's last power to resist. Suddenly, in all the world, only this man existed. Nothing else mattered; all else was, for the moment, forgotten. She nodded, first weakly, and then with greater assurance.

"Yes . . . yes," it seemed someone else said in a soft shaking voice. "I will be . . . be your wife."

She felt his arms tighten around her as his face flooded with pleasure. She had done it, she had promised, but it didn't seem even slightly real, only words in a vast ocean of pleasure. What did words matter when he made her feel like this? Then his lips were on hers again, and this time Juliette offered no resistance.

Brandon's senses throbbed. Never had he wanted a woman so intensely, and never had one dared put him off as Juliette had. His need to possess her had grown ravenous. He had come here planning to take her to the *Black Hawk*. But now his decision wavered. At last she had consented to be his wife, and holding her surrendering body and seeing her angelic face turned up to his as it was now, his frustration took on a new dimension of gentler feelings, those still unfamiliar feelings which only Juliette evoked, and which drew him to her like a child reaching for a fascinating new treasure.

Forcefully he curbed his desires then, and moving his hands to her shoulders, held her away from him.

Hungrily his gaze roved over her bright hair, her parted lips, her limpid loving eyes, before dropping to where her breasts rose and fell beneath the tormentingly sheer material. Not yet—not now, he thought, taking a new grip on himself. To take her now might always flaw her feelings for him. Tonight he would let her go, but tomorrow night—tomorrow night all the waiting would be over. And imagining the infinite pleasure of having Juliette willing and desiring in his arms made it possible to let her go one last night.

Chapter 35

Dearest Brandon,

I call you Dearest because you are dearer to me than anything else in the world besides my own cherished independence.

Please forgive me when I tell you I cannot be your wife. Last night was beautiful, the most exquisite and moving experience of my life. However, being impetuous, as you know I am, I promised more than I can ever keep.

Please understand if you can. I have the special opportunity to be as completely free as I have always dreamed of being, and I cannot give that up.

I know you must think me a fool and perhaps you
are right. But I am determined to remain unmarried
for a very long time to come.

> My fondest regards, now and always,
> Juliette

P.S. If you wish, please meet me for tea on the terrace
at four o'clock.

> J.T.

After setting down her pen, and rereading the note, Juliette sealed it in an envelope and rang for a steward. Then,
taking the packet in her hands, she lightly ran her fingertips over its edges as she walked to look out the window.

There was no blue sky this morning, only depressing
gray clouds formed a thick ceiling as far as she could see.
Since dawn it had been raining large cold droplets that
splattered against the glass before running down like tears.

Wasn't it inevitable that her determination be tested? she
asked herself. Hadn't she already learned that life required
certain sacrifices? If she wanted to be independent, then
she must give up the prolonged attentions of any one male.
There could be no wavering. Falling in love was out of the
question. She had experienced a certain fascination for
Brandon Phillips, nothing more. It had been a valuable lesson, and in the future she would know better how to avoid
emotional entrapments.

Still, there was a pang in her conscience at the knowledge that she *had* promised, even if under pressure, even if
she never intended to promise. It was the first promise she
could ever remember breaking, but lifting her chin with a
sniff, she quickly pushed this thought out of her mind.

She had been a fool last night, but it had been his fault,
too. Why was he always making her do what *he* wanted,
always manipulating her and thinking only of his own desires? Just what kind of man was he always to corner her—
to be so forceful? Maybe a rejection would be just what he
deserved, and yet. . . .

There was a knock on the door, and opening it she found a steward holding another bouquet of flowers, this one being so large and elaborate it nearly eclipsed the blue-capped man.

Obviously Rodney was trying to apologize for his behavior yesterday, she thought, as the man said, "Flowers, miss."

"Yes, I see. Thank you. If you would put them on the table, please."

The steward complied before giving her a quick bow. "Will that be all, miss?"

"There is one more thing—could you see that this letter reaches Monsieur Phillips?" Juliette felt awkward, suddenly realizing she couldn't say where Brandon was staying. Indeed she had promised herself to someone whose address she didn't even know. Imperceptibly, she shuddered.

"You do know where he is staying, don't you?" she inquired holding the envelope toward him and relieved to see him nod.

"Yes, miss. The villa along the cliffs south of the hotel. I know the one."

"Good. I'll leave it to you." Juliette pressed several pesetas in his hand and again he bowed and turned down the hall.

Quietly, Juliette closed the door behind him, feeling apprehensive as she walked to smell the roses and touch their shiny leaves.

She had sent the letter. There was no going back now, and something within her stiffened. What would Brandon's reaction be? She hadn't completely considered that. Certainly he was not one to take rejection easily, and there could be a scene.

Agitatedly she rearranged the long-stemmed roses in their large Venetian vase. Oh, why couldn't he be more like Rodney, never pushing her, always being patient, always sending her these lovely flowers. Yes, if she ever married anyone it would be dear dependable Rodney. He was always such fun, like a brother she never had. And there were never any of these complications, these feelings that so upset her and made her do and say things she did not intend. Anyway, hadn't she promised she would marry Rodney if she married anyone?"

"Ouch!" She pulled her hand out of the bouquet and popped it in her mouth where a thorn pricked her finger. Then her eyes enlarged as she saw a jade box hidden among the roses. These flowers weren't from Rodney, she suddenly realized, but from Brandon.

Quickly she took the box in hand and lifted the lid, drawing a breath as the light revealed a ruby ring on a pedestal of velvet, an elegant heart-shaped ruby that danced with unearthly brightness from its refracting depths.

Wonderingly she lifted it out and, without thinking, slipped it on her hand, holding it up and spreading her fingers.

It fit perfectly, as if sized for her alone. But in spite of its beauty, the weight sent a shiver up her arm, and abruptly, she slipped it off, noticing as she did the inscription on the inner side.

"*Beloved*," she whispered aloud. Her heart swelled and then beat with a wretched pain. And seeing now there was also a note, she reached for it with trembling hands, unfolding it to read;

Dear Juliette,

This ring comes to you with all my love, my heart, and my very life given once and for all into your keeping.

Two weeks ago I didn't know what love was. But in you I have found a new meaning for life—my sweetest angel, my fragrant rose of beauty, my lovely wayward child. You have brought a new fragrance into my life, a peace to my soul, and a love into my heart that will keep me yours forever.

Your devoted lover now and through all eternity.

Brandon

In the deep comfort of a leather chair within his private study, Brandon puffed on a pipe of fine English tobacco as he looked out the wide-flung windows where rain was falling lightly.

Rain, he mused. In the desert it was considered a fortunate sign of life, of the earth replenishing itself, of the coming of spring, and of birth and rebirth. It pleased him that his wedding day would be a rainy one, and the weather would not interfere with his plans. Already he had prepared for a discreet ceremony on board the *Black Hawk*. There would be a reception later, and then, before anyone had recovered from the shock of Juliette's speedy marriage, he would have whisked her away.

By waiting this way he was losing another precious day when he should already be sailing, but if the winds were favorable, he could make up the distance and intercept the guns en route.

Lightning flashed through the sky. From across the ocean came distant thunder. A light breeze blew the fresh rainy fragrance into the room. "Juliette," Brandon whispered recalling an Arabic poem,

> *Reason is powerless in the face of love.*
> *Love is the truth.*
> *Allah is never seen. But the vision of*
> *him in woman is most perfect of all.*

An hour passed before he left his private sanctum and, walking into the hallway, he found an envelope set out for his inspection which was addressed in a round girlish hand.

Brandon had never seen Juliette's handwriting, but immediately he guessed it was hers. What had she to say? he wondered while breaking the seal—words of love, no doubt, of thanks for his gift. And withdrawing the paper, he read.

Brandon had always considered Juliette unpredictable— a trait not lacking in charm. But he found nothing charming about *this*! On the contrary, his eyes hardened as they traveled down the page, and after reading the last line, he crushed the paper in his fist.

He was in no frame of mind to see the love her note contained. Only one thing was clear. He had been rejected! He, Brandon Phillips, Sheik of El Abadan, a man of awesome wealth and enormous power, he who had been given his every desire without question, to whom women had always given themselves, freely, eagerly, while begging him to love them if only a little—*he* had been cast aside!

His face turned to stone. Her last line had been most insulting of all. "Tea at four o'clock." What did she think him—a serving boy to meet her at some appointed hour—a man with milk in his veins instead of blood? His jaw locked, slanting cheekbones growing pronounced. He would meet her. But the tryst wouldn't wait until four. This time, she had gone too far!

"Have the *Black Hawk* made ready," he ordered in a clipped harsh tone to Rashid, who was standing in an alcove. "We leave for Africa within the hour." Then, nearly knocking down the servant who scrambled to open the door, Brandon strode out into the rain.

Juliette sat in her bath, a vaporous dew rising around her head as she lay against the high-backed tub.

Occasionally she turned to look again at the boldly scrawled letter placed upright on a stand beside the tub. The words leapt out at her, *my sweetest angel, my fragrant rose of beauty, my lovely wayward child.*

Juliette moaned and rolled her head to face away. If only she were different. If only she had never wanted, had never wished so bitterly long to become her own mistress. She couldn't give it up. And now, miserably, she wished she had never tasted the sweetness of wealth, never learned to love her joyous freedom. If only I were just Juliette Clayton again, she thought mournfully, an orphan, then I would accept his devotion with love.

With a wretched sense of weariness, Juliette rose and stepped out of the bath, patting the water droplets off her arms and body before giving her hair a vigorous scrub. Then, picking up Brandon's note again, she carried it to her vanity and laid it face down on the polished surface before taking up her brush and, with a sigh, starting to brush her hair.

From down the hall then the sound of footsteps came closer. They paused outside her door and abruptly Juliette drew a short breath as a knock came firm and resounding against it.

The color drained from her face. Brandon! And it was still hours until four o'clock. She couldn't see him!—not now!—and certainly not like this! She bit her lip as the knock came again, this time louder, bouncing the door against its hinges and making the barrier seem suddenly vulnerable. A deep voice followed, commanding with a snarl that made her cringe.

"Juliette! Open this door or I'll break it down."

Silently replacing the brush, Juliette ran on tiptoe to her closet, and slipped into a dressing gown.

If he thinks I'm not here, maybe he will go away, she thought. She couldn't open that door.

There was a long thin silence while neither of them spoke or made a sound. Had he gone? she wondered. But with startling swiftness the door was smashed through by a single splintering blow, the lock smashing out of the door frame as the wood gave way beneath Brandon's shoulder. Then brushing loose bits of wood from his white shirt, Brandon stepped imperiously through the opening.

A lock of raven hair had fallen in a curl against his forehead, somehow making worse the look of concentrated fury on his face as he came toward her, speaking between clenched teeth and holding her crushed note out in his fist.

"What do you mean sending me this? Are you trying to make a fool of me?"

Juliette's eyes were enormous. How could he have actually broken down her door—dared come in here like this? He was capable of anything!

Unconsciously she pulled her dressing gown tighter to her throat and, determined to remain calm said, "Brandon . . . please. You must try to understand. Everything is just as I wrote. I care deeply for you, but last night I became . . . became carried away. I've been both rude and foolish.

I've promised to marry you when I really have no intention of marrying anyone. It's not that I don't care for you, I—"

His hand interrupted with an impatient wave. "I'm not interested in excuses. I want you to be my wife!"

Unsmiling, Juliette raised her chin. "It isn't an excuse," she said coolly. "It is what I intend. I am unmarried now because I enjoy my present state and I . . ."

"Bah! That's not what you said last night!"

His flexing jaw, the mixture of fury and pain in his face made Juliette suddenly sorry, and her voice softened. "But last night I couldn't have refused," she began. "Don't you see? Last night you were kissing me and . . . and I had no choice . . . and . . ."

Immediately she regretted her words as he stepped closer, his menacing eyes moving to her lips and then her breasts which, even now, burned beneath the thin dressing gown. He moved to pull her into his arms but she quickly stepped out of range, placing her vanity chair between them and saying, "Brandon, please! It would do no good to kiss me now. I don't feel the same. I am . . . I am in control of myself now. While last night I wasn't. Last night there was nothing but you, and I'm afraid you rather . . . well rather swept me off my feet." Her breath came in little pants.

His laugh was cold and hard, and his eyes blazed. "You toy with me," he said dangerously. "You toy with me as you do with Rodney and the other fools who moon over you. You have promised to marry me, and you are going to keep that promise!"

He had never seemed so large—so full of power. "I cannot and I will not," Juliette said losing her patience. "A woman has the prerogative of changing her mind."

"It is not a privilege I intend to allow."

"But it is one I intend to assert!"

Brandon didn't reply, but his face grew darker as they stood deadlocked, staring at one another, Juliette's jaw as firm as Brandon's, her violet eyes glaring into his black ones.

The silence lengthened while the air heated with tension.

Juliette was the first to become abruptly conscious of the scene they were making. Glancing at the broken door, she wondered how she would ever explain it. Then lowering her voice she said, "I told you I would see you at four o'clock. Please Brandon, leave me now. This afternoon I will meet you."

"I will leave, but you will come with me. My yacht is waiting. We can discuss this when you're on board."

"I'm not going . . . I've told you before . . ."

A swift movement of his leg sent the chair between them skidding across the floor, two legs breaking like match sticks. Juliette recoiled, backing away but his hands encircled her upper arms like a vise, pulling her up on tiptoe and giving her a shake.

"You will come now or I'll take you over my shoulder."

Juliette's anger and defiance turned to fear. Any other man would have been bluffing, but not Brandon. "I can't now—can't you see, not like this."

"Then put something else on, but you are coming now."

Juliette was afraid to hesitate. Should he actually shoulder her and carry her out past all the gaping hotel staff and whatever guests might be available to witness her degradation, the scandal would force her to marry Brandon or resign herself never to facing polite society again. Her eyes dropped.

"You must allow me to dress properly first. You can't expect me to just put something on over this."

"I'm not interested in what you wear."

"But I am," Juliette said, and then more softly, "Brandon . . . please," and there was a desperate tone in her words. "You have me at a terrible disadvantage. Do you want me to beg you? Just ten minutes and I will come."

Some of the fury left his face as he studied her. "All right, ten minutes. I'll wait in the hall for that long, but no more."

Juliette only nodded as he gave her a parting look that underlined his commands. Then making his way to the doorway, he stepped back through the splintered opening into the hall.

PART VI

DISCOVERIES

Chapter 36

As Brandon disappeared into the hallway, Juliette stood looking after him; her submissive expression melting away like a waxen mask as another, quite different, face emerged—a defiant face whose riveted eyes became beacons of outrage as she kicked the fallen vanity chair sprawling another yard across the floor.

She stalked to her wardrobe, flinging the doors wide and roughly searching through the multicolored array.

Violent thoughts possessed her, and retorts she might have made began to form in her mind pouring more fuel on the tinder of her fury. "If I'd known you were still in the garden I never would have gone," she said, reliving the conversation as it might have been. "I want nothing to do with you! Is what happened my fault? First you offer me no choice but to say yes, and then you dare to be furious when it isn't what I want!"

Her searching hands paused, and hauling out a white silk blouse with mutton-leg sleeves, and a pair of broadcloth breeches, she dragged them into her dressing room and slammed the door. Then stripping off her dressing gown, she pulled on the blouse, breeches, and shiny leather boots before pausing and trying to collect herself.

For a full minute Juliette remained seated before, abruptly, she raised her head, her mouth rounding as a plan materialized in her mind. "Of course!" A smile curved her lips. "How infuriated he'll be. And it will serve him right!"

She stood up then and, opening her dressing room door a crack, looked toward the splintered doorway.

The smoke from Brandon's cheroot drifted in the opening. Slowly, keeping her footsteps silent, she pushed the door wider and moved to the balcony, looking quickly over her shoulder as she eased open the door handle, subduing the squeak that emitted from one hinge.

She stepped through, shutting the door softly. Then swinging over the railing she secured hand and foot holds in the gnarled vine there and, without difficulty, backed down to the ground.

It had stopped raining and the sun shone between parted clouds as Juliette approached the wooden dock lined with yachts and local fishing craft bobbing on the blue-green swells.

It was easy to spot her own yacht, *Whimsy*. It was small compared to the others and entirely white, and half a dozen men were moving over her decks, laying in stores for the voyage due to begin the following day.

On the bow, Captain Buckman stood, stout and blocky, his blue hat pushed back on his head as he shouted orders to his men. His back was to Juliette as she walked down the narrow gangway, and he didn't see her until several crewmen tipped their caps and wheeled around.

"Aye! So it be Miss Thorpe," he said, his bulldoggish frown disappearing.

Taking his hat off, he held it crushed against his rounded belly with one meaty hand and smiled broadly. "I s'pose ye come ta see how we be farin', miss. And I'm tellin' ye we'll be ready ta sail first thing in the mornin'. Most the men be still ashore. But I'm roundin' 'em up tonight so there won't be no delay." His eyes twinkled as he spoke, frankly mopping his round weathered face with a large red kerchief.

"That is exactly what I came to speak to you about, captain," Juliette began. "I've changed my plans. I want to leave for London this afternoon—immediately if possible."

Captain Buckman's mopping hand stopped in mid-wipe, his smile disappearing. "Immediately, miss?' he questioned as if not hearing right—and when she nodded, "Well, if that be yer need it can be arranged. We are a mite unprepared 'tis all . . . and can ye be meanin' to sail with no luggage?"

His dubious look made Juliette realize how ridiculous she must appear, standing here on the deck and demanding to leave immediately without her maid or Mrs. Welwright, or so much as a handbag. But she must not act suspiciously, she must not let anyone suspect the real reason for her hasty departure. Bravado was the only answer, and raising her chin she said, "That is my affair, Captain Buckman. Please assemble the crew and inform each man he'll receive a bonus if the ship can set sail in less than an hour." Juliette was pleased to hear her voice was firm, and her eyes never wavered as they looked into the captain's questioning ones.

"Very well, miss," he said at last. "This be yer ship, and I be only the captain . . . I guess I has me orders."

Juliette smiled then, "Thank you, captain. I will be in my cabin." She started to walk away when, as an afterthought, she turned and said, "And, captain, be sure not to allow visitors on board. I don't want to see anyone."

"Yes, miss," Captain Buckman nodded again and tipped his hat as she took the stairs below decks. Then waiting until her blond head disappeared, he gestured with annoyance.

"Quality!" he announced with a mixture of frustration and awe. "There never was any use trying ta understand 'em when they all were unpredictable as the sea itself." He shook his head, and, pushing his hat back further, turned to one of the nearby seamen.

"You, Smitty. Git up to that damned whorehouse, sober the men up, and fetch 'em down here. We be sailin' in an hour."

The seaman looked uncomprehending.

"Now move yer arse, lad," the captain roared at Smitty's blank stare. "The ledy ain't got all day ta wait. And don't be asken no foolish questions neither, cause it ain't none yer business."

Satisfied that the yacht would be ready to sail as quickly as possible, Juliette hurried down the corridor to her cabin and turned a key in the brass latch until it clicked open.

Her quarters were modest, containing a four-poster, a desk, and a wall of drawers, and closing the door behind her, she walked to a porthole and turned the carved handle.

Brandon's yacht, the *Black Hawk* was berthed only a few ships away. From here she could see its crew moving about the decks and climbing the rigging, though none of them glanced in the direction of the *Whimsy*.

A steady breeze came in from the open porthole, bringing the smells of saltwater, damp wood, and a trace of smoke from the small braziers the crewman used to cook fish. From somewhere out of her view came the cries of a boy selling candy and tobacco.

Yes, it all seemed peaceful enough. Apparently no one had given any notice of her coming on board her yacht, and by the time Brandon realized where she had gone, it would be too late. She would travel home to London, and be rid of him, and all this ridiculous talk of love, for once and forever.

A half-hour had passed when she heard shouts from the deck, and glancing out the porthole again, Juliette noticed the men were arriving. She hoped they were sober and could get the ship underway without further delay.

A knock on the door interrupted her musings. "Yes, come in."

The door knob turned and Captain Buckman's large face appeared. "S'cuse me, miss. You said there was ta be no visitors. But there is a gentleman here asken for ye. Pretty determined, too, he is, miss. Caused quite a fray with the men when we told 'em he wasn't ta be allowed ta see ye."

Juliette swallowed thickly, her mouth abruptly dry. So, he *had* found her. Not even an hour had passed! How did he know? But no matter. *Now* she had no choice but to deal with him.

"Did he state his business, captain?"

"No 'fraid not, miss. I asked 'em. But he wasn't sayin'. Only says he knows ye well and that you'd see 'em."

Juliette's mind raced. It would be difficult, if not impossible to calm him. Perhaps if she agreed to stay another week. No, that would be giving in to his bullying. She frowned. She would try to reason with him, try to make him see the wisdom of what she did. If he was foolish enough to be forceful . . . well, he was on *her* ship this time. She had a dozen men at her instant command. If necessary she could . . . and would, have him physically ejected.

"Very well, captain. Send him in."

"Yes, miss. I'll tell him directly, miss."

The captain left, and it was only a few moments when she heard him returning, his footsteps echoed by another pair following.

Juliette held herself erect as the color drained from her face, her throat constricting.

There was a small deferential knock at the door before it opened.

The captain's face appeared first, frowning, and in his wake, to Juliette's surprise, Rodney's blond head bobbed into the room.

A wondering smile spread over her face, and Captain Buckman, seeing the guest was in fact welcome, nodded in both their directions before backing out the door and closing it behind him.

Rodney rushed forward to take her shoulders. "Juliette! Are you all right? I saw your door this morning. Your maid said it must have been a burglar. But she said nothing was missing but you. I came on the chance I might find you here. That old rot Buckman almost didn't let me on."

"You!" Juliette said, "But I thought . . ." Then pausing, she composed herself before continuing. "It's nothing to be concerned about, really. Perhaps it was a burglar, but I'm all right. I've decided to leave early and not wait until tomorrow, that's all. I just haven't had time to send word to anyone."

Rodney's blue eyes searched her face. "It's Phillips again, isn't it, Juliette?"

Juliette's gaze veered away. "Rodney, I'm surprised at you. I didn't think you were the jealous type."

"Call me what you want. I won't have that man troubling you. He has already done enough damage."

Juliette stiffened. "He isn't 'troubling me,'" she said with a warning in her tone. "And if he were, it would still be none of your affair. But since you seem so interested, I'll tell you that I plan never to speak to or see Monsieur Phillips again."

Rodney continued staring into her face. It took a moment, but then his shoulders visibly relaxed their bearlike hunch, his voice becoming conciliatory. "Of course you are quite right. I'm aware you are capable of handling your own affairs. But just this morning I heard straight from Lord Linley all about this 'Monsieur Phillips,' as he calls himself, and whatever you've had to do with that fellow, you're well rid of him. Lord Linley has just discovered that he only passes himself off as a Frenchman while he is actually a half-breed Arab. Soon there won't be a decent family who'll receive him."

For a moment Juliette thought Rodney was playing some horrible tasteless joke. Oh, let it be only that, she told herself as the set of his features told her he was sincere.

"I don't believe it," she said at last, waving her hand in a manner meant to dismiss the entire matter. "All those gossips make up the ugliest things about everyone. I think they have all stooped quite low to say such things about Monsieur Phillips."

In spite of the sureness in her voice, the word "Arab" echoed over and over in her head. Brandon an Arab? But why hadn't he told her? Why had he let her think. . . . She felt suddenly numb, as if her heart had turned to wood.

"But it *is* true!" Juliette heard Rodney insist.

She turned on him. "How can you be so sure? All those people are the same—monsters! All of them! You should realize how eager they are to hurt with their evil tongues. Don't you think I know some of the things they've said about me? And now you expect me to believe these ridiculous charges. I'm disappointed that you give credence to such nonsense!"

Rodney placed a hand on her shoulder. "It *is* true, Juliette." His voice was gentle. "Can't you see what he is? Hasn't his secretiveness and his Arab servants made you wonder? Or have your feelings for the man clouded your usual good sense? Haven't you ever thought he must have something to hide?"

The truth in Rodney's words made her throat constrict. She stifled a moan. Could it possibly be true? Everything Rodney had mentioned had entered her mind. But always she had passed off Brandon's silence as dignity—his Arab servants as eccentricity. But what if she were wrong?

"And that's not all I have to tell you," Rodney said silently savoring his final *coup de grâce*. "You may not believe what the others say about his Arab blood, but I know myself he is keeping a mistress."

Juliette's head snapped up so her incredulous regard met Rodney's firm one.

"It's true, Juliette. I've seen her myself. She is an actress, they say, and just the sort you'd expect—vulgar, with loads of ghastly red hair."

Juliette turned deadly pale. It was impossible, unbelievable. Rodney must be wrong, even lying. Yet just the possibility it was true made a fiery rage form like an explosive ball in the pit of her stomach.

"I suppose you won't believe me," Rodney went on. "You've already said I'm jealous, and I suppose I am. But I'm only telling you these things for your own good. Anyway, if you think I'm lying, you can go and see for yourself. Just this morning she was at his villa. Several people saw her. They say Phillips is very open about his women and allows them to parade themselves about under the noses of gentlefolk."

Juliette's voice was strained and cold. "Oh, that is what 'they' say, is it? Well, I will tell you, I don't know what to believe. But considering Monsieur Phillips and I are merely acquaintances, I can't see why any of this should matter to me as much as you seem to think it should."

Juliette walked stiffly across the room and sat very straight in an armchair facing away from him.

"Now, if you would be so kind, I would like to be alone. I have several letters to write and I must have them posted before I leave."

Aware he was being dismissed, Rodney walked to stand behind her. "I hope I haven't upset you," he began, wishing he hadn't told her so brutally. "I only wanted to prevent something from happening that . . . well, that you would regret."

Juliette continued staring rigidly ahead. "Please, Rodney," she said in the same hollow voice. "If you have said what you wanted to say, please go!"

Rodney clenched the hands he held behind him, unsure of how to rectify what he had done. The silence continued and his uneasiness grew. Perhaps it would be best just to leave her alone and let her absorb the news, he decided, backing toward the door. "Of course," he said finally. "I hope you understand my intentions were only for the best. I mean, I would never want anything to come between us."

He waited for an answer, but the time stretched out without a sound. He continued back, scuffling his boots on the carpet, opened the door and stepped out, carefully closing it behind him.

Chapter 37

Long ago Lucille Madeaux had discovered that information was money, particularly information concerning prominent figures, and especially those in politics. Even as a little girl, Lucille had learned how men loved to confide, particularly after drinking. Any woman who made them feel strong and clever and so very appealing could find out anything she wanted to know.

And when Lucille accepted a "friend," she always did so considering what he might be able to tell her—at least she usually did. Brandon Phillips had been an exception. With him she had been too filled with foolish romantic notions to concern herself with learning his secrets, at least, that was how it began. But as Brandon's passion cooled, and Lucille found herself dropped firmly on her lush buttocks into cold reality, it was only a short time before she remembered that she *was* a practical woman.

It was Monsieur Phillips's silence that had first convinced her he must have something to hide. But even in their most intimate moments, he was in control, and while she had easily induced other men to divulge their secrets, she had no power over him. She used every trick and device she knew, even resorting to drugging his wine. But in spite of all her practiced methods, Brandon remained silent, implacable, and finally, it became necessary to seek out his servants.

Lucille's experienced eye spotted the traitor immediately. Abdul was young and handsome, in an adolescent way, and his dissatisfied manner and shifting eyes told Lucille all she needed to know.

Abdul himself found the bargain particularly attractive and agreed at once. He was the lowest of the house servants. His pay was little and his hours long and tedious. And how much easier, he reasoned, was it to be paid in little gold coins for telling the master's plaything information known by all the master's household.

Yes, his master was an Arab, he informed her, a sheik from the great desert where his father before him was richest among the faithful, while his mother had been a woman with hair of fire, a woman brought by Allah from a distant land.

Abdul did not concern himself with what could be so valuable about this common knowledge. He only cared it pleased the woman, who smiled like a hyena does after gorging itself on its kill, and dismissed him with a wave of her painted fingers.

Lucille was pleased, very pleased. And already the information had been sold to a certain anonymous gentleman who she was sure by his accent was upper-class English.

Now the damage was done, and profitably so. There had been rumors and conjecture about Brandon before, but now the whispers would be turned into an outright scandal.

Tomorrow she would return to France. But today she had come here unable to resist seeing Brandon once more. Maybe she would even tease him by hinting at what she had done. The thought delighted her. How would it suit Brandon to be turned out of society for reasons none of his wealth or charm could mend? Her expression soured then. Perhaps, she thought, he would discover just how bitter rejection could be.

It was then Lucille looked up from her place on the terrace and saw a slender blond girl coming toward her across the lawn.

She was dressed in a simple white yachting dress that was nevertheless elegantly tailored, and as the girl came to a stop on the opposite side of the terrace railing, her face was a study of disbelief.

Entrancing eyes, Lucille thought—so large, and lovely hair and skin. Yes, a real beauty, though too thin. But what was she doing here? Lucille cocked her head. She had long suspected another woman had been responsible for changing Brandon's lukewarm liking to chilling disinterest in less than a week. And there was a certain bright innocence about this girl. A quality that men often found irresistible, particularly men like Brandon who had grown cynical enough to value virtue.

"Who are you?" the girl suddenly demanded in well-enunciated English.

Lucille raised her finely plucked eyebrows. This girl's bearing, her dress, and her refined speech all confirmed Lucille's suspicions. Indeed this was just the sort of woman Brandon would take seriously. But how much did this one know of Brandon's wild doings in Paris and elsewhere? she wondered. Probably nothing, at least not from Brandon. Had someone else told her perhaps? Was that why she was here—so surprised and so furious? A slow poisonous smile spread over Lucille's features.

"My name is Lucille Madeaux," she said at last. "I am an actress and here by the personal invitation of Monsieur Phillips—as I imagine you are." She swirled the brandy in her glass before taking a bit in her mouth and letting it dwell on her tongue before continuing. "He really is quite careless, don't you agree? Most men take infinite trouble that their mistresses never meet. *Et voilà!*" She gave an airy wave and smiled deprecatingly. "But there is no need for a scene between us. I yield to you. It appears that you have replaced me—for the time being, that is. But don't think I am too jealous. I will content myself knowing that sooner than you realize, someone will replace you. Monsieur Phillips is quite fickle, I'm afraid. Or haven't you heard?"

Revolted, Juliette could only stare, trying not to believe what was plainly before her, coarsely displayed in a décolleté gown and emerald earrings. It was horrible enough that Brandon had lied about everything. But to realize that his lips had caressed this woman's as well as her own was nauseating, and the fiery ball in the pit of her stomach flamed with outrage.

"Yes. I think now I'm beginning to understand," she said in a voice steadier than she expected. "But I assure you I am not here because I have any relationship whatever with Monsieur Phillips. He did not invite me."

"Ah! But of course—I see," Lucille said taking more brandy from her glass. "There are many he doesn't invite, but they come anyway. He is much too difficult to resist, *n'est-ce pas? Un beau idéal.*" She sighed in a mocking gesture before smiling again.

A searing pain stabbed Juliette's chest so her breath came quickly. It was all true—all of it. What a fool she had made of herself, and worse, now fully realizing Brandon's deceit, she was also ironically and mercilessly aware of her own deep feelings for him.

Inwardly she squirmed at her own folly that so easily might have been the prelude of even worse degradation. She shuddered, and without another word, turned to go silently as she had come.

A dignified retreat was suddenly made impossible however, when she saw Brandon quickly approaching from the opposite side of the lawn.

For a moment Juliette hesitated, noting the series of questions and emotions playing across his usually composed face. Then, throwing him a look of utter contempt, she continued in the direction of the hotel.

He was behind her then, keeping pace even as she continued stalking ahead.

"I want to speak with you—now," he said though she continued on as if not hearing. "You will stop and I will explain. . . ." But Juliette didn't let him finish. Spinning around, she pointed a shaking finger back toward the terrace. "Go!" she spat. "Go back to your . . . to that woman. How dare you *ever* talk of love to me when you . . . when she . . . You are vile—detestable! I hate you!" And turning, she started again across the lawn.

Again he was behind her, and before she could elude his hand, he had her arm and whipped her round to face him. Their eyes met as he jerked her hard against his chest. "Don't you dare touch me!" she screamed, no longer caring about anything but the waves of rage that consumed her. She wanted to kill him, yes, kill him if she could!

Brandon looked at her evaluatingly. How much had Lucille told her? Enough, it was plain. There could be no renunciation of what had passed. All his efforts to win her in a civilized way had failed, and now, after this, she would never give herself willingly. But of course the time for negotiation had already ended. And looking at her now, Brandon's senses churned. Her hair had come loose from its pins as she tossed her head so it looked like a wild mane. She was magnificent—an enraged lioness. And with a short, ironic laugh, he took her in his arms, forcing her head back against his shoulder as he kissed her with devouring lips. Still she struggled, kicking with determination and strength he had not suspected. And when that did not succeed, Juliette bit him viciously on the mouth.

Startled, Brandon pulled back, transferring Juliette's flailing body to one arm, and raising the other hand to dab at the wound. Indeed his fingers came away wet with blood.

"Bitch! She-devil!" he said in Arabic. And though Juliette couldn't understand what he said, she could hear the almost amused mockery in his tone.

How could he insult her now when he . . . "I won't do this!" she demanded. "If you don't release me immediately I'll scream for help. Someone will hear me! And you'll . . . you'll pay for this!"

Brandon paused, cutting short an urge to carry her off then and there. The hotel was only a few yards beyond a nearby hedge. And there was also Lucille watching everything. Damn Lucille anyway. Damn her to Hell for the whore that she was!

Miraculously then, Juliette felt herself released, and stepping away stood rubbing her bruised arm while catching her breath.

He was smiling at her, and now he touched his forehead,

each breast, and his lips in a salute that was decidedly Arabic as he said, "*Au revoir, ma petite.* And I assure you, *we will* meet again."

Beyond words, Juliette only glared at him. Then turning, she resumed her pace across the lawn, wanting to run, but forcing herself to remain dignified as her head throbbed in counter beats to her heart. And just as she was about to disappear round the end of the hedge, she heard him laugh soft and deep and suddenly she felt more frightened than ever before.

Chapter 38

Before the first rays of coral sunshine pierced the slate sky, Sheik Karim al-Sharif stood before his assembled men delivering a series of orders, clipped and precise, that divided them into several groups and sent them hastening from the room.

Moving then to an ivory box on the sideboard, the sheik withdrew a cheroot, and lighting it, exhaled the smoke from his nostrils like tusks before walking the length of the dark woven rug, past the brass lamps to the sideboard and then back again, over and over.

In only a short time, a trio of men returned, bowing low before their master, a disturbed expression on their swarthy faces.

"Well?" the sheik asked.

There was a troubled silence before one Arab stepped forward bowing lower than before. "Master," he said. "The yacht belonging to the English lady is no longer in the harbor. It has gone."

"Gone?" the sheik repeated, his eyes traveling from one face to another.

They all nodded, their brown faces dropping.

The sheik's eyes darkened, emitting the piercing glow of burning steel.

His men shifted uneasily from one foot to another.

Obsequiously the spokesman bowed again, his voice

barely audible as he said, "We inquired, master, and were told the English lady left yesterday after sunset."

The sheik inclined his head, his jaw twitching as his hand waved to dismiss them. "Go now," he said. "Later I will have instructions."

The servants all bowed low and salaamed, backing toward the door. But Brandon was hardly aware of their silent exit.

Again he walked to the opposite end of the room, opened the ivory case and withdrew another cheroot. His eyes unfocused as he placed it between his lips and lit it, puffing several times until smoke surrounded his head. Then the corners of his mouth curved upward in a slow smile.

She had outmaneuvered him again! Again he had underestimated her! She was only a girl—not yet a woman, and yet she had developed the will and deceptive cleverness of a man. Only last night he had learned of the existence of the *Whimsy*, even as she had been using it to elude him. What other secrets had she kept? And how strange that she could seem so soft, almost fragile, and yet be capable of such quick-witted decisiveness.

Karim raised a hand to touch his scabbed lip as he paced up and down. He had no intention of letting Juliette go. Thankfully he had already sent a force of men to delay the ship carrying the rifles from Marseille, so now he had the choice of intercepting her yacht before she reached England, or waiting and waylaying her somewhere after she landed.

Both ways had their risks and advantages. She was already hours ahead, though the *Black Hawk* would be able to catch her. It would save time, but then he would have her crew to deal with. Her disappearance could be carried out far more discreetly in London. She wouldn't have her regular servants with her, and temporary ones—people already employed by him, could apply for the positions and, if necessary, bribe the other applicants.

A knock on the door interrupted his planning, and when the sheik acknowledged it with a meaningless syllable, the door opened tentatively to reveal Rashid offering a letter from his tray.

Karim took it, immediately recognizing it as a letter from his investigator, William Sleth. What had the man found out? he asked himself, tearing away the seals. His attention lately had been so consumed by Juliette that he had given few thoughts to revenge.

Now, pulling out the paper and unfolding it, Karim nodded to dismiss Rashid as he read the letter once, and then again, doubting his eyesight for the first time in his life.

Monsieur Phillips,
    This is to inform you concerning one Juliette Clayton and his wife, Elizabeth Thorpe Clayton, a woman
    Miss Clayton was born in England to Captain Clayton and his wife Elizabeth Thorpe Clayton, a woman of the highest birth and connections who died while giving birth.
    Juliette was orphaned eight years ago, at the age of eleven, when her father succumbed to wounds received during his assignment in hostile Arab territory.
    Most recently, Juliette Clayton attended Miss Fayton's Girls' School. She changed her name after graduation to Juliette Clayton Thorpe as a stipulation for receiving her inheritance. At present, Miss Clayton Thorpe is touring Spain.

                Forward any further instructions.
                William Sleth

For an instant Karim reeled before standing perfectly still, like a man shot and waiting to fall. Then his teeth clenched. Only two words stood out from the ink-scrawled page like a curse, *"Juliette Clayton."*

Juliette? George Clayton's daughter? Was it possible? Violently Karim threw the cheroot onto the rug, heedless as it burned. And now, suddenly, everything seemed clear. Of course! Clayton had been sent home after he was wounded, and Clayton had known the name of the young Arab who gave him that mortal wound. Yes, Clayton had known *his* name, Karim al-Sharif, and he must have told his daughter Juliette!

Now everything fell into place—their meeting—everything had been planned. It had all been a game—Juliette's own form of revenge. But what else should he expect from the daughter of George Clayton!

Karim's face blackened with rage as he walked to a carved antique table and, picking up a decanter, poured himself a generous Scotch.

Yes, it was obvious now. It was too much of a coincidence that he should have met Juliette by mere accident. She had known all the time who he was and that he had killed her father. He thought she was resourceful. But he had never conceived her capable of such duplicity. All along she had tricked him—mocked him. Even that day they had lunched in the orange grove. How naive he had been not to understand when she had so cunningly asked, *"Have you a lot to forgive, monsieur? Is that why you detest the English?"* And, *"I am an exception, are there others who aren't exempted? Some special English enemy list perhaps?"*

Then he had concluded her questions could only be offhand, or, at best, insightful. How wrong he had been! And now, suddenly there was a growing scandal about his true identity as an Arab. He had blamed Lucille, but had it been she?

Karim's pride writhed under the realization. *And I played along. How she must be laughing at me, a foolish Arab who she could have dancing to her tune and then expose and reject!*

He gripped the table's polished wooden edge. He had been so gullible, so charmed by her feigned innocence. Of course she and Rodney had been accomplices in the scheme, and lovers too, no doubt. While Juliette had played him like a puppet on a string, Rodney had also been spinning his own schemes, dangerous schemes that only recently had come to his attention.

He paused, picturing her in his mind—Juliette riding horseback at his side—Juliette laughing as the wind tossed her hair—Juliette in his arms, her lips warm and open and moist. And every image of her lacerated his exposed nerves. There was a long silence. Then blindly he picked up the table and threw it crashing into the wall, shattering its legs, and jarring loose a picture that fell on top of it.

He laughed then, a short, hoarse laugh, and, lighting a match, set the letter afire, watching it flare and crumble into brown ashes which he flicked from his fingers. His smile was cruel and twisted. Of course, Juliette had gambled that he would never know *her* true identity. But this time—this time she had underestimated him!

Chapter 39

"Isn't it positively exciting?" Millie asked as she sat with Juliette in her large London house. "Look at all these invitations you've received and you have been home less than a week," she continued, her accent decidedly more English and less American since her recent marriage to Lord Robert Clintridge.

Juliette tried to look excited though she felt absolutely no enthusiasm for any of the balls or suppers being given almost nightly now since May had arrived. Still she dared not beg off. Lady Linley had just returned from Las Flores and with her came the story of Brandon's Arab blood. Gossip like that would soon make the rounds and now it was more important than ever that she give the appearance of not giving even two pins for the man. Everything depended upon it. So for the next week, Juliette threw herself into the round of suppers and dances where many times she was guest of honor. But she could not stop her thoughts from turning to Brandon Phillips.

She had tried to be rational by reminding herself he was not only a detestable Arab, a fact that was unacceptable both to her personally and to her society at large, but that he was also undoubtedly Muslim. And then there was the relatively trivial matter of Lucille. Of course it was better it had ended this way, she told herself. She had been shocked, yes, stunned. But it would make everything easier in the long run. Now at least she was cured of him and nothing could ever bring them together again. Now if she

could only stop reliving the same astonishment and fury
that, even now, could quicken her pulse. They had been
like animals that last time together and, worst of all, Lucille had seen it all! Inwardly Juliette twisted with the agony of it. It was all Brandon's fault. Why had he shown
love to her when from the beginning he knew nothing
could ever be between them? Why had he made her feel
things that he had no right to make her feel? He had led
her on. She had suspected he could be cruel but had never
wanted to believe it. Silently then she cursed him even as
the pain redoubled in her heart. Yet she must not let anyone even suspect what had really happened—not even Millie. And what would happen when William Bond heard?
Unfortunately his reaction was as harsh as she'd feared:

> *Dear Miss Thorpe,*
> *Recently your relationship with a certain Monsieur*
> *Brandon Phillips has reached my attention and, as*
> *your legal guardian, I am writing to warn you against*
> *any further relationship with this man. Not only is his*
> *reputation with women unsavory but recently his*
> *background has been called into question.*
> *It is imperative that your name no longer be linked*
> *with his and that no scandal cloud your name and*
> *thereby mine. I trust you recall our agreement on this*
> *matter. If a scandal should occur and you are still un-*
> *married I will be forced to revoke your privilege of*
> *independence. I trust however this option will not be*
> *necessary and that you will untangle yourself from*
> *this man so that his reputation no longer affects*
> *yours.*
>
> > *Sincerely,*
> > *M. William Bond*

Revoke her independence, Juliette repeated with silent
horror. He couldn't . . . not over this when it was for her
freedom that she had refused Brandon in the first place.
Oh, what a mess!

And so with the sense of doom hanging over her head,
Juliette now became doubly careful never to mention Bran-

don's name and to be completely casual when others brought him up in conversation. She made sure to have many partners at the balls, to smile and to chat a lot and make everyone believe she didn't have a care in the world. It was an act that became more automatic with practice, and she discovered that when she laughed, only *she* heard the hollow note. And when she danced, only *she* knew that her movements and smiles were mechanical as a metal doll's. And tonight as she waltzed and polkaed, and danced the quadrilles and schottische in a haze of champagne, Juliette silently blessed Miss Fayton's for training her to perform so well without thought or attention.

"Haven't you heard? It's all over London tonight."

"I haven't heard a word," the Countess Landry said. "What about Monsieur Phillips? Surely no one has been ridiculous enough to condemn him for his mistresses. At least he has always been reasonably discreet."

"Not that certainly, Countess. It is much worse than that. So horrible in fact that I only am telling you because I know you had considered him for your niece Anne. Now of course, you must put any such ideas out of your mind. You wouldn't want her involved in a scandal and just think of poor Juliette Thorpe. Her dear mother must be turning over in her grave."

"Well, what is it, Elizabeth?" the countess asked, now thoroughly curious.

"So you haven't heard." There was a note of elation in Elizabeth Wolsey's voice that belied her serious countenance. "I'm so afraid for the girl. All alone in the world and now faced with such a ruinous scandal!"

"What scandal? What are you talking about, Elizabeth?" the countess demanded. "Nothing you say makes any sense."

"Well, there is no gentle way to put this," Elizabeth answered. "All I can tell you is that people are saying he is an Arab, a half-breed. Everyone is talking about it. I thought because of your niece you should know."

At the word "Arab" the countess's ostrich-plume fan stopped in mid-swish.

"But that is ridiculous. An Arab! And what has Juliette Thorpe to do with all this?"

"Well, no one knows for certain the . . . ah, extent of their relationship," Elizabeth whispered glancing across the room to where Juliette was dancing. "But I can tell you that she blushes whenever the man's name is mentioned, and they were seen together so often in Las Flores del Mar that now the poor girl's name is linked with his. I always thought something like this might happen to her. It is simply not right for a young woman to be so independent. And with a scandal like this behind her, many of the matches she might have made will automatically be closed to her. I wonder what her guardian William Bond has to say about this. He should have been more responsible in his duties. I think I'm going to write him so myself."

As the party continued, Juliette became aware of the controversy surrounding her. Several women had mentioned Brandon's name in conversation and watched her sharply as she claimed no knowledge of his whereabouts with what she hoped seemed a lack of interest. It was a horrible night. Several times she entered a group only to cause an embarrassed silence, and often women let their fans shield their words when she was near. And where was Rodney? She had heard someone whisper that he was gambling tonight, but she had never known him to play and dismissed the remark as idle chatter. It would have been some comfort to have had him with her. He had been so kind these past weeks, never mentioning Brandon or anything that might embarrass her. Perhaps all the parties had exhausted him, she thought, recalling he had difficulty dancing two nights in a row. Well, she told herself, you will just have to do this alone.

Hours dragged by until midnight came and she could gracefully excuse herself. She felt stiff all over—even her mouth felt sore from the forced smiles. Bidding her goodbyes she had her coach called and drove home through the streets of London feeling hardly able to hold herself upright in the seat. Oh, how long would this last? She had never been the subject of such a furor, not even when she had first started seeing Rodney and already William Bond was threatening to take away her freedom. Oh, he couldn't, he must not! She would not be confined again.

Inside her carriage Juliette felt chilled to the bone and, though she wrapped herself more tightly in the fox lap robe, when she finally entered her house on Windbury Street, her teeth were chattering.

Immediately she ordered a fire built and a cup of hot tea sent to her room. Then with a heavy hand on the bannister, she walked up the stairs.

From the window of her suite on the third floor she could see a large section of London, the street lamps marking the skeleton of its streets. Leaning against the window she wanted to cry. There was such a strain, a horrible digging pain within her. But the cramped fullness in her throat refused to give way to tears. The champagne she'd had made her dizzy and the dimness of the house depressed her further. She had intended to redecorate the Thorpe mansion herself when she returned from traveling. But she never imagined that would be this soon or that she would have to live in such a cold atmosphere of darkness and heavy furniture and portraits of stiff, cold-eyed relatives long dead. But now there was no help for it. She had to stay here, at least until this scandal died down. To flee now would be tantamount to an admission of guilt.

She sat down heavily in a large winged chair. Of course later in the year she would go traveling again. But now even this prospect seemed uninteresting. Life, which had for a short time been so enchantingly wonderful, had suddenly become difficult and sad again, just as it had been after her father's death.

At last a maid, a temporary one hired until more permanent staff could be found, came in bringing a pot of tea on a tray. Rose was around forty, with a thin, sharp face that gave her a harsh appearance. She did not smile, but only dropped a curtsy in greeting and helped Juliette out of her gown before undoing her long blond hair.

When it was done, Juliette smiled weakly. "That will be all, Rose, thank you," she said. And when the maid had gone she gratefully crawled into bed.

It was then that she struck something stiff just under the covers, something that crackled like paper when she felt it. How odd, she thought, pulling it out even as her heart quickened. And laying the paper above the quilts and taking a candle she held it so the glow washed over the note, illuminating the firm masculine handwriting that sprang out at her like a slap.

WE WILL MEET AGAIN JULIETTE CLAYTON AND THIS TIME I WILL HAVE MY REVENGE!

Juliette read it again, and a third time, as all the horror of this night surrounded her like a net. Instantly she was hot and perspiring, her heart taking leaps.

What did he mean? How did he know her name had been Clayton? And why did he call her that now? She swallowed and steeled herself. Was he still here?

With shaking fingers, Juliette lit the two lamps flanking her bed and looked around.

The shadows reflecting against the opposite wall seemed distorted and sinister, but there was no sign of anyone.

Juliette jerked the cord by her bed.

Instantly Rose appeared as if anticipating the call.

"Yes, miss?"

"Call my carriage at once," Juliette commanded. "I want to leave immediately."

"Yes, miss!"

For the second time that night, Juliette found herself riding through the streets of London. She had given the driver no specific instructions and rode aimlessly for twenty minutes, sitting rigidly erect, her mind racing, her hand still clenching the note.

Her servants had been bribed. That was certain. How else could the note have gotten in her bed? She couldn't trust any of them. And what kind of revenge did Brandon mean? He was unpredictable. Even a public scene would probably not be enough to salve his wounds although it would ensure her ruin. William Bond would waste no time in taking her independence and this she must avoid at all costs. But how? she asked herself. How? And it was then she suddenly thought of Rodney. Yes, Rodney! He would understand and she could trust him. And banging on the front wall of the carriage, Juliette gained the driver's attention.

"To Eaton Square," she shouted. "With all haste!"

Daverson, the Keiths' family butler, was stunned to see Miss Juliette standing on the porch of the Keiths's ancestral home. But after a moment's confusion, and blessing the fact Lady Keiths would not return this evening and witness her most inappropriate conduct, Daverson showed Juliette to a sitting room and bade her wait while he roused the young master.

It was ten minutes before Rodney rushed into the room and immediately took her two cold hands in his. At a glance he could see she was deadly white with a dreadful pinched look about her. "But what has happened?" he asked.

Wordlessly, she handed him the crumpled note.

Curious, Rodney took it, his eyes widening as he read.

"What is he talking about? How does he dare threaten you?" he said at last. Rodney had known the business at Las Flores had upset Juliette, but recently she had seemed so recovered that he had rejected the idea that there had been anything serious between that half-breed and Juliette. But now. . . .

Juliette's face was tight and she clasped her hands together to steady herself. "I . . . I promised to marry him," she blurted out. "I . . ."

" . . . you what?" Rodney looked askance at her.

"I . . . promised to marry him. But I never meant it. It was all a mistake, you see. I . . . well, rather he . . . I never intended to agree."

"You mean he forced you to agree?"

"Well, not exactly forced. But yes . . . he was . . . well . . . I thought I had no choice."

"And then what happened?"

"I told him the next morning that I couldn't . . . that I wouldn't marry him."

"Yes, and?"

"He was furious. There was a terrible scene. It was after that I saw you at my yacht. I went back to his villa to see if it was true about that woman. I . . . I . . . you were right about everything." Juliette grew whiter and her eyes filled with tears as she remembered the scene again and her voice faltered.

Rodney looked back to the note, rereading it as he walked to the fireplace before crushing the paper and tossing it into the dying embers. Silently he watched as a tiny flame blazed larger to consume it.

"He is furious, I'm afraid," Juliette began again. "And since I promised he wouldn't let me take it back. I tried to explain but . . . but . . . It is really all my fault for being so naive. I didn't know about Luci—. I didn't know about his mistress, or that he was an Arab until you told me. I didn't know anything about him. But now I have insulted him. And the man is capable of anything. He won't stop before I'm disgraced, and William Bond will . . . well, he has already threatened to retake control of the funds I receive." Juliette knew she was shaking. She hadn't slept well for nights now and had eaten almost nothing. She felt light-headed and her stomach turned so she felt weak. "Oh, Rodney," she finished. "I really am afraid of what he might do."

Rodney spun around to face her. "That is ridiculous! Phillips is only a man, and a half-breed at that. There is nothing to be frightened about. I'll arrange everything."

He seemed gravely serious and in command as Juliette had never seen him. He would help her—yes, she had been right to come to him.

"Maybe I should leave London immediately," she said leaning back in her chair. Then suddenly she could no longer hold the tide of confusion that came out in a torrent of tears.

Rodney smiled as he studied her bent head. At last his luck had taken a good turn. He put a comforting arm around Juliette's slim shoulders and handed her a handkerchief.

"Leaving London won't help. In fact you'll be more vulnerable away from those who care about you. A man like

Brandon won't let anything stop him. There is only one permanent answer. You must marry me."

Abruptly Juliette pulled away and looked at him with round streaming eyes. "Marry you! Rodney! But that is absurd." She sniffed and wiped her nose. "You know I don't want to marry anyone. My freedom is exactly what I've been trying so hard to keep."

Rodney took her hand. "But don't you see? It is the only solution. If Brandon does what he says, and I'm certain he'll do something typically vulgar, then William Bond will take away your independence and perhaps even force you to marry someone else. But, if you married me you could maintain your independence totally. The scandal would be stopped and it would end this engagement business with Phillips. From what I understand of Arabs, they do have some respect for marriage."

"But Rodney, I don't love you, I love . . . ." Juliette began, before stopping herself as she realized what she was about to say. Somehow tears filled her eyes again and she was sobbing. Was it really true? Did she love Brandon? But Rodney gave her no time to think.

"You *must* marry me, and quickly! I know you don't love me," Rodney said forming the words bravely. "But it doesn't matter. We will be man and wife in name only."

Juliette stared uncomprehending.

"I mean," Rodney said, looking directly into her violet eyes. "I mean there would be nothing between us that could . . . that would lead to children. You would be free to go your own way. I would not hinder you or demand anything. You would, in fact, be just as you are now, your own mistress, only you would be Lady Keiths. Then no one could question you, and most of all Brandon Phillips won't have any claim on you."

"But will it work, Rodney?" Juliette asked feeling numbed by the swiftness of events. "He is . . . is an extraordinary man. And clever. . . ."

Rodney took her other hand in his and squeezed it. "Trust me," he said.

Juliette stared at him standing before her, his blue eyes intense under his crown of blond hair. Now he seemed like a knight come to save her, just as he had done so long ago when he had come to her at the ball at Miss Fayton's when, taking her hand, he had transformed her from a poor orphan into a beautiful young woman. He had always been so good, so considerate, always understanding, and now, once again, he was unselfishly offering himself in her time of distress. This time she couldn't put him off. She had only to choose between a scandal that would ruin both her reputation and her independence or this desperate alternative. So silently, seriously, still looking into his questioning blue eyes, she nodded.

Chapter 40

"I tell you, I *know* what I'm doing!" Juliette's voice was raised and indignant. "Everyone always knew I would marry Rodney, didn't they! People have been gossiping about it since before I graduated from Miss Fayton's. And now that I'm doing exactly what they have all been expecting, you seem to think I've gone mad!"

"No one thinks you are mad, dear," Mrs. Welwright replied, trying to calm Juliette. "Quite the contrary, you have made a brilliant match. It is only that you seemed so completely against any sort of permanant relationship just a few weeks ago, and now, suddenly, you are rushing into marriage."

Mrs. Welwright paused and bit her lip. She wanted to question Juliette about Monsieur Phillips and what had happened at Las Flores del Mar, but she hesitated for fear of sending her into even greater distress. How sensitive and moody she had been lately! Happy one moment and sullen the next. But it wasn't her moodiness that worried Mrs. Welwright as much as her complete disinterest in the wedding preparations. When asked her preference on almost any matter, she would only reply, "Well, yes . . . whatever you think best," or, "I really don't know—be a dear and decide for me, won't you?"

The whole ceremony seemed of no consequence to her.

And lately, a new distance had come between them, making even discreet questions impossible.

"I was only suggesting we might delay the ceremony for a time," Mrs. Welwright began in her calm voice. "You would still be engaged, naturally. But I think it would be better to wait until you are feeling better."

"I'm feeling fine!" Juliette flared. "I've decided to get married, that's all, and in three weeks. I'm not a bit tired, and what is the point of waiting, anyway? I just want to do it and get it over with," she finished flatly.

Mrs. Welwright looked startled.

"I mean," Juliette fumbled, searching for words. "I mean, what could be more natural than bringing about my happiness and Rodney's as soon as possible?"

Mrs. Welwright studied her young friend before finally expending a deep sigh. "Yes, of course, dear. I . . . we all only want your happiness. If this is what you want, then I will do everything in my power to make your wedding as perfect for you and Rodney as possible."

Immediately, Juliette's expression altered in that abruptly changeable fashion that also seemed so uncharacteristic. Then coming close, she linked their arms together.

"I do want to thank you so much," she said, assuming once more her normal tone and manner. "You have been so sweet and helpful. I can't ever repay everything you have already done to help."

Mrs. Welwright smiled. "It has been little enough, really," she said. "And I'm glad to do it. I once told you I would be happy to be the governess to your children. It only surprises me that it is to come about so quickly."

Mrs. Welwright was sure Juliette flushed then, her eyes rimming with tears before swiftly looking down.

Mrs. Welwright frowned. "Maybe you should go and lie down," she offered, remembering how, only a few weeks before, Juliette would often dance most of the night, then rise at dawn to ride her horse without ever seeming to tire. "I'm sure these plans and decisions and your excitement have all exhausted you."

"Yes, I believe I will." Juliette's voice sounded small. "I

really am very tired. You will forgive my rudeness, won't you? I do appreciate everything you have done for me."

"Of course, dear," Mrs. Welwright said, giving her a motherly hug. "I was once a bride, too, you know, and I realize the strain it can be. Now go ahead upstairs and get a good long rest. Three weeks is such a short time, and before you know it, you'll be standing at the head of the stairs, a happy bride."

"Three weeks," Juliette had repeated. Three weeks seemed an aeon then—an aeon when each day she could never really think about Brandon, but never could completely forget him either or stop wondering how he could carry out his threat.

So each night, Juliette fell into bed exhausted, though she never slept long or deeply. And each moment she was dominated by fear, and the absolute certainty that he would come. Yet at the same time she was so busy with fittings and the choosing of flowers and colors and her own trousseau, that everything ran together in a blur. But then, at last, sooner than seemed possible, Juliette did find herself standing at the head of a flower-festooned stairway, leaning on Rodney's uncle's arm, and looking below her at the assemblage of smiling faces and glowing candles filling the Thorpe mansion from stately wall to wall.

"I will be married but I will be free," she told herself, as she had all afternoon, trying to calm the churning in her stomach. "I will be free!" But now the words had become meaningless syllables as she heard the wedding march begin, seeming to come from a different world.

Her eyes drifted slowly over the sparkling, bejeweled throng and her legs felt weak and difficult to control.

Looking down she saw the toes of her white high-heeled slippers peeping from beneath the white satin gown covered entirely in chantilly lace. It had a flowing train and long pointed sleeves each hooked by twenty-five buttons—a wedding dress—*her* wedding dress.

Sudden waves of cold dizziness swept her. "What am I doing?" a small voice within her asked. "Is it possible I've carried this folly so far?"

"Juliette, Juliette," she heard another faraway voice say. "It's time dear. Now don't be nervous. Take my arm."

It was Rodney's uncle, Lord Salisbury, a stocky, distinguished Englishman with thick gray muttonchops.

Slowly, Juliette turned to him, swaying slightly as mechanically she circled her hand around his elbow.

"Smile, dear," she heard him say. "This is not a funeral. It is your wedding, and the happiest day of your life!"

Juliette smiled automatically with only her lips. Then reaching a foot outward while keeping her chin high, she started down the long winding stairway, slowly stepping in time to the wedding march.

"Slowly, remember, walk slowly, Juliette," everyone had repeatedly reminded her.

The walk seemed interminable, and Juliette's knuckles grew white, clenching her orchid bouquet as she descended first one flight of stairs, a landing, and then another. The fragrance of perfume and the brightness of candlelight surrounded her as a maze of eager eyes followed her every movement, every glance and smile.

Her eyes recorded brief glimpses of Lady Linley with her diamond-encrusted lorgnette, the Countess of Devonshire smiling her mask of brittle sophistication, Mrs. Welwright, her eyes already moist as she twisted her lace handkerchief, and finally Rodney's mother, Lady Keiths, a smile fixed on her face as firmly, Juliette knew, as the exact figure of the Thorpe fortune was fixed in her head.

At the end of the aisle, there was Rodney, his blond hair stuck to his perspiring forehead, his face solemn, his eyes glowing with pride.

As she reached him, their gazes met, and unable to return his look of unspeakable joy, Juliette dropped her eyes to the polished wooden floor.

The music quieted, and the bishop began the ceremony, intoning the same words Juliette had heard beginning a hundred weddings before. Then they were praying and everyone's head was bowed.

Juliette tried to pay attention, but could not, her thoughts unwillingly traveling to Brandon's face as it rose in her mind's eye. Brandon Phillips, his chiseled cheek

bones, his strong jaw, his dark penetrating eyes. If everything had been different she would already be Mrs. Brandon Phillips—Madame Phillips—Juliette Phillips. How she
had trembled in his arms—just as she was trembling now.
But that had been a wonderful soaring sensation instead of
this horrible sinking one.

She felt so removed, so far away as she vaguely heard
the bishop ask if there was anyone who had reason that she
and Rodney should not be joined as man and wife.

There was a pause and, in the silence, Juliette closed her
eyes and thought she heard a deep voice resonating above
the crowd as it said, "I do!"

All heads turned in one movement toward Brandon silhouetted by moonlight in the doorway. Then he was up the
aisle, shouldering aside a stunned Rodney who gaped openmouthed.

Her eyes were drawn and held by his black ones as suddenly he announced, "This woman is already promised in
marriage to me."

Rodney gasped, as did the bishop, and there was wild
muttering in the crowd as Juliette turned to speak but
could say nothing. It was exactly what she had hoped in
her most secret heart.

Then, after the pause, the bishop's words droned on
again, bringing Juliette back to reality with a jolt of horrible empty despair. She listened as Lord Salisbury gave her
away, and then she felt Rodney's clammy hand tentatively
take hers.

The bishop's voice continued before there was a chill of
metal against her hand.

Mesmerized, Juliette stared blankly as Rodney slipped
the ring on her finger. It was a huge diamond, one of the
Keiths's ancestral jewels, its flashing facets reminding her
of the heart-shaped ruby ring that Brandon once had sent
her. That ring she had refused while now, this one seemed
riveted to her finger, impossible to remove, and with it Juliette realized her fate was sealed.

The bishop was reciting the vows, and Rodney repeated
them, his voice shaking with emotion as he promised to

love her, to cherish her, to give himself to no one else until death do them part.

Then it was her turn, but Juliette found she could not concentrate on the words, and the bishop had to repeat them before she replied in a voice barely audible.

There was another pause. It was almost over. In a moment she would be Lady Keiths, wife of Lord Rodney Keiths, forever . . . until death.

Blankly, Juliette raised her face to look at the bishop as he pronounced them man and wife. Rodney's voice was whispering in her ear, reassuring her, asking her to turn toward him.

She felt stiff as wood as Rodney took her shoulders and turned her gently to face him. Then, with his heart in his eyes, his hands visibly shaking, he lifted her lace veil and kissed her.

His mouth was soft, like a woman's, and, in spite of herself, Juliette remembered another mouth that had once covered hers in a blazing caress so different from this trembling peck that barely touched her and left her wondering if, in fact, she had been kissed.

The orchestra crashed suddenly into the wedding song, and with a cold emptiness in her stomach, Juliette realized it was over.

Head down, unable to look at any one, she turned and, at Rodney's side, started down the aisle. It had all happened just as she planned, Juliette told herself. Now Brandon couldn't hurt her. She was Rodney's wife . . . forever and ever, and no matter what she did, or how long she lived, Brandon Phillips would never take her breath away with his burning kisses again.

Desperately she tried to blink down the tears that sprang to her eyes as a shaft of pain stabbed her heart.

"But what is it, my love?" Rodney asked gently as he turned and saw Juliette's overflowing eyes staring up at him.

"It's just . . . it's just," she began, looking down again and fumbling for words. "It's just that I'm . . . I'm so happy."

Chapter 41

It was after midnight before, mercifully, it was over. And as the half-moon was sinking through thick fog toward the western horizon, Juliette stood arm in arm with her groom, bidding good-bye to the last of their guests.

Exhausted and wordless then, Juliette climbed the stairs beside him, past the drab portraits of the Thorpe ancestry, and along the hall until she reached her room. Then flushing self-consciously, she turned to Rodney and, tiptoeing, kissed him on the cheek. "Good night. It was a . . . a beautiful wedding."

Juliette thought there was an oddness about Rodney as he looked at her now, but she was too exhausted to consider it. If something was bothering him, morning was soon enough to discuss it. So she smiled, turned, and reached for the doorknob to her room though his hand pulled her back and as he whispered, "Don't you think we should spend the night in the same room? I mean, what will the servants think? We *are* newly married you know."

Juliette's flush darkened. "Don't be ridiculous. There is only one bed in my room."

Rodney frowned. His feet shifted uneasily, scuffing the carpet as his gaze dropped to the floor. "It's quite embarrassing for me," he began. "I wouldn't touch you—I swear. But if we sleep apart, everyone will think that I . . . that you . . . that we haven't . . ."

". . . But we agreed," Juliette hissed. "Why should we set a precedent that can't be continued? Anyway, who cares what the servants say? People have been gossiping about us for years. Frankly, I've learned to live with it," she finished starting to turn away.

"Well, I haven't," Rodney flared indignantly. "Things like this have a way of getting around, you know. I won't have it said at my club that I was turned out on my wedding night."

Now it was Juliette's forehead that knitted in a single vertical line between her brows. A long silence followed.

She understood his discomfort. With servants required in every element of a person's life, they tended to know everything, and their present staff was filled with many new and temporary additions who could not be trusted to keep quiet.

It would be cruel to embarrass him, she thought, particularly after his consideration for me. She smiled wanly.

"Well, all right, then. Just for this one night to avoid the gossip."

A glow of pleasure and relief spread across Rodney's features. "Shall I come with you now?"

"No! Wait until my maid has gone. Then come."

"But I could help you."

"Rodney! No!" And with that, Juliette crossed the threshold alone and soundly shut the door.

She was relieved Rodney didn't follow. What had gotten into him? But of course, there was his masculine pride to consider, and after what he had done for her, how could she refuse such a concession?

In a moment, the maid came and helped Juliette remove her gown and slip on a silver nightgown elegantly embroidered with a multitude of white roses. Then, letting down her mistress's golden curls, she brushed them vigorously.

After a time, Juliette dismissed her. "That is enough, Ellen. Thank you and good night."

"And a pleasant night to you, madam."

The maid had no sooner closed the door when there was a discreet knock and Rodney entered, smiling shyly, dressed in pajamas and a heavy burgundy robe.

Juliette had already climbed into bed and sat up clenching a sheet modestly beneath her chin as she peered between the velvet bed draperies. She pointed to a huge overstuffed chair in the corner. "I'm not sure it's very comfortable," she whispered. "But I'm afraid it's the best there is."

Indeed the chair was a monstrosity of ugliness. But now, seeing how useful it was going to be, Juliette was glad she hadn't had it removed as had been her first inclination.

Rodney's jaw twitched and his smile faded. "But I thought. . . ."

"Please, Rodney!" Juliette said with a note of irritation. "No one will know if you sleep in the chair." He stood staring at her. "Certainly you hadn't imagined anything else!"

Rodney did not answer, and grumbling words too low for her to hear, made his way to the chair and curled in its large seat beneath a blanket.

He spent the night there, jockeying for a comfortable position before finally dropping off and snoring discontentedly until dawn when he rose cold and cramped and, leaving the room, closed the door behind him with more than necessary force.

That same day at noon, Juliette's elegant white coach, strapped high with trunks and band boxes, headed down Windbury Street carrying the newlyweds to their country house where a two-week honeymoon was scheduled.

In an hour they had reached the countryside. A bank of low clouds had covered the sun, ruining what had earlier promised to be a sunny day. The clumps of wild daisies did not show their faces, remaining closed in the dim light, and a lark perched on the high grasses trilled three high notes and three low, over and over in a series of forlorn cries for its mate.

Inside the carriage, Juliette leaned back against velvet cushions, glancing occasionally at Rodney, who had taken the seat on the opposite side of the carriage, his chin plunged into his fist as he gazed absently out the window. He had not spoken beyond a civil "good morning" in front of the servants, and now he seemed to Juliette like a dejected puppy.

She sighed. No doubt he already regretted having married her. Obviously he had deluded himself into thinking that once they were married she would relax the terms of their bargain. But if she had not been sure of her feelings for Rodney before, last night had proven to her she could never have more than platonic relations with Rodney Keiths. It was a fact both of them would have to live with. She would try to make it easy. She would make no demands on Rodney or ask any questions about his affairs. She glanced at him again. He would be as completely free as she would be. In time it would all be easier. But whatever happened, they were man and wife, and there was no going back for either of them.

It was nearly midnight when, at last, the carriage rolled through heavy iron gates thrown wide by a boy wearing a red uniform and a small black cap. Huge oaks towered over them like sentinels and the horses' hooves echoed as they trotted along the cobblestone drive.

Inside the elegant manor a series of lights blinked on like eyes from the windows, and lanterns were brought out onto the porch.

Rodney helped his bride out of the coach and, with dignity, presented her to the assembled staff who all bowed or curtsyed in turn. Then, leading her up the steps, he walked inside, not bothering to lift her over the threshold, a fact not missed by the servants, Juliette was sure. And while she hadn't expected it, abandoning the custom made Juliette even sadder.

Rodney did not ask to sleep in her room that night and, after consuming a light meal in silence, he simply went to his own room, squaring his shoulders as he headed up the stairs.

Juliette did not see or speak to him again that night and, the next morning, Juliette found Rodney decidedly absent at breakfast.

There was only Daverson, Rodney's butler, dressed impeccably in gray coat and tails who served her tea.

"M'Lord has gone shooting, madam," he informed her. "He left quite early this morning and has been gone several hours, although I don't expect him to return for several more."

"I see," Juliette said. "Then Daverson, could you have my horse saddled for an hour after breakfast. I think I will go riding."

The butler nodded his balding gray head. "Yes, madam. Very good. I will tell the stable boy. And, madam," Daverson began with another bow. "Should you require anything else, anything at all, please, don't hesitate to ask. We are all pleased and honored to serve you."

Juliette smiled at the old servant. Certainly he had seen enough to draw his own conclusions about the situation and, during the last two days, he had been extremely efficient and kind, anticipating her slightest whim.

Juliette was grateful. "Thank you, Daverson. You've been most helpful in every way. It is a comfort to know you are running the household."

Daverson bowed again. "Of course, madam, and thank you."

He moved off, leaving Juliette alone again in the overlarge dining room where a huge dark clock marked the time with a ticking pendulum that echoed in the empty room.

She felt deserted, although she couldn't really blame Rodney. Now it was up to her to follow his example and find something with which to occupy herself while they endured this farce of a honeymoon before going their separate ways again.

A ride on High Times seemed the most obvious means of escape and sometime later Juliette found herself cantering over the lush green countryside, the manor receding behind her.

High Times was in blooming spirits, pulling constantly at the bit until finally Juliette released her tight grip on the reins and let him carry them at full gallop over the hills.

The wind whistled past her ears and brought tears to her eyes until at last slowing of his own accord, High Times relaxed into a slower canter.

Several miles passed under the big horse's hooves before Juliette pulled him up on the summit of a grassy knoll.

From there she surveyed the valley below, a breeze tossing her blond curls. The meadow was blanketed with orange and yellow poppies and daisies, and the buzzing of busy bees mingled with the bright calls of quail.

To one side, the grassy sea of flowers stretched to meet the blue horizon, and on the other, the meadow terminated after a half mile in a dense forest of oaks and maples.

The invigorating air brought roses blooming in her cheeks, and for the moment, her problems forgotten, she propelled High Times into a trot that took them down the hill into a narrow valley.

A stream ran there several yards wide and, turning down it, they trotted along its banks where the calls of birds blended with the sound of High Times's hoofbeats against the soft earth.

The water bubbled on for a mile or so before picking up speed. The terrain inclined and the stream bed narrowed and deepened. A half mile further, Juliette was forced to pull High Times to a stop as they reached a cliff where the stream spilled over in a narrow splashing waterfall.

Glancing down at the muddy bank, Juliette was surprised to find hoofprints of other horses. From the way the grass was still pressed tightly down in the shape of the print, Juliette knew they had been made only a short time ago.

Suddenly, she felt uneasy, pricked by an inexplicable sense of danger. Her eyes darted around. They could be above her, she thought. Anyone out of the valley could easily escape her notice. A warning throbbed in her veins and she felt urged to run away even as she tried to restrain the impulse. What if others are here? Certainly it doesn't mean they intend to harm me, she told herself. But even High Times was prancing uneasily and, once given his head, wasted no time in leaping up the steep sides of the valley to the top.

Quickly Juliette looked around, her heart plummeting as, from across the meadow, two men on horseback came galloping toward her.

PART VII

REVENGE

Chapter 42

High Times snorted as he leaped forward, his flying hooves marking the turf as he bolted into a headlong gallop away from the two men.

Over the rolling meadow they went, Juliette's heart pounding.

Brandon! Of course. It was he, or perhaps his men. They had come to do whatever it was he planned. Oh, why had she been so foolish not to have taken a groom with her?

In spite of High Times's courage, she knew his energy had been depleted by the previous long gallop and she guessed the mounts of her pursuers were fresh.

Leaning forward, Juliette urged the big horse on before looking wide-eyed over her shoulder at the riders closing the distance.

No, she couldn't hope to outrun them. The only possible escape was to reach the trees before they did and lose them there. Another nudge of her spurless heel sent High Times toward the forest, his long strides eating up the distance in a series of extended bounds that soon found her entering the dense growth.

Luckily, there was a path before her, narrow and partly obliterated by fallen leaves but still discernible, and bending low over the horse's neck, she urged him along it.

Again Juliette looked over her shoulder, seeing the riders just entering the trees behind her. The path ahead turned a corner and dropped down into a ravine so she was concealed from their view. At the bottom of the ravine Juliette pulled the big horse to a halt. Then spinning him at a right angle to the path, she sent him along the bottom of the ravine where fallen logs and exposed roots threatened to tangle the horse's legs at every step until they reached a large boulder and moved quickly behind it.

Jumping from her horse, Juliette stepped to his head,

holding his soft muzzle cradled in her arms to keep him from calling to the other horses as she waited.

The thundering of hooves drew nearer, and in only a moment, the two riders also dipped down into the ravine.

Juliette held her breath, peering from her hiding place and praying for them to continue past. She heard one of them curse as his horse stumbled over an exposed root and fell to the ground in a confusion of flailing limbs.

From behind the rock, Juliette watched the man roughly haul the horse to its feet. He looked quite tall though his face remained hidden beneath a hat, and she didn't recognize him.

He leapt onto his horse, and to Juliette's relief, both riders continued along the same path, galloping away in the distance.

High Times was in a lather of sweat when they finally arrived home and, jumping from the saddle, Juliette tossed the reins to a groom before running up the stone steps and through the massive door.

Once inside, she didn't even acknowledge Daverson's formal "Good afternoon" before asking,

"Where is my . . . my husband?"

"M'lord returned while you were out, madam. But now he is gone again himself. He left word that you should not expect him for dinner. I took the liberty of informing the cook."

"Yes, of course," Juliette said, inwardly frustrated and hurt. But what had she expected? Surely she didn't imagine Rodney would be at home waiting for her. They hardly had spoken in two days.

"Thank you, Daverson," Juliette said, recovering herself and realizing she must seem like a madwoman.

"Is there something wrong, madam?"

"No, nothing!" she said too quickly.

"Will that be all, madam?"

"Yes. For the moment at least."

"Very well, madam." Daverson bowed stiffly.

In a brief flickering expression, Juliette smiled in return, wondering if she should confide in the servant. What if the men followed her here? No, she concluded after a moment's thought. Not even Brandon would be so bold. So raising her chin, she turned and with as much calm dignity as she could manage, climbed the stairs to the privacy of her bedroom.

That night, after midnight, when Rodney still hadn't arrived home, Juliette began to worry, and by two o'clock was pacing the floor and nearly driving herself mad with unanswered questions. What could Brandon want from her now? Her marriage to Rodney was supposed to have prevented just such an occurrence. Well, so much for that! But maybe it wasn't Brandon at all. Maybe they were highwaymen trying to rob her? Would they try again? Well, she would be sure never to ride alone, at least for now. But where was Rodney? Had he been waylaid, or worse? She dared not even think further, but continued to pace until the wheels of a phaeton and the hoofbeats of a single horse told her Rodney had arrived.

Having hours ago dismissed the servants for the night, Juliette let him in herself. But even as she opened the door, she could smell the reek of liquor and she didn't need to see his bloodshot eyes or disordered clothes to know he was unscathed except for apparently losing a contest with tremendous portions of Scotch.

Squinting, Rodney peered at her in the dim light and seeing it was she and not Daverson, he swept an arm before himself in a wide courtly bow that mocked her.

"Good evening, Madam Keiths," he slurred, grinning drunkenly. "Or shall I still address you as Miss Thorpe?" He leered up and down her pale lavender dressing gown.

Fear, rage, frustration all collided within Juliette as she stood there, fists clenched at her sides trying to control her temper. "Where have you been? And what do you mean coming home in this . . . this disgusting state?"

Rodney's face twisted in a grimace. He smiled cockeyed as he took her arm, unsteadily propelling her through the hall and into the library before shutting the double doors behind them.

Juliette let herself be led until they were assured of privacy, then, jerking loose from his hold, she silently crossed the room to close the tall windows blown open by the wind that filled the draperies like sails.

Oh, how could he? she thought, trying to control her boiling fury. And when she turned back to Rodney, she found him bending over a decanter of Scotch, gracelessly slopping a portion into a glass, and leaving behind a brown puddle on the table's shiny surface.

"Where have you been?" she repeated. In the lamplight she could see he was even drunker than she first thought.

"With Squire Longsworth," he slurred. "We've been having a little chat, he and I, and I've been telling 'im all about you and me."

Juliette's face darkened. She could only imagine what Rodney had confided in his present condition. No doubt when he sobered up, he would be as mortified as she.

"He says I'm a bloody fool," Rodney rolled his eyes in her direction. "And I . . . I agree with him," he finished, downing the drink with a practiced flick of his wrist that Juliette found even more aggravating.

She stood watching, her arms crossed, all her fear now turned to anger. "I suppose it doesn't matter to you that I was attacked today?" she began. "That two men, and I don't know who they were, chased me home."

Rodney paused and sat down heavily as he peered at her through glazed corneas.

"Two men?" he asked stupidly.

Juliette came toward him like a fury. "Yes! I narrowly escaped. And all night I've been worried to death about you. I see that I should have known better!"

Rodney looked blank, appearing not to have heard. In frustration, Juliette twisted her slipper heel into the carpet and glared at him. "You are disgusting," she said. "If you had any decency you could at least be interested in what I'm telling you. Don't you care that your wife was almost waylaid, or robbed, or even raped today?"

Her words seemed to rouse him. "Yes, my wife . . . my wife," he mumbled. "That is just what Squire Longsworth said. You aren't really my wife."

"Rodney, you are talking nonsense, and I'm disgusted and—"

"No!" Rodney shouted as he shook his head drunkenly. "No! That's just what I said. But it's true, you see. I have it on the authority of the squire. People aren't really married until the ceremony is *consummated*," he finished, watching with satisfaction as Juliette's face changed. He poured himself more Scotch.

"What are you trying to say?" Juliette began. "We are married in just the way we agreed. There is nothing in our bargain that includes . . . that includes anything else!"

"Ah, but Juliette," his voice was suddenly gentle as he made an uncertain path to her and took her by the shoulders. "We are married in name already. What can it matter if we make it a fact? Only one night, that's all I ask. Then we will be man and wife for once and all, and I won't bother you about it again."

His grip on her shoulders had grown painful and Juliette jerked away, her sense of uneasiness growing. Tilting her head higher she said, "You are drunk, Rodney, and hardly able to discuss such a serious matter intelligently. First you make a bargain, and now you ask me to go back on it—to engage in something that would disgust me. If I had known you could behave this way, I assure you I would never have consented to any marriage between us. Now I'm tired of your foolishness, and I'm going to bed, *alone!*"

She turned then and headed toward the door. But Rodney followed, his shoulders hunched, his fists clenched, his eyes suddenly hard. As she reached for the doorknob he was there, spinning her around and pulling her against him until she gagged from the stench of alcohol on his breath.

"It will be done, Juliette! I've a right to your maidenhead, and I mean to have it!" His face was puffy and red as his bloodshot eyes leered into hers.

"Is it to be rape then?" she asked coldly. "It is certain I'll never give in to you. I find you disgusting, a cad and a liar, and I believe at this moment I hate you."

"Yes, you hate *me!*" Rodney said in a low accusing voice. "I'm not Phillips, am I? I know how you feel about *him*. You love him, don't you? But you found out he had a mistress and it hurt your damned pride. So you married me. I was convenient, wasn't I, and fool enough to keep you respectable while all the time you've been mooning over him, just waiting for a chance to find him again and open your legs for that bloody *nigger!*" Rodney's body was heaving now as though out of breath. "Well, that may be so. Phillips may have you," he continued spitting the words at her. "Perhaps I can't prevent it. But I shall have you *first!*"

He lunged at her then, but Juliette jumped away so he fell flat on the carpet.

"Rodney, stop it!" she said with all the bravado she could muster. "This is absurd. You will wake all the servants with your drunkenness!"

Rodney crawled to his feet, his face suddenly so filled with malice that she hardly recognized it as his. "I don't care if I do," he said. "Let them know . . . let them all know! It will create a nice scandal, won't it? Lord Keiths rapes wife, eh? But I'll tell you a secret, Juliette. You haven't made quite so big a fool out of me as you think. You've been congratulating yourself haven't you? You think I married you because I really care for you, love you, eh? But you're wrong. I have debts, Juliette, huge ones. My mother doesn't even know. She doesn't approve of gambling, you see. And she certainly wouldn't approve of the company I keep. But I had to do something to amuse myself while you were off prancing about and showing everyone just how free you are. Gambling is a marvelous pastime, even if it is expensive. I like it quite a lot, and now there's no reason anyone has to know about it. I was desperate, you see, and then you came to me so upset about Phillips that you were desperate, too. I saw my chance and took it, and now that we're married, Madam Keiths, you'll have to pay my bills or see your reputation ruined right along with mine. And now there isn't any reason to stop my fun, either. With your money I can go right on playing. Of course it will be expensive. You probably won't be able to travel so much as you planned—maybe not at all. But you *will* pay. Those thugs that followed you this afternoon—they were a warning. My creditors, you see, are not the most scrupulous characters. I can't pay them. I'm absolutely broke. And they are growing impatient, I think.

Undoubtedly they meant to give you a little example of what it could be like if they don't get their money. So you see, my dear, it is *you* who have been the fool!"

"Don't be ridiculous, Rodney! You have your estates and your mother's jewels. I don't think the crown jewels are worth much more. What are you talking about, you can't have gambled all that away!"

"No, I haven't gambled it away. For the moment it's invested. Do you think those jewels my mother wears are the real thing? Oh the gold is real enough, but the jewels are paste, copies I had made while I borrowed money on the real ones. I plan to make money, lots of money. I'll be so rich I won't care if you do go back to that filthy Arab of yours—that spy!"

"Spy—what do you mean spy? Brandon may be a lot of things, but he is certainly no spy," Juliette said shakily.

"So you want proof, is that it?" Rodney came menacingly forward. "Well, I'll prove it to you. Brandon Phillips is a spy and leads an alliance of Arab natives resisting our forces in the Sahara, and the French forces as well."

"I don't believe you."

"Don't believe if you like. But how well do you really know him? And how can you say you don't believe this when everything else I've told you about him is true?"

Juliette stood stunned. Brandon did seem so mysterious and traveled a lot, she thought. And what was he doing posing as a vacationing Frenchman when he was an Arab? "What do you mean?" she repeated.

Swaying on his feet unsteadily as a midshipman on his first cruise, Rodney made his way to the desk, pulling open a small panel and withdrawing a scroll of paper that he waved. "It's all here," he said tossing it at her. "I had his mistress steal it. No one knows yet, but everyone shall. I would have told you before if you hadn't been so bloody upset about your precious Monsieur Phillips's woman. I know who Phillips is and what he is doing, at least part of it, and I intend to find out everything. You want to know where the money has gone, well, I've invested the last of it in rifles being sold to the French for shipment to the Sahara—guns that will be the downfall of this Brandon Phillips, or 'Karim al-Sharif' as he is known in the desert. The French pay triple the price of rifles upon safe delivery. But even if I didn't need the money so badly, I'd gladly give them rifles just to see that bastard destroyed. It's going to be the end of your damned half-breed."

Juliette was looking at him as if he were someone she didn't recognize, an intruder that she happened upon where she least expected it. "But Rodney, selling guns to the French is treason. You can't! And your mother's jewels, how could you . . ." But before she could go on, he grabbed the front of her dressing gown and ripped it open to the waist.

Instantly her round, pink-tipped breasts appeared through the opening as a hand clapped over her mouth and he dragged her to a velvet couch. He threw her on it then, covering her squirming, kicking body with his own.

With his free exploring hand, he was quick to discover she had only a chemise under her gown and, propping a knee between her legs, he spread them apart.

Juliette's eyes bulged as she struggled, trying to breathe under the hand that held back her screams and her oxygen as well.

Everything was a blur, revulsion filling her at the feel and smell of his sweating body. Then, in that moment, everything stopped, as above Rodney's ragged panting, Juliette heard a voice.

"It seems I missed the wedding," it said. "But luckily I'm not too late to witness the newly wedded bliss."

Juliette gasped and felt Rodney leap off her with surprising agility as they both turned to see Brandon standing above them on the sill of the tallest window, his hat at a jaunty angle, his black cape swinging from his wide shoulders.

There was a kindling fire in his eyes that touched her like a brand as white teeth flashed in a smile. "And you, Juliette," Brandon continued, sarcastically indicating her gaping gown. "You are looking lovely."

"Brandon!" Juliette breathed in a hoarse whisper as she drew the torn material together across her breasts.

"But you seem surprised," he said. "I thought surely you were expecting me. Didn't you get my note?"

His tall black boots mirrored the pale light of the room as he stood balanced and alert, like a wolf ready to spring and yet waiting. Then he stepped down from the window to stand beside Rodney who seemed to have grown abruptly sober.

"How dare you, sir!" Rodney began. "You . . ."

"How dare I?" Brandon interrupted. "Indeed, how dare you!"

He gave a scornful perusal of Rodney whose pants were still vulgarly open, although his hardened appendage had wisely retreated out of sight.

"But my business is not with you," he continued dismissing the young man. "I am here strictly to do business with the lady—your wife, so they tell me." And turning from Rodney, Brandon walked to stand hovering over her, seeming the devil himself. Deliberately he bent, picking up the scroll of paper Rodney had thrown at her, unrolling it and quickly reading. Then over the top of the sheet his eyes came back to her, his expression so brutal it made Juliette's back teeth clench with fear.

"Get up!" he snapped. "You're coming with me."

Juliette felt numb, her legs immobile. No, he couldn't be serious, he couldn't be expecting her to go with him—and what had the paper said? She hadn't even looked at it and yet now he would think she had a part in stealing it.

"This is unforgivable," she heard Rodney begin. "You will not take her from this house! I am her husband. I have certain rights. You can't just come in here like this . . ."

But Brandon was ignoring him as he held her gaze in a willful vise of black. "Get up!" he repeated.

"I won't," Juliette answered barely whispering. "I won't go with you. I wish I'd never laid eyes on you . . . I . . ."

A look of disgusted impatience crossed Brandon's face, and reaching down, he captured her wrists together and hauled her up. setting her on her feet like a doll. "I'm not asking your opinion. I am giving you an order. It would be best for you to learn to obey me, *chérie*. People consider it essential where I'm taking you."

Rodney was between them suddenly, a small pistol shaking in his hand. "All right, Phillips! Against the wall before I shoot you where you stand!" But before Juliette could release the strangled protest that lodged in her throat, Brandon had already taken the gun into his own hand.

Rodney leaped after him, pinning the pistol between them. There was a quick struggle as Rodney's hand closed around the gun.

A deafening explosion rocked the room. For a brief silent moment no one moved. Then, slowly, Rodney's head began dropping, his form sliding downward along Brandon's legs to finally lay before the tall man's black boots, a scarlet hole in his chest.

Juliette stared, her arms hanging limp at her sides.

He was dead. Brandon had murdered him! But she was given no time to think. Stepping clear of the body, Brandon came to stand behind her. "Apparently, Madam Keiths," he observed dryly, "you have become a widow."

Chapter 43

Desperately fighting with all her strength, Juliette was hauled through the window, over cypress bushes, and dragged stumbling across the dew-damp lawn to a pair of horses in the shadows of hulking oaks.

"Brandon, stop this . . . you're hurting me! You can't just . . . you can't . . . you've murdered Rodney. My God, Brandon, stop!"

He didn't answer, throwing her onto a gray mare, gagging her, and tying her wrists to her saddle. Then taking her horse's lead rope, he mounted his own stallion.

Her gown was gaping open. A shout came from the direction of the manor. Grabbing a hank of mane in one hand she fell forward on the gray's neck, aware of the ground dappled by a pattern of moonlight and shadow that whirled and melted together beneath the horse's feet as they galloped away.

No, it wasn't possible. He couldn't be kidnapping her!

He was just trying to scare her, it couldn't be true. But the next hours became for Juliette all too horribly real as ahead of her Brandon rode purposefully erect over hills, through gullies, and across streams. He never even glanced back as she was scratched and cut by brambles and thorns. Her long skirt was torn away, piece by piece, revealing her knees and calves. Then she was further scratched and splattered with mud.

Still she clung to her mount, afraid that if she fell, he wouldn't stop but would let her be dragged by her wrists. He was insane, yes, insane! He would welcome some mishap and no doubt was planning to kill her anyway.

They made only one stop, apparently prearranged.

The moon was shining between the branches overhead, and tossing her scattered hair out of her eyes, and sitting up, Juliette saw what appeared to be a common Englishman waiting beside the road with two horses. It was only when the man salaamed that she recognized Brandon's servant Rashid.

As Brandon dismounted an owl took silent wing overhead. Together the two men's shadows merged into one, their conversation low and brief and in Arabic.

Then Brandon came to her, wordlessly untying her hands and dragging her from her horse.

His callous roughness renewed her fury, and with one fist she managed to glance his jaw before his arm surrounded her ribs, abruptly squeezing the air from her lungs and giving her a shake. "Hold still!" But he need not have spoken. At once she hung limp in his grasp, offering no resistance as she was thrown into the saddle of the new horse.

Her wrists were tied as before and she was agonizingly aware that the full length of her thighs, and most of her breasts were plainly displayed now beneath what remained of her gown. Yet he seemed not to notice, or care, as he mounted the other horse and they galloped off again.

They traveled faster now, often out in the open, and the horses' necks were lathered with sweat and steaming by the time the smell of salt air told Juliette they were near the coast.

When they stopped at the edge of a cliff and Juliette looked down, she saw Brandon's yacht far below, bobbing in the swells.

A damp wind blew in gusts, and above her, fierce black storm clouds had gathered. The wind blew faster, harder now, the first large droplets of rain quickly reaching a crescendo in a downpour.

Plucking Juliette from the saddle, Brandon stood her on her feet, removing the gag and untying her wrists before shoving her toward a narrow path down the cliff face.

Lightning flashed overhead, illuminating the ship, the cliff, and Brandon's demonic countenance for a brief instant before thunder rolled. "Walk!" he commanded.

"I won't go!" she screamed, choking against the rain. Then shielding her breasts, she dodged him in a desperate leap and made a dash for the horses.

In a single bound he had her, his hand threatening to crush her upper arm as he flung her round to face him.

"You try that again and I'll drag you down this cliff," he snarled.

Juliette stood panting, her hair dripping in rivulets. It seemed impossible. There was no resemblance between *this* Brandon and the one she had known before. This man was a savage, and, by the cold look in his eyes, was willing to do exactly as he threatened and probably would enjoy it.

Turning, she started down the path which was steep and rough. The rain pelted down harder, transforming the cliffside into mud that slipped from beneath her feet. Twice she fell to her knees and was brutally pulled up again. The third time she heard him growl like a beast.

Lightning flashed and, in that instant, she saw his set and rigid features as he snatched her up roughly and deposited her over his shoulder before continuing down.

Along parts of the path, the footing was extremely rocky and treacherously narrow, and Juliette was torn between the fear that he would stumble and drop her head first down the precipice, and a wish that he would do just that and end it all now.

But his hold didn't slacken, nor did he lose his footing. He stopped only once, wordlessly wrapping her in his black cloak like a mummy before shouldering her again and walking the last hundred yards to a skiff where two Arabs waited at the oars.

With a sure foot laid steadily in the center of the boat, Brandon stepped in and sat down holding her across his lap. She lay still, unable to move, hardly able to breath, and leaning against him, she slept or fainted, she never knew which, since the next thing she knew, she was being hoisted up the side of the ship and pulled on deck.

Then once again she was in his arms, this time carried like a child. The cloak had fallen away so with one eye she saw stairs and wood paneling and bowing Arabs all passing in a blur before there was only a room, dimly lit by the glow of a brass lantern, and the door crashing closed from a kick of his boot.

Juliette had just started struggling again when she felt herself tossed sprawling with a bounce on a large circular divan.

Righting herself, she cringed as he stood above her, one black boot propped on a low table at the edge of the divan, his arms crossed.

He had never seemed so tall, so proud, so utterly furious as he scrutinized her for a long ominous moment.

"So, you have had *your* revenge, *chérie*," he said at last. "But now it is *my* turn."

"What are you going to do?" she whispered huskily.

His charcoal eyes burned into hers as he laughed shortly. "You don't know? Has marriage taught you so little, madame?"

Juliette's eyes blinked wider—eyes that Brandon recalled now had once enchanted him. Now they only reminded him of her father's eyes. Why hadn't he realized the resemblance before?

"Don't touch me! Murderer!" There was sudden panic in Juliette's voice as she crawled as far away as the limits of the divan would allow.

He didn't try to stop her. "It's too late for mercy." His smile was the snarl of a wolf. "Certainly you showed none to me—nor did your father to mine. And you call *me* murderer? I think you're forgetting the facts!"

"You're mad!" she said. "I don't know what you're talking about! I haven't committed any crime. It is you . . . you who . . ."

". . . So you admit nothing! I imagined you wouldn't. You are too clever for that. And you know I can be weak where you are concerned. But I'm afraid this time your charming innocence won't help you."

His fingers reached forward to twine themselves in the cape before tearing it off and slinging it across the floor.

Juliette cried out, frantic hands trying to catch the garment back to herself. But then suddenly she was crouched, naked, his gaze moving slowly over her.

Quickly she drew up her arms to cover her breasts, tucking long legs beneath her and rolling to sit on one side of her slender flanks. She bit her upper lip, one lower tooth gnawing at the corner. I will not beg him, she ordered herself, though she was shaking uncontrollably and felt her courage ebbing.

His eyes drawing up and down her form, Brandon felt his blood pulsing, and didn't bother to slacken the powerful surge and hardening in his groin.

During the month since he had seen her, she had lost none of her appeal. Her added slenderness gave her fine bone structure a feline grace, and the childlike quality that had marked her before had given way to a new womanly sense of maturity. Now with her hair wet, and silver, and falling against her trembling flesh, she was like a primitive wild thing.

How good it was to have her, he thought, to own her, and to make her pay. . . .

"Once I wanted you in *your* 'English' way," he said in a low deadly voice. "But you wouldn't have me—an Arab. So now I will take you . . . in *mine!*"

Then casually, deliberately, his eyes never leaving hers, he removed his clothes, letting them fall on the carpets, and revealing in turn his powerful scarred chest, his arms, hard and heavily corded, his long muscular legs. Then as he removed his last garment, his hardened member sprang into sight.

Taking a quick gulp of air, Juliette pressed herself

against the woven hanging on the wall behind her. She had never seen a man naked, and, while it horrified her, at the same time, she couldn't take her eyes from this engorged manhood.

A jagged flash of lightning came through a window, illuminating him as suddenly he laughed. Then in two long steps, he was on the divan.

It was impossible to evade his arms that immediately dominated her, pulling her beneath him. And even as Juliette squirmed and struggled, she was aware of his firm flesh against her nipples, of the crisp hair of his groin, and of that hot appendage pressing against one thigh.

"Brandon. No. . . ."

But then his mouth stopped her words.

She kept her teeth clenched until with animal fierceness he forced them apart, his hot demanding tongue plundering every inch of her mouth before finding and dominating hers.

She couldn't struggle or think or breathe, and when his mouth eased its pressure on her swollen one he murmured, "I should have done this the first time we met. It would have saved me a lot of trouble."

His fingers intertwined themselves in her hair, forcing her struggling head back and down so the long slender expanse of her throat was exposed. His lips pressed there, and she felt his teeth impress her skin as if tempted to tear out her jugular. Then still holding her head motionless, his mouth continued downward to her heaving breasts.

She tried to twist away as he reached the trembling flesh but it was useless and suddenly he had taken a nipple into his mouth and was sucking, teasing it until it grew enlarged and taut; a quivering prisoner beneath his tongue.

Juliette heard the blood pounding in her ears as he moved to the other breast and bit the already erect nipple before sucking hard. His hand was moving down along her silken belly then, his strength leaving her no choice but to open her legs to his fingers as they searched, found, and opened, the inner lips, slowly circling them before entering into the tight mouth where nothing had ever touched before.

She moaned, her heart thudding with outrage, fear, and now a new tremor of ecstasy as she grew shamefully wet and her loins filled with a strange ache.

His fingers explored the inner rim of the opening then slid further to test the inner softness before slipping out.

Lightning flared from the window, silhouetting him in blue-white light as he suddenly shifted position, placing both his knees between her thighs and parting them helplessly wider.

Juliette felt the thick head of his rod push against her, inserting its fiery heat just inside the opening. She gasped, feeling herself stretched taut around the pulsing of his member as he paused as if to savor his conquest.

Then, as thunder pounded overhead, he rammed forward.

A horrible searing pain shot through her followed by pressure and fullness that threatened to tear her apart.

She screamed, but it was muffled against his chest—struggled, but couldn't move, her body shaking and quivering beneath his as she panted. For a moment she thought she would faint. But then the agony receded and when she lay quiet, beaten, he slid out almost all the way before moving in again, his largeness stretching the inner walls to the deepest length of her.

He moved slowly then in and out, again and again as each time the feeling of pain receded further to be replaced by sensations of a different kind, rippling wonderful feelings that had just begun to churn and grow when his husky voice came in her ear.

"There will be no pleasure in this for you, madame!"

He rode her swiftly then, pounding, until the wild ecstasy that so unexpectedly swept her was interrupted by a sudden inward explosion. His movement slowed then and he pulled out of her immediately to stand up beside the divan, his hands on his hips, his manhood shiny now with the mingling of her wetness and his.

Closing her legs she shrank from him.

"So! You were a virgin," he said. There was surprise and a touch of triumph in his voice.

Her horrified gaze followed his to the wet stickiness

dripping from between her thighs onto the divan. Slowly, staring, Juliette reached a finger to touch the soiled fabric and suddenly realized it was blood.

Of course, she thought numbly. She had heard somewhere virgins bled, but she had never understood exactly what was meant until now.

"You are a heartless bitch," he was saying. "Not only have you cheated me, but your foolish husband, too. We have both been fools to care for you," he finished with a shake of his head that seemed almost sad.

Then retrieving his clothes and quickly pulling them on, he abruptly opened the door and stepped out, banging it behind him before a key clicked the lock closed.

Chapter 44

"Damn him!" Juliette said aloud the next morning when her eyelids snapped open with a start, and brushing back the hair straggling into her face, she rubbed her still tear-swollen eyes.

Yes, she must have slept finally, since now the daylight streamed through the window, revealing a large cabin, luxuriously appointed with silver and black draperies and thick Oriental rugs.

Instinctively she covered her nakedness with a pillow before turning to hastily glance around the room. No, Brandon was not there. The cabin was empty, and through the window beside her, a thick shroud of fog made it impossible to gauge their direction though the ship rolled regularly back and forth beneath her.

Sliding to the end of the divan, and dropping her feet into the deep softness of a sapphire-blue carpet, Juliette went to retrieve the cape Brandon had torn off her the night before and, shivering, wrapped herself in its dark folds. Then walking to a porthole, she twisted the latch, pulling inward, and stood on tiptoe to look out.

The gray-green water splashed high against the hull as the bow sliced through it. The masts creaked overhead, and the smells of salt water, of well-scrubbed decks, and the sharp tang of the wind against her face all seemed familiar from her voyages on the *Whimsy*.

Her head spun. Had they been traveling all night? Where was he taking her and what more would he do?

Unconsciously she touched between her thighs, finding herself caked with blood and semen. No, he hadn't finished with her yet! There would be more of the same, or worse, to follow last night's assault. And knowing this made the air seem suddenly thick and heavy in her lungs.

Squaring her shoulders, she walked to a chair thrown with gold and black spotted pelts and, sinking down, her fingers pressed her throbbing temples, pain coming from every part of her body.

Her wrists, her buttocks, her scratched legs and ankles all ached. What hadn't been bruised in her struggles with Rodney, or during that wild ride across country, had apparently been injured by Brandon last night. Already she was turning black and blue where his fingers had gripped her shoulder.

Devil! Murderer! Liar! Last night had been the final degradation. And yet—she had to admit—it had not been altogether painful. There had been something else. And this morning, even now, she was peripherally aware of a mysterious new feeling. Where he had filled her the night before ached, and yet there was also an awakening of an untried element of her being—a powerful force able to sweep her away until, for a fleeting moment last night, she had forgotten her hatred and terror and pain, and there had been only *him*.

The realization made her quiver and she refused to dwell on it. Again she whisked her thick mane back from her face and a pain shot through her wrist.

"Damn him!" she said rubbing it with the other hand. "I won't be treated this way, like his thing, his *slave*! He wants to dominate me, to make me cower!" Her teeth clenched. "But next time he tries to touch me, he'll have to murder me, too," she swore aloud. "I'll never give in to him. Just wait until he comes again. Then he'll find he hasn't kidnapped a spineless wench, but a serious enemy to be reckoned with!"

Seeming in answer to her thoughts, footsteps came outside the carved Moorish door.

Her heart jumped and, standing up, she pulled the cape closer. But to her surprise, it wasn't Brandon who came through the portal as it widened, but a girl, seemingly her own age, buxom, with skin the color of browned butter, who paused and bowed deeply from the waist, her palms pressed together at her chest as if in prayer.

"Who are you?" Juliette asked.

The girl raised honey-colored eyes. "*Je m'appelle Cassia*," the girl answered in thickly accented French. "Our master has sent me to serve madame."

Juliette's lips compressed. "He is not *my* master!"

Cassia's smile faltered as she noted the dangerous tone in the white woman's voice and the bright fury in her eyes. She opened her mouth to speak, but then closed it again.

Juliette hesitated also. Oh! To be forced to appear a willing guest before this girl was insufferable. Yet what choice did she have? More hysterics would do her no good. Besides, this girl was in Brandon's power—willingly too, or so it seemed by the reverent way she said "master."

Juliette crossed her arms. "He is *not* my master," she repeated for emphasis. "And you . . . you are one of Brandon's . . . I mean, Monsieur Phillips's. . . . You are one of his . . . his harem?" Juliette blurted out before biting her lips at her own artlessness.

She should have remained silent, dignified. But even so, Juliette waited expectantly for the answer.

Surprise crossed Cassia's face before she looked down at the floor. "Oh, no, madame. I am too insignificant to be given that honor. Only ladies of rare beauty are honored so. I was given to my master as a servant, which itself is far too great an honor for one such as I."

Juliette turned to hide her face and strode to the thick-legged table, stopping there and leaning against it. She had been hoping to hear this girl laugh, to say her "master" did not keep a harem. Now there could be no doubt. It was true! He was an Arab, a Moslem. It was all a lie when he said he loved her as none other. But she had hurt his pride, and so he had chosen to hurt her, to degrade her until his anger was expended. And then . . . ? Her heart gave a little thud. How could she predict what he might do with her then?

Cassia looked cautiously at the white lady's back. "Madame is hungry perhaps?" she asked. "She will eat now?"

"Eat?" Juliette echoed the word forlornly. Eat when her world had crumbled around her? Eat as if she were a guest and not a prisoner?

Shaking her head, she turned back to face the girl. "No."

Cassia looked at her as if she had not heard correctly. "No?" she questioned.

"No," Juliette repeated. "I'm not going to eat, and you can tell your master I don't intend to either!"

Juliette could see the girl was trying to hide her surprise. Brandon's female guests were usually more docile, she surmised with a grimace.

"Perhaps then a bath, madame," Cassia asked, as unconsciously her eyes wandered to where the cape parted to reveal Juliette's mud-splattered legs.

Juliette did not have to follow the girl's dubious expression to know that she was filthy, more filthy than she had ever been in her life. Yes, a bath, she thought. How good it would feel to cleanse herself everywhere *he* had touched her. So, even while part of her regretted accepting even this from him, she nodded.

To her surprise, a bathroom which she had not noticed before came into view at the end of the room as Cassia parted a long black drapery. It took only minutes to fill the tub with warm water from a boiler situated above the tub. And when it was done, Juliette needed no urging to strip off the cloak and step into the scented water, letting herself down into a sitting position.

Her acquiescence seemed to please Cassia, who would let her do nothing for herself.

"*S'il vous plaît, madame,*" she said in her sweet childlike voice. "It is my place to serve, and madame's place to be served."

They were words spoken with the gentleness of a kitten

and, Juliette realized, the inflexibility of a rock, and feeling unable or unwilling to fight anymore, Juliette sighed and did lean back, closing her eyes as the girl set about scrubbing every limb with delicately scented soap and a soft sponge.

The balm of the warm water eased her sore stiffness, and for a time, refusing to think anymore, she let herself be pampered. Moments stretched long, and the water had begun to cool by the time she was brought to awareness again by Cassia saying, "If madame wishes, I will wash her hair now."

Juliette leaned forward, letting her hair tumble heavily into the water. The Arab girl poured a liquid from a flagon onto it, carefully working it into every strand before she massaged her scalp with educated fingers that made Juliette's head tingle all over. Then, at last, she was rinsed thoroughly with more warm water and helped to rise before being wrapped in a black towel, undoubtedly one of Brandon's. And after Cassia had dried her, the girl led her back to the divan and, with a bow, indicated for her to sit on it.

Just the sight of the divan made Juliette uneasy again. The two dark spots near its center had seemed to grow larger. Her virgin's blood, she thought. And while someone else may not have noticed them, Juliette saw the stains as if nothing else existed.

She veered away and sat herself instead in the large chair draped with a leopard pelt.

Cassia followed, giving no reaction or comment but, producing an ivory-handled brush and comb, began the task of untangling her blond mane.

It seemed almost hopeless. But Cassia was as gentle as she was relentless, and finally, the long mass once again fell down her back, drying and curling softly in the warmth from the tiled stove.

Setting the brush down, Cassia now unrolled a bundle to reveal an ankle-length white robe with a low scoop neck and wide sleeves. It was cut in a shapeless tube, but seeing the lightness of the silk, Juliette realized it would cling to her every curve.

"But is there nothing else?" she questioned. "What about some of your clothes," she indicated the wide trousers and shapeless cotton top that Cassia wore. "Bring me some of those."

Cassia backed away, shaking her head. "Oh, no, madame. These are for those who serve, not for those who would give pleasure to the master."

"I don't intend to give your master pleasure!" Juliette said with a hiss in her voice.

Cassia stared wide-eyed before dropping her eyes to her own sandaled feet. She had never known a woman like this one—she seemed almost like a man with her defiance and flashing looks. But the master himself had bid her serve this woman, and so it was her duty. Cassia shrugged. All was the will of Allah and determined by fate. And who could tell what secret plan might be unfolding—even now.

"Madame must please forgive me for angering her," she said. "But this gown is all that is suitable."

"Very well, then," Juliette said finally waving a hand with irritation and chewing her lip. What use was it to resist anyway. Damn him! And with that, Juliette let Cassia slip the gown over her head and down her naked body.

"Now madame will rest perhaps," Cassia said softly. "And if she grows hungry, or wishes for something," she lifted the end of a cord by the divan, "pull this and I will come." Then Cassia bowed again, and going to the door, closed it noiselessly as she went out.

Chapter 45

It seemed endless hours had passed before Brandon came, so silently that Juliette, lying sick with anxiety on the divan, had to quickly scramble up to face him, the depths of her round eyes sparkling with fear.

At once she noticed he had changed from the European garb of the night before into white Arabian robes, so now he looked every bit an Arab as he salaamed so gracefully with his long hands that the very gesture was insulting.

"Mademoiselle, or should I say madame." he said pointedly surveying those curves Juliette knew to be distinctly outlined beneath her white silk gown. "It appears you've survived last evening without undue damage."

Boldly she raised her head. "It's no credit to you if I have," she snapped. "What did you expect?—to find me cowed and ready to lick your boots?"

Oh, how she longed to rake his face with her fingernails until he dared not look at her as he was looking now as he said, "No, you are not easily cowed, are you? It would have surprised me if you were. But I did expect that you would want to eat. Self-denial is hardly like you."

"Well, you're wrong! But this has nothing to do with self-denial or a lack of it! Certainly you don't actually expect me to accept this charade—this absurd role as your guest?"

Brandon was looking at her like a person he hardly knew and liked even less as he braced a hand against an overhead beam. "No, I expected you to struggle senselessly. But then you will learn, and that will please me."

"Is that what you think? But it seems to me that under the circumstances I can only imagine it would 'please' you most to watch me starve to death!" Juliette said glaring directly into his black eyes.

Imperceptibly she recoiled then as a slow, wicked smile spread across his features. "*Mon Dieu!* How you underestimate me! I assure you I'm not so blood-thirsty. And I have much more amusing things in mind than watching you starve. In fact, it would 'please' me most for you to eat. I'm sure you are going to need your strength."

Juliette colored at his innuendo and swallowed hard before she said, "But I won't!" curling her lip sarcastically. "I never will do anything to *please* you! And you can't keep me on this ship forever. When we land, and we shall have to eventually, I will escape!"

He came toward her, laughing in a cold humorless fashion that made Juliette fall suddenly weak-kneed as he roughly lifted her chin so their eyes interlocked. "You will escape only if it *pleases* me to let you." His hard gaze roved over her features and then dropped to the thin gown, pausing where two rounded protrusions thrust forward at the centers of her breasts. "And at the moment, it pleases me to have you as you are!"

Juliette wanted to shield herself from his insulting looks, but she would not shrink, and forced herself to meet his eyes squarely when once again he raised them.

For a long moment each measured the other. Then, with a grimace, Juliette wrenched her chin from his grasp, her stare going to the floor.

He turned away, walking to a sideboard and pouring himself a glass of wine, his movements slow and casual as he sipped the rosy liquid.

"Eighteen seventy-two was a particularly good year for French wine, although not for Italian. Do you enjoy wines?"

Juliette raised her head. "Wine?" she repeated wonderingly, and then furiously, "Wine!" She was prepared to fight, to scream, to die if that was what he intended, but not to stand here discussing wine. He was insufferable!

"What a hyprocrite you are," she hissed. "And tell me how is it that you are Arab, and proclaiming to be Moslem even as you defy the precepts of that religion by drinking alcohol?"

He laughed again, and this time there was a new touch of light in his eyes. "So, you aren't so ignorant after all. And you are correct, true Moslems are forbidden wine. But I found when I began traveling in France that it was impossible to seem French without learning to enjoy their wines. Fortunately it hasn't led to my moral downfall," he laughed again, "although you might disagree with that. Now I accept it as one of life's joys, along with fine food." His eyes looked her up and down before he added, "And, of course, women." He toasted her and sipped again, his eyes hardening as he continued. "Cassia tells me you aren't hungry, but you won't mind if I'm served my meal here, will you?"

"I can hardly imagine you care what *I* prefer," she screeched, her self-control slipping. "You mock this intolerable situation. And you should know I *mind* your presence. Eat here if you must, but I won't touch a bite!"

That was her final word. She did not even look at him again but went to the far side of the room and huddled herself in the alcove of the window where the fog had thinned to reveal the moon, half full, and glazed with a hazy golden mist as it rose where sea and sky blended as one.

It was approximately an hour before dinner was served, and her stomach growled incessantly as tantalizing fragrances wafted past her upturned nose. She couldn't resist peeking out of the corner of her eye at the dishes Cassia deftly set on the table before removing the silver cover. She offered each dish to Brandon so he could select whatever he wished before discarding the rest.

"Glutton," she said to herself, seeing how much he seemed to be eating, and determined not to let temptation get the better of her resolve, she turned away further, refusing even to look. But all her stoic display seemed lost on him as the click of china and silverware continued and he appeared absorbed in savoring the contents of each dish. Then, at last, he was finished, and Juliette heard Cassia clearing away the dishes until only the smell of coffee remained. Then Brandon dismissed the maid, leaving them alone again.

Juliette felt her skin flush and then turn to gooseflesh as the power of his presence emanated from behind her. She stiffened as the silence grew and her pulse quickened, reverberating in her head.

Minutes ticked by before, holding her breath, Juliette heard him rise from the table. She waited to feel his fingers encircle her shoulder as an inward tremor rushed through her stomach. But then, to her relief, he didn't come in her direction, but rather toward the bathroom. And in a moment, she heard water tumbling into the brass tub.

Was he going to take a bath? Here? Now? Of course he would. There was no limit to his audacity. So she remained facing away toward the window and discovered that, with the moon now overhead, the glass panes became a mirror backdropped by the black of night and she couldn't help watching him undress and step into the bath.

Her face grew hotter and she dared not move or speak as she could see him looking at her.

Minutes seemed extended to hours, and when his deep voice finally broke the silence, she jumped.

"Come here, *chérie*," he said simply.

Juliette didn't move, but another tingling rush of emotion slid up her spine.

"Come here," he repeated.

Still Juliette remained motionless and erect. She wouldn't go . . . wouldn't do his bidding.

"Damn it!" he swore. "Come when I call you!"

Juliette's breaths grew short as she turned to face him, the cold anger in his eyes gripping hers. "I warn you," he continued, "I'm not above beating you into submission."

Juliette clenched her teeth as venomously she spat, "It would appear that there is nothing you are 'above,' monsieur. Murder, kidnap, rape, they are all nothing to you!"

His eyes became slits. "And you," he said ominously. "Are you giving lessons in sainthood? What are you above, lying, stealing? You may have been a virgin, but don't think that makes any difference. You still have the heart of a whore!"

The last word cracked in the air like a whip. Juliette's breath left her lungs in a rush. "And spare me your indignant looks," he continued. "We have both sought revenge. I had to forfeit the first round. You are an expert in the art of duplicity and clearly made a fool of me. But the second round you have lost. Now it's your turn to suffer the consequences."

"You are insane," she flamed, seeing he was perfectly serious. "I've done nothing but injure your pride, while you . . . you've done murder!"

He was infuriatingly calm as he sat with arms casually stretched along the edges of the tub. "It may interest you to know that it was your beloved husband that pulled the trigger, not I. He succeeded not only in being stupid enough to marry you, but also in killing himself. Anyway, I thought you would be pleased to be rid of him. It appeared your marriage was already beginning to bore you. I think marriage vows wouldn't have prevented a woman like you from pursuing other interests. Perhaps it's better Rodney's dead. There's nothing more ridiculous than a cuckolded husband. And you have a way of making a man a laughingstock."

Juliette opened her mouth to speak, to tell him the truth about Rodney, but in confusion she hesitated when he said, "Now come here!" the warning in his voice worse than an outburst.

Fear rose within her but, determined not to cower, and careful not to lower her gaze below the surface of the water, Juliette advanced to the tub.

She paused near him, but out of reach, and Brandon's mouth curved upward slightly as his eyes measured her with a hint of amusement.

"I have difficulty reaching my back," he said at last, producing a large sponge and holding it toward her. "You will scrub it for me."

Juliette stared at him astonished. "The devil take you!" she said taking a step backward. "I'll not do anything of the kind!"

His smile evaporated. "You will do as I tell you," he said factually.

Blinking back tears, Juliette realized that no matter what she did to the contrary, he could make her do whatever he wanted. It was too much—unendurable! He would have to *make* her then.

"I won't," she said. "You won't make me a slave. White women don't follow the orders of . . . of . . . *half-breds!*"

She spoke with venom that shocked even herself, and the word "half-breed" hung in the air with the violence of a thunderclap.

Still she faced him in the dangerous silence that followed, the sudden opacity of his eyes and tightening around his mouth telling her she had at last penetrated his self-control.

There was a low growl and a splash, and he was out of the tub and beside her, a bronze naked savage. Then in a quick movement, she could not evade, she was in his arms, and just as quickly splashed full-length on her back in the tub and scrambling to get out.

Brandon's fist gathered her robe at the neckline and held her underwater until, sputtering, he raised her face barely above the surface.

"You will learn to obey," he said between closed teeth. "There are ways to teach you." His fist tightened. "And you will begin by calling me 'Master'—in Arabic. Say it now—call me *Sayyid*."

He dunked her again roughly so the water splashed onto the floor. He pulled her out then, his features seeming carved of stone. "Now say it!—*Sayyid*!"

Courage and defiance Juliette had not known she possessed coursed through her. "You can kill me," she said, coughing. "I swear I'll never give in to you. I hate you!"

With a straightening of his arm, the water closed over her eyes and she held her breath. Her determination was strong, but as her oxygen ran out her arms came out of the water to push against him, her legs thrashing.

His hold was as unyielding as a stone pillar. Juliette pushed harder, flinging her arms about, wildly clawing at him, her lungs feeling as if they would burst.

Abruptly the arm slackened, and with her robe still clenched in his fist, Brandon heaved her out of the water, the heaviness of her sodden hair tilting her head backward so her back arched, outlining every detail of her breasts beneath the wet silk.

"*Sayyid*!" Brandon repeated.

Juliette's eyes stung from the soapy water. Her outrage and hatred had taken her beyond fear as she sputtered catching her breath. She would not! She would not give in! It was unthinkable. Better he should kill her. And squeezing her eyes shut, and compressing her lips, she shook her head furiously.

Immediately the arm stiffened and the water closed over her in a blocking out of sound as his hand moved around her throat as if to choke her.

Again her arms struck out, beating his arm, his chest, and scratching at his face. But this time he continued hold-

ing her down until her lungs burned as she sloshed about
the tub, dizzy and disoriented.

Her hands made fists and beat on his arm, but already
her lungs had reached their limit even as, in her mind, the
same words repeated themselves of their own volition. "I
will not! I will not!"

Then even the words faded, her arms suddenly falling
limply in the water at her sides.

Vaguely she felt him pull her out again, and heard him
speak. The words meant nothing to her as her head lolled
backward.

He plunged her under again and everything reeled,
whirling in a kaleidoscope of color that slowly became a
tunnel of black where she was falling . . . falling toward
a diminishing pinpoint of light—which then abruptly vanished.

Chapter 46

A fire crackling; the splashing of water; a regular swaying
back and forth; the smell of wood burning; all, one by one,
nudged their way into Juliette's consciousness before suddenly she remembered.

She was dead. She must be. And her heavy eyelids struggled to open.

The room's incandescent glow was revealed. Above her
the beam ceiling swayed and occasionally creaked. She was
lying back down on the divan, and turning her head, she
saw Brandon across the room.

He was wearing only a pair of tight-fitting suede
breeches, the lantern glow casting a relief of light and
shadow onto his bare torso as he leaned so his hands
pressed flat against a table where a large map was spread.

For a time his countenance concentrated on the map,
eyebrows drawn together over the bridge of his nose. Then,
as she watched, he unbent, instinctively aware, it seemed,
that she was awake as he strode to the divan and stood over
her, bracing an elbow against a low beam overhead, as he

said, "So! You've come around. Are you surprised? Did
you really expect me to let you die so easily?"

In spite of the dry warmth coming from the tile stove, or
the thickness of quilts heaped over her, every muscle of
Juliette's body shivered. She wasn't dead, though she felt at
least half dead and beaten in every bone as she watched
him shake his head and continue.

"No, madame, my plan isn't for you to die. And I've had
enough of your foolish games. It is time to eat something."

Juliette did her best to glare at him, though the practical
side of her mind was saying, "What difference will it make
to eat? You can't fight if you starve yourself."

The smell of food tantalized her nose, as Cassia suddenly
appeared from somewhere, her doe eyes filled with worry
as she set a tray of silver plates on a nearby table.

Juliette hoped the girl would stay, wanting the protective
presence of another nearby, and her heart sank when
Brandon's voice dismissed Cassia and they were alone
again.

"So you're sorry to see her go." His expression was almost amused. "Did you think she would interfere with anything I chose to do?"

Coming close, he slipped a strong arm behind her, lifting
her into a sitting position against propped up pillows. Then
he set the tray in front of her. "Now eat," he commanded.

With a feeling of fathomless weariness, Juliette noticed
the *poulet à l'orange* was precisely cooked and attractively
served with a garnish and glazed carrots. Brandon remained beside her seeming ready to force the food down
her throat if he saw any sign of flagging. So she picked up
a fork and began, moving it mechanically from plate to
mouth and back again in an even cadence until the portion
was finished. Then pulling the quilt higher under her chin,
she leaned back heavily against the cushions in sheer exhaustion and looked toward the wall.

Against his will Brandon's half-hooded eyes roved over
her pale face and slender limbs outlined beneath the quilt.
What kind of woman was this? Most men would not have
the courage or tenacity to fight in the face of such over-
whelming odds. And yet, this woman, hardly more than a

girl, was prepared to die if necessary rather than to give in, even as a pretense. How complicated she was and how full of contrasts. All at once she was as fragile as a flower, as lovely as an angel, and yet she possessed a heart of ice. And still, with her blond hair fanning in a halo around her face, she seemed like some fair waif. He shook his head. What a trick fate had played, crossing his stars with this most desirable and treacherous of women, this one woman who had moved him as none other of her sex.

"What a pitiful looking creature you are," he said at last.

The nourishment had renewed Juliette's energy and, in spite of her fatigue, she felt a sense of returning fury rumbling inside her like inner thunder. Her eyes glared open to find him still watching her with infuriating calm, so much the *master*. Again she imagined clawing his face.

"And how else could I look after all you've done?" she asked. "And if I were a man, Monsieur Phillips, or whatever you call yourself, you would not be smirking so!"

His face did not change. "So, even that dousing hasn't cooled your hot head. And let me assure you, if you *were* a man I would already have killed you. No man lies to me and lives."

"I lie? You dare accuse me?" Juliette countered sitting up in spite of her dizziness and throbbing head, and clutching the quilt tight around her. "*You* lied, didn't you? At least you didn't tell the truth. You with your mistress—and you knew I didn't realize you were an Arab. How could you be so . . . so *deceitful!* You had no right to say what you said . . . to make me feel that . . ." She dropped back, bracing herself on one elbow, fighting to control the tears springing in her eyes, ". . . to hurt me like that."

Brandon pulled his attention from those soft curves beneath the quilt, attempting instead to concentrate on her crimes. Still he couldn't deny the awakening in his loins. How she sapped his resolve, he thought. Her beauty was like a curse that set him against himself and, realizing his own weakness, angered him.

"So now you accuse me of hurting you, is that it? Do you expect me to believe that? I'm no English prig like your Rodney. This isn't the first of your kind I've known.

But I must congratulate you. Your true nature is well concealed. Just don't expect to fool me twice."

Juliette's overly bright eyes stared at him as she threw her head back challengingly. "And you think you can judge me! You pretend such dignity, such *honor* when it is obvious, monsieur, you have none!"

There was a pause as they faced each other. What had happened? Juliette asked herself. Could this be the same man who once had made such tender love to her, who had called her his fragrant rose of beauty, who had made her want him?·A pain pierced her pounding heart like a red-hot knife.

"Honor? You dare talk to *me* of honor?" Now Brandon's voice was ominously quiet as he stepped closer, his fierce look penetrating.

Juliette tilted her head higher. They were only inches apart, so close Juliette saw his eyes were not completely black, but ringed with gray. Eyes that had once been so different, shining with a wonderful light. Oh, what difference did that make now, she thought, that or anything. Her voice was low as his, "Go ahead. I don't care what you do. Blood? Is that what you savages need?" she asked, imagining him crushing the life from her with his bare hands. "Kill me then!" she finished with a sneer.

Brandon's hands reached to encircle her neck so his thumbs stroked where it pulsed.

Juliette neither cringed nor cried out, but squeezed her eyes shut and, unaware of the single tear running down her cheek, waited.

But moments lengthened, and when she looked at him again, his expression held a strange spark. "You have the most irreverent tongue I've ever heard. Arabs cut out the tongues of women like you. But I'm not going to kill you, *chérie,* not now."

Juliette grimaced and, knocking his hands away, withdrew further back on the divan. But he was coming nearer, grasping the quilt and wrenching it out of her hands.

Crouching in an attempt to cover herself, Juliette screeched, "I hate you!" before edging further into the corner of the divan.

Still he came, leaning forward to capture a wrist in each hand before spreading open her arms like the wings of a bird. Juliette, unable to meet his gaze, looked away with a low moan.

"I don't need to kill you," Brandon was saying, his voice containing a husky note. "My revenge is sweeter to have you like this."

Juliette did not speak, but her huge luminous eyes stared at the divan's satin surface as it blurred and swam through tears.

"It would be better," he continued, "if we could begin by being honest. I could respect you if you were. But this masquerade is absurd and insulting to both of us. I wanted revenge and so did you. Admit what you have done and everything will be easier."

Juliette shook her head weakly, squeezing her eyes shut against the tears that rained onto her knees. "What do you expect me to say? I've told you before. I never wanted to marry anyone. I wanted to have the right to my own choices. I thought *you* of all people would understand people wanting to dictate their own lives."

"Damn!" he swore as the grip on her wrists tightened until she winced. "You will not lie to me! Do you expect me to believe you? Yes, I suppose you do. But then explain to me why you took Rodney Keiths as a husband no longer than a month after you swore to me you would never marry anyone—and what were you doing with a document stolen from my possession, an order for guns to be sold to my enemies?"

Juliette tried to squirm away. "I don't know anything about that document. I never saw it before until Rodney showed it to me. And it's all your fault I married him. I only did it because you sent me that horrible note. It was to get away from you! And Rodney said . . ." She stopped short then, biting her lip. She hadn't wanted to give Brandon the satisfaction of knowing she hadn't loved Rodney.

Brandon's hold slackened only slightly. "And I suppose you deny knowing my name, Karim al-Sharif," he said watching her with steady concentration. But there was only a look of confusion on her face as she repeated the name.

"Karim al-Sharif?" Her eyes unfocused. Karim al-Sharif—yes, she remembered Rodney called him that and the name did strike some other familiar chord though she couldn't place it. A wall thick with years stood in her way, leaving her memory blank.

"Don't look so innocent!" His fingers dug painfully into her shoulders, shaking her as he demanded, "Do you deny it?"

Juliette gasped from the bruising pain. "I . . . I don't know!" she was trying to remember what the name meant to her and realizing it was somehow the key to this elusive puzzle in which she was uncomprehendingly playing a role. "Rodney did call you that. And I think . . ." she paused, but try as she might, her thoughts remained jumbled. She felt at any moment she would remember. It was so close, and yet the catalyst floated just out of reach of her grasping mind.

"Bah!" he said at last holding her at arm's length, his frown deepening to a heavy scowl as bright hawk eyes probed the depths of hers. "I want the truth, Juliette!" He gave her another shake that snapped her neck like a whip. "Do you deny it? Do you deny knowing who I am?"

"No . . . I mean yes! I do deny it!" Juliette finally wailed, wanting only to escape the sinewy fingers that crushed her shoulders. "Why is it so important that I do or don't know your name? It was enough to find out you were an Arab, and to realize there could never be any . . . anything between us."

Humiliated, frightened, all understanding drowned in confusion, Juliette stifled a sob as tears cascaded onto burning cheeks. Oh, what was the use!

The pressure of his fingers relaxed now as he appeared to consider her. His face darkened, his jaw twitched dangerously. A meaningless syllable ejaculated from his lips as he flung her, belly down, and stepped off the divan to stand towering over her for a long moment. Then, grabbing a heavy cape and stepping out the door, he gave her a last look of disgust before closing it with a resounding bang.

Chapter 47

Brandon did not come again, nor did Cassia, and the next morning when Juliette awakened from a troubled sleep and looked out the porthole, she saw dark clouds covering the sky from horizon to horizon, blotting out the sun.

The wind was stiff. A storm, she thought, closing the porthole and going to the stove to warm her hands. Already the ship's cradlelike sway had given way to bucks and bobs, and in another fifteen minutes, Juliette was forced to balance herself against table and chairs when she moved about the cabin.

By midday, the first rain began, gathering momentum until it was an unbroken sheet of water.

Another hour passed and the ship tossed like a tiny cork as the storm increased. Overhead the beams creaked and popped in a chorus of agonized cries as the swelling sea became endless mountains of gray that rolled in smooth slides.

The cabin lurched with each roll, and after being thrown off the divan, Juliette stumbled to the Persian carpet in front of the stove, and gathering woven cushions beneath her, huddled before the warmth.

Through the window lightning flashed. From the decks above came the muffled shouts of the crew as the rain pelted furiously.

Day passed into night, and the gale worsened until Juliette, still bundled as near to the stove as she could squeeze, put her hands to her ears, blocking out the terrible moans of the ship and praying it wouldn't shatter to pieces. She had thought that Brandon would kill her. Never had she considered dying like this, sinking to the sea's fathomless depths, the fare of crabs and sharks.

By midnight the stove's fuel ran out, and ravenous with hunger and numb with increasing cold, Juliette was tossed about in complete darkness, unable to see even her hand before her face as everything pitched chaotically, making her dizzy, disoriented, and nauseated until she lay down full-length on the carpet, her fingernails clenching its softness to keep herself from sliding across the deck.

It was nearly dawn before the wind stopped howling, the masts began to creak less, and the ship's wild plunging resumed a less violent rhythm. Curling into a ball among the cushions, Juliette fell asleep at last.

Hours passed then and she knew instinctively that it was much later when she became aware, first of the gentle rocking of the ship, and then of a brightness that reached the insides of her closed eyelids.

Juliette stirred, absently flinging back the quilt and turning onto her back before rising on one elbow.

Automatically her eyes blinked against the morning light—sunlight, and she brought a palm to her forehead.

Had the ship been sinking or had she dreamed it? Outside there were shouts and, getting up and pushing her hair back, she walked to the porthole and twisted open its fastening.

Outside a flock of seagulls was following at the stern, screeching, flapping, and diving into whitecaps as hungrily they fought over fish cast out by the crew.

Puzzled, Juliette listened to the rapid Arabic spoken by the men who were conversing excitedly. Then, in a flash of understanding, she realized the full implications of the birds. Gulls didn't live in the ocean, but on land. And not bothering to relatch the porthole, Juliette ran to the one overlooking the bow.

Not more than a mile away there were yellow and green hills crowding close upon a buff strand of beach. Directly above it thunderheads hung suspended against the blue sky, and as they sailed closer, Juliette could make out the rolling surf tumbling up the naked sand in licking tongues of pearly foam, a dock, and bay cliffs, topped with the great walls of a ruined fortress.

Had the storm blown them off-course? Where were they? Juliette could hardly bear to think. "I'm not afraid," she told herself firmly. "Now that we've reached land, I'll have an opportunity to escape. There must be a way . . .

I'll make one! And once I'm free," she concluded, raising her chin and pausing, not sure what to add, "then I'll contact the British consul and seek protection from him," she finished.

She leaned closer to the window, watching the beach loom larger. A flurry of small boats was being rowed toward the *Black Hawk* by grinning boys in faded turbans.

Cheerfully they called to the crew and the smaller boats flanked the larger one as they swept into the harbor, gliding more slowly now that the sails were lowered. Then, carefully, the *Black Hawk* was maneuvered alongside the dock.

From her vantage point, Juliette could see a myriad of children skittering and shouting along the pier and pausing with others to stare at the impressive craft, until a crowd formed.

The people wearing white robes or shirts and pants shortened to knee-length appeared to Juliette to be men. But there were others, clothed from the tops of their heads to their dark-sandaled feet in black shapeless garments with hoods that covered their faces so they looked like priests, or possibly children masquerading as ghosts.

Juliette studied them as they converged into a group directly across from her porthole, and noticing now that several of them were slung with babies, Juliette realized they must be women.

Indeed, their robes were ridiculously modest, more so than any nun, Juliette thought. And wondering why women would wear such confining clothes in so hot a climate, Juliette listened to their high-pitched singsong voices as they gestured and pointed, obviously excited by the *Black Hawk*'s arrival. The only word that Julliette could understand was "sheik, sheik," which was repeated over and over.

Nearby a number of small boats, curved up at both bow and stern in the shape of crescent moons, were anchored about the sunlit water. Each had a tall single mast and another support at a right angle to the mast that held a colorful canvas and acted as the boatman's tent. From under these awnings, happy, curious faces peered, the occupants fanning braziers that spiced the air with frying fish.

"Tripoli—a charming sight, isn't it, *chérie*," a voice said behind her, making her jump and whirl round in one motion.

It was Brandon, impeccably groomed, freshly shaven, and wearing robes and turban of black so he looked more sinister than ever.

Juliette clutched the quilt tightly about herself as she watched him scan the room, pausing at the pile of pillows by the stove where the curl of her body was still imprinted. Then he turned back to her, holding out a bundle.

"Take this," he said shortly, "and put it on."

She glowered at him, stepping backward and tossing her head. "I want nothing from you."

He laughed softly. "It is not a gift, *chérie*. It is a necessity where I am taking you. I doubt if you'd prefer parading past my men in that." He indicated her silk gown. "Now put this on. We're leaving immediately."

"Leaving? Where?"

"We are to be the guests of the Arab governor of Tripoli."

"But that's absurd!"

"Your opinion is immaterial."

"Indeed? And what does the governor think of kidnapping? Don't think I won't tell him. I'll see you punished for what you've done. And if he isn't prepared to help me, I'll find someone else who will!"

Brandon smiled with only one side of his mouth, as if her threats were those of a child. "You may tell whomever you please, although I doubt if you'll see the governor. We Arabs are more possessive than you're accustomed to. It is not customary for one man to see the women of another, so you will be kept out of sight in a harem, where you can amuse the other women with your tales to your heart's content. Now put this on," he finished, holding the dark bundle toward her again. "I'm in no mood today for your shrewishness."

Juliette stood as if frozen to the floor. "A harem," she repeated.

Purposely Brandon misunderstood her. "Yes, you'll be quite safe. You will stay there until we are ready to travel. And, of course when we reach our destination, you will live in my own harem." He watched the frantic disbelief rise in her eyes. "Hadn't you expected it?" His eyebrows raised sarcastically. "I thought you were informed about Arab customs."

Juliette stared at him, her mouth slack. She prayed he was joking, but at the same time, knew he was not. And now, no longer waiting for her to take the bundle, he unrolled it himself and held it up to her.

Juliette's eyes passed from his face to the garment, seeing, to her horror, that it was none other than a replica of the black shapeless dresses she had seen the women on the pier wearing.

"You can't be expecting me to wear . . . to wear *that*! You can't be serious. I'll suffocate . . . I'll be blinded . . . like a walking mummy!"

"I told you before," came the answer. "I expect you to do what pleases me." His eyes were hard as he continued. "It would have been quite different if you had married me. But as it is, you are just another servant of my household. And here, my will passes for law."

"Really," Juliette said. "And what did you do to make your other women do your bidding . . . beat them . . . torture them?"

She wanted to strike him when he only chuckled. "I was not speaking of 'women,' *chérie*. All other women have been eager to please me—eager to give themselves. It is only you who have been so reluctant. But you will change. And if you don't, there is plenty of time to decide what to do with you."

Juliette knew he meant what he said. If she didn't wear the robe, if she didn't go peaceably, in a word, if she didn't *obey*, she would be forced, humiliated in front of all those curious brown eyes that pressed ever tighter around the yacht.

Her position was untenable, and he knew it. So she didn't protest further when Brandon dropped the dark stifling robe over her head, allowing it to fall to her heels before bringing up the hood and fastening it.

Surprisingly the garment was not uncomfortable and she could see through the fine mesh over her eyes better than she guessed, though she still felt degraded to be treated in this way, to have no choices whatsoever—to *belong* to him.

Now his hands were on her shoulders, drawing her close. She looked up.

"'This robe offers you protection that should be welcome," he said. "But as usual you are thinking only of your own wants and can't grasp the obvious."

"Protection!" Juliette burst out. "How can you speak of protecting me!"

But he didn't seem to hear. "Once we reach the governor's palace and his women see you, rumors will spread concerning your white skin and blond hair and the color of your eyes. Here a woman's worth is measured by such things, and your coloring is rare among these people. I will not always be with you, and my men here are few. There will be many eager to taste your charms, or to sell you to others for the same purpose." He paused and his eyes narrowed seeming to measure her as she stared back, mute, her lips rebelliously compressed.

He gave her a single shake. "Are you really so foolish, madam? This is not England, and Arabs see things quite differently. Here you are a profitable piece of merchandise. Do you understand? Women are stolen here, imprisoned and sold over and over to an endless stream of men— old men—sick men—diseased men."

At his words, Juliette's eyes lost some of their defiance. He held her at arm's length. "Do I shock you? Yes, I see that I do. But I know how stubborn you are. You've made no secret that you want to escape. But think well, Juliette, before you employ any of the clever plans that I'm sure are in your mind. You call me villain, but you have led a sheltered life. There are many far, far, worse than I."

Chapter 48

Sometime later it was Cassia who conducted Juliette above decks and down the railed gangway to where four men waited beside a sedan chair.

Through the mesh of her hood, Juliette noticed these men were as rounded and muscular as wrestlers.

As they reached the sedan chair the men's eyes lowered. They salaamed profusely, then politely ignored both Juliette and Cassia as the servant lifted the silk curtain draping the entrance of the vehicle. "Madame will please seat herself," Cassia requested in a firm tone that suggested she had been warned to expect resistance.

Juliette would have refused if she could see any advantage in balking, but there was none. So mounting the three carved steps, she climbed inside the conveyance and sat herself on the small brocade-covered couch.

Through the haze of fluttering silk curtains, Juliette saw the men reach for the platform's long poles. It swayed under her as they lifted, and finally, shouldered it.

A small Arab boy took the lead, holding a pot of incense that drifted toward her in a soft curl of smoke. Then, stepping in unison, her bearers moved onto a path that gradually wound up the hill ahead like a sandy serpent.

Making a narrow part in the silk draperies, Juliette watched everything pass by. There were houses, or rather, shacks, with a few scrawny chickens pecking the ground outside and strings of fish drying on lines.

The children, who were playing together in a large gang, wore pitifully dirty clothes and their smudged faces stared curiously at the men and the sedan chair, and craned to get a glance of her.

Further along, the path widened so to accommodate two sedan chairs traveling abreast. Here there were whitewashed buildings and, on the hill's summit, substantial residences appeared, surrounded by more whitewashed walls and overhanging palms and wild rose vines.

Against these walls, turbaned men leaned and dozed while more children darted about, playing tag among the carts now congesting the wider street.

In another kilometer, they came to a marketplace, which was a hubbub of high-pitched voices and twanging music and the bleats and brays of small herds of goats and sheep.

Shops and small stalls lined the streets shaded by posted awnings and from beyond a particular dark doorway came the sounds of flutes and tambourines and the provocative beat of a drum.

The atmosphere grew dusty from the stir of traffic, and the air rang with cries of merchants hawking their goods. Peddlers on foot were moving up and down the street carrying their own less bulky merchandise of threads and incense, and Juliette heard a huge red parrot call out loudly in Arabic as she passed.

It seemed almost like some biblical street, she thought, camels, swarms of goats, and nameless dogs all milling about. There was a smell of fried fish and rotting vegetables and drying camel hide that seemed an incongruent atmosphere for the rich silver and jade and pearls that appeared in the booths and shops along the twisting tangle of streets.

The street narrowed again and divided into a maze of portable booths. The dust and hurry and shouting voices all combined in a cacophonous din, and after some minutes, Juliette was surprised when the sound of voices slowed and quieted as, inexplicably, everyone on the street paused and one by one began taking up a chant, *"La Ilaha Illa Allah— La Ilaha Illa Allah,"* syllables repeated rhythmically, over and over and even her bearers stopped, moved to the side of the road, and set down the sedan chair before joining the others, all kneeling to face the same direction.

Fascinated, Juliette peered from between her parted curtains. She had heard that Arabs were religious, but she was not prepared for this overt show of devotion, this kneeling and abject supplication that continued for several minutes, the devotees all chanting in unison and bending to touch their foreheads to the ground, then rising erect again, and repeating this several times, until it was apparently over.

Then they all rose to their feet, brushing dust from their robes and continuing their business just as before.

The bearers came forward then, assuming their former places, and they were reaching for the rails of the platform when a sudden shout drew their attention up the street.

A charging mule, eyes wild, ears laid back, came squealing between the booths. The crowd quickly scattered in its path as it raced through the marketplace. A man came in pursuit, his torn robe dragging as he shouted a flurry of Arabic after the beast.

Undaunted, the mule dashed forward, upturning booths so that angry merchants raised their arms to the sky as if imploring their God to witness their ill fortune.

Twice the mule was surrounded, but each time it eluded its would-be captors. It seemed to delight in making fools of everyone—quickly lashing out with hind hooves whenever any man came close enough to grab its tattered halter.

The bearers stood in a row between her and the defiant animal, watching the chaos as some of the growing crowd tried to help subdue the destructive creature.

Looking past the spectacle, Juliette suddenly covered her mouth to prevent a cry of surprise from escaping as, down a side street, she spotted an Englishman. Yes, certainly he must be English, she told herself, since he didn't wear robes, but a white drill suit and sun hat, and he was flourishing a walking stick in that certain familiar way, apparently unconcerned about the fray to his back.

Juliette could hardly keep herself from shouting to him and, checking to make sure her bearers were distracted, she realized that, even before she had expected it, a chance for escape had come. Then carefully, and for the first time grateful for the disguising robe, she picked up the hem and noiselessly slipped out of the sedan chair, glancing to see the bearers were still facing away before resuming a normal gait down the street.

Her heart was pounding and keeping her head lowered, Juliette made her way along the street and around a bend until she was out of their sight before picking her robe up to ankle height and speeding after the white-clothed figure already disappearing around a distant corner.

"Dear child!" the gentleman said as Juliette dashed to his side, grabbing his sleeve and bursting out in a garbled version of her circumstances before imploring him to save her.

"But we must get you indoors at once before your guard misses you. Merciful heavens! What might have happened to you if I had not been passing by? Here, follow behind me as the Arab women do. And keep your head down!"

The man started off again and, with her heart racing and her hands shaking, Juliette followed him past beggars and children until they reached a narrow door in a white-washed wall that opened by pulling a black ring hanging in its splintered center. Beyond this door was a narrow flight of stairs terminating at yet another door which the man opened, this time with a single large key.

Stepping inside, Juliette found a casual combination of east and west, with a large British flag on one wall, and pillows and Arabic hassocks arranged on a single rug around a low brass table.

Juliette's head whirled. Had anyone seen her? Could it really be this easy? But yes, yes it was! And with a spasm through her chest she thought, I have escaped! She smiled as she imagined Brandon's anger when he found out. Oh, he would be furious. And it served him right!

The Englishman showed her around his rooms, a sitting room, a primitive bathroom, but a bathroom just the same, a myriad of small bedrooms occupied with young boys—orphans, he informed her, and a dining room.

"But this is wonderful," he said. "A real English lady—and in this house. How lucky I am to find you. Do you know how long it's been since I've heard the voice of an English lady? And you must meet Billy. He is my business associate and partner. And how lucky you are, my dear! Have you any idea what might have happened if you had been captured by one of these Arabs? Do you realize a runaway slave is punished by . . ." He paused, grimacing then and waving a hand as if to wipe out the unpleasant thought. "But never mind that! It's foolish to scare you when you are safe now. I'll invite Billy for dinner. I must

send a runner immediately. He would never forgive me if I
failed to introduce you."

"Dinner?" interrupted Juliette. "But I must go—
immediately, if possible. There are guards, and they will
certainly be searching for me. And if they find me. . . ."

"Ah, my dear lady. Please don't upset yourself," said the
Englishman smiling as if her fear were childish. "Long ago
I . . . uh . . . shall we say, made *arrangements* with
everyone living nearby. As far as they know, I don't exist.
You are perfectly safe, at least as safe as anyone can hope
to be among these devils. What harm can come from enjoying yourself? And anyway, I'll hear nothing to the contrary. It has been too long since either poor Billy or I have
even seen an Englishwoman, let alone spoken to one. Oh!
And do take that horrid hood off. I think of all Arab inventions, these robes their women wear are the most barbaric—don't you agree? They are all so jealous, you know,
so possessive. And isn't beauty something to be enjoyed, not
hidden away?" He smiled with delight and turned to a
young Arab boy who had just brought in a tray holding a
pot of tea. Then with evident enthusiasm, he poured them
both a cup, holding hers toward her.

"Now, you must sit down over . . ."

The Englishman had returned his gaze to Juliette, who,
taking his suggestion, had removed the hood, and stood before him flushed, her blond hair falling around her shoulders.

His hands wavered as they tilted the saucer, nearly dropping it before he recovered. He licked his lips. "But my
heavens," he said at last. "I haven't introduced myself." He
bowed. "I am Henry Farthington."

That night became a celebration, and Juliette found
Henry's friend Billy to be about her age, shy and with-
drawn until fortified with a generous portion of wine.
Henry had sent a servant to see about arranging passage
for Juliette on one of the ships leaving port the next day.
The three laughed and talked as they awaited the man's

return and Juliette felt her tensions ebbing with each glass of wine.

Finally the servant returned and Henry conferred with him in low tones before rejoining Juliette and Billy with an enthusiastic smile.

"It's done! It's done!" he announced beaming. "You're good as home right now! I have your passage on a ship sailing early in the morning from here to Spain. And once there, you can book yourself onto a ship sailing straight for England!"

"Then why don't you come, too?" Juliette urged him, seeing his enthusiasm. But he looked away, his smile fading.

"I have a business here to run," he said. "And anyway, it's useless to go back where no one wants you. Family problems, you see. But what does a young girl like you know of such things?" he finished looking into his empty teacup.

Juliette glanced up at the older man, hearing her own heart somehow expressed in his almost bitter tone. She nodded sadly. "I do understand, Henry," she said softly. "Most sincerely I do."

"Both of you are going to so much trouble and endangering yourselves for me," she continued. "How can I ever repay what you are doing?" And coming forward, she gave them each a kiss on the cheek and thought of the huge reward she would give both men when she was back in England.

Both men looked uncomfortable. Henry cleared his throat and gave Billy a piercing look and, coughing, Billy stared at his plate. But then conversation resumed again with more questions about England, and after a time they were exchanging stories and all laughing. But the carefree air had flown and by midnight had been replaced by tense silence. The darkness of the apartment was broken only by a tiny flickering candle as Billy and Juliette took up opposite ends of the table, both watching Henry, who paced smoking endless cigars, the lines around his mouth deepening.

What a terrible risk they were taking, Juliette thought. What if *he* found out? Had he posted a reward for her return, or sent messengers about the city? But now was no time to ask as the ticking of the large English clock became the only sound.

It seemed hours had passed before a knock came at the door. Immediately they were all on their feet and, putting her hood in place, Juliette followed the men down the stairs and into the star-speckled night.

The hour was late, and the streets deserted except for shadows' that darted from the alcoves and side streets and back again, and eyes that peered from niches and stairways. And moving quickly along, Juliette kept in mind Henry's assurances that they were only stray cats and dogs.

The streets were covered by thick dust, and twisted and turned until she lost all sense of direction and the smell of camel dung and urine grew stronger. Then, after walking further than Juliette could ever remember walking before, they finally turned off onto a side street and wound narrowly up an incline terminating in heaped garbage which rustled loudly as rats scattered at their approach.

Only the flame of a single candle flickered within a rag-shrouded window a short distance up the hill and Juliette bit her lip uncertainly as Henry began leading them directly toward it.

Weren't they supposed to be going to the harbor? She clasped her hands together to keep them from shaking. She looked both left and right over her shoulder. Yesterday, feeling safe, she had taken a moment to delight in imagining Brandon's reaction when he found she had escaped. *Then* she had savored the thought of his frustration and anger. But now, vulnerable again, the memory of those devilish black eyes was a different matter. He had raped her for denying him, nearly drowned her for insulting him. No doubt his guards were searching for her. And what might he do if he found her now?

Pressing her palm against her fluttering stomach, Juliette glanced at Henry and Billy who seemed tense as she. Certainly they must be taking all possible precautions, she thought, and not wanting to increase their burden by asking foolish questions, she remained silent.

The darkness obscured the details of the house as they reached a wooden door which Henry opened and held for her.

The room was small and, in the dim light, Juliette could see the walls were mud blocks, chipped and ragged, and dirty palm mats covered the floor. The air was dank with the smell of unwashed bodies and a sweet musky odor and, though she could see no one, Juliette sensed the presence of others.

Reaching for Henry, she touched his sleeve. "I thought we were going straight to the ship," she whispered, her eyes expanding as they swept the shadowed walls. "Why have we come here?"

Fondly, Henry patted the hand that clung to his arm. "I'm picking up two additional crew members," he said. "It's part of the captain's conditions for letting you aboard."

"Oh," Juliette said, although the squalor made her uneasy and the smells a little nauseated.

"It seems the men we're expecting haven't arrived yet," Henry continued. "It may be a wait of an hour or more. These Arabs aren't exact about time. You'll need a place to rest. It's still a long walk to the ship." And turning, he spoke in low Arabic to the darkness.

Like magic, a face melted from the shadows into the candlelight. It was a coldly emotionless face, a man's, with a scar running the length of his cheek and across one eye so it squinted half-closed.

The man answered and Henry appeared to thank him. Then Juliette felt the Englishman's sure hand in the middle of her back propelling her forward.

"But I don't want to leave you," Juliette whispered as they moved along a hall.

"Nonsense. You'll be perfectly safe here. Safer in fact, since we won't risk anyone seeing you."

He was right, of course, Juliette reasoned. This was a sailor's den of some kind, frequented by many, and someone might spot her and ruin everything. She nodded, a movement she soon began to regret as they neared a door at the end of a short hall. Beyond the illuminated ring of Henry's candle there was a scuffling and a squeak, which Juliette assured herself was not a rat.

A small push against the door revealed a small room, a narrow bed, and a single stool in the middle of a straw-strewn floor.

Henry held the candle high and sighed with disappointment. "Well," he said, "these are hardly accommodations for a lady, but they will have to do. I'm sorry better arrangements weren't made, but at least you won't take a chance of being seen here, I can assure you of that."

Glancing around the cubicle, Juliette forced herself to smile good-naturedly even as a shiver crept up her spine. "I suppose it is the best there is to offer," she said. "Anyway, now is not the time to concern oneself with luxury." So taking the candle from Henry, she used its flame to light another candle stub that sat in a broken pottery bowl before sitting on the stool.

Too quickly, it seemed, Henry turned back toward the door. And perhaps it was the look he gave her now—the unreadable expression that crossed his face and made him seem a stranger. But, when he stepped out, closing the door soundly behind him, suddenly everything seemed wrong, terribly wrong, and ugly suspicions came to mind that proved immediately correct when Juliette shouted Henry's name and the door didn't spring open.

She ran to the door, pulling the leather thong that served as a handle until it broke off in her hand. Then she was beating it with her fists and screaming, "Henry! Henry! Let me out!"

The sound of his footsteps was diminishing up the stairs before fading away to leave everything horribly quiet but for the occasional rustling of unknown creatures in the dark corners as the small candle sputtered suddenly and then went out like the last ray of trust in her heart.

Her teeth clenched and her temples pounded. No, Henry couldn't do this. No . . . not to me! With frantic hands she battered the door, screaming again, "Henry, Henry," until her arms were numb and her fists bleeding. Her voice rasped with tears. It was no use, she was trapped and betrayed. The hopeless pain of her rage made her stomach cramp until she fell against the rough surface of the door. Then sliding downward she lay sobbing against the straw.

PART VIII

SLAVE GIRL

Chapter 49

That night Juliette spent alternating between fits of rage and terrified weeping, and the next morning when the sun came up even hotter than the day before and the straw on the floor began to reek with filth, she beat her scabbed fists against the splintered door calling, "Henry, Henry Farthington! Let me out!"

She was hardly aware of the pain, and only able to think that he couldn't leave her like this. It was a matter of money—that was all. Oh, why hadn't she told him before she was wealthy? She would pay whatever they asked. If only they would give her a chance to explain!

It must have been near noon when she next heard several sets of footsteps coming down the stairs and, with her breath catching in her throat, Juliette backed away from the door as it was flung open and four Arabs filled the small room.

Immediately Juliette recognized the scar-faced Arab from the night before. With him were two burly guards with short black whips coiled in their meaty fists and also a richly robed man, taller than the others, who eyed her appraisingly.

Backing away until the wall stopped her, Juliette pressed her palms against its crumbling brick.

Already the rich man's eyes were pleased. He nodded to the scar-faced Arab, who spoke a few words in rapid dialect, so that the two guards came toward her, lusty grins spreading slowly over their broad faces.

Juliette blanched, evading them with a leap toward the opposite wall where she clung until, just as quickly, the guards cornered her, each of them capturing one of her arms and dragging her back to the center of the room as easily as if she were one of the straws on the floor.

Still she struggled between them. "Stop this! Let me go! If it's money . . . money you want, you'll have it," she panted. "Just release me and I'll give you whatever amount you demand!"

She did stop fighting then as she looked from the scarfaced Arab to the wealthy one, waiting for a look of interest but seeing only surprise and annoyance.

She began again more angrily, "Don't you understand? I have enough money to make you all rich. You have only to name an amount and . . ."

This time one side of the scar-faced Arab's mouth turned as he stepped forward and slapped her hard across the lips.

The burning sting brought tears to her eyes and her own hand automatically to her face. Then, before she could recover or protest, the fastenings of her robe were ripped away and, in a flash of dark material, her only garment was snatched over her head.

Juliette cried out, fighting to cover herself with arms still painfully held in the guards' grip.

Slowly Abdul ibn al-Mehridim's half-closed eyes moved over the white girl. She aroused him, this one, with her ivory limbs and those firm, rosy-hued breasts that jiggled as she writhed and strained between the guards. And that gold-furred triangle of womanhood promised even more delights. Unconsciously he touched himself now, thinking the price this Englishman asked was not so great after all.

"You have not spoken falsely. She is perfection," he breathed at last, bending his head to the other Arab before adding, "but she is spirited."

Kaleb's scarred face smiled. "Perhaps. But we have methods of subduing her without damaging her worth. Leave the details to me, and I assure you she will be ready whenever you say."

A conspiring smile crossed the face of Abdul ibn al-Mehridim. "Tonight then," he said, withdrawing from his robes a weighty bag that clinked, setting it in Kaleb's outstretched hand.

Juliette's face blazed red, her flesh crawling with revulsion as she turned away.

Cold sweat covered her as she anticipated any moment being thrown down and raped. But to her surprise, a wave from the scar-faced Arab caused the guards to release their bruising hold and set her free.

Immediately she retrieved the fallen robe, clenching it to her breasts. The wealthy-looking man was moving toward the door, which a guard opened and held for him. As he passed through, he paused, turning back for one more look, his heavy lips parting slowly in a smile that showed a gold tooth glowing dimly, before he disappeared, the others following, and the splintered door banging shut.

All that day, Juliette expected the men to return and do any of a hundred horrors she couldn't help but imagine, while again and again, Brandon's words repeated themselves in her head, "Continuously . . . all night . . . old men . . . sick men . . . diseased men. . . . Do I shock you? But there are many far far worse than I."

A paralyzing dread formed in her stomach as she sat on the filthy straw, the robe clinging wetly to spots under her arms and between her breasts. In the torrid heat the cell's one tiny window was inadequate and, leaning against the wall, she fanned herself with an open hand. How long would they leave her here? She couldn't remember ever being so hot or so intensely thirsty in her life. Yet there was no relief from the heat, and no water in the squalid little cell.

Again it seemed hours before footsteps came and Juliette, languishing on the floor, tensed, lifting herself to lean against the wall. But this time she saw only a hand and forearm as, in a flash, the door opened and a waterskin was tossed in before it was closed and locked once more.

Suspiciously Juliette waited until the footsteps diminished before crawling through the straw to grasp the sack. To her surprise, it was half full of water and, quickly unstopping the neck, she raised it to her mouth and gulped deeply.

In her mind she knew that the water was foul. She could even feel particles slipping down her throat. But this made no difference to her parched mouth or thickening tongue. Any wetness seemed sweet and the bag was nearly empty before she regained control of her convulsive swallowing.

With effort she pulled the waterskin away, letting it drop in her lap and savoring the moisture remaining on her lips. Better to save the rest, she told herself. There was no certainty that she would get any more.

Then crawling back to her former position, she leaned against the crumbling plaster wall.

The heat seemed less suffocating now, and tilting her chin, she looked up at the ceiling. It was only rough rafters mortared with mud and straw so it offered shade, though it would never stop rain, and through its occasional cracks and holes bright blue sky was visible. Juliette could hear a chicken walking up on it, clucking occasionally, its feet disturbing the roof's powdered earth so it fell through the cracks to the straw floor in a dusty trickle which shimmered in the sunlight.

Rolling her head against the bricks, Juliette sighed, her eyes dropping to her hand which had also taken on a certain luminescence. Every vein seemed to stand out, throbbing red, and her skin seemed alive, even breathing.

A warm euphoria swept her. The stench of the room had evaporated and she felt suddenly a deep relaxation melting through her blood like warm honey. Why fight? she thought. They hadn't really hurt her, at least not yet, and maybe they would let her explain who she really was.

Minutes ticked by unnoticed. Every part of her was tingling with refreshment as if from a long sleep, and yet she felt so lazy she didn't want even to raise her arms or move her legs though, automatically, her fingers reached again for the bag.

She laid down on her back, putting the neck of the waterskin to her mouth and drinking deeply again before wiping away the drip that gathered on her chin with the back of her hand.

It was so good, delicious in fact. And wasn't it lovely just to lie here on this crisp straw that really looked a little like gold and reminded her of the barns she played in as a child. The memory made her happy and she smiled. Why had she thought it so awful before? What was it again? What had frightened her? She tried to think. There was something else . . . far more important . . . but what was it? She squeezed her eyes shut, trying to concentrate, to turn her thoughts backward, but when her eyes closed, a carousel of visions spun in her mind and she was suddenly lost in a sea of color and light.

Chapter 50

Several nights later, a snake dancer, the defloration of three twelve-year-old Sudanese virgins, and an orgy of dwarfs all preceded the secret sale of a mysterious white slave girl at the notorious Club Rayseyn.

The sale was to be at midnight and, near that time, various figures presented themselves at the back entrance of the club to be examined, first through a slit in the door, and next under the light of a foyer, before being admitted down the winding stairway to the "room below"—a private den where entertainments were held for the enjoyment of certain patrons by invitation only.

It was a large room, blue with the smoke of incense and hashish, and candles in tall brass holders cast the shadows of those seating themselves on the low chairs against the heavily draped stage.

As the numbers grew and they waited, rumors circulated in low murmurs.

Some men claimed to have seen the girl, reporting she was beautiful beyond their expectations, while several others whispered she was, in fact, a highborn English lady. There was a third story, too, that insisted she was none other than the stolen property of the Sheik of El Abadan, and all three stories added a tense air of mystery to the proceedings as the minutes passed.

A Turkish woman entered and seated herself in the rear of the dim room where she applied skilled fingers to a zither, sending a slow sensuous melody swimming through the thick smoky atmosphere.

Abdul ibn al-Mehridim entered from one side of the stage, nodding to several patrons he knew. Then signaling to an attendant, who pulled a cord, the plush curtains were drawn apart and, through the haze of smoke, the slave girl appeared.

The white girl's eyelids were seductively half-closed and diaphanous peach veils gave a flush to her skin, both obscuring and revealing her smooth body as she stood gracefully, one knee slightly bent, her head tilted back, her lips parted in a tragically innocent, yet provocative pose. Her full breasts rose defiant and firm beneath the light covering, and long wavy hair tumbled to her waist, reflecting like pure gold in the glow of the candles.

For a moment the crowd caught its breath, before craning eagerly forward, commenting in hushed voices, and there was laughter as a lusty comment was made.

The conversation paused as Abdul ibn al-Mehridim stepped forward, pointing out the slave girl's shimmering hair and rare-colored eyes, her firm breasts and rounded buttocks before calling for the first bid.

"Three thousand dinars," someone shouted from near the stage.

It was a staggering figure. But undaunted, other voices called out in rapid succession, doubling the bid in minutes, and then again, until it reached twelve thousand dinars and only three men remained bidding.

Abdul ibn al-Mehridim was pleased. His fleshy tongue touched the corner of his mouth as his eyes darted between the rivals.

One was an Ethiopian, Gessat Nassid, who owned several secret diamond mines to the south and was known for both his cunning and his wealth.

The second was the governor's indulged son, ibn-Abad, who sat on the far side of the stage, drawing on his hookah, his glazed eyes narrowing to see through the clouds of smoke as he stared at the girl.

The third man sat in the rear of the room, darkness shrouding his face so that only the red-hot ember of a cigarette betrayed a presence.

He was an Englishman called Jack Player who owned the most notorious brothel in Tripoli and had just made the last bid in a hoarse gravelly voice.

The Ethiopian's black eyes gleamed beneath his red turban as he evaluated the girl's worth. There was a certain African chieftain whose lands Nassid had to cross on the way to his diamond mines and, in the past, Nassid had found it both wise and profitable to flatter this particular chieftain with occasional gifts.

As recently as their last meeting, he had promised to bring the chief a girl as beautiful as the morning. Certainly this one matched that description and, offering such a treasure, Nassid reasoned, would insure peaceful crossing to the mines and guarantee a peaceful return as well.

Gessat Nassid cocked his turbaned head, weighing the value of a safe expedition against the price of this slave girl, while mentally counting his gold. And when Abdul ibn al-Mehridim leaned toward him and asked for a bid of thirteen thousand dinars, the Ethiopian nodded.

In the back of the room, the red-hot ember of a cigarette bobbed suspended in darkness. And for the first time in years, a spark kindled in Jack Player's cold reptilian eyes.

Many times before he had purchased white women to satisfy his customers' lust for pale flesh. But this one was different. She had none of the others' hard seasoned looks but seemed an innocent under all the makeup and drugs. And feeling a sudden eagerness to himself taste her charms, he called out, "Fourteen thousand!"

Ibn-Abad drew on his hookah, puffing bluish smoke toward the plaster ceiling. His bloodshot eyes crawling slowly up and down the white slender body, pausing again and again on the girl's smooth and rounded buttocks.

He had always preferred boys to females of any age, but seeing this girl. . . . His eyes focused again on her boyishly slim flanks and then rose to her perfectly formed breasts. This girl had the best attributes of both. And what a delight to dominate such a body—to have it writhing beneath him and also cheat the Sheik of El Abadan out of the pleasure at the same time. It would be sweet revenge. How he hated Karim al-Sharif with his smooth looks and fastidious European ways. Even now the man was staying in the palace of ibn-Abad's own father, who showed the sheik more affection than he did himself, his own son. And taking the pipe out of his mouth, ibn-Abad called in his high-pitched voice, "Fourteen thousand five hundred dinars."

Abdul ibn al-Mehridim nodded, repeating the bid as his eyes shifted between the Englishman and Gessat Nassid as if to read their thoughts.

The Ethiopian sipped from a thimble-sized cup of syrupy black coffee. It was an exorbitant price to pay for any girl, he reasoned. But her fairness alone made her an exceptional treasure, exactly the type to tempt an African chieftain grown bored with the dark skins of his own women.

It was true, of course, he might match her coloring with another brought by nefarious means across the Mediterranean, but he would be unable to match her beauty. Nassid adjusted his wide sleeves and, glancing at the dark end of the room, noticed the red glow of the cigarette ember bobbing up to Player's mouth, burning for an intense moment before paling and dropping downward. Then, looking back to Abdul ibn al-Mehridim, the Ethiopian said, "Fifteen thousand dinars."

Jack Player shifted uneasily on his thick cushion, his eyes fixed on the girl. Surely it must be true that she was a wellborn lady. The way she held her head and shoulders, and the pose of her arms reminded him of rich English girls he had seen in London. But none of them had ever been interested in him—a bastard, even if his father was an English lord, yes, a bastard all the same.

He dragged again on his cigarette, bringing the ember to flashing brightness before calling out in his harsh voice, "Be done with it! Twenty thousand dinars!"

The zither twanged discordantly and the room grew hushed before heads pulled together and whispers rose to a fevered pitch.

"Player must be breaking himself to have her," whispered one man. "The girl is a rare gem, but twenty thousand dinars! It is the price of a ship and crew!"

From the stage, smoke hazed and blurred the gaping throng, and barely conscious, unseeing, uncaring, and filled only with dreams, Juliette heard the haunting melodies of the zither as if from another world, the music leading her bemused mind down the labyrinths of time, and once

again she was a young girl standing at her father's bedside.

"It's only a scratch after all," she heard him say.
"Scratches heal. That young Arab, Karim al-Sharif, didn't
realize how tough we English can be." He laughed infec-
tiously. "Now be a good girl and keep me company."

"I will, I will," she heard herself say. "I love you. What
a wonderful Papa you are. Always stay here," her childish
voice pleaded, "Never, never leave again. See, I'll dance
for you." And as she spoke, she raised her arms overhead,
suddenly swaying to the twanging chords.

The crowd paused at this unanticipated sight. Never had
they seen a slave so beautiful, and now those luminous eyes
were blinking heavily, and her full, pomegranate lips spoke
without sound as delicate limbs lifted and moved in a
graceful interpretation of native dance.

A wave of whispers swept the audience. Again ibn-
Abad's eyes traveled to her buttocks. And feeling himself
grow hard and painful beneath his robes, he imagined parting those cheeks and driving himself into her. Then suddenly he was on his feet, unconscious of the odd angle at
which his robes protruded and, rushing to the stage, he
grabbed the slave girl's ankle as he shouted, "Twenty-five
thousand dinars!"

Pandemonium followed. Jack Player's voice calling
above the din as he too abruptly dashed from the protective
darkness into the uncertain candlelight.

"The merchandise will not be molested!" he shouted over
and over.

Gessat Nassid was suddenly out of his seat, too, protesting
loudly in his native tongue as others did, shouting louder
and louder to be heard above the chaos. Then a dozen men
were clamoring at the girl's feet and Abdul ibn al-Mehridim
was calling for his guards.

The surge of noise startled Juliette, who felt something
touch her ankle and, from beyond her dreams, a congealing
of thought drew her nearer reality.

Looking down, she saw a thickset man with bloodshot
eyes caressing her calf, while a second man was struggling
in the arms of guards. Through swirling clouds of smoke,

ghoulish demons emerged, staring with leering grins and clutching the edge of the platform where she stood.

"Papa! Papa!" she screamed. But her voice was lost in the fracas and her father faded as another face appeared, a mocking face that she recognized immediately by his black cape and hard laugh as the Arab who had murdered her father.

She tried to rouse herself, raising hands to press against her checks. Surely this must be Hell. Karim al-Sharif had murdered her father and now had murdered her, too, and brought her here to reside among demons. Her mind echoed "Karim al-Sharif, Karim al-Sharif." Her head spun dizzily and the images blurred. Then with deafening suddenness, the music and voices ceased. There was a single scream and then only a low murmur.

Shaking her head weakly, Juliette closed her eyes. When she opened them again, all the demons had turned to look across the room where a lone figure stood.

It was him, something told her, her father's murderer, Karim al-Sharif, just as she had always imagined him, dressed from turban to boots in black, a large burnoose hanging from his shoulders that floated behind as he advanced down a parted aisle of bowing figures.

Juliette's heart pounded violently. He was coming for her and there was no escape. Her vision blackened, then cleared, as she swayed. He reached the edge of the platform and in a single step was up beside her.

There was the rushing of the sea in her head, or was it her father's voice whispering a thousand times, "Karim al-Sharif," over and over. But as she looked at him, she inexplicably saw Brandon, a half-triumphant, half-mocking smile on his handsome features.

Her thoughts tumbled in confusion. She had not the capability of reasoning and only knew that he reached out and took her wrist before pulling her toward him, his dark eyes glimmering like polished mirrors.

Again her father's voice came echoing through the walls of her memories, "Karim al-Sharif, Karim al-Sharif," followed by the memory of Brandon's own voice saying, "And

I suppose you deny knowing my name, Karim al-Sharif. . . ."

Juliette stepped backward, her eyes rounding so the whites circled huge violet centers as the width of his shoulders blocked her view of everything but him.

Her mouth opened to scream, but no sound came out. There was only the strength of his arms encircling her, pressing her against thick enveloping robes.

"Come," he said simply.

Hearing him speak somehow broke the spell and, with it, an understanding sprang to Juliette's mind.

She pounded him with her fists and screamed, "Brandon . . . Brandon, Karim al-Sharif!" But her cries were muffled against his great burnoose as his arms tightened and an overpowering dizziness swept her. Then she was being carried through grotesque lights and figures that parted for them to pass.

Outside the stars were veiled by misty fog, or was it her misty eyes. She never knew, because she fainted.

Sharif lifted her to balance on his saddle before mounting behind her. Her cheek fell heavily against his arm as he spurred his horse and they burst away, Juliette's unbound blond hair streaming past his shoulder in the wind.

Chapter 51

The mellow tones of a bell echoed down the polished marble halls of the governor's palace, summoning Zalla to the special suite prepared for the Sheik of El Abadan.

Immediately Zalla went hastening toward his chambers. She was a tall woman whose advancing age didn't conceal her grace or completely disguise her once sumptuous beauty. Since puberty, Zalla's one occupation had been the pleasure of men, and having learned her lessons well, she was now keeper of the governor's harem and the only woman of any importance inside the palace besides the governor's short-reigned "favorites," who came and went as swiftly and easily as the seasons.

Her position secure and long standing, Zalla was well acquainted with those most delicate conduits of palace gossip—those particularly secret and reliable sources to be found among any large servantry, which often seemed to transmit an event almost as it was happening. But at this moment, Zalla needed none of her fine informing methods to know what every occupant of the palace, from the royalty to the lowest stable attendant knew—that *this* girl could be none other than the one who had kept the household in a storm of speculation for days—that same girl who had mysteriously run away from the Sheik of El Abadan when so many others plotted to gain even a glance of his attention.

Zalla herself had been present when the news was first brought to the sheik of the girl's escape. She had seen with her own eyes the lieutenant of the guards turn pale beneath his dark skin as he bowed deeply and reported the loss. He paled to an even lighter shade when the master came to his feet with a spring like that of a cheetah stung by a wasp. "Four men could not keep one girl!" he said. "Where did you lose her?"

From his prostrate position, the guard began, "It was in the market place, Sayyid. There was a disturbance—"

But the sheik didn't wait for the rest of the answer. Already Rashid was bringing the sheik's rifle and his burnoose, and his personal guard was hastily falling in behind as he strode out of the hall.

The search lasted for days and nights while men combed the streets and criers were sent about the city telling the people of the girl, the dire consequences to anyone who might harm her, and the reward of gold to that one who would return her to the Sheik of El Abadan. But five days passed while each hour the master's face grew darker and his eyes more dangerous until all the household feared even to speak in his presence. And, in the end, they were all grateful to a certain beggar who on the sixth day was seen breaking through the palace guards to speak to the master.

"*Sayyid, Sayyid!*" the beggar cried out, falling to his knees. "I pray only that you listen to a poor beggar who serves you as faithfully as the richest of your subjects."

Already two guards had taken the old man by his shabby robes and were preparing to drag him from the royal presence while another guard bowed, apologizing for the interruption.

The sheik's voice was clipped. "Let him speak. Don't you think beggars hear and see more than all the servants and guards of the palace combined?" Then he turned to the crouched figure whose fallen hood had revealed a deeply lined face sparsely bearded with straggling gray hair.

"What is it, old man?" the sheik demanded. "Speak. But pray that the information you bring is worthy of the disturbance you cause."

The guards released their painful hold and the beggar fell forward to his hands and knees. "Oh, great and noble lord, defender of the faith." The beggar raised his grayed lips. "If the eyes of the slave girl you seek are truly the color of the desert sky in the evening as I have heard described, then I have seen today such as she taken to the Club Rayseyn. She is to be sold there tonight at midnight."

The sheik studied the old man's face with such sudden intensity that the beggar recoiled and said, "My words are true, *Sayyid*. I swear in the name of Allah the merciful and compassionate and also in the name of your beloved father, for whom once I was a warrior before the pain of a wound gave me over to the disgrace of drink, may Allah forgive me." Rolling his watery eyes skyward, he salaamed.

The sheik's face was expressionless for a moment before a certain light glowed behind his features. "Zayed ibn-Rafik—I remember. You rode with us the day my father was captured."

Zayed bowed so deeply that his gray beard dragged in the dust. "My master does me great honor to remember, and with him I spit on those English infidels who that day committed the infamous crime for which they can never be forgiven."

"Nor shall they be forgiven," the sheik added. "But my father has been avenged, his murderer sent before Allah to be judged." And leaning down, the sheik helped the old man to his feet and pressed a rich coin in his palm. Then over his shoulder he said to Rashid, "Get my horse, and signal the men. And see Zayed ibn-Rafik has food and work if he wants it."

Again the old man was prostrating himself and kissing the hem of the sheik's robes. "*Sayyid, Sayyid.* I did not believe a man could be wiser or more generous than thy father, but before Allah, I have seen it is so."

The sheik shook his head. "It takes little wisdom for simple matters," he said shortly. "What man is so powerful that he does not need another faithful subject?"

Then the master's horse was there, already prancing even as Karim al-Sharif mounted him in a single movement and rode galloping from the palace gates, a complement of warriors streaming behind.

For hours after that, all the household held its breath. If the slave girl had been harmed, they sensed a bloody vengeance and each feared the worst. In a rage the master was more dangerous than a hungry lion. And so they waited until at last the sound of horses' hooves clapped again against the courtyard flagstones, telling everyone they had returned.

Even before Zalla had answered the royal summons, she had heard whispered that the sheik had taken revenge on his enemies, that those responsible for the abduction of the girl had been executed, and the Club Rayseyn destroyed. And now as Zalla watched him lean over this girl, who had already taken more trouble than fifty slave girls, she saw a new look in his face.

Zalla bowed low, listening carefully to the sheik's orders, only nodding before bowing again as he left. Then she rose from her knees to strike the small bell twice more.

At the signal, three giggling serving girls entered and peered curiously at the white girl. She was beautiful, was she not?—so fragile—like a butterfly of heaven all in gold and white and pinks. And what strange words she murmured in a tongue they could not understand as she seemed first awake and then asleep again. But Zalla gave them little time for idle wondering, setting them immediately to work undressing the girl's limp body and slipping her into the master's luxurious bathing pool, already filled to the brim with fragrant scented water.

Slowly they scrubbed her inch by inch, until she was washed clean and her skin glowed a rich rose. Then, lifting her out, they dabbed her dry with soft cloths before laying her once again on the couch so that Zalla, with the care of an artist, could brush color on her lips and nipples and even rouge her sex while the girls added perfume of a light exotic scent before dusting her with powder that made her skin as smooth as a newborn babe's.

At last satisfied with the result, Zalla moved the white slave to the master's bed, arranging the clouds of golden hair that now was her only ornament, and letting down the mosquito netting that fell from the ceiling in a filmy mist of white.

The slave girl's eyelids began fluttering with fresh life as the lamps were dimmed to a soft orange glow. Then together, they tiptoed out of the chamber, the three girls whispering and giggling among themselves and only wishing they could be the fortunate one offered to the master like a rare treasure.

Later, when Juliette's eyes blinked narrowly open, she was still dizzy and disoriented, and bringing a hand to her forehead, she didn't realize for several minutes that a figure was standing over her, a bronze god, wearing only white pants drawn tight at the waist by a black silk cord.

There was no past, only the present, and after a time, a shadow parted the milky curtain surrounding her, and lolling her head in that direction, she saw Brandon who, like a dream, did not speak, but silently came onto the huge bed.

She was in his arms then, pressed against his body so much larger and harder than her own. He was warm, so warm, and of their own accord, her arms wrapped around his neck.

She couldn't help lifting her starry gaze to his, at once hypnotized by those penetrating eyes, mysterious, and dark as midnight. Yet something nagged at her brain as he drew her closer, an understanding not clearly formed. She only knew she didn't want to feel so helpless, and struggled to make sense of the tangled threads of her mind. But still lost in a strange fogginess, she could only watch him wonderingly as she felt his long fingers caressing her throat and sliding downward to her breasts as his mouth took hers in a scorching kiss.

She did not want to be changed, but sensations erupted that dissolved any question of will. His lips were playing against hers, teasing, soft, then demanding, his tongue running along her teeth before pushing through, exploring her inner recesses so she blazed and trembled by turns. He was the sun, and she the sea, his touch glimmers of delight against her undulating need. Together they became light and shadow, a mingling soaring oneness.

She heard herself moan under the onslaught of whirling colors circling her head as all movement, all knowing narrowed down to only one irresistible demand.

His mouth lifted to hover over hers and words were whispered against her flesh as he moved down her throat to one breast, his mouth taking the nipple and rolling it with his tongue, pulling it with his teeth, sucking it until it was swollen to erect bursting before he moved to do the same with the other waiting breast.

Her heart pounded crazily and her thighs opened themselves even before his tongue had moved to explore her navel, expertly circling it again and again. She was no longer her own creature, but his, brought alive so that desire was all that existed as his hands took her hips firmly, his lips slipping in soft kisses down her silken belly and lower.

Moaning, her head turned slowly from side to side. She was mesmerized—his slave as she let her thighs be lifted over his shoulders, a sinking surging dizziness spreading outward from his plunging tongue that burned hot like the sun's radiance from the inner core of its central furnace.

She arched her back and moaned again as wave after wave of shimmering pleasure peaked and fell away only to rise shimmering again, building each time higher and more wonderfully full—an overripe fruit ready to burst at the slightest touch. But then, just when a new incomparable height was within her grasp, he pulled away, his lips traveling down the inside of her thighs that fell open wide in offering.

She moaned, weakly reaching to pull him back, but he

was suddenly above her again, her own feral scent upon him. And slowly, so she knew each burrowing inch of his taut and throbbing hardness, he filled her with himself, her own body rising to meet what he thrust forth.

"Brandon," she whispered against his lips as he found her mouth again. Then he was driving and gliding, in and out, building a momentum of wild sensations that climbed steadily toward an unknown dimension, each thrust seeming to penetrate deeper than the one before so she could feel herself opening wider, deeper, to take all of him.

He paused then and, fearful the wonderful sensations would stop, her own hips swirled up to match his movements as she whispered hoarsely, "Brandon, Brandon . . . don't stop. I want . . . I want . . ." But then he began again, faster, harder. And just when she imagined she could endure no more, a wrenching wonderful ecstasy exploded, so stabbing, so triumphant, she pressed against him in wild abandon as fulfillment drowned her in rapturous spasms.

It seemed then she teetered between life and oblivion, beyond time or knowing as the world hung by a gossamer fiber that at any moment would dissolve. But like ocean waves rolling up the sand, her senses surged to their highest point before slowly declining until only a wonderful peace and satisfaction remained. And with him still a part of her, Juliette murmured, "Brandon," and breathed a sigh of velvet softness before falling into deep sleep.

Chapter 52

"Where am I? What am I doing here?" Visions of her father—of the Arab devils—of hands groping about her ankles—and of Brandon, were all scrambled in confusion as her eyelids fluttered open and she found herself lying on her back in a wide bed.

Automatically her hands raised to rub her eyes as she peered through the milky netting all around, unsure for a second if she was still dreaming as she saw Brandon across the room. Or should she think of him as Sharif now that she knew *who* he was—Karim al-Sharif, her father's murderer, looking sinister in his black robes as she had always imagined him.

He must have known she was awake, since in three steps he was parting the netting and leaning over her, his eyebrows drawn together in concerned questioning.

Handsome! Yes, despicably so. Sheik Karim al-Sharif! Desperately she had not wanted to understand, or face the truth. Why else could she have been so completely blind not to realize everything that first time she heard his name?

Truly he was a murderer, and this time he couldn't deny it!

Twice he had shattered her life! Twice he had plunged her to the deepest despair. So easily she could remember her father and those happy times before he died—his smile, his warm words, those little gifts he brought home in his uniform pocket. He was the source of all security, all loving in the world, her shining god, far greater and more noble than any other father. It was his memory that kept her from despair during all those hard times that followed his death. And when, as if by a miracle, she had become an heiress and achieved freedom, she had gloried in it, trying to make up for all those earlier days. Yet not only had this man killed her father, now he had blotted her life a second time. Juliette's face hardened and the hairs prickled at the back of her neck. Murdering her father had not been enough. Now he had killed her husband, too, and like a thief in the night carried her off, ruining her—degrading her. She wanted to scream, to cry, to claw his black eyes, to kill him. But now, "You!" was all she could croak, scrambling to get her legs over the edge of the bed and pulling up the thin sheet to cover her nakedness. The room spun and carved wall paneling, wine-colored draperies, and Sharif all became a whirling of color and she fell down on the bed with a bounce.

The light of expectation left Sharif's face as he straightened, arching an eyebrow. "Indeed, madame? I'd thought, under the circumstances, you'd have more to say."

With deliberate movements he reached over to a bedside table and poured a generous glass of liquid from a jeweled flask, and turning back to her, he drank it.

His calm manner was exasperating. And as the dizziness receded, Juliette gained control of her tongue at last.

"But now I understand," she said in a scathing tone. "You can't lie to me any longer! I know *who* you are and I know what you have done! Yes, admit it! You murdered my father!"

Sharif finished the drink, setting down the empty glass and meeting her eyes directly. "I killed him," he said quietly, and his cold admission astonished Juliette almost as much as what he said next. "And your father murdered mine. But, of course, what would that matter to you any more than it mattered to him. My father was only an Arab after all, a *bloody nigger*. And what does one more or less of that sort ever matter to you *holy* English."

Juliette's jaw slacked, the momentum evaporating from her attack. She must not have heard correctly. "Your father?" she questioned, unable to focus his words or believe them. This was a part of the story she had never heard.

Sharif set his glass down with a sharp rap. "Truly, madame, your conversation grows tedious—'you . . . your father.' Is that all you have to say? You disappoint me. But it isn't the first time, is it?"

Juliette's eyes constricted to flashing slits. That he had the audacity to mock her now—that he made light of the enormity of what he had done was unforgivable. But when she spoke, her voice was suddenly calm and coldly serious. "It is fortunate for you I didn't realize before who you really were," she began. "Because if I had, Karim al-Sharif, I would have killed you myself!"

His face did not change as he watched her steadily. "So now you admit wanting revenge. That's some improvement at least—a basis for discussion. Maybe you would have preferred I left you to the mercy of Abdul. Or were you so drugged you didn't know what they were doing?"

"It doesn't matter!" Her head throbbed but she ignored it. "Whatever they would have done, at least I would be rid of you! Anyone else would be preferable!"

A wicked smile curved Sharif's mouth. "You didn't seem to think so last night." He leaned closer, his smile mocking her. "Or do you always give yourself so readily?"

Juliette's eyes dropped under the sparkling light that danced in his. Though her recollection was vague, try as she might, nothing could blot out the lingering sense of rapture touching her with fairy fingers, especially between her thighs where tremors like the aftershocks of an earthquake still rumbled.

She blushed scarlet. "I'm not in the habit of being drugged."

"Obviously, *chérie*. But the state becomes you. You lose that stiff Englishness and become a woman for a change." A hand reached to stroke the hollow of her throat and trace the line of her breast. "And last night you became a woman—*completely*, whether you like it now, or not."

Juliette pulled away. "Of course someone like you would have to resort to drugs."

He shrugged, "I only took advantage of a convenient circumstance. I find it much more pleasing to have you beneath me crying for more than listening to your barbed tongue. Usually you are quite insulting. If Abdul weren't already dead, I could ask him for his concoction. But then perhaps we won't need it. As you will discover, last night served only to spark a new appetite—not satisfy it."

Juliette gasped. "Certainly you don't imagine that I could ever . . . would ever want . . ." She drew herself supremely erect. "You underestimate me. You are wrong, and you shall see!"

Sharif's hands came to rest on his hips as he laughed shortly. "You have a lot to learn, *chérie*, both about me and yourself. I will try to be patient—that is, to a point. And I think I won't underestimate you again. A fine horse is one trained slowly so it is molded by the trainer's hand, not broken."

"You can be patient till doomsday! I'll never do anything but loathe you. And I'm not one of your horses! You might as well kill me because, if you don't, I'll find a way to kill you, or myself, before I let you touch me again!"

He gave her a long considering look, then shrugged. "*In sha'Allah,* what will be is the will of Allah."

His shift from the attack to apathy made her even angrier. "Damn you. You can't keep me like this! Where are you taking me? What are you planning to do?" Juliette exploded, pulling the sheet higher and snatching the end of it free to throw over her shoulder like a toga. She came to her feet and faced him. Her hair was in a tangled mass that flew tempestuously as she tossed her chin higher. But he didn't change expression and only reached down with infuriating familiarity to capture a waving curl whose end he brought to trail across his own cheek.

"I'm taking you to my desert city. *What* I do with you remains to be seen. And I hope you've lost any foolish notions of escape. You may not be fond of warming my bed, but I think you will find it preferable to servicing all the others."

Juliette tore the golden lock out of his grasp and glared at him, her mind racing in search of a retort to his horrible cutting truths. But she was forced to remain silent as no suitable answer presented itself.

In this last he was correct. She had not forgotten the callous betrayal by Henry Farthington. The experience had been bitter, and had taught her how completely alone and among strangers she really was. She knew nothing of these people. Their customs and religion were all a mystery. This world was one apart, barbaric and unexplored. Indeed she was both helpless out of his protection and helpless within it. And to add to her dilemma Sharif had awakened a new untried dimension of her being that made everything all the more confused, a power he could use against her. And now, looking down, she curled her bare toes as she thought. It's true, I can't trust anyone. And as another, still foreign, tingle of delight darted through her loins, a voice within her added, "Not even myself."

Chapter 53

Outside the palace, the sun shone bright and mercilessly hot as Juliette found herself perched on the pommel of Sharif's saddle and galloping at the head of fifty men to the outskirts of the city.

A caravan was assembling there amid a choking stir of dust, and Juliette felt that she couldn't even open her mouth without getting grit in it as Sharif pulled his horse to a stop.

A dromedary was kneeling there, one of the white variety she had heard the Arabs refer to as *mahreh*. It had an elegant pavilion strapped to its back that reminded her of the other vehicle from which she had so disastrously escaped. Sharif chuckled disconcertingly and, seeming to overhear her thoughts, said, "This time I won't be so far away."

Averting her chin, Juliette pretended not to hear, and not waiting to be helped down, jumped from his saddle, climbed into the pavilion, and whipped the transparent draperies closed, refusing to meet his knowing expression.

What was the point of making a fool of herself arguing, she thought, crossing her arms tightly against her chest. And so she said nothing, only glaring at his receding back as he galloped to the head of the column, horse and rider seeming as weightless as a large bird borne on the wind of his billowing blue-black burnoose.

They traveled until midday, the sun beating down on the soft earth that stretched as far as her eye could distinguish. Only the slightest breeze stirred, and signs of life were limited to occasional scrubby bushes and lizards dashing from rock to rock as they were flushed from cover by the caravan.

The sway of the dromedary, so different from the movements of a horse, was difficult to master. But Juliette did her best to move with it, swaying from side to side and back and forth in a circling movement though it made her stomach queasy.

By the time the sun was directly overhead, she was parched and her head ached though, defiantly, she refused to ask for water. But finally, just when she thought she couldn't endure the terrible dryness or her thickening tongue any longer, she heard Sharif's voice from the front of the column shouting a command.

Her *mahreh* halted, like the others, lurching forward and down to its knees so Juliette had to grasp the pavilion's frame for support as the animal settled to the ground, its long neck high in an aloof pose as it gazed into nothingness, calmly chewing its cud.

Pushing aside the silk drapery, Juliette scanned the monotonous stretch of desert to her left, noting that Sharif was not within sight before dropping the material in place again. "Good!" she said aloud, hoping she would be spared the ordeal of his vile company. He was mad! Anyone would be mad to live in this godforsaken place!

A shadow suddenly fell across her, and she jumped and turned to find an unfamiliar Arab bending to look through the curtained opening. The end piece of his black head scarf dangled to one side of his seamed leathery face, reaching to the tip of his gray-flecked beard. His small black eyes squinted to sharp points that seemed already to know everything as for a moment he scrutinized her. Then, apparently satisfied, he motioned her to follow with a certain intrinsic sense of command that made it somehow unthinkable to refuse. So stepping out of the pavilion and down the three wooden steps, Juliette followed as he led across the sand without looking again in her direction.

He was Rashid, Sharif's servant, Juliette realized as she moved quickly to keep up with his long-legged strides. Her robe made the work more cumbersome, and she lifted it ankle high as they moved between white-robed boys unloading burlap-bound supply packs off camels held by a ring piercing one nostril.

Off to the side stood a group of warriors who ignored her with polite deliberateness as she passed, though one younger than the others did glance curiously over his shoulder as she passed before a curt word from Rashid made him flush and turn away.

Finally, at the entrance to a shaded awning, Rashid paused, not speaking or salaaming as the rest of Sharif's servants always had, but merely pulling aside the drapery before dropping it back in place as soon as she had stepped inside. Then he sat himself cross-legged just outside, his hand casually resting on the hilt of the knife sheathed Arab-fashion at the center of his waist.

Apprehensive, Juliette sat on one of the several large tasseled cushions arranged on carpets over the sand, but she barely had time to wonder what might happen next when the curtain was lifted again and, looking up, she was surprised to see Cassia coming toward her, salaaming deeply and kneeling in front of her.

"Madame! Oh, how I have prayed! And the master. . . ." She rolled her eyes. "We were all so frightened! But Allah is merciful and you have been found." She smiled brightly, her gold earrings glittering. "And you are in great favor. Perhaps now you are happy?"

Juliette had been returning the girl's smile, surprised to find she had sincerely missed her too. But her smile disappeared with Cassia's question. "Happy? Of course I'm not happy. Is *this* what Arab women call favor?"

Cassia looked startled. "But of course, madame. Does not Madame sit in the shade of her own pavilion and ride in comfort when many walk? You are to be served only the finest delicacies of cakes and minced dates and rice." She indicated the Arab at the doorway. "And doesn't the master's personal guard, Rashid, watch over you? You are being treated with great favor, madame. Many would give all they possessed to be as you are now."

Juliette looked levelly into Cassia's wondering eyes. "I'm not surprised you don't understand. But if you were raised the way I was, you *would*. It's not right to take a woman against her will. It is against the law and well—barbaric—an evil thing to do!"

Cassia shrugged. "Perhaps. But the desert is different. You are lucky to be desired by such a powerful man—a man who will someday rule all of the tribes of the desert. And the stars confirm it will be his line of as yet unborn sons that will unite all Islam. It is a glorious destiny, is it not?"

Juliette didn't answer. Instead, trying to wipe everything out of her mind, she concentrated her attention on the tray of pita bread, dates, and fruit that another bowing black-robed woman brought in, and which Cassia served.

For an hour the caravan did not move as the Arabs ate their dates and rice concoction. Some dozed for a time, their faces veiled by black turbans, while others hunkered on their heels, speaking together in low voices while drinking coffee in slow meditative sips.

There were prayers later, each man kneeling on a carpet, shoes removed, forehead bending to touch the sand as he chanted. Then the carpets and cooking bowls and food were all packed in bags by boys and a half dozen veiled women.

Cassia left and Rashid came again, indicating that she follow him. He led her back to her own *mahreh*, indifferently helping her into the pavilion before bringing the animal to its feet with a sharp command.

After that they traveled steadily southward, as the sun slowly set over a low range of mountains before dropping behind them.

It was twilight then, a glorious red glow spreading over the cloudless sky before slowly shrinking to a red-orange band above the mountains, silhouetting their jagged peaks like the points of church spires. Then, to Juliette's bewitchment, the sky turned, a shade at a time, to lavender and darkened to violet, and a sparkling veil of stars came to mist the deepening sky and grow brighter as the heavens blackened to a velvety matte.

Beneath the winking light, the caravan halted and, once again, Juliette's dromedary knelt and Rashid appeared. But this time he didn't lead her to an awning, but rather to a tent that was already erected, apparently by campmakers sent ahead of the caravan.

Outside, Sharif's stallion, Fadjar, had been unsaddled and was being rubbed down by an Arab youth. In the pale starlight, the horse's shiny blackness made him almost disappear so only the whites of his great eyes showed as he threw his head and danced, pulling on his rope as they approached. The boy, careful to keep out of range of his hooves, spoke sharply to the animal. But it had no effect, and the horse continued to dance as Rashid lifted the tent flap and motioned her in before again taking up his station just outside the doorway.

Hungry, exhausted by the heat, and dizzy from the sway of the dromedary, Juliette waited with growing apprehension. Obviously she was to be treated like a prisoner, a slave, in spite of what Cassia called "favor."

Warily, she glanced around the tent. In the light of two large wax candles, she could see the room was larger than any tent she had seen before, and regally furnished with a small carved table inlaid with ivory, an embroidered brown hassock, and piles of cushions scattered on carpets that seemed luminescent in the flickering light.

Apprehensively, Juliette walked to a pair of striped draperies and, parting them, discovered a second room taken up almost entirely by a bed tossed with leopard skins that made it seem like a stalking animal.

Involuntarily, Juliette's throat tightened. Then dropping the drapery, she turned back to the main room, eyes suddenly rounded and glancing aimlessly about.

A gold and silver hanging—a brass vase—a trail of smoking incense, all passed through her vision. But she could concentrate on nothing. This was *his* tent, and *his* bed. He might come in minutes or hours, or possibly, not at all. He was unpredictable, and she could only wait on his coming—his bidding—his pleasure! And when he did come. . . . The thought sent her pacing the carpets and wringing her hands.

Outside she heard the same litany, *"La Ilaha Illa Allah— La Ilaha Illa Allah,"* the men's voices rising in prayer like that of a single beast. She shuddered. Did he expect that after what happened last night she would be willing? she asked herself. How she hated him—more than ever. But of course, he would do whatever he pleased. No one would stop him, and he had left no doubt concerning his intentions.

She ran her fingers through her hair, drawing herself to full height. Of course last night had not been *her* fault, she assured herself. And tonight she wouldn't be drugged. Tonight she would fight!

She froze then as voices outside interrupted her thoughts. Prayers had ended and suddenly he was there, bending his tall head to step under the tent flap, and hardly glancing in her direction before going into the bedroom.

Was she to follow? No, never! Stiffly she stood her ground, waiting for his voice to penetrate the curtains with an order. But when moments passed and he did not speak or return, Juliette sat down on the hassock, very straight—a difficult matter since the hassock was constructed to recline upon and, at best, she could only perch on its edge. Damn these Arabs, she thought angrily. Even their furniture encouraged seduction.

When Sharif came again, he had washed and changed into clean robes and his head was bare of the dark turban so only his crop of raven black hair remained. Still he didn't glance in her direction before walking to the tent flap and clapping his hands.

Almost at once a meal of skewered mutton, steaming rice, and minced squab with cinnamon was brought and painstakingly served by Cassia, who now was carefully veiled, her eyes demurely downcast.

Intently, Juliette watched as several dishes were presented, their silver covers removed, and it seemed an afterthought when Sharif looked up and motioned her opposite him at the table.

Unable not to, Juliette came forward. The hard day of riding left her stomach empty and craving nourishment. It was impossible to refuse, as much as her pride wished she could indifferently turn away. But why should she go hungry and only hurt herself more when it was he she really wanted to kill? she thought. So, silently she obeyed and, with as much dignity as possible, sat down cross-legged on the black silk pillows.

Sharif personally served her a portion of each dish but, though she was hungry, her anxiety made eating difficult and twice the tightness in her throat made her choke when attempting to swallow.

She waited for him to speak, to issue some further ultimatum or insult. But throughout the meal, he remained silent and inscrutable, and by the time it was over and coffee was served and consumed, Juliette was torn between relief at his silence, and a desire to hear him speak—to be given some hint as to what she should expect. But he said nothing.

It was only later, after he had ignored her most of the evening, relaxing on the hassock and reading a book in which he occasionally scribbled notes, that suddenly he seemed to remember her and, looking up said, "Juliette, come here."

The deep pronunciation of her name sent a shiver flying up her spine. She had been facing away from him, cross-legged, and pretending to be occupied with a book of her own, though for hours the print had jumped and blurred on the page and she hadn't read a word.

She was afraid. Yes, she had to admit it. Why shouldn't she be? She was helpless to prevent anything he might do, and he hated her. It was impossible to know to what extent he might go for revenge and, now that he had called her, she had only to think of his hands about her neck, and water closing over her head, as it had when she had defied him before, to make her rise and start toward him.

He's training me, she thought, training me like a dog to come at his call. But she was already near him, although still out of reach, her lips compressed, her eyes mutinous. This far she would go, but no farther.

He leaned back then, both hands round the back of his head so his elbows pointed out to the side. The muscles on his inner arms were carved in light and shadow, and stretching out his long booted legs, he crossed them as his eyes made a leisurely path over her body, seeming to evaporate her robe.

She stood stiffly, her breasts rising and falling more rapidly as a slow smile spread across his chiseled features. "I've forgotten how pretty your body is under those cumbersome garments, *ma chérie*," he said at last. "Take them off now and remind me."

Chapter 54

Juliette's face blanched as her mind flew furiously at the audacity—the impossibility of his request.

Automatically her fingers raised to press against her pulsating temples, utterly enraged, yet strangely fascinated by the light in his dancing black eyes. Was he mad? Did he really expect that she would docilely comply? That she would strip for him like a common woman of the street, or perhaps one of the members of his harem?

"I won't," she burst out finally. "I'm not your slave!"

Sharif sighed mockingly, shaking his head. "I don't think you understand, *chérie*. Or do you like to have the clothes torn off your back? Some women do prefer it."

Juliette's teeth clenched. "My preference has never varied. I have wanted only to be rid of you once and forever. But has it ever mattered what *I* have wanted? No! You are interested only in your own desires, not mine. Let us be frank at least!"

He paused, seeming to assess her words. A muscle jerked in his arm. Then the matter for him was apparently settled as, rising to his feet, he said, "Very well, madame. Indeed let us be frank!" Calmly he stood over her, his face serious.

Juliette's lips trembled. "You can't . . . you can't treat me like this. I won't let you."

"No?" His gaze was steady. "By Allah, all that English upbringing has made you stubborn. And what a shame when there could be so much pleasure . . . for both of us. Haven't I already shown you?"

Juliette backed away, stumbling over a cushion and recovering herself. "I don't care. I hate you," she said hearing the desperation in her own voice. "And if you were a gentleman, instead of a barbarian, you would have some . . . some sensitivity!"

Her words made him pause before throwing back his

head to laugh loudly. "Gentleman?" he repeated. "And I suppose you would like me better if I were more like one of those simpering dandies who so gratefully jumped at your every call and whim. To them you weren't a woman, but an untouchable virginal temple." He came closer, shaking his head. "And I suppose you think you'd be happy with that. *Mon Dieu*—You *are* slow to learn!"

"I don't know what you are talking about. Do you think I'm happy now after you have . . . have," Juliette could hear her own heart's galloping rhythm. She must stop him. She must get away. It couldn't happen again. Only pride kept her from begging for mercy and bravado seemed all that was left.

Assuming a wide stance she tossed her chin. "If you come any closer I'll scream. I swear I will."

Amused surprise came into his face. "Poor *chérie*. And do you think someone will come to your rescue?"

Then, with the swiftness of a striking serpent, he had her arm and, though Juliette pulled with all her strength, he held her fast, drawing her so near she could smell the masculine scent of his neck.

"You can't prevent what is to be between us, Juliette, what has always been inevitable. Didn't I once tell you I never go without something I want and, in spite of everything you've done, I've never stopped wanting you."

"Everything *I've* done!" Juliette said feeling her brave facade cracking. She leapt away from him then, taking refuge behind the small table so that it blocked his path.

He never took his eyes from her or changed expression, but, with one hand, pushed the table aside.

Immediately, Juliette burst toward the tent flap. But Sharif was a menacing step behind, and, before she could reach it, a steely arm encircled her waist, pulling her hard against his broad chest.

She was helpless—a puppet in his hands. For an instant she heard the deep drumming of his heart under her cheek. But then, before she could resist, her robe was pulled off and hung limply in his hand, and she was naked but for the dainty sandals on her feet.

He released her then, the force of her own struggles sending her stumbling backward.

For a moment he stood observing her, a sardonic grin on his face. But then she was in his grip again and flung on the carpet flat on her stomach.

She tried to scramble, to kick, to claw, but already he was holding her between his knees and pinning her wrists over her head.

"Damn you!" she sobbed. "Is rape what you need? Barbarian! Half-breed!" But the sound of her protests was lost in the soft carpets as his weight forced her down and his free hand roamed up her back, caressing the soft skin, and tossing her thick hair aside to kiss, and then bite, the back of her neck, her shoulder, her ear, so that chills tingled in waves along her body. And, over the pounding of her own heart, Juliette heard him whispering teasing jibes, then love words . . . sex words.

Juliette clenched her teeth, determined to feel nothing. But oh, God—it was happening again, this sense of being taken beyond herself—of tiny shivers shaking her from head to toe like ripples over her warming flesh.

His hand slipped beneath her, touching her erect nipples and playfully teasing the lobe of her ear with his tongue. And feeling her resistance ebbing, she kept reminding herself it would be over quickly, "as soon as he has what he wants," she told herself. But when his caressing fingers reached between her legs where, already, she was growing wet beneath his exploring, she forgot to repeat the reminder as a long breath was released and a tide of yearning set in motion which she was powerless to deny or control.

A moan escaped her lips and she held back another. Her mind swirled and she was hot and cold and shaky as slowly the world faded, leaving only Sharif. And when he turned her over on her back, she knew her breasts were flushed with passion and her feverish protests were really against herself. And when his lips took her mouth, Sharif found it parted and open to his demanding tongue that found and subdued hers until she surrendered to his plunder.

He freed her hands then and they came to push halfheartedly against his chest though somewhere in Juliette's mind she called herself a hypocrite. "Stop . . . Brandon . . . Karim . . . I hate you . . . please stop." But the words sounded embarrassingly breathless and did not prevent his full length from covering her, or his knee from nudging further apart her unresisting thighs.

Every inch of her awaited him, craving the completion of what had begun. Again his magical hands slid down her form, testing her skin before reaching again between her legs and teasing the red fruit there that swelled larger under his touch until it throbbed as if to burst and Juliette arched, resistance forgotten in the swirl of mindless pleasure.

Abruptly then his hands were gone, his lips were gone, and the sensations slowly receded leaving only their hot brand.

As if startled awake from a pleasant dream, Juliette dropped to earth, gasping for breath, her blood still rushing in her ears like the sea, as looking up, she found him on his feet, his eyes glittering enigmatically in the candlelight.

Panting, Juliette raised on one elbow, her face bewildered. What had happened? Hadn't he been seducing her, and now. . . .

He was laughing softly. "You see, it won't be so difficult to rid you of your stuffy English ways. And you must admit none of your dandies ever made you feel like *that*."

He remained standing above her, arms crossed, his regard taking in every curve of her body. Juliette gasped as his purpose dawned on her.

He had only been toying with her—amusing himself, and now he dared make fun of her!

Fury and humiliation combined in a sudden explosion and, without thought for her weaker state or nakedness, she leapt up and attacked him, fingernails bared. But he caught her easily, twisting her arm behind her and dragging her through the striped curtains to the foot of his bed where he threw her down. It was a brief struggle and, before she knew what he was doing, he had clamped a metal shackle around one ankle that was fastened to a post driven into the sand.

"Usually I tie hunting cheetahs like this," he informed her factually. "As long as you scratch like one, you'll sleep like one."

Juliette sprang up, bruising her ankle as she reached the end of the chain with a violent jerk that brought her to her knees. Her face was animated with fury. "Damn you! Damn you to Hell for the devil you are!"

Sharif's grin deepened. "Damn *me* indeed, madame. And I think I'm not alone now in my 'devilish' needs. It seems with some encouragement you display . . . would you have me call it, a warmer side of yourself?"

"Ohhh," Juliette's breath expelled all her anger and humiliation in the single syllable. Her fingers tightened into fists and she longed for a weapon to wipe the fiendish grin off his face. But how could she deny it? Hadn't he just proven that he could make her want him? Besides, another denial might bring yet another demonstration. So, controlling herself, she only looked daggers at him as for a moment neither spoke.

Then he turned away again, perfunctorily stripping himself of his robes, his skin flashing bronze in the flickering light as the muscles of his back played like the workings of a well-oiled machine. From a trunk he withdrew a rough woven blanket that he threw carelessly at her. Then, not giving her a backward look, he tumbled into bed and, to Juliette's astonishment, moments later fell asleep.

Chapter 55

The next morning, Juliette awoke to Fadjar's impatient pawing outside and to the sounds of voices coming from the outer room.

Wondering if her aching head would split from the pain, she sat up warily.

How could he have left her here, chained to his bed, and still sleep so soundly when she, filled with fury, had only been able to drop off from exhaustion an hour before dawn? God—and to have to face him this morning. But what was he doing now?

She came to her feet, noticing only then that the shackle had been removed, though her reddened ankle still bore its mark.

Wrapping the blanket around herself, she stepped to the doorway dividing the rooms and stopped there as she heard voices coming clearly through the drapery.

"But I cannot blame you for not wanting to let the girl go. She has bewitched you, is it not true?" The black Ethiopian kissed his beringed fingers. "Such rare beauty. And never in all my travels have I seen eyes that color."

Gessat Nassid reached within his robes to secretly weigh again the small bag of diamonds he kept hidden there as his smiling eyes regarded the Sheik of El Abadan. "But you, my friend—it is said you have many lovely women in your desert city and also that you often travel to places where fair coloring such as hers is as common as pebbles along a road. But think, my friend, what a rarity she is to me, and what I am willing to pay." The Ethiopian's eyes enlarged with his show of teeth and he continued to secretly finger the little leather bag. "And I will tell you that it is most important that I have her. Already I have promised her to a certain chief. You may know his name— Hazrat Khan?" Again the Ethiopian raised his eyebrows. Despite Sharif's stony expression, Nassid felt sure that the sheik was interested. "A powerful chief, you will agree," he continued. "A man who might also be able to help you. I propose that together we give this girl as a present from ourselves. And just between us, I am willing to also impart to you the price I offered at the Club Rayseyn." He waved his hand. "A mere trifle to you, of course. But doesn't every small amount add to a man's wealth? And wars are expensive, are they not?" Again Nassid smiled, his eyes locking with Sharif's before dropping slowly to sip his coffee.

Sharif's face was inscrutable as he, too, tasted from his

own cup, wondering as he did of Nassid had come to his
camp only to make an offer on Juliette or if there was
another motive. Indeed this Ethiopian was no fool and apparently knew what offer would be most tempting. Hazrat
Kahn was the chieftain controlling the passages south of El
Abadan. When war finally came with the French or English, it would be across this chief's territory that he could
best supply his men. Nassid offered a perfect opportunity
to join in friendship with this chieftain. But then, frustrat-
ingly, Sharif had no time to explore the options or extract
any further information from his guest since a rustle at
the curtains told them both that *she* was there, even before
Juliette jerked the divider aside.

Setting his coffee cup down with a click Sharif bit back
a curse. By Allah! He *did* have half a mind to sell her!

Of course her entrance stopped the discussion, as the
Ethiopian's eyes slipped easily over Juliette's bare shoulders
scattered with tangled hair and down to her bare legs
standing astride below the blanket she kept tightly held to
herself.. Then courteously Nassid looked away smiling
slightly as if to himself and nodded, half bowing, before
excusing himself so as not to impinge upon the imminent
domestic collision.

Ah, he thought to himself as he reentered the sunshine,
so this houri of paradise was here, right in the sheik's own
tent. And, from her attitude, it was obvious she had not
been completely tamed. No wonder Sharif was not anxious
to let her go. In the dim lights of the Club Rayseyn she had
been lovely, but in daylight her freshness took on a new
dimension. Now her eyes sparkled with a kind of fire and
her face was animated instead of bland and drugged. Exquisite, yes, her brilliance reminded him of his diamonds
and, indeed, once he had her, he would not be so quick to
make her a present to Hazrat Khan. But Sharif, for his
part, had given no sign to suggest his interest in the proposal, though instinct told Nassid he was considering it.
Well, possibly it still all could be arranged, and now, having seen the girl again, his mind was settled. He must have
her, and would—one way or another.

*   *   *

That day, the caravan traveled steadily southward up a long sandy incline, a light breeze fluttering the silk curtains of Juliette's pavilion as she rode.

She had expected today to be the same as all days—that they would travel until midday, rest, and then continue on until dark. So she was surprised when instead Sharif's voice halted them only an hour after beginning.

Pulling back the curtain, Juliette peered out, seeing they had stopped near the edge of a plateau where the desert floor stretched three hundred yards below in a desolate plain for as far as she could see.

Why were they stopping here? And she was even more curious when the camels were quickly hobbled and those horses, that so far had not been ridden but had been led tethered to camels, were saddled and mounted by the men.

No one spoke to her, nor did Rashid escort her to the awning. But Juliette dared not even stick her head out to try and spot Cassia for fear of seeing Sharif instead—and she couldn't, no, wouldn't face him—not after this morning. She had thought he was going to strike her, even strangle her with his bare hands that flexed occasionally at his sides as he had lectured her with quiet, horrible calm. "Women are to be discreet," he told her. "They are never to appear before a man's guests—never! And you will not again."

Oh, how she hated him. But what choice was there but to nod, cringing inwardly as he impaled her with a last look before he shouldered his way under the tent flap and was gone. No, she didn't want to see him again, not until she had to. So she didn't look out, but stayed in her pavilion until Cassia came, offering her a small tray of tea and plump dates.

"What is going on?" she asked. "Why are we stopping?"

"We are to wait here, madame. The master is traveling ahead to another caravan carrying rifles and ammunition to the French fort at Ihir. The master has gone to bring back these guns."

"Bring them back?" Juliette questioned. "Do you mean steal them?"

Cassia cocked her head. "Perhaps steal, yes, madame.

But this is Arab land, not French. Yet the French have come—have built fortresses, and, if they have more weapons, they are more dangerous. The master will not permit this. He will capture the weapons and take them to El Abadan." Cassia touched Juliette's hand lightly and reassuringly. "Please do not look so frightened, madame. The master never fails. He will return to you unharmed."

"But he must fail sometimes!" Juliette said indignantly.

A volley of shots interrupted them and, though they were not loud, Juliette held her ears. Murderer! Attacking innocent people just to rob them. How could he?

The shots were returned by another volley of fire that rolled across the open sand plain like thunder. But it was short-lived and in minutes the shooting stopped.

It was an hour before the party of men returned, conspicuously without prisoners and leading a line of camels laden with crates.

There was a brief rest while horses were watered, unsaddled, and tethered again to camels as the other mounts were resaddled. Then, as if nothing important had occurred, the camels were unhobbled and urged to their feet with a lurch, and the caravan moved off again in long rhythmic strides.

The sun paled to burning white, the sand and sky blending into one as heat waves rose off the desert floor in filmy streaks flowing upward and veiling like ghosts a herd of gazelles as they ran along the open plain in the distance.

In spite of the water she drank before, Juliette's throat was already parched, her tongue feeling thick. Oh, God, this was torture. She had nothing left to lose. Instead of cringing, why hadn't she accused him of bargaining to sell her to that swift-eyed little man. And now in his typical matter-of-fact way, he had murdered those Frenchmen. Oh, how could he? she thought, putting her hands to her eyes and wanting to whip her emotions into a fury. But somehow, she felt too hot even to think further and, leaning her head back, she closed her eyes and wished that somehow her temples would cease throbbing.

When the caravan halted for the night, it was Rashid

who, as usual, appeared to escort her to Sharif's tent, his hard sparse body striding effortlessly over the sand.

In the last hours the weather had finally cooled and now rare clouds dotted the cooling sky in puffs of salmon against turquoise as she stepped inside the tent, looking from side to side and half expecting to see *him* there. But he was not, and a quick perusal of the bedroom told her he had not yet arrived.

Wearily she leaned against the middle post of the main room, a part of her feeling beaten, defeated, without hope, even as another part of her was infuriated by her own weakness. Could anyone despise another as much as she did him?

Her eyes shifted toward the open tent flap where, outside, a *mahreh* was being led past, the last sunlight playing against its white coat. Then turning away, she began pacing the floor, her feet sinking into the soft rugs as she traveled up and down, one small fist pounding into the palm of her other hand.

She couldn't just sit here, waiting like a snared animal for him to do whatever he planned. She couldn't allow him to take her whenever he wished and to wring, in spite of herself, a response from her traitorous body.

A noise outside brought her up short and, running lightly to the entrance, she peered outside.

It was Sharif, his stallion prancing and snorting as it was reined to a stop.

A groom jumped to the horse's head as the tall man swung nimbly down, tossing the tasseled reins to the salaaming Arab and giving the animal an affectionate pat before it was led away.

Juliette withdrew out of sight, shuddering as he came forward, the end of his black head scarf hanging loose against one shoulder.

Her hands entwined, whitening her knuckles. He was coming, just as before . . . to hurt . . . to humiliate her. She couldn't, she wouldn't bear it, no, not any longer.

Stormy eyes swept the room, settling on the large candleholder sitting on the low table. Then, driven by sudden impulse, Juliette quickly reached to grab it and moved to the doorway, stepping up onto another table there and waiting, the candlestick raised like a cleaver.

If only she could kill him. He deserved it! He deserved worse! And when Sharif entered, she brought the weapon down with all her might.

Chapter 56

Some instinct must have warned him, or he saw the blow coming—Juliette never knew which. But he was suddenly beyond the reach of it and grabbing her just above the elbow to jerk her off the table and beneath one of his arms.

"Bastard! I hate you!" she screamed as he wrenched the candleholder free and replaced it on the table. Then carrying her to the hassock, he sat down pulling her across his knees.

"Let me go! I'll kill you! I hate you—murderer!"

Sharif held her easily, letting her wear herself out.

"I think it's time we understood each other, Juliette. I consider you *my* woman, but that makes you no better than any of my servants. And you will call me *sayyid*; as they do."

This was too much! He was no master of hers—no, never! Yet she feared him and, flushing, she turned her face away, shaking her head.

Immediately Sharif's smile disappeared. He stood up, letting her tumble off his knees onto the floor, and she didn't attempt to rise, automatically drawing up her legs and arms as a shield as he loomed over her, his scowl making her quiver.

"How shall I convince you?" he asked quietly, his hands rising to ride his hips. "What do you hate most?"

He didn't let her answer, but merely pushed her further down on her back, straddling her, pinning her between his knees. She didn't have to see his hands unfastening his robes to know what he planned. And suddenly anything was preferable to his touch, to his presence within her, to the shame of her own renegade responses. "Please!" she cried.

His eyes shifted to her face and, leaning forward, he pressed her shoulder blades to the floor, his thumbs resting on her breasts. *"Sayyid,"* he pronounced softly through clenched teeth.

For a long moment steady ebony beams met her faltering gaze before she jerked her chin so he had only her profile to study. What remained of her pride was revolted by her surrender, but still she found her lips forming the word *sayyid* in a scathing hiss.

Magically she was released and pulled to her feet so again the robe fell to her ankles. Her legs felt weak, shaking so she could hardly stand and, swaying, she looked up.

"So you really hate me that much. You surprise me!" He laughed shortly. "I've never encountered a woman who wanted so much to resist, particularly when her own body is so willing." His smile deepened, and his hand tilted her chin up as he studied her wordlessly. Then his hand dropped and, walking to the tent flap, he lifted it, indicating from east to west with a sweep of his arm.

"This is the desert, *chérie,* and I see I must explain that here exists a place worlds apart from England or France or anything you have known before."

His arm swung to the east. "There is the most rugged territory in the world, nothing for miles but crushed rocks burned black by the sun. Arabs call it the gravel pit of Hell since no one dares live there, and no one crosses it unless he must. It is a border more formidable than if it were patrolled by a thousand armies."

His arm indicated northeast. "There is Egypt, a land already subjugated by Europeans, a place easily used to supply those English armies that are already competing for territory with the French and Italians in the north.

"And last are the Hussar," he said pointing south, "waiting, I suspect, until we get closer before they attack. Abu Hussar's tribe and mine have been at war for generations now, and there will be no peace until one of us is dead."

He turned back to face her, his hands on his hips. "Hostility is all around, *chérie.*" He opened his arms outward. "And here I am in the middle, only a man of flesh and blood. You call me murderer, but just to live in the desert is a constant war between the elements and the people. In war there is always death. Today I killed—is that why you are so angry? But you will learn that sometimes it is necessary to kill to prevent being killed. Why do you think the French are arming themselves? Not for peaceful purposes, I assure you. In a way it is your fault I had to kill them. If you'd come with me willingly months ago, I could have avoided this much trouble. As it was I had to make sure the ship was delayed in Marseille long enough so I could catch up with them here—but no matter. Whatever you call what happened today, it is a fact that in the desert only strength has value. Arabs are a tough breed, and if I am to lead them, then I must never demonstrate either weakness or sentimentality, especially where a woman is concerned. It is only fortunate this incident tonight was not witnessed and can remain a private matter between you and me, and if you are wise, you will not provoke me again, madame." His piercing appraisal riveted her in a vise of black. "I would rather not have to demonstrate just what a savage I really am."

PART IX

HUSSAR

Chapter 57

The desert sun blazed high overhead, a white-hot furnace blending the boundaries of sky and sand into a single sea of undulating waves. It might have been a lake. Certainly, from a distance, the endless stretch of sand seemed to sparkle and dance with lights as it must have ages ago, when it was a huge water-covered plain.

Under a shaded awning, poised cross-legged on a pillow, Juliette sat drinking tea and eating dried meat—her portion of the food which had been rationed ever since several pack camels were lost in a sudden sandstorm three days before.

Sandstorms. They were a new phenomenon, like nothing she had ever seen. Wind blowing dust into gritty waves that turned the ground into rivulets resembling the ridges of a washboard, and sand, sand everywhere until one could not move outside the tent and even the animals were brought inside with the people.

The wind, the dust, the very power of it had frightened her at first. But later, after the first storm had passed and Juliette stepped outside the tent, she found the desert transformed into an oddly beautiful infinity of wavy patterns as pristine as a new fall of snow.

There had been two smaller storms since then and now she was more fascinated by, than afraid of, the howling wind. It seemed impossible that only a month had passed. Hadn't she been traveling forever in this endless, frightening, yet magnificent desolation? Yet lately she was forced to admit that the desert did have a certain magic—a sense of total presence that made the appalling dryness and the sudden rains seem only a part of a great mystery. And sometimes now, when the night was still, she would slip from Sharif's side and tiptoe to the tent's entrance to watch the twinkling stars, to feel the sheer magnitude of space and the silence so complete, so empty, that it reached the depths of her soul.

Yes, a month had changed everything, and she, like the Arabs around her, had learned to survive, to obey this man and, with a shrug of her shoulders, she accepted it. Why bloody herself against an obstacle she had no hope of overcoming? Why make herself unhappy when she could concentrate instead on the beauty of dawn when the sky turned from red to orange and finally to a strange haunting pink before clearing to blue as the sun peeked over the edge of the endless sand.

But within this mystery and magic there was danger. As they penetrated deeper into the desert, the terrain changed from sand to endless fields of gravel dotted by sporadic upheavals of rock. It was a land more forbidding, more majestic than ever Juliette imagined. She also noticed the guard was doubled now, and the careless talk and laughter that characterized the men earlier had changed to silence.

They no longer wore their rifles slung on their backs, but rested them instead in the crooks of their arms, their constricted eyes scanning the expanse. And, when they did speak, they often mentioned the name Hussar.

Scouts were sent ahead any time the column neared a hill or pass that might hide an ambush, and sentries climbed the cliffs and signaled back to the caravan with mirrors that tossed the sunlight from point to point in a code of their own.

Just this morning, in fact, scouts had ridden off toward a stone formation that crouched like a huge animal in the distance and, having a view of the camp from her awning, Juliette noticed now that a mounted group was galloping toward them.

Squinting, Juliette had just realized these were not the returning scouts, when Sharif's men began reaching hastily for their rifles and again she heard the name Hussar.

Sharif appeared among the men, also looking toward the riders, a curt word from him instantly easing the tension.

There were a dozen riders, two of them at least being women, and, as they came to a halt, Juliette saw their leader jump from his horse and prostrate himself in the sand before Sharif's boots.

Sharif said something Juliette couldn't hear, and the man rose again and, with chaotic wavings of his arms, began a stream of rapid Arabic.

"They are entertainers—Gypsies, you would call them," Cassia translated in a whisper. "They were with a caravan from Algiers that was attacked by Hussar. They are the only survivors and beg protection from the master."

Juliette heard Sharif's voice deep and clear across the open space. She could understand more Arabic now than she could speak, and knew he had granted their request.

Again the man fell at Sharif's feet kissing the hem of his robes before rising and leading the group of horses and riders away.

False alarm—for now, Juliette thought, though she knew the news of the Hussar warriors being nearby would have an additional unsettling effect on the men and wasn't surprised as they all checked their rifles and added crisscrossed bandoliers of cartridges across their chests.

Looking at Sharif, Juliette found him thoughtfully watching the receding backs of the Gypsy party, his profile etched against the white heat of day as clear as the face on a coin.

The sun had bronzed his complexion until it was only a shade or two lighter than the other Arabs and, within his robes, his body lost all its civilized graces. Now he bore little resemblance to the man she had once called Brandon. Those same hands that had once formed genteel salon gestures now seemed just as natural wielding a dagger with deadly accuracy or pulling the clothes from her with slow deliberateness before exploring her as no gentleman ever would.

The days he spent at the head of the caravan, fully erect in his saddle and apparently heedless of the intense heat and glare. The nights he passed meeting with various lieutenants or studying maps by candlelight until finally coming to bed near dawn, throwing back the covers to bare her naked body, and taking her wordlessly. Then rising again he would dress for the day and was gone.

His preoccupation and silences that often lasted for hours or even days wore on Juliette. What was he thinking?

And feeling irresistibly curious one evening she asked, "You are so silent, Sharif, you hardly speak. What occupies you so?"

A frown passed fleetingly across his brow. "A man's mind is not the business of a woman," he said flatly before returning to the maps laid out on the floor of the tent where he sat cross-legged.

Then, as always, his casual insults left her speechless, her anger throbbing for ventilation. But what was the point of showing him how furious he could make her when he would only win in the end? So remembering this, and her promise of obedience she said, "I was only wondering. Sometimes you say so little." Then wanting to make peace she added, "I'm sorry if I've displeased you."

The edge around his mouth seemed to soften. His eyes were knowing as he nodded. But still he said nothing, ignoring her the rest of the evening until, once again, he called her to him and took her, this time more gently and slowly so that her passion rose with his, so that once again Juliette found herself drowned in the same rapture as before, and shamelessly craving release—so blindly drunk with pleasure that for those moments she forgot how he hated her, that he was an Arab, her father's murderer. And it was only afterward, when the cloud of euphoria receded, that she remembered it all again and, stiffening, told herself firmly that she despised him too, while denying the deep emptiness gathering inside her. And turning over, she silently sobbed herself to sleep.

After that she refused to think about the past or future. She could not dwell on what might come when they reached El Abadan, Sharif's desert city. She couldn't think what would happen when the journey was finished and she became only one of Sharif's many women and one whom he would one day grow tired of humiliating. What might happen then was too abhorrent even to consider. If I think of that now I will go mad, she told herself. So she put the future out of her mind and lived only for the present. It was part of being Arab, she was once told, to find pleasure in simple things, to savor the wind against her face, to taste the sweet goodness of water on her tongue, and to see the

fine sculpture of the distant mountains, experiencing each
wonder to its fullest, neither wanting more nor less, and
questioning nothing. And as much as Juliette was able, she
stayed within the balm of the present to find a certain
peace.

Now, Juliette tasted her tea again and tore another bite
of meat from the hardened slab with her back teeth.

From outside a sudden sound caught her attention and,
looking up, she found Cassia running toward her, wild-
eyed, disheveled, her modest black robe torn. Stumbling
under the awning, the girl fell at her feet.

"Madame! In the name of mercy . . . help me!" she
wailed between sobs.

"Cassia!" Juliette's mouth rounded. A young Arab man
followed hard after the girl and paused now at the edge of
the awning, apparently reluctant to trespass within it. From
where he stood outside he uttered a series of curses, most
of which Juliette did not understand though they made
Cassia cringe and cover her ears.

Juliette hauled Cassia up by the shoulders. Tears were
streaming down the girl's face and pooling at the corners of
her mouth.

"I have sinned, madame. I have sinned and Rafik is
going to kill me."

"Don't be ridiculous. No one is going to kill you. Who is
this man? What does he want?"

Cassia was quivering all over as if from a violent chill
and there was a red imprint of a hand across her face.
"You do not understand, madame. I have sinned! I have
dishonored my father and my brothers and uncles. It is
right to kill me but . . . but, madame, I do not want to
die. I'm afraid. And I am not a bad girl, only an unlucky
one."

"What do you mean?" Juliette asked, the truth slowly
taking shape in the form of Cassia's robe curving over her
rounded abdomen. She remembered thinking that the girl
was thriving in spite of the rationed food, but now her apparent health was explained in a very different way. "Oh,
Cassia, I had no idea," she said with a faint blush. "When

did it happen, I mean who is the father—not *this* man surely!"

"No, madame," Cassia replied, her face blanching as another abusive volley of language fired from the man.

"How does this man dare follow you here?" Juliette asked, her temper rising as, like a tigress, she strode forward, throwing back the hood of her robe to face him.

"No, madame!" Cassia screamed grabbing her mistress's ankle and a handful of her robe.

Juliette looked down. "Do you think I'm going to let this man treat you like this?"

"But he is Rafik, my brother, madame. He has seen the evidence of my crime. To wipe the shame from our family he must kill me. But, madame, this is not my fault. I am not an evil girl. It was months ago in Tripoli. I was sent to the marketplace for silk. I stayed later than I thought. It was a long walk home and two men followed me. We were alone. What could I do? There were two of them. . . . Please believe me, madame!"

Juliette winced, imagining Cassia, helpless in the grasp of these two men. Rafik was cursing again. "And now that you have been raped, your brother has the right to kill you, is that it?" she asked incredulously.

Cassia moaned. "Please, madame!"

"No one is going to kill you, Cassia," Juliette said evenly, "that I promise." And this time when she turned toward the Arab, Cassia didn't cling to her, but kissed the hem of her robe.

Juliette's eyes were slits of light-struck glass as she straightened and confronted the man as if an army stood at her back instead of only Cassia, crouched, looking out from behind her knees like a child.

Surprised, Rafik took a short step back. So, he thought, *this* was the bold white woman of which there was so much gossip—the one who had caused the death of Abdul ibn al-Mehridim and the destruction of the Club Rayseyn—the one who had become the most favored of all Sharif's women. She made no move to cover her face or lower her gaze. No, this one spoke in faltering but understandable Arabic and looked him right in his eye.

"Why have you come?" she asked, and Rafik was forced to admire her dignity and proud bearing for all its immodesty. Was not this woman to mother sons? But the woman would not distract him from his mission and, pointing a lean finger at his sister, he said, "I have come for her."

The white woman seemed to grow taller as she said, "You cannot take her! Even if she is your sister, she is my maid given to me by the master. I will not see her harmed."

"This is a family matter," Rafik said firmly. "She has disgraced my father and my father's father. For this she must pay."

"You would punish her when what has occurred took place without her consent and by force?" Juliette stared indignantly.

Rafik was embarrassed. This white woman was frank as a man. He averted his eyes. "She must die," he said between clenched teeth.

"But surely there must be some other solution than to kill her," the white woman began again in a conciliatory tone as a moment passed. "If Cassia were to marry, then surely . . ."

Rafik waved a hand as if to sweep away her words and leaned closer. "What man would marry a woman so dishonored? No man would take her. She has only the choice of becoming a public woman, a *sharmûta*, giving further dishonor to her family."

"But you can't kill your own sister. And she is not a . . . a *sharmûta*. She is my maid, I tell you!"

Rafik felt furious at this woman's lack of understanding of principles that seemed to him elementary. "Doesn't a white man feel dishonored when others pay to copulate with his sister?"

Now it was Juliette's turn to flush with embarrassment. And it was then Juliette saw Sharif riding down the face of a dune a short distance out of camp

Thank heaven! Juliette thought. Now he would put this horrible mess right—or would he? But it was too late now, already he was nearing them and reining Fadjar to a halt.

His face was expressionless as his eyes moved from Juliette to Rafik to the cringing Cassia. Then his gaze shifted again to Rafik. "Come, ibn-Rafik," he said simply. "We will discuss the affairs of men in private."

Rafik's expression lost its anger and grew more dignified. He gave Juliette a glance down his narrow nose before salaaming the Sharif. "It is as you say, *Sayyid.*"

Sharif's eyes fell momentarily on Cassia. "You will come too," he commanded. Then turning his horse, he rode in the opposite direction.

Cassia cried out as Rafik reached to pull her from behind Juliette. But Juliette did not dare to protest. What more could she do without making more of a scene that could force Sharif into a position against her. Her only choice remained to helplessly watch with both fury and fear turning her stomach as Rafik followed the sheik, dragging Cassia after him.

Chapter 58

Juliette waited, terrified that at any moment a single shot would signal Cassia's end. But the dry air remained still as the caravan moved on and Juliette, fearful, frustrated, looked through her pavilion curtains, twisting her neck in search of some sign, some indication of the girl's fate.

Isn't it just like Sharif to keep me in torment? she thought to herself. But there was nothing to do but wait in dark apprehension. And, as it turned out, she didn't learn what happened until that night, after Sharif had silently eaten dinner and coffee had been served in thimble-sized cups and he had lounged back comfortably against the cushions reading, ironically, Shakespeare's *The Tempest.*

Juliette feared asking outright what had happened, but finally unable to bear the tension any longer she blurted out, "What have . . . what has been done with Cassia?"

As he looked up from his reading, Juliette felt sure he would simply tell her it was none of her affair.

"Please!" she began before pausing to bite her lip. "Don't keep me wondering. It's so cruel of you. I've been frantic with worry all day."

His eyebrow half cocked in that infuriating way that always made her want to slap him. "Really," he said, "you surprise me. What difference does the life of one brown-skinned girl more or less make to you?"

Juliette's jaw slackened before her face stiffened indignantly. "A great deal of difference! How can you think otherwise? It's you who are callous, you and the others. Her own brother wanted to kill her, and for reasons I'll never understand."

"You don't understand because you are ignorant of Arab customs," he commented lazily. "In England honor is little more than an idea to bandy about, while here, a man's reputation is everything. Arab tribes live closely together for generations, each knowing the others all their lives. Here a man's reputation and family honor is more valuable than gold."

"I don't know how you can say honor isn't important to the English. It's just that we don't believe in killing a girl for . . . for what happened to Cassia. You Arabs treat women like something that gets thrown away when it is soiled."

Sharif's expression was unmoved. "Yes, and what do you English do when a girl has been 'ruined'? That is what you call it, isn't it?" he asked with a nasty ring in his voice. "Bah—what hypocrites you are! You don't kill the poor girl but instead doom her to being the constant subject of gossip—to a life without the protection of a husband, and to have a child which likewise will be the subject of scorn—an embarrassing fact that everyone wishes would disappear. Arabs are more brutal perhaps, but also more direct. We choose a quick end rather than prolonged misery."

He turned back to his book then, unconcerned, the discussion, from his point of view, over. And still looking at the back of his head, Juliette's white teeth worked on her lip, feeling cold to the pit of her stomach as the truth sank in.

It seemed impossible, yet he had killed Cassia—killed a defenseless pregnant girl for a crime committed not *by* her, but, rather, *against* her.

The unfairness and cruelty of it all was unendurable and, thinking again of Cassia being dragged stumbling away, brown arms outstretched back to her in silent supplication, Juliette felt a sudden compelling rage rush through her.

She stood up, her fists clenched at her sides, all her vows never to anger him again forgotten. "How can you sit there justifying murder. Is there nothing that revolts you? And if you are so keen on quick endings then what about *my* misery. Why prolong *my* pain when you could end it. When will you let me go? I can't stand this. You're driving me mad, and anything would be better than living like this and watching you become an animal before my eyes!"

"I don't let you go, *chérie*, because I wish to have you here and alive." There was a hint of a grin on his lips. "Anyway, I'm the one who 'ruined' you—remember? Now you are my property, and I keep what belongs to me."

"Property!" Juliette flared. "You may think so, monsieur. But to me I have been kidnapped and taken against my will. I am no more at fault for what has happened to me than poor Cassia was responsible for what happened to her. I am no one's property except my own. You are disgusting . . . all of you—nothing but a pack of barbarians!"

Sharif shrugged, maddeningly unmoved by her outburst. "Perhaps you would prefer to belong to anyone." His arm swept to indicate beyond the tent walls. "If all of them were free to take you, then you would be common property—although there are more colorful words to describe such a woman. My men would be pleased, no doubt. But I wonder if you have the strength to service them all. Even *you* have some limitations."

And before she could think of a scathing comment, his two hands had pulled her down beside him.

"But you'll get used to our Arab ways. Arabs and English are not as different as you think. You may even decide you like this life, given time to grow accustomed to it." A glimmer in the depths of his charcoal eyes assessed her closely.

"Never!" she flamed trying to jerk away. "I can't prevent how you treat me, but I'll never like it. You're wrong. Nothing has changed. And I'll escape. You'll see! I'm not beaten yet! I'll never become an Arab woman, no matter what you do, and I'll never stop hating you!"

She was breathing hard now as she tried to stand up, but he held her firmly, so finally she turned her head away, leaving him only a pink ear to study.

Already she had said too much, and now her heart quickened with fear as she suddenly remembered Sharif's temper. Angered, he was capable of anything, and she braced herself as, for a moment, he neither moved nor spoke.

His hold on her arms relaxed before his fingers encircled her chin, raising her faltering gaze into alignment with his steady one. "Don't be a fool," he said flatly. "Do you think your English friends would take you back? You may not ever become an Arab. You may hate me till the day you die. But your English society won't have you. Not now because, just like Cassia, you are 'ruined.' And not just by a white man of their own kind but by an Arab, which they consider much worse. So, you can forget about your English 'friends.' " His eyes drew into penetrating focus. "And what if *you* should have a child?—*my* child—an *Arab* child? Have you thought of that, *chérie?*" he asked with a look that impaled her.

Juliette's eyes were wide open, her quick intake of breath rasping. She jerked her chin free then, refusing to let him see her face and the confusion his words had provoked.

It had occurred to her of course. Yes—she had thought—but then refused to think . . . A baby! *His* baby!

Her thoughts tumbled tumultuously one over the other. No . . . Oh, God! Such a catastrophe was impossible. She swallowed hard. Yet her body was no longer her own. He used her as he would—whenever it pleased him. Even now she might carry his child and, glancing at Sharif's firm jaw, his broad shoulders, his sleek animal body sitting beside her, she realized abruptly that he would plant his seed within her whether or not *she* would have it there.

A sudden numbness crept over her and she wasn't prepared when Sharif laughed softly, scooping her up into his arms and bending closer to reach for her lips.

"Damn you!" Kicking her legs, Juliette beat fists against his chest. But he only laughed again.

"So! You aren't so subdued. I thought not. How well you pretend. You never fail to amuse me." He took both her wrists in one hand again, pulling her closer. And in spite of her protests, kissed her, forcing her lips open to receive him before he withdrew.

"You can't . . . I won't let you . . . It won't happen again!" she wailed, struggling in vain against his hands, which did not hurt but would not give way.

He seemed not to hear and, lifting her higher, shouldered aside the drapery to carry her into the bedroom where he laid her on the bed with a firm sense of purpose that sent Juliette's pulse throbbing. Already the sign of his desire was hard against her knees, and his fingers pulled open her robes and traced her nipples, and pulled them into erection.

Sharif felt his need throb as he unfastened his garments. How her beauty taunted him, he thought. And today, even as they had ridden southward, none of the dangers and pressing matters of business could keep his attention as again and again he found his eyes trying to glimpse Juliette between the pavilion's blowing draperies. Juliette, this strange girl-woman. Would night find her submissive or rebellious or simply silent in the way she often was—as if a shutter were drawn down between herself and the world? Most women told everything they thought, all their secrets in a constant chatter. But this one was a puzzle, constantly changing, one moment seemingly content, and another as savage as a Zulu princess.

What was she thinking during those long hours when they didn't speak? Did she think of England, or Las Flores? Did she ever recall those days before they had learned to hate each other so well? Did she ever think of that night in the garden, that night she had promised to marry him as she had lain trembling in his arms, not just wanting him, but loving him.

He gritted his teeth. How could she have deceived him when she seemed so incapable of duplicity? And he recalled another night, blue-black as this one, when he had taken her in the governor's palace in Tripoli. How easily then her hot blood had blossomed into passion matching his own. Then he had been surprised, even awed by the warmth and wonder he felt from her surrendering body. And with this new awareness growing within him, he had played her body like a fine instrument until, at last, everything had exploded in a shower of pleasure before, satiated, she had fallen asleep in his arms.

"Don't touch me! I won't do this again!" Her voice pierced his reverie as she writhed and squirmed beneath him like a young animal. "I won't have your child! I won't! Don't you know I hate you? And even if I can't help what happens, I swear I'll drown any baby of yours! I will . . . as soon as it is born! Do you think I would have *your* child when it is *you* who murdered my father? I hate you . . . you dirty . . . you filthy . . . you . . . you . . . *nigger!*"

Her breast were heaving and her dilated eyes had grown to polished jewels. His grip stiffened, his face suddenly turned to stone and, in his opaque eyes, she could read nothing but chilling hardness as a long moment silently passed. Then suddenly she was tumbling out of his arms and onto the floor with an unceremonious thud as he stood up, never seeming so tall, so proud as he towered over her.

Juliette sprang up, backing against the tent walls, his look scathing her as he said, "Ah—so you do have your prejudices, if not against your servant Cassia, then against the more general population of what you English indiscriminately call 'niggers.' As you might someday understand, though our customs differ from yours, it does not make us inferior. And since you seem so interested, I might add that the Arabs of this region, the Tawarigs, are all descended from the same Caucasian ancestors as you."

"Sharif, I . . ." Juliette began feeling ashamed that she had called him that horrible word when she didn't really

think of him that way, not at all. But he had cut her off
with a wave of his hand.

"*Bon soir,* madame. You may keep your precious white
hide to yourself. There are others, women instead of little
girls, who welcome my attention." Then noiselessly turning,
he passed beyond the curtains without another glance.

A sharp pain chopped into her heart as she blinked
wildly. Others indeed, she thought. "Well, let them have
you then!" she shouted after him. "You and your children
too!" But there was no answer, and she knew he had already gone.

Tears filled her eyes, droplets running down her face
and falling onto the big bed. Enraged, hopeless, and suddenly empty, she didn't even bother to brush them away.
She hadn't meant to call him that, but somehow it had happened. Still he was such a beast, and worst of all, there was
no where else to go, no one else to help her. Yet she
couldn't remain, not with him. Oh, God, how she hated
him. Curling herself into a ball of misery, she held a pillow
in her arms and sobbed against it.

Chapter 59

When Juliette finally sat up again, brushing the tumbled
hair from her tear-streaked cheeks, it was because she
couldn't endure the sounds of tambourines and drums and
the shouts of men any longer.

It was those Gypsies who had started it, she thought angrily. Standing out in front of their striped tents juggling,
they had challenged the warriors to best them at hitting
circles marked in the sand with thrown daggers. So they
had competed. But then, as the night sky had darkened,
the knives were sheathed and the winners congratulated
and, with shouts of encouragement, the music had begun.

Oh! How could all of them be enjoying themselves when
she was so miserable. And, rising to her feet, and wiping
her swollen eyes, Juliette half walked, half stumbled to the
open tent flap.

Outside, some distance away, the men had built a fire larger than usual and now were sitting around it circled by musicians. The sounds of their drums and tambourines thundered in Juliette's head and she was about to turn away when she heard the men begin shouting again.

Craning her neck, she saw a woman appear from the darkness to the circle of firelight—a tall Gypsy woman kicking her feet to the beat of the drums, and holding her arms above her head as she danced out into the open space.

Now the men shouted louder and more eagerly. She lifted her face veil, swirling it above her head and moving around the outer limits of the circle with the supple grace of a snake.

The woman seemed neither old nor young, and she was not beautiful. But her bare feet danced time to the music, kicking up the dust, her mane of black hair framing her slanting cheekbones and wide red mouth in a wild mass that made her seem at once utterly sensual and challenging.

Undulating her lavish body, she looked from one man to another, a large white smile flashing across her face from time to time that said more clearly than words, "Here I am—you can take me—maybe—if you are man enough."

Juliette's head throbbed and, bringing her palm to her brow, she thought, now why doesn't Sharif choose someone like that? Someone who would welcome his vulgar attentions. Why does he insist on having me instead, when I hate him? But wasn't that just like a man to want what was not easily given?

Again Juliette thought of going back within the tent, but something about the woman kept her watching as the music slowed to a more sensual tempo and the Gypsy's voluptuous undulations became more blatantly suggestive.

Her bright smile sneered slightly now as she brushed close to one of the men, at once inviting and repelling. Her large scarf floated between outstretched arms, accentuating the heavy bouncing of her large-nippled breasts.

The men shouted less often then until the only remaining sounds were the music and the whisper of the Gypsy's veils and mesmerized "ahs" of appreciation from around the circle.

No, the woman was not beautiful, Juliette thought, but she possessed a feral essence that would kindle any man's desire. And now she noticed that even Sharif, who had been conversing with several of his headmen, had stopped to take notice.

Apparently the girl noticed him, too. The drums and tambourines quickened the pace, and she paused directly before him, her feet keeping time as she twirled faster and faster until the light veils draping her body lifted out, revealing all her lavish curves.

Faster, yet faster, the beat increased, until bare legs flew. Then, in a jarring halt, the music ceased, and suddenly the Gypsy was kneeling at Sharif's feet, her head bowed submissively.

He smiled, and the man beside him nudged another as a murmur raced over the crowd. Juliette held her breath as Sharif reached to lift the woman's face. She couldn't see the woman's expression, but imagined her knowledgeable eyes bright with invitation.

Suddenly it was too much and refusing to watch any more, Juliette jerked the tent flap closed and began pacing up and down in front of the hassock.

Well, at least she didn't care! Let him take his pleasure where he found it. She couldn't hate him any more than she did now. He had treated her like an animal and worse, all the while acting as if *he* were the injured party.

Well, let him have his women. She was just the sort he was meant for, one who made her living dancing for coins, one who would willingly pleasure him.

Defiantly she wiped away a tear. But when the music started again, she found herself at the doorway peering out with lips pressed firmly together.

Now it was another woman who danced and Sharif and the first woman were not around the fire or within sight.

Of course he had already taken her somewhere, perhaps behind one of the sand dunes surrounding camp. Yes, that was just what he would be doing, rutting like an animal on the ground. In a burst of fury, Juliette kicked a bundle of clothing lying on the rug halfway across the tent.

The blow broke the twine that held it together and scattered pieces of clothing across the rug.

Surprised, Juliette noticed they were not Sharif's, though they were men's breeches, a top, and a burnoose. No, they were not nearly large enough for him, but they would, she realized immediately, fit her.

Why would he have brought this here if not for me? she wondered. And why men's clothes? And bending to pick them up and clutching them to her one by one, an idea took shape.

Quickly she pulled off her hot robes and slipped on the clothes, finding the wide-sleeved shirt a bit long, though the burnoose and pants were satisfactory. And twisting the long dark length of fabric around and around her head, she formed a turban before knotting it just behind one ear and letting the end drape onto her shoulder. A pair of soft kidskin boots completed the costume. Then, picking up a hand mirror, Juliette studied her reflection.

Dressed this way, who would notice her? she asked herself with growing excitement. And tonight, Rashid was not outside but apparently occupied with the entertainment. It was an opportunity to escape, and this time disguised as a man.

Lowering the mirror, her sparkling eyes stared straight ahead. Of course, who would realize she was a woman? And there was a small oasis only a few hours back where they had stopped at midday. She would find water there and with the gold from Sharif's trunk she could bargain for passage with a caravan going north. She was not as naive as she once was. She spoke the language now and couldn't be fooled as she had been before by Henry. Of course there was still a risk, but what was her alternative? Now Sharif would be crueler to her than ever. She would not be his slave, to be rejected or even killed at his whim or, worse, to bear his children. Wouldn't it be better to die from thirst, or at the hands of bandits? Yes, even that would be preferable.

Looking out the tent flap she noticed even the guards had joined the throng around the dancing girls, abandoning their posts and making everything almost too easy.

Just outside the doorway, Sharif's stallion Fadjar was staked.

It was an Arab custom never to herd horses together, since having them in one place made them too easily stampeded by an enemy tribe. So each man kept his mount by his own tent, where the horse doubled also as watchdog, alerting his master to intruders.

Fadjar snorted as Juliette carefully ducked around the side of the tent. She firmly said the Arabic word that Sharif used with the animal and, to her relief, he quieted immediately, making no further sound as she ran lightly across the open spaces from one tent to another until well out of reach of the fire's glow. Then pausing, she moved stealthily toward a small tent where a horse was outlined against the sky.

The mare detected Juliette almost at once, raising her slender neck, pricking forward sculptured ears, and turning a finely etched face to look at her with intelligent curiosity.

"Easy, girl," Juliette whispered, "easy." She stretched out a hand toward the mare as if having something in her palm, at the same time berating herself for not bringing anything with which to bribe a mount.

Hastily she searched through her robe pockets, delighted to find a dried date.

It was withered as hard as a rock, but Juliette held it toward the mare, whose eyes grew brighter as her neck arched forward in a play of muscles, and her nostrils opened and closed before reaching for the tidbit.

Velvety lips brushed Juliette's palm as the mare sucked up the date, chewing and swallowing it pit and all. Juliette stroked her fine neck. Certainly these Arabians of Sharif's people were the most beautiful horses she had ever seen, small, graceful, hardy, and as fiery as the desert for which they were bred. "Easy, girl," she repeated softly looking over her shoulder and hoping no one in the tent could hear.

Inexplicably she felt an odd sense of being watched, although she could hear no sound or see any movement to indicate a presence. So bending, Juliette silently untied the fastening, and with only the lead rope and halter as a bridle, mounted the mare bareback with a leap. Then clapping her heels to her sides, Juliette only half heard something like a shout as she galloped away toward the north and freedom.

Beyond the circle of tents the mare quickly moved into the long-strided, tireless gallop for which her breed was famous, moving up and down the dunes as effortlessly as a bird. The sand was cooler and therefore firmer now. But while it did not suck at the horse's feet, Juliette knew the coolness also brought a sea of poisonous vipers roaming over the sand, hunting for rats and fennecs and each other, and trying not to think of this, she pulled her mare to a stop at the summit of a dune.

Glancing over her shoulder, Juliette assured herself no one followed. The oasis they had rested at during midday was perhaps five miles ahead. Searching for the north star, she breathed deeply in and out.

She had escaped—quietly, easily, and no one would be the wiser for hours. With any luck, by the time her disappearance was discovered, she would already be a safe distance ahead, and anyway, they would not be sure which direction she had taken. Would Sharif even delay the caravan to search for her? she wondered. Now that he had the rifles and with the limited supply of food, he seemed especially eager to reach El Abadan.

A surge of euphoria swept up from her toes, through her stomach, and into her throat. Freedom—she could feel it—yes, taste it in the air.

Still, looking for the north star, her eyes were drawn by the silent flight of an owl to the east, and she saw *them*, silhouetted against the crest of a dune, a large band of mounted figures, their rifles unslung and ready as they came ever closer. And feeling a frozen knife stabbing her guts, Juliette breathed aloud, *"Hussar!"*

Chapter 60

A cold wave passed through Juliette's stomach and even the trembling of her fatigued legs stopped as she looked again.

No, it wasn't her imagination. The force was moving steadily forward, their horses' hooves making no sound in the sand.

Hussar! Of course! What better time to attack Sharif than now, when even the guards were distracted by the Gypsies, and the camp could be overrun before any defense could be mustered.

In her imagination Juliette heard the gunfire, the surprised shouts of men and cries of women. And Sharif—they would want to kill him most of all. Who could tell what barbarous tortures these people used. He would die, and horribly, and, with a mental image of Sharif lashed to a stake and bleeding, Juliette was suddenly wheeling the mare and heading back toward camp.

Someone had to warn them!

Sensing the sudden new urgency in her rider's commands, the mare responded, immediately bounding back down the dune and sliding most of the way as if skiing on her hocks.

Clinging to the mane, Juliette prayed the Hussar had not seen her. Yet, in the moonlight, the mare's whiteness made them an easy target.

The waves of undulating dunes standing between herself and camp, that only a moment ago had seemed short, now stretched endlessly in the distance as, leaning forward to encircle the mare's neck with her arms, Juliette expected every minute for an accurate rifle shot to knock her from the horse.

But there was no fire as the animal bounded up the face of one dune and then another, finally nearing camp until, at the top of a last dune, the mare suddenly shied, turning unexpectedly in the opposite direction so abruptly that Juliette fell off to hang by the one knee still hooked over the horse's back.

The mare stood still while Juliette righted herself with a heave of her thigh and, in doing so, she noticed a small detachment of black-robed men coming toward her from the direction of Sharif's camp.

Sharif's men! Not more than twenty yards away—men already searching for her though, oddly, they were on foot and not mounted.

They appeared calm, apparently unaware that the Hussar were so close and not wanting to risk shouting Juliette reined the mare and urged her toward them.

The mare snorted, refusing to go and tossing her head rebelliously as Juliette urged her harder. But it didn't matter, the men had seen her and, in a few running strides, were circling the mare, which continued to dance and pull against Juliette's hold until one of the men grabbed the animal's halter.

Juliette looked from face to face. She didn't recognize any of them. Then someone grabbed her leg and she was falling onto her back in the sand with a soft thud.

Instantly scrambling to get up, she saw the mare's foreleg strike out at one of the men. The man jumped back, avoiding the blow and drawing his dagger in a single motion. Then leaping forward, he took the mare's bridle hard and, twisting her head aside, plunged the blade into her throat.

Blood spurted and the mare fell thrashing into the sand as the man turned back to lean over her again, his knife raised and flashing in the starlight.

Juliette's scream was loud and high-pitched. "No!"

Abruptly his blade paused in midair.

"Don't you realize who I am?" she began in rapid French.

The Arab seemed startled and frowned and the others, who had ignored her until now, turned to see.

Lowering his knife, the man reached forward and knocked the turban from her head, spilling her blond hair out onto the sand and baring her face.

Now they all leaned closer making guttural sounds of surprise as several faces broadened into leering grins.

Juliette sat up, propping her elbows behind her in the sand. "I am the English woman," she began in faltering Arabic. "I am Sharif's . . . your sayyid's woman."

They laughed. One of them roughly grabbed her robe about the neckline and jerked her face so close she gagged from the stench of his breath.

"Karim al-Sharif. I spit on his name," he snapped in a voice that cut like a whiplash. "We are Hussar, foolish woman."

Juliette's terrified eyes grew even larger. Of course—Hussar—spies dressed as Sharif's men. They had been observing the camp, signaling the attack! Again Juliette looked from one face to another, cold sweat beading her forehead and dripping from her underarms.

In a burst of strength she lunged, breaking the Arab's grasp and dashing away as she suddenly heard a volley of rifle shots from the direction of camp.

Hussar had attacked. Even now Sharif and Rashid, and the women and all the rest were being slaughtered!

She ran with all her strength, but the Arabs were right behind her. Her ankles were grasped and held so she fell face down into the sand.

As she turned over, a weight fell upon her. It was the same Arab who had so brutally killed the mare now pinning her down, his lips drawn back in a kind of smile, his front teeth missing, his hands, like fat insects, sliding under her robes and crawling over her flesh. Then his mouth opened in an O of delight as, holding the tip of his tongue between his thick lips, he squeezed her nipples between thumb and fingers.

Gulping for breath, Juliette fought harder. They were all over her now, all of them, their rough hands on her breasts and legs even before a ripping sound came and her pants were jerked off.

She screamed again, wildly flinging arms that were captured and pinned over her head as a foul-smelling rag was stuffed into her mouth.

A blow to her forehead made the world reel with flashing lights and colors, and there was a vague awareness of fingers and hands everywhere and a pounding at her temples that drowned out moans she dimly recognized as her own.

Brutally her legs were pulled apart and held as a weight crushed her. Black clouds and dots of light swam in her head, blurring everything.

There was an explosion then, followed by others as her befuddled brain fought for consciousness. The weight was removed and her face slapped and she knew the sensation of water running into her eyes and nose and mouth.

She sputtered, and the light returned, making shapes in the darkness. A hand took her robe that hung in tatters from her neck and she was pulled up like a rag toy before being hurled onto the back of a horse.

Her bare legs clung to the skittish animal as, in a flying leap, the beast plunged away, scattering a spray of sand over five motionless forms left in its wake.

Instinctively, Juliette's arms circled Sharif's waist like a child grasping a rock of support in a careening world.

He was alive when she had thought him dead, and just knowing this somehow gave her a soaring feeling that there was not time to explore as rifle fire behind them made her turn.

There were more men galloping hard after them now, their white robes billowing, their rifles leveled and taking aim.

Sharif turned too, dropping the reins and controlling the charging horse with his knees as he raised his rifle to fire past her at the men.

The explosions were deafening but, clinging tighter to his waist, Juliette saw one man after another fall while those remaining returned his fire in short bursts of flame exploding orange against the night sky.

Bullets pelted the sand around them. The stallion raced on. Then in a whirl of gunfire and shouting and the stench of gunpowder, they charged up the last dune into camp.

Sharif's warriors were dashing about, reinforcing the piled supplies that served to block the Hussar's bullets.

Fadjar plunged to a halt near the center of the makeshift fortress and it was Rashid himself who lifted her to the ground, quickly wrapping her in a blanket.

Rapid Arabic was exchanged over her head before Sharif's eyes were suddenly on her as he spoke French.

"Go to Cassia," he was saying. "She has been calling for you." And that was all before spurring his horse into the fray, rallying his men to what seemed an impossible defense.

"Cassia?" Juliette questioned turning to Rashid. Wasn't she dead? What could he mean? But Rashid did not disclaim the remark and, bending double to avoid the rain of fire overhead, he led her across camp to a quickly erected defense of piled supply packs from where numbers of men were firing steadily.

Between saddles and more piled packs, Cassia was lying, alive—but looking nearly dead as she rolled her head from side to side and moaned softly.

"Cassia," Juliette said. "Cassia, it's me. What has happened? What have they done?"

The girl's eyelids opened slowly halfway and there was recognition and a faint smile. "Madame," she whispered hoarsely. "You have come."

"But Cassia—I thought you were dead! I thought that your brother. . . ."

"No . . . no, madame." Weakly Cassia squeezed her hand. "Did not the master tell you? He bought me from Rafik. I am to be your slave now. I was filled with joy when I was told. But it was then the pains began."

"But why are you bleeding?" Juliette persisted. "Are you wounded? Where are you hurt? Let me see."

The girl shook her head and the wan smile came again. "Madame does not understand. It is the child being born too soon. For hours I have pain, and now there is only blood. I am dying, madame. It is Allah's will. Now I will not disgrace my family." Cassia's eyes opened larger. "But I am so frightened. I have sinned, and now I will burn forever in the fires of damnation."

Juliette patted Cassia's small brown hand. "You are *not* going to die, Cassia. Don't even think it! And you certainly are not going to hell. I don't believe you really sin unless you want to. And what happened was against your will. It's those creatures who attacked you that are damned if anyone is. Your God doesn't damn the innocent, does he?—no! I'm sure he understands."

A bullet singing close overhead interrupted her and behind them a shout turned to a liquid rattle.

Juliette ducked her head, peering between ammunition boxes.

On one side of camp the Hussar had broken through the piled boxes and packs and, through the smoke of rifles, Juliette saw Sharif charging into the oncoming Hussar with Rashid at his back.

In the close combat a scimitar replaced his rifle, and Sharif swung the curved blade in circles, cleaving the white-turbaned men as they came until a semicircle of bodies were forming beneath Fadjar's high-stepping hooves.

More of Sharif's men joined him, and the attack was beaten back until no more Hussar charged through the opening, which was once again blocked, and Juliette heard victorious yells from the warriors as Sharif spurred his horse to the other side of camp, making an easy target above the others.

A volley of bullets whizzed overhead, hitting a man nearby, who made no sound as he dropped his gun before hunching over to hold his bloody arm.

Automatically Juliette rose to his side. Always before, Sharif's warriors had frightened her and she had never considered touching one. But now, bound together by a common enemy, things seemed abruptly quite different.

She examined the wound and, even in the dim light, she could see the bullet had gone completely through the arm. So tearing what remained of the sleeves of her robe, Juliette tied off the limb so that the bleeding slowed and pooled and finally stopped as around them the battle continued to rage.

There was gratitude, if not worship, in the man's brown eyes as he salaamed and spoke words of thanks that touched Juliette in a way she had not expected.

Close by, three women bent their heads, their hands holding their mouths to stifle screams.

Seeing them, Juliette called them in Arabic, motioning them to her just as another man nearby abruptly spun around and fell into the sand.

The women came and, together, they half dragged the man behind a shelter of crates. And with the women hovering beside her, Juliette ripped his pants to reveal a gash on his thigh nearly to the bone.

"Look," Juliette said in Arabic. "You must press here and the blood does not come. All of you must do this so these men will not die."

As she demonstrated, pressing hard on the artery until the spurting blood trickled then stopped, the women's eyes grew larger and they nodded with understanding. She knew from Cassia that most of them had lived inside the harems of Tripoli and were "presents" from the governor to many of Sharif's men. They were terrified by the desert's hostility, having never seen violence like this. But now they seemed willing to help and watched her movements carefully.

Another wounded man stumbled and fell on the sand and again the women looked over her shoulder as Juliette tore away his shirt. But already it was too late, and Juliette tried to control the wrenching in her stomach as she saw the gaping hole in his chest and realized from his open eyes that he was already dead.

Juliette shook her head and motioned the women to help another man while she turned her attention back to Cassia.

From watching the cook at Miss Fayton's tend the wounds of gardeners and workmen, she had learned basic first aid. But Cassia's miscarriage was beyond her knowledge and in spite of all her brave assurances to the girl, if the hemorrhaging did not stop . . . well, she would try not to think of that now. If the Hussar couldn't be thrown back, it wouldn't make any difference, they would all die one way or another.

For the next hour the battle continued while Juliette tended the wounded, directing the women who unquestioningly obeyed.

From somewhere she heard *"Allahu akbar,"* which Juliette could translate as "God is great," and knew it to be a triumphant battle cry.

She bent lower, covering Cassia's body with her own as another round of bullets sang overhead. But what did God have to do with this sort of killing? she asked herself. What did God ever have to do with men murdering men, no matter what the cause? And yet wasn't it true that inevitably God was always used to justify it?

She peered again over the crates and packs surrounding her. Now there was more shouting, but to her surprise and sudden relief, it was Sharif's men swarming out from behind their own defenses to chase the Hussar back into the desert. *"Allahu akbar! Allahu akbar!"*

Then, except for a few last shots fired at the routed Hussar, there was no more shooting and now only the moans of the wounded remained.

As abruptly as it all began, it was over and, as the dust settled, Juliette's gaze searched among the collapsed tents and scattered packs before realizing that unconsciously she was searching for Sharif.

Always before he had been clearly visible, galloping up and down the lines of men. But now he was not to be seen and, when Juliette spotted Fadjar riderless and grazing on a scrubby bush a short distance from camp, she felt a cold sinking in the depths of her stomach as she stood up abruptly.

He had been such an easy target on horseback! Always above the others and he had been so reckless.

Heading across the camp in quick steps, her eyes cast furtively among the fallen weapons and broken sacks and supplies and scattered bodies wounded or dead. Was Sharif somewhere like this? she asked herself, taking a closer look at each one of the bodies. It seemed impossible, inconceivable that such a man could be . . . could be . . . Her mind paused, refusing to think further while her heart beat wildly. Her steps quickened and she dashed about aimlessly, hardly seeing where she was going when she ran against a tall figure, and, looking up, realized it was Rashid.

Her wide searching eyes bright, Juliette wasted no time on either dignity or formality. Her fingers gripped the older man's sleeve. "Rashid! The master? Is he wounded? Where is he?"

Rashid's eyes studied her, a knowing expression emerging as he said, "Yes, madame. He is wounded." Rashid raised a long sinewy arm to point across camp. "The master is there, madame."

Juliette did not wait to hear more, but dashed in that direction, her feet flying, her heart filling her throat as a voice within repeated the same prayer over and over, "Please God, don't let him be dead! Please, in the name of . . . of . . . Allah. Don't let him die!"

Then rounding the corner of a pile of camel packs, Juliette stopped short, feeling at once ridiculous.

He was there, a short distance away, sitting on a bundle and even smiling at the Arab woman who was deftly attending his bared upper arm for what seemed a minor wound.

Of course he wasn't dead, she told herself defiantly. Yet, as she stood watching, she could not deny her overpowering emotions or trembling hands that only a short time before had calmly tended the others.

It is just that I'm grateful to him for saving my life, she told herself, hoping that he had not seen her. She headed back toward Cassia then, and looking up at the horizon, noticed there was a pink glow in the east that signaled the approaching dawn.

PART X

THE HUNT

Chapter 61

Two hours after dawn, the dead were buried with the most violent display of grief Juliette had ever witnessed.

The women screamed and cried, tearing at their hair and clawing their faces while the men stood by, tears running down their cheeks, and declared oaths of vengeance, brandishing their rifles in the air.

It was only after the bodies were finally covered over in sand that attention could be given to the practical consideration of their own survival.

Feeling stiff and sore and not quite sick yet not well, Juliette found the women once again around her, still dabbing at their eyes as they salaamed, calling her madame and obviously awaiting instructions.

Juliette glanced around them at the scattered packs, the broken bundles, and torn tents. She noticed that already some of the men were retrieving the few animals remaining alive and it seemed obvious to Juliette that food must be their first consideration. So motioning to Fatima and Karile to come, she asked them to gather together into one place all the food that was still edible.

At her side Tasifa was speaking to her in rapid Arabic and Juliette's attention was drawn to her next as the other two hurried away.

"What did you say?" Juliette asked in Arabic. "Speak slower."

"The tents, madame. What shall we do? Most of them are ruined and will give no cover from rain or blowing sand."

Juliette looked at the remnants of the tents that Tasifa had brought to show her. There were the stakes of one, the ropes of another, all still intact. But no whole canvas or skins remained. Her brow puckered as she thought before saying, "Go about the camp and gather all that remains of any of the tents. Perhaps parts of many can be made into a single whole tent."

"Yes, madame." The girl salaamed before leaving on the assignment, carefully holding up the hem of her own robe that was severely torn and was dragging on the ground.

Juliette turned back to Fatima and Karile who were already stacking the remainder of food before her, and it was not difficult to see they had almost nothing left.

Juliette sighed and ordered these scant rations packed together so a few animals could carry what remained while at the same time she asked herself how so many were to survive on so little. Moments passed until she felt a sense of eyes upon her and, raising her head, she was surprised to find Sharif watching her from over the heads of his gathering men, an odd look on his face that made Juliette realize he had been watching her for a long time.

Without knowing why, Juliette felt herself blush and, not wanting him to see how, even now, his perusal affected her, she turned away, retreating to where Cassia still lay between the piled crates.

As she bent and examined the Arab girl, Juliette discovered that the bleeding had miraculously stopped, though her pulse was weak and her skin hot to touch.

Earlier Juliette had been rationed a small waterskin and now she unslung her precious supply, pouring some onto a cloth and dabbing Cassia's face before placing it across her forehead.

"That may be the last water you see for days, *chérie*. Such self-sacrifice hardly suits you."

Juliette started before turning to find Sharif standing behind her, his hands on his hips in a ridiculing swagger.

What does he think he knows about self-sacrifice? she thought, biting back the words. Her eyes stung. She had wanted their reunion to be different than this. He had risked his own life to save hers, and it seemed she should thank him and apologize for what she had thought about Cassia. But now his barbed words made her gratitude stick unuttered in her throat and she only glanced up into his critical countenance for a serious moment before turning back to Cassia, hoping he would simply go away.

But he didn't, and, in a moment said, "I thought I'd seen all manner of stupidity among women But *you*, madame,

have displayed a completely new dimension. Even if the
Hussar hadn't found you, other bandits would have, and if
not them, then the sun, since you didn't even bother to take
a water sack. I imagined your adventure in Tripoli taught
you something. But it appears your intelligence does not
take easily to facts, however elementary."

His aloof condemnation, delivered in clipped French,
made the hair at the back of Juliette's neck prickle. Whirling, she threw back her head so their eyes met. "What do
you care what I do? Wouldn't it be a relief to have me off
your hands? Anyway, wasn't your Gypsy wench keeping
you occupied? You disgust me!"

Sharif didn't change expression, but crossed his arms.
Then he shook his head and spoke as if to a child. "Do you
think I am quite a fool? My spies told me days ago when
the Hussar would attack. It was you who nearly exposed
everything. When you rode off Rashid wanted to go after
you but I stopped him. If the Hussar had seen one of my
men armed as he was they would have suspected a trap.
And anyway, a woman disobedient as you deserves the
consequences!"

"Well, then why did you bother to come after me? I
didn't ask for help, and anyway, the Hussar weren't doing
any more to me than . . . than you have done!"

He came closer, a burning light in his eyes and Juliette
wondered if he would slap her. His voice was controlled
when he spoke. "Haven't I told you that a man protects
what belongs to him, or have you forgotten that, as you
seem to have so many other things. By Allah, you are an
ungrateful wench. But I don't have time for this now. I
only came to tell you you're coming hunting with me tomorrow. Be ready to leave at dawn."

Cassia moaned suddenly and Juliette, unwilling to react
to Sharif's insulting orders, turned to her, pouring another
amount from the water sack to wipe the girl's perspiring
face and dab at her temples and eyes.

"Cassia, Cassia," Juliette whispered softly. But the girl
had fallen unconscious again and, taking her small brown
hand, Juliette leaned closer, forgetting Sharif for the moment as she said, "Poor Cassia, poor, poor girl."

Behind Juliette's back, Sharif watched, a brooding light of puzzlement coming into his eyes that disappeared as soon as Juliette turned again to face him. "Please," she said with a note of desperation. "Do whatever you want to me. But go away now and leave us in peace. There has been enough violence today."

Unexpectedly, he nodded and surprisingly turned to go. But then he paused as an afterthought. "By the way, *chérie*," he said evenly. "You shouldn't be jealous of that Gypsy girl. Perhaps it would have saved me a lot of trouble if I'd told you before that those Gypsies were all Hussar spies. Affeda, if that was her real name, tried putting a knife between my ribs at her first opportunity." He laughed short and hard so that a tingle ran up Juliette's spine. "Probably even before you rode out of camp, she was already dead."

The sun was a red ball frozen on the horizon of the chilled desert morning when Sharif, five other men, and Juliette trotted away from camp.

Still it warmed up quickly and, by the time an hour passed, the sand was burning beneath the horses' feet as they swept toward mountain peaks just visible to the east.

Numb, yet strangely wide awake, Juliette sat her horse, determined not to fall behind even though this hard pace made the speed of the caravan seem sedate by comparison.

They stopped only once, briefly at midday, but now, instead of a shaded pavilion and a leisurely lunch, Juliette squatted apart from the others, holding her own horse and accepting a portion of dried dates out of the gnarled hand of one of the warriors.

A common waterskin bag was passed around to wash down the tasteless fare, then once again, they were in the saddle riding even harder.

That night it was an hour after dark when they finally stopped and dismounted. Juliette was still standing beside her horse when Sharif tossed her a heavy blanket with such force that catching it made her sit abruptly down in the sand. "This should keep you warm," he said. "Get used to it. There's no time for you to be pampered."

Juliette wanted to answer indignantly, but her arms and legs felt rubbery and it didn't seem worth the effort. So she said nothing, but took the blanket and forced herself to walk a dignified distance away from the others before rolling herself in its rough folds and lying down facing away from camp.

She didn't hear Sharif coming toward her, his footfalls as silent as a cat's, but then he was beside her, casually rolling himself into his own blanket before curling around her back, his arm wrapping possessively across her breasts.

She thought of struggling, but she had not the strength and only gazed down at his bronzed hand thinking of the pain and pleasure it could give. Then she must have fallen asleep. It seemed only moments had passed when she was startled awake again and Sharif was unceremoniously depositing her on a horse.

The sky had hardly grayed in the east as they started out. They traveled even harder that day, but Juliette, hot and clinging to her mount, refused to complain or let him see her weakness. So with all her determination she kept her back erect as she rode, though he only glanced at her once without expression and didn't seem to notice her again.

How she continued that day she never understood. She was faint with hunger, her legs and arms and buttocks all felt bruised and numb—as if the blood had stopped pumping through them, and her head ached with a blinding pain that only worsened the hotter it became. Still, somehow, she kept the pace and that night found them camping unbelievably at the base of those once distant mountain peaks.

A small seep trickled through the red rocks making a stream so slow it took several hours to fill a single *guerba*. But finally it was full and was passed around, and Juliette thought even its brackishness seemed sweet as, carefully, she restricted herself to only a few swallows before passing it on.

There was no more sleep that night than the one before. Only a few hours and they were up again. And this time Juliette rode in a stupor so that she didn't even notice the narrowness of the rocky ledge that switched back and forth

across the face of the jagged peak. She never looked over
the edge of the cliff at the dizzy drop to the desert floor,
or noticed the vultures that circled them curiously. She was
not even aware of the heavy breathing of the horse or the
occasional sound of a rock being kicked off the ledge and
tumbling down the bare rock face.

That night they ate the last of their dates and Juliette,
who fell immediately asleep, was surprised when it was the
bright sunlight that awakened her instead of Sharif's rough
hands.

Opening her eyes, she knew at once something was different, and raising on an elbow, she saw they had gone.

A start jarred her stomach. He had left her!

Scrambling to her feet, the blanket fell circling her ankles.
She kicked it free and quickly climbed to the highest point
of rock, shading her eyes as she scanned the area.

They had camped in a narrow valley between long rock
formations that seemed like the skeletons of enormous
stone dinosaurs and, looking back the way they had come,
the plain of rock and sand seemed endless, terminating
only in curtains of waves shimmering ever upward.

She had wanted to escape, but not like this, lost. She
would never find her way back and panic was overcoming
her just as she spotted Sharif in the maze of rocks leading
the others toward her.

Quickly Juliette scrambled down from her observation
point, not wanting him to see her fear and contrived to be
folding her blanket when he came toward her.

Casually, he tossed the headless body of a snake at her
feet.

"Here," he said. "It's about time you made yourself useful. We need someone to cook."

He didn't stay to hear the sputter of protests rising in her
throat. Automatically she had jumped away from the thing.
A snake! He couldn't mean he wanted *her* to prepare it
to . . . to eat.

Completely at a loss she stared after him but was quickly
rescued by the youngest member of the party, a boy about
fourteen who immediately took up the prize with an excla-
mation of awe and, withdrawing his knife, slit the belly of

the thing to its tail, skillfully peeling off the skin in a single swift operation.

Juliette felt her empty stomach knot, a shudder moving through her. But the boy only smiled and began building a small fire of acacia thornbush and *Aristida* grass. And when the meat was finally sizzling upon heated rocks, Juliette could not help finding the aroma attractive. And when it came time to divide it among the group, the painful cramps in her belly would not let her refuse. So, gingerly, she nibbled at her portion, surprised to find it tasted like mild fowl and, with no more hesitation, she ate until it was gone.

It was a small amount of food, but even this seemed to revive everyone. And when it was finished, the men took up their rifles again and, splitting into groups, set out in opposite directions.

It was hours before they returned, once again empty-handed. And that night, as they sat around the low smokeless fire, passing the *guerba* so each could drink, Juliette was aware of how casually these warriors had come to treat her, more like a boy than a girl, and she had grown used to them, too, no longer finding them strange or frightening. And lying on her blanket now, and staring up at the stars she thought again of the vultures flying overhead that day, a constant reminder that without food, they all would soon die. So what did it matter, she asked herself, if she ate and slept and traveled with these Arabs? What did it matter if she ate the flesh of the snake or if she no longer struggled when Sharif, took her silently after all were asleep? No—what did it matter now, when these were probably her last days on earth? And that night, Juliette fell faster than usual into a deep peaceful sleep.

Chapter 62

Juliette had lost track of time. A succession of blistering days all blended one into the other, leaving behind parched mouths and gurgling stomachs.

The men hunted every day, but the mouflon continued

to elude them and the mounting sense of desperation grew more intense as the sun's burning heat turned the land into a furnace.

"How long will it be before we sight mouflon?" Juliette asked Rashid one night across the campfire. After riding together these past days, she no longer feared this lean and dignified man and occasionally sought him out rather than Sharif when she wished to ask a question.

Rashid frowned, his bushy gray brows drawing down over his crinkled eyes. "There are no mouflon here," he told her firmly.

Juliette, who had been mending her burnoose with an acacia thorn and grass fiber, looked startled. Certainly she must not have heard correctly. "What do you mean? Isn't mouflon what we've been hunting all these days?"

Rashid's frown deepened as he leaned closer, talking low between his teeth. "There are no mouflon near here," he stated. "And if there were, we would not be hunting them."

His words were definite, yet insanely incongruous. And both hungry and indignant, Juliette felt in no mood for jesting and would have raised her voice to this firm-jawed Arab had she not suddenly remembered what Cassia had said.

"Mouflon can smell for miles and have the power of the genies and spirits of the desert to warn them of danger. One must never speak of killing one since a genie might overhear and warn them."

Yes, superstition, of course, Juliette thought. To these desert people, things did not just happen, but happened magically, and, thinking this now, she nodded to Rashid.

"Mouflon are very rare," she began, closely watching the old Arab's leathery face. "Even if they were nearby before, they must have all gone by now."

This time Rashid's dark eyes screwed to even smaller points before he said, "The wind of the desert carries thoughtful and unwary words alike. Who can tell who might hear?" Then his eyes focused firmly into hers, as if seeing through her. "You are not so foolish perhaps as you seem," he stated flatly, but Juliette saw he was smiling, and, feeling herself color under the man's fleeting look of approval, she said nothing more that night.

The next day camp was moved and the hunters started out again searching up the narrow rocky ravines that bordered this seemingly endless plain.

Again Juliette was left alone and, climbing to the top of a large, round-topped rock, she lay in a narrow niche of shade near its summit, facing the opposite direction from the way the hunters had taken into a labyrinth of rock columns.

Before her stretched an ocean without limit, the silvered sand of the desert spreading farther than sight could reach and glittering like steel struck with a bright light. A fiery vapor carried up in streaks made a perpetual veil over the quivering land. There was not a cloud, not a breath of air, and the horizon ended as the sea on a clear day, with one line of light as definite as a dagger cut.

It all seemed familiar now, although the immensity and silence still tugged at her soul. As she looked now, she felt again as she had once days before, totally alone. But now her awareness of this fact did not make her shiver or recoil. Death had seemed so close so often that facing it had made her realize she had always been alone, even before her father had died, even at the moment of her birth she had been alone. And when she died, she would die alone. And somehow, realizing this changed everything, although she couldn't have named exactly how. There was a new freedom, a new strength welling up inside her. She was alone, but she was no longer afraid.

Turning over onto her stomach, Juliette looked over the edge of the rock into its shadow where beetles stumped about, shaded from the sun. She closed her eyes then, feeling the warm breeze caressing her face like a velvet glove. An hour passed and then another, and it was after that when, slowly, as if by some newly formed instinct, she realized something was wrong.

Rising on one elbow, she scanned the sand, the rocks, the sky, noticing only that the sun had passed its zenith and now had begun a burning descent. And though nothing seemed out of the ordinary, she reached for the rifle beside her.

As a child, she had always been afraid of guns, and Miss Fayton's had certainly not included marksmanship in its curriculum. But the unpredictability of this land had changed her attitude, and now she was relieved to have a rifle at hand and thankful for the shooting lessons Rashid had given her two days before.

Now from somewhere to her back, from among the forest of rock pillars, a shot rang out, and then another.

Juliette peered in that direction, but could see nothing as the sound echoed between the rocks before diminishing in a roar.

The sun beat down on her head, and her skin was moist even as the dry air blew around her. Was it the men firing at mouflon, or Hussar?

She strained her ears to hear, but there was nothing.

Quickly she scrambled down, dragging the rifle behind her and, running lightly to another rock formation, molded herself to its base.

To her left she caught a movement, and carefully drawing the rifle forward, she rested the barrel on a promontory of rock and waited.

The tumble of boulders and pillars was such a tangle of shadows and shapes that she couldn't be sure she had seen anything at all until it moved again.

It was a shadow, or so it appeared, the head of someone who wore a helmet that was raised and curved backward.

Another rifle shot fired and hung in the air before echoing against the rocks.

In a flash the shadow bolted from cover and Juliette breathed in a quick rasp, realizing that it was not a man, but a mouflon.

Her response was swift and automatic, as if she had done it a hundred times and it seemed to Juliette that she watched herself from a great distance as she leaned down over the rifle's long barrel and lined up the sights as the mouflon came bounding forward. Carefully, without jerking, she held her breath and squeezed the trigger until an explosion made her ears ring and the rifle butt recoiled with a jerk against her shoulder.

The mouflon dropped in a tumble of gray fur and legs before another mouflon followed it, dashing from cover. It was another ram, as large as the first.

Lining up the sights again, Juliette prepared to fire. But, before she could pull the trigger, another shot burst in the air and the second mouflon crumbled into the sand.

Jerking her head up, Juliette saw it was Sharif, yards away, poised on top of a low rock and lowering his still-smoking rifle as his men ran forward, first to inspect the two mouflon that indeed were dead, and then to look disbelievingly at her.

Juliette walked to the dead sheep, her knotted hair fallen down her back in a blond coil as she stared at the animals.

A murmur was passing among the men. For the master to kill a mouflon was not surprising and to be expected. But a woman . . . Never, never before had they seen a woman hold a rifle so—or aim so precisely. It had never been done!

Each man looked to the others. It was a miracle someone suggested. A miracle sent by Allah who, in his wisdom, had spared them through a miracle performed by this female.

Herself astonished, Juliette felt Sharif take the rifle from her hand. Rashid was suddenly beside her too, his eyes bright with pride as, spontaneously, a happy shout came from one of the men. Then the others followed, all their relief and joy expressed in their cry as they stood round her and cheered.

The next morning they wasted no time in returning the meat to camp and to their hungry comrades. It took two days to reach them and, once there, Juliette found to her surprise that everyone considered her shooting the animal something quite amazing, though she tried to tell them it had been hardly more than an accident . . . luck perhaps, she insisted. And when, stumbling, she tried to tell them in Arabic, they only laughed good-naturedly and congratulated her further.

So it was taken out of her hands. She was the center of attention and treated like a youth who had made *his* first kill, and was presented with the carefully skinned hide of the animal. And that evening when she retired to what remained of the tent (it was re-erected to be only one room now, so the hassock and table and bed were all crowded together) several women came and salaamed deeply, offering her gifts and praise.

After the women left, Cassia helped her undress, and the moon was already halfway across the sky when she slipped into Sharif's big bed.

Outside the Arabs chanted prayers, a pleasant, now familiar litany. Strange that people so capable of ferocity were at the same time so fastidiously religious, she thought.

Her mind drifted then from one thing to another, reliving again the days in the desert. And it was with a certain satisfaction that she considered the fact that the attention she received now was given not because she was Sharif's favorite slave, but rather because of her own accomplishment. And with this thought smugly in her mind, Juliette turned over, snuggling deeper into a pillow and, feeling a growing lethargy, fell asleep.

Chapter 63

When Juliette opened her eyes again, she was surprised it was still dark. They had camped at an oasis, and above her the moon cast the shadow of a palm tree on the ceiling of her tent. The smell of dead ashes from the camp fire hung in the air, and the stamp of a restless horse combined in the distance with the haunting notes of a flute.

Throwing back the covers, Juliette sat up naked on the wide bed. She knew what had awakened her—a dream— Sharif surrounding her—engulfing her, his hard body close, his warm lips parting hers, his arms holding her so nothing else mattered and all else was forgotten.

There was the touch of a hand on her breast, a bold caress along her thighs, and, when she could endure the waiting no longer, the thrust of him hard and hot between them.

But satisfaction had not come. Instead she had awakened feeling feverishly hot, the silk sheet clinging damply to her body.

Once he had warned her their times together would only awaken a new appetite, not satisfy it. She had not realized he meant this—that she would find herself wanting him. And, to her despair, the days spent near him on the hunt had sharpened her feelings until the warmth of his body curled round her back had brought a new aching desire that spread over her like an invasion, thawing away what remained of her icy fortress of reserve. So now, in her dreams, she welcomed those very caresses she would have fought against in a waking state.

This fact was humiliating enough, but worst of all, lately she had begun to wonder if he knew, if he could possibly read her thoughts now, as he had so often in the past.

Since she had shot the mouflon, he had ignored her. And thank heaven he was spending the night away from camp, she thought. This foolishness of hers was only a physical reaction. She didn't really care for him. But then her thoughts were interrupted by a sudden uneasiness stemming from the sense of being watched—a feeling that made her skin quiver with gooseflesh.

Her eyes swept the tent. "Cassia?" she whispered into the black. But there was no answer beyond the abrupt pause of a cricket that had been making solitary chirps.

Then, with a tremor in her voice, "Sharif?"

He did not answer, but stepped closer, his features a relief of light and shadow, his chin a slant of shadow in the play of darkness and light. But it was he.

The cricket had not begun again and the air was so silent she knew he heard the catch of her breath. Her pulse gathered momentum as she drew the sheet high above her breasts.

A thrill dashed up her spine as, in two strides, he was beside her bed, hunching slightly to keep from brushing the top of the tent in a posture that made him seem like a hulking bear.

She thought to scramble from the bed—to run from him, but where? So she remained, her breasts alive, her abdomen quickening with a spreading liquid that warmed her skin and made it tingle.

Did he know? she asked herself again. Had some animal instinct of his sensed her desire? Had he changed his plans and come, knowing that she wanted him?

No! Impossible! But the thought made her blush darker.

He couldn't know how I feel, she assured herself. And hoping the presence of light would bring some calm to her jumping heart, Juliette reached to the inlaid table beside the bed and lit the candle there.

Illumination flooded the space, turning his bronze features to a fiery gold.

"Get up!" he said finally, his husky voice deceptively soft.

"Get up?" Juliette echoed disbelieving.

"Yes. Had you been expecting something else?" His eyes brightened with a devilish gleam.

"No—no, of course not!"

"Then get up. I want to talk to you and it's damned distracting when you're on your back."

Juliette found herself somehow standing, wrapping herself in the sheet as she moved away until her back brushed the sides of the tent.

"It's never been my choice to be 'on my back' as you put it. It has only been because you have forced me there!"

"Still the sharp-tongued one, aren't you?"

The bed stood between them, and Sharif's eyes, half-hooded, were watching her with the intensity of a cat watching a cornered bird.

Juliette's heart hammered so loud it drowned out all reasonable thoughts except one . . . she must not let him touch her—not now—not when excitement rushed over her in waves she couldn't quell.

Her fingers dug deeper into the sheet as she pulled it closer, unaware that it pressed her impudently high breasts even higher to spill over the top of the sheet in a swell of white.

She watched him laugh softly. "What a difficult woman

you are. Any self-respecting Arab would have taken two others by now and traded *you* for something useful."

Juliette opened her mouth to speak . . . to protest. But then she could only murmur and turn away from the half-mad light glowing in his eyes.

Sharif gritted his teeth against the strength of his desire. She was exasperating—impossible. She had resisted him with all the power of her resilient mind and body and insulted him with her scathing tongue. But instead of hating her more, he found himself still wanting her, until now he wondered if he had not become *her* slave.

And he was not alone in being charmed by this girl. Now he could see admiration for her in the women's eyes and sometimes he wondered which one of his men he might have to kill as now they openly admired her too.

They had not forgotten how, during the hunt, she had never flagged, never bent the erect posture of her spine as they had gone mile after mile.

"If the 'little one,' " they had said, "can go on, how can we give up?" And then, when many murmured that they had been forsaken by Allah, it was *she* who had shot the first mouflon, she—a woman, and already the story had been recounted scores of times and was taking on the character of a legend and she had become a *mar'a muharibah*, a warrior woman.

Thus she had gained the respect of his people, holding power over their hearts as well as his own. How neatly she had accomplished it—she who had deceived and rejected him and still would not bend to his will. And now he gave her a sudden shake that snapped her head on her neck, causing her hair to fly about in a tangle of golden threads until Juliette wondered if indeed he had gone mad as the fierce light in his enigmatic eyes glimmered brilliantly.

He jerked his chin to indicate beyond the walls of the tent. "Do you know what they think?" he asked as if she should know what he was talking about.

Juliette stared wide-eyed before managing to shake her head.

"They think you are favored by Allah—that you per-

formed a miracle, or at least have the services of the desert
genies. And do you know why?"

Again Juliette shook her head. If only he would stop
looking at her so . . . so. . . .

Sharif touched his temple. "Because they don't believe a
woman could accomplish such a thing without the help of
spirits or Allah." He leaned closer. "Ha!—they don't know
you as well as I do!"

Juliette's mind struggled to reconcile his words. Contrary, as always. What the others treated as a triumph, he
considered a crime. "I tried to tell them it was an accident.
And I don't know why all of them should think . . ."

Sharif waved a hand that cut her short.

"No. Don't be so modest *chérie*. It doesn't suit you."

He pushed her away, withdrawing his hand with effort.
She was infuriating. He hadn't intended tonight to come here
but instead to visit the chief of a tribe camped half a
night's ride to the east. Then he had spent an indecisive
hour. Twice he was going to call for his horse but the
weather delayed him. He felt a storm brewing, and a storm
could pin him down for days and waste more time. His
spies had informed him that Hussar's main force was still
somewhere to the south. And of course there was the matter of Juliette. Maybe he should take her with him. If he
left her behind Rashid could keep an eye on her, of course,
but she was unpredictable and even Rashid's eyes had begun to rest on her as he had never seen that stoic Arab's
eyes rest on any woman.

Perturbed he had waved away a second plate of mouflon. Had he gone mad? he asked himself. He was beginning not to trust anyone. Was it jealousy that made it so?
And pondering the question, he made the rounds, speaking
to the camp guards before finally finding himself at his
own tent, lifting the flap to see her there—in bed, and naked. Had she been waiting? Tonight he sensed something
more in her than hate. There was a certain spark joining
the rebelliousness in her eyes—something unmistakable—
yes, and in the part of her lips.

A warm laughter suddenly filled his insides with that

returning sense of pleasurable wonder he had experienced
only with this woman. So . . . he thought, and said aloud,
"Wasn't it your English Shakespeare who wrote, 'Me-
thinks the lady doth protest too much'?"

Catching his meaning, Juliette stepped backward, tossing
her blond mane defiantly as she said, "You're being ridiculous with all this talk of genies and mouflon and Shakespeare and the rest. I don't know what you mean!"

"I think you do, Juliette. But all this talk is wasted.
Sometimes words are superfluous."

Juliette could feel him closing in, even if he hadn't
stepped closer. Again she backed away. If only she could
somehow keep him away. If only she weren't so confused.
"What right have you to accuse me of anything," she cried.
"What of your lies . . . and your killing and the rest?"

His voice was calm, factual. "I never lied to you," he
said. "I never made promises I didn't keep. It was you who
promised to be my wife—you who broke faith with me."

"Why must you always bring that up and throw it in my
face? Yes—your wife in the company of how many *other*
wives and how many mistresses? Wife! You make a mockery of the word. Any woman would be a fool to become
your wife."

His lips curved sarcastically. "But now it no longer matters what you think. Now you are mine—wife or mistress.
And by Allah, you are going to act the part!"

He came closer and Juliette stumbled over a wave in the
carpet as she stepped backward, losing her balance as his
arms encircled her.

A sparkle of tears silvered her eyes like mirrors as his
fingers, rough from the handling of leather reins, reached
round her throat, his thumb passing down the front until it
pressed threateningly against the hollow. "Do you know
there is no one else who would dare insult me as you do?
No one!" His thumb pressed harder. "Damn you!" he said
at last. "Does nothing frighten you? Are you really so im-
pervious?"

With an abrupt sweep of her arm, she tried to dash his
hand away but found her wrist caught, and held in his
other hand. "What do you care whether I'm afraid as long

as you can throw me on my back and use me as you please?"

"But a woman doesn't need to be always on her *back*—haven't I shown you before?"

One hand slid lower, while her arms remained in the iron hold of the other, and with splayed fingers he moved across her belly and down to stroke, enter, and test the secrets of her softer recesses, shamefully open and welcoming.

She tried to wrench free, but he was already laughing triumphantly. "What do you English say about the spirit being strong but the flesh weak?" He grinned wickedly as two fingers took the place of one.

Juliette nearly swooned, absurdly clinging harder to the sheet. He couldn't . . . he wouldn't . . . the tent seemed to spin crazily in a carousel and a dry sob caught in her throat.

It was a relief when she was suddenly lifted, his arms circling her hips, and she would have fallen backward had her legs not automatically opened to girth his waist. And then she was in . . . oh! such a position!

His breath scorched her cheeks. "How strong is that English stubbornness?" he asked, "I wonder . . . Perhaps you can resist my desires, but what about your own?"

Then suddenly everything was a swirl of searching lips and burning, demanding caresses as his mouth found the ripe nipples already flushed red with passion even before his lips and tongue sucked them hard to swollen fullness and tingling anticipation.

She was lifted higher then so his throbbing need pressed hot against her own opening desire. Burning sensations licked through her abdomen, destroying all resistance so the sheet slipped from between them and fell unnoticed to the floor as she curled long arms around his neck and drew him closer, pressing her hungry, parted lips to his.

She felt the large swollen head enter her first. Then grasping the globes of her buttocks tighter and tipping her further backward to allow him free access, he slowly filled her.

He was so enormous she wondered if she could contain

all of him. Then, still holding her by her slender hips, he slowly, skillfully drew himself out nearly all the way before sliding inward again so that her tightness relaxed to become exquisite pleasure.

He repeated the delicious movement, effortlessly guiding her along the shaft, first slowly out, then in again, more joyfully deep each time. He pushed higher to touch at her womb, then lower, then side to side, opening her to the fullest.

On fire, she moaned as his tongue thrilled her mouth in rhythm with his plunging manhood as now he drove faster, sending her to peak after peak of unbearable pleasure so that each time she wondered if it was possible to go on, even as each jeweled wave swept her higher, then higher, until at last it crested, whirling downward with such explosive force and fathomless joy that she didn't know her cries held his name as she buried her face in the dark fur of his powerful chest.

Chapter 64

The next Juliette knew, she was awakening to the sound of the wind howling like a jackal as it pelted sand against the outside of the tent.

It was day. The air was warm against her flesh and, opening her eyes, she found herself just as she had fallen asleep, naked, face down on the divan.

Stretching slender arms, she brushed the tangled hair out of her face, aware then of the feral smell of their lovemaking still clinging to the air and the subtle glow of warmth still radiating from her loins.

Last night they had mated, there was no other word for it, not once, but again and again, their passions gathering momentum as he swept her along in that timeless union of male and female.

It was a oneness without words or shyness—a wanting that brought their bodies together, forming and reforming

patterns on the leopard pelts. Silently, feverishly, they bat-
tled before soaring together beyond themselves and back
again, panting and perspiring, their longing only satisfied
for a short time before at last there was one final moment,
a rising and falling—a coiling and uncoiling in her belly
that took her to oblivion. A relaxing followed, a melting.
Then she must have slept, since that was the last she recalled. And now here she was—but where was Sharif?

Rising on one elbow, she looked through blurred eyes
around the tent. He was sitting comfortably on a cushion at
the foot of the bed reading a large chart and writing something with thoughtful concentration. As if aware of her
eyes then, he looked up, their gazes becoming one, and
there was amusement in his.

"So, you've decided to wake up. Good! Cassia wanted to
come and tidy up. But you were hardly able to receive
even a maid." He toasted her then with his cup of coffee,
nodding to where, Juliette abruptly realized, her legs were
still positioned to offer him a direct look at all that had
once been her most private. "Though don't mistake me," he
was continuing. "I find the view charming."

As he downed the full cup with a flick of his wrist, Juliette immediately drew her legs closed with a slap of
knees. How could he! Then she heard him laugh.

"So—you still blush. I thought last night might have rid
you of self-consciousness. But it doesn't matter. Soon
enough we will. Today there's no reason for you to dress
anyway. We won't be traveling."

The barb of mockery in his voice was no different than
before, but this morning Juliette felt more stung than ever.
After last night how could he be so flip, so coarse, so utterly casual about everything? But then, what had she expected? Over and over his lust had been followed by his
hostility, or, at best, indifference. Still her pride squirmed
knowing that last night she had been like a puppet whose
strings he knew how to manipulate with such accomplished
mastery. Again he had proven he could make her feel as
she never knew feeling could be. They had seemed almost
like lovers then, and now. . . . Oh, why was she so weak?

she asked herself, glancing again at his indifferent profile. Well, she wouldn't give him the satisfaction of seeing the torment he inflicted.

Crawling off the divan with as much dignity as her nakedness allowed, she retrieved her black burnoose and wrapped it around herself, pulling the waist tie closed. Then, walking to the tent flap, she unlashed a corner of it and peered out.

The wind was blowing in fierce gusts so that the sand flew by in rivers that rippled in waves three feet above the surface of the dunes and covered everything in a thick layer of sand. Even the horses were brought inside the tents and, though the flying grit blocked out the sun, the heat and brightness were still intense.

Yes, obviously they wouldn't be traveling today. And now he was apparently planning to wait out the storm *with* her.

"How long will it be like this?" she asked dropping the flap in place and lashing it shut with several turns of the braided camel-hide cord.

"All day certainly, tomorrow too, perhaps. We've been lucky it hasn't happened before. But since we can't travel in a sandstorm, it gives us all a chance to rest."

Recrossing the tent, Juliette paused at the table to pour her own coffee, unwilling to look up since she felt his scrutiny still on her.

Today and tomorrow too, she repeated to herself silently. And they were alone. Even Cassia would not be interrupting them. She dared raise her eyes then to glance at him over the rim of her cup and found him still watching her—reading her thoughts, or so it seemed, when he said, "Don't worry, *chérie*. I have much more pressing matters than molesting you . . . that is, at least until tonight when it's too dark for anything else." Then, without waiting for a reply, his attention returned to his charts, his face becoming serious and immediately absorbed in his work.

Juliette blinked with surprise, her eyebrows arching. He made it sound so simple. And what was *she* supposed to do?—wait placidly until he desired her?

But, in the end, as the wind continued to whistle, there

was nothing else but to help herself to more coffee and a portion of dried meat which she did before sitting down with her back to him.

Well, thank heaven, now at least they weren't starving, Juliette thought, gnawing at a slice.

The wind gusted so the tent swayed and the ceiling flapped. It blew hard, then harder for a moment before dying again. When her meat was finished, Juliette turned from her place and studied what she could see of the charts.

Kufra—Sebha, and *Tripoli* were the only words she could understand. The rest was a mysterious squiggling of red lines.

Carefully, Sharif measured one point to another with the use of a large gold compass, apparently unaware of her now. Opening her eyes innocently wide she asked, "What are you doing?"

"Measuring," he gave his answer, not looking up as he drew another arc with the compass, rolling the junction of the instrument between thumb and fingers.

"Oh?" she said, shifting her weight to the other side of her buttocks. "Measuring what?"

Only his head lifted. "I'm judging the distances between ourselves and El Abadan, the Hussar, the nearest European force, and the next oasis."

"You need to know all that?"

"If you were in a cage of tigers wouldn't you want to know where everything was?"

"Oh, of course," she said, but his attention had already turned back to the charts.

Juliette walked to the opposite side of the tent. "Well, where are the Hussar? Are they ahead of us?"

"No, they are moving steadily east into their mountains. But their main force is still intact and can't be far. Still, I don't think they can get reinforcements and attack us again before we've reached El Abadan."

Taking up his pencil again he scribbled numbers on a small white paper while Juliette rose and traversed the distance between the table and the tent flap.

"Explain to me," she said and paused. "Explain about

the Europeans? Why do you hate them? It isn't all because of my father, is it, but about other things, too?

Annoyance on his face Sharif raised his head again. "You are a strange woman, Juliette. I thought you hated all Arabs. Why would you care about my reasons for anything?"

Juliette lifted her shoulders evasively. "I don't know. After living with you for these weeks, don't you imagine I would be at least curious? I've heard people say in London that the presence of Europe in Africa has resulted in modernization. I'd like to hear your side of the story."

Sharif gave her a long considering look. Then, apparently sensing her sincerity, he said, "It is true the Europeans have brought positive inventions and improvements. But with these improvements they've also brought a form of slavery and exploitation. As their power has grown here they have confiscated all the most fertile and valuable land and resources and bribed our government officials, so that now the wealth of the Sahara exists for the profit of foreign governments. In addition, the very presence of Europeans in our marketplaces has driven the prices higher on everything, so fewer and fewer can afford to buy even necessities. In short, they are turning us into a country of beggars, and while we need European goods we must force Europeans to trade with us as equals."

Sharif leaned back against the hassock and continued, his eyes never leaving her face.

"But any negotiation at this point is futile. The Europeans control the government, which will put down by force those who challenge them. And the Europeans are not willing to talk away what they already have in their possession. It is much more profitable to increase their empire by adding our wealth to theirs, than to have to trade as equals."

"But the tribesmen must not let this continue," Juliette burst out. "The Europeans must realize you will not be treated as inferiors, but as an independent power. The tribesmen must unite, and then Europe will be forced to obey their will."

"Yes!" Sharif said. "In this case, it is the only solution.

You understand as I thought you would. Sometimes I think it is a pity you weren't born a man—although I wouldn't have preferred it." He smiled ironically before rising to his feet and lighting a cheroot, then exhaled very slowly.

"But there are two things which keep all the tribes from uniting. One is Abu Hussar, who constantly blocks the formation of a strong alliance by retaliating against any tribe that joins me. The other is the constant bickering between tribes, which weakens their numbers and power and keeps them from considering the larger problem. In this way the Europeans have, unknowingly, helped us. Their domination has given all the tribes of the desert a common enemy, when before they had only each other. One day the Arabs will throw off their shackles and take the helm of their own destiny. One day we will send the Europeans home and we will be as equals instead of conquerer and slave."

Juliette felt frightened. "And that's what you are planning," she said. "That's why you stole the rifles and ammunition from the French, to lead the tribes against the Hussar, and later, the French and English!"

"Exactly," Sharif answered. "But first there must be total unity among all the tribes, not just twelve."

"But why fight with Hussar. Why not just make an agreement with him?"

Sharif shook his head. "What is between us is generations old. I would never trust him to keep any agreement. He and his tribe care nothing for unity and have made their living by robbing for as long as anyone can remember. They must be destroyed before any forward step can be taken. Only then, when we speak with one voice, can we hope to overcome the Europeans. But it will be done, and the world will understand that we are a free people, and not a conquest."

The cold determination in his face sent another chill through her. So *this* was what those secret meetings and low conversations were about. And he could learn all the English and French plans by mingling with them while they had no idea who he really was. He had fooled them as easily as he had fooled her into thinking him no more or less than a spoiled playboy. But if he were ever found out, his intentions exposed. . . . And suddenly she blurted out, "But you're not ever going back to France, are you? What if they find out, and Rodney knew—he told me. And there must be others!"

Sharif emitted a deep disgusted note from his nostrils. His black eyes were both amused and very hard. "Rodney did know, and there was one other. Both have been silenced," he finished flatly.

Juliette swallowed hard, her throat cramping so she couldn't ask any more before Rashid's voice was at the tent entrance speaking quick Arabic words that Juliette could roughly translate as, "Master, please—there is trouble."

"I will come," Sharif answered, pulling on his burnoose and deftly wrapping a long scarf several times round his head, before pulling the last eighteen inches across his face so only his eyes remained visible through a narrow slit. Then lifting the tent flap, he was gone, the gale sweeping in with a short blast of sand before the flap fell closed again.

He didn't return that day, or nearly until the dawn of the next. But then he was beside their bed, silently checking his revolver before lying at her side, his arms crossed behind his head as he stared at the tent ceiling.

Staying still and observing him through mostly shut eyes, Juliette recalled how she had once thought him completely mad, a kind of monster, while now he seemed familiar and somehow necessary.

The warmth of his body touched her beneath the sheet that was pulled over them, and feeling strangely content, she sighed.

Today he had been different, a leader, even an idealist, she thought. Yes, he could be human sometimes. And wondering if she would ever understand him, she turned over and listened to the wind blow the sand until the sound blended with her dreams.

PART XI

EL ABADAN

Chapter 65

Yes, Sharif could be almost human sometimes, Juliette had thought. And yes . . . it almost seemed he saw her as more than a thing with which to satisfy his lusts. At least that was what she had thought.

As she looked back on it later, she knew she should have known what would happen. But those days during which the sand continued to blow in rivers around them, forcing them together, had thrown her off guard.

The second day of the storm was even worse than the first, and tucked snugly in their tent, Sharif had treated her almost as his wife, a friend at least, talking with her of the past and his plans for the future, disclosing little anecdotes about his childhood, about his first cheetah hunt, and a beloved old mare that had died.

Many times he made love to her, gently though, not like the fierce way he usually possessed her. She should have been warned of course—at least later when he left camp for two days without even letting her know. But it wasn't until they reached El Abadan that she was reminded again that, in spite of everything, he still hated her.

El Abadan—when Juliette first caught sight of the city it seemed a queen enthroned on the rocky heights above— impenetrable, mysterious, as it overlooked the wide desert plain that stretched beneath its feet to infinity.

Its surrounding high wall was dotted with parapets and turrets, and huge gates were visible while, inside, appeared a maze of the Oriental; darker mud walls, endless arched windows and towers and even taller minarets reflecting the sunlight from their tiled domes. Aloof, even sinister, an ancient entity standing alone, it seemed the last outpost at this forgotten end of the earth.

It took another day just to climb to the top of the cliff, a ride that illustrated the invulnerability of the fortress. Certainly no enemy could take this city by force. No army could surround it without being at the mercy of the armaments on the walls above them.

No wonder El Abadan had controlled this narrow pass that led the caravans south to the African interior, Juliette thought the next morning, as she rode through the wide-flung iron gates.

And as they entered, the populace thronged in the streets, cheering, chanting, all straining forward at once to catch a glimpse of their sheik, or better, to touch his horse or burnoose.

Pouring out of the houses along narrow streets, heavily veiled women came, picking up the hems of their robes as they trotted toward the column, craning in an attempt to spot someone. Then, shouting in high-pitched voices, they lifted sons to display, and several warriors dismounted, taking their infants and tossing them in the air. Then someone was shaking a tambourine and the voices rose to be heard above the barking dogs and stamping horses.

Disguised by her male garb, no one noticed Juliette as she found herself an unobtrusive place to observe from behind a cluster of palm trees on the edge of the crowd.

Peering between palm fronds, she watched as the jubilation continued, and the men were welcomed and the crowd chanted, "Sharif, Sharif, Sharif," before switching to *"Allahu akbar,"* and then coming back to "Sharif, Sharif, Sharif."

It was only when another sort of chant came from the minarets and floated down over the crowd that the jubilation paused and the crowd divided between men and women and all faced the east, kneeling and reverently taking up the singsong phrases, *"La Ilaha Illa Allah, La Ilaha Illa Allah,"* which by now Juliette could translate as, "There is only one God, he is Allah," which was the beginning of prayers.

Having heard this familiar litany a hundred times without the slightest variation, it seemed to play itself in Juliette's mind the way all things do that become familiar. She knew each rhythm, each word by memory, and though she always remained aloof, she found, strangely, that the

chanting gave her comfort of a sort, the same deep quiet
that came after listening to the chanting of monks.

Prayers lasted for several minutes as they all bowed
prostrate in the dust, chanting, bowing, rising, and bowing
low again. And when it was finished, they all rose a last
time together before getting to their feet and continuing as
if there had been no pause at all until the cries of celebration dominated all else again.

She noticed then that Sharif had disappeared, and she
was searching for him among the crowd when Rashid came
and motioned her to follow.

He guided her along a stone-paved street worn smooth
by hundreds of years that wound up a continuous incline to
the north side of the city. It was bordered by mud-brick
walls that sometimes were draped by vines or an occasional
coral-flowered oleander.

Ahead, at the end of the incline were even higher-walled
gardens and wide swinging gates that were unmistakably
the palace's.

They rode through these to a porch with a staked awning
before the large carved doors.

A thickly veiled woman of sizable bulk ushered her inside. Then, wordlessly, the woman's kohl-lined eyes swept
her from head to toe, seeming to miss nothing before she
nodded with a slow, graceful inclining of her head. But
Juliette was given no chance to speak, since the woman
turned and waved her to follow before taking the lead with
a serene glide.

The hallways were set in intricate patterns of blue
mosaic tiles and, as they went, Juliette had peeks of several
elegant sitting rooms decorated in muted shades of red and
blue with low, shiny brass tables scattered between hassocks and floor lamps.

They traversed a garden, cool and lovingly manicured in
the speckled shade of palms. They entered a long hall
again on the opposite side of the garden. A guard stood at
the end of the hall, protecting two gilded doors. He never
looked directly at them, but stepped aside as they approached and opened the doors.

Until now, instinctively, Juliette had tried to keep in mind the numbers of turns and changes of direction. But now, as she stepped inside and the doors were closed behind her, even these thoughts were jolted out of her head. She hardly even noticed the deep blue tiled floors or the embroidered diaphanous luxury of the place, her eyes locking instead on a group of young, very beautiful girls who were all looking at her.

She drew herself up stiffly. Of course! A harem—*his* harem, with silken rooms of shimmering draperies, soft cushions and divans, and even softer women—*his* women. Hadn't he admitted to having them? Hadn't he even threatened to put her here one day—at least she *thought* it had been only a threat. She never had actually considered what it might mean to stand here, staring at his jeweled, vaporously veiled women who seemed quite curious, though obviously less surprised to see her than she was to see them.

It was the realization of her worst fears. She wanted to scream, to cry, to run, but refused to yield to those impulses, even as her stomach contracted into a knot.

Masking her surprise and humiliation as best she could, Juliette continued past the other women, noticing as she did the poisonous scrutiny of the loveliest among them, a fiery beauty whose certain animallike aura reminded her of Sharif. And later, in her private room at the end of a narrow carpeted hallway, Juliette kept all her fury and humiliation to herself as she asked Cassia, "Who was that woman? The one who seems to hate me?"

"Oh, you must mean Zenobia," Cassia answered as she folded silken gowns into cedar-scented drawers.

"I don't know her name, but she has extremely long black hair, almost to her knees, and very large gold hoops in her ears."

"Yes, that is Zenobia. She *was* the favorite," Cassia answered with special emphasis on the "was." "That is before madame came. . . ."

Cassia frowned, her eyes taking on a worried expression. "Zenobia is a foolish and spoiled daughter of the chief of the Assar and his first wife, who is a witch, a woman who keeps her husband's love by the use of devilish magic. The name Zenobia means dark one—and so she is, dark as a devil. When she was given to the master a young Berber princess was favorite. But it was not long before this girl was attacked in the night, her face permanently disfigured by a potion tossed in her face." Cassia cast down her face, anxiously fingering her robes before continuing. "Three days later, the girl hanged herself."

Involuntarily, Juliette shivered. "And you think Zenobia was the one responsible for the attack?"

Cassia shook her head with grave eyes. "I don't know, madame. But many swear it was she, even though a dagger bearing the mark of the Hussar was later found in the hall outside the girl's room and the Hussar were blamed. Still, I think it was Zenobia that planned it. Certainly she became favorite quickly afterward and has remained so. Now the other women fear being favored by the master because of Zenobia's jealousy."

"Does Sharif know about this?"

"No, madame. All are afraid to tell him. And madame must be careful not to anger this one. She is more dangerous than a scorpion."

"But Zenobia has no reason to hate me," Juliette said. "I assure you Sharif has no intention of favoring me."

The few dark hairs that acted as Cassia's eyebrows raised and came together. "Madame must be careful," she repeated. And that was all she said before fluffing up the pillows on the bed.

The next day Juliette began a daily routine that was to be repeated again and again. Cassia awakened her in the morning and, propped against pillows, Juliette was served breakfast.

Fruit was common, or precious juice or melons, and mint tea usually followed. Then she was taken down a marble stairway to the bath, consisting of two large underground tanks, one of warm water, and one of cool.

She was bathed in these pools, first the warm, and then the cool and, from that first day, her toilet afterward became a routine social affair.

There was no privacy in the harem, and Juliette found out there was nothing to do but accept the numbers of curious and not unfriendly eyes that watched her, that fingered her hair and then, more shyly, brushed her skin with their fingers, smiling and declaring she was beautiful, a warrior woman. *"Mar'a muharibah,"* they said over and over and giggled self-consciously under her look.

But Zenobia did not join this throng of admirers. Most of her time she spent in the harem's common room, separated from the other girls and reclining on a low couch in the midst of solicitous servants.

She rarely spoke, and almost never to the other girls, who ignored her too except for an occasional wary glance. And after a time, Juliette lost any idea of becoming friendly with her, occupying herself instead by watching the numbers of jugglers and snake charmers and other entertainments that came to the harem.

Indeed, exhausted from the journey across the desert, in a few days time Juliette had discovered the harem to be the essence of pleasurable boredom. The deprivations of the desert had given her a new appreciation of luxuries of every kind and she found the many savory delights prepared by the palace kitchens beyond comparison to the weeks of dried dates and mouflon. So, fed and pampered as constantly as Zenobia, Juliette felt herself seduced into laziness.

For now there was no hope of escape, she told herself. Later she would decide what to do. So, for the first few weeks at least, Juliette found it was easy to forget about everything unpleasant.

One lazy morning Juliette sat contentedly at her toilet, eyes closed as her hair was brushed. How good the bristles felt against her scalp, and how lovely the rose incense that floated through the hall. But then her reverie was broken by the sound of footsteps and the voices of the girls dropping to an anxious murmur.

She looked up, somehow not surprised to see Zenobia coming toward her, the other girls melting out of her path.

The Arab girl's eyes were brimming with fury as she paused a few feet away, standing astride, arms akimbo, as she said, *"Sharmûta,"* throwing the word like a knife. "It is *you* who has stolen my gold bracelet!"

Another whisper rushed over the watching girls like a breeze in dried grass.

Still sitting, Juliette faced the irate girl, her expression calm as she answered, "I have stolen nothing from you, Zenobia. I have no gold bracelet, nor do I want one."

"I do not believe you. You have stolen my bracelet, the master's gift to me. You have taken it!" Fury flamed brighter in the girl's perfect brown face and, in an explosive gesture, she tossed back her long black hair. "It is true," she insisted. "You are a thief and a white she-devil! You rise up in the night in a cloud of mist and stalk through the palace bringing evil upon all true believers!" Zenobia stamped her small bare foot in a tinkling of ankle bracelets before crossing her arms and glowering at Juliette. "You have stolen what is mine and I will stand here until you give it back!"

Now there was not a sound from anyone as the two women regarded each other. Juliette remained seated. "Please believe me, Zenobia. I would not steal what is yours. Besides, of what use would it be to me? I am told you have sharp eyes. If I stole something from you, I would never be able to wear it. So why would I take it from you?"

The gathering of girls nodded in a fanning of head veils. The white *mar'a muharibah* was correct, no? The sharp eyes of Zenobia would prevent anyone from wearing her stolen jewelry. And of what use was a thing if one could not adorn one's self with it?

Zenobia's rounded arm shot out like a sword as she pointed straight into Juliette's face with a henna-stained finger. "You would steal just for evilness. And the master will not allow stealing." She leaned forward so Juliette could smell her hot mint-scented breath. "He once sold a woman who stole from another. And she was never heard of again!"

Still Juliette appeared unmoved by the venom of Zenobia's attack. "I have stolen nothing," she said. "Therefore the master has no reason to be angry."

Zenobia's eyes constricted further and her face grew scarlet with anger as her neck stretched forward and down. *"Infidel,"* she spat. And with a movement so swift and unexpected it couldn't be prevented, one of Zenobia's hands grabbed the neckline of Juliette's robe and with a jerk, split the garment to the waist.

That was shock enough. But when Cassia jumped between them, Zenobia threw the girl sprawling with a slap across her face. Then she bent closer to Juliette. "The bracelet is mine. And you will give it back!" she finished with a hiss.

This was too much! Amid shrieks of surprise, Juliette sprang forward capturing Zenobia's long hair and twisting her arm behind her. She tightened her hold, turning Zenobia's screams to sudden whimpers as Juliette's voice came short and angry. "I have not taken your bracelet, or anything else that belongs to you. And if you dare lay a hand on me, or on Cassia again, I will cut off this fine hair of yours!"

For effect, Juliette lifted a pair of scissors from a nearby table and snapped them open and closed beside Zenobia's ear before releasing her with a shove.

Now the fury in Zenobia's face was mixed with fear, and she made no further resistance, allowing herself to continue in the direction she had been pushed. Some distance away then she turned, her fingers splayed like claws. "I warn you," Zenobia said. "This is not over. You, whose mother copulated with the devil. Another time you will find I do not give up what is mine so easily."

Zenobia faced her, panting. Then suddenly her face inexplicably changed, the ugly twist to her lips disappearing to reemerge a smile.

Immediately Juliette realized it was not for her, but for whoever was behind her. And then the Arab girl was running with open arms and crying out, *"Sayyid! Sayyid!* At last you have come!"

Chapter 66

Indeed it was Sharif, striding into the room with panther-like grace before settling himself on a large black cushion as his women gathered around.

Immediately, Juliette whirled to face away, humiliation replacing fury as she realized he must have seen it all. Oh, what a good laugh this would give him, catching her brawling with his women, and over him! She gathered together what remained of her shredded robes and, head high, started for her own room.

Unfortunately she had only taken a few steps when his voice rose above the happy chattering girls.

"It pleases me for you to stay, Juliette."

Juliette stopped, her back to him. What would he do if she didn't obey?—call the guard and have her physically deposited at his feet? And unwilling to go to him, yet not daring to risk his retaliation, Juliette lowered herself on a nearby cushion, a cold shoulder turned toward him.

To Juliette's surprise he then ignored her, turning his attention to his women instead, speaking affectionately to them, as if they were children, and listening with a slight curve to his lips when they answered his questions in soft, sometimes shyly hesitant voices.

Upon request one girl sang a short composition, accompanying herself on a mandolinlike instrument, and another girl was asked to dance for him but this was cut short when a large tray was brought in.

Risking an eye in his direction, Juliette saw the tray was piled high with gifts and, when it was set down, Sharif distributed them offhandedly to each girl.

There were jewels, carved ivory combs, new veils as fine as butterflies' wings, and feathers that all combined in a confusion of brilliant colors with shiny limbs and long swinging hair as each girl tried on her gift, modeling it before Sharif, and even shedding little tears of joy as they kissed his hands in gratitude.

Sickening! Juliette thought. But at least he didn't expect

her to participate in such a degrading spectacle. No, he seemed satisfied, at least for the moment, with demonstrating the completeness of his power over her. Well, perhaps *this* would show Zenobia and the rest of them how he really felt about her and stop this ridiculous gossip about Sharif making her the favorite, she told herself clenching her jaw tight. Yes, *favorite*, that's what they called it—like a horse or falcon—a favorite toy. And nothing could be further from the truth—everyone could see that now. But later, even knowing this, didn't prepare Juliette for the next shock.

"A wife?" Juliette found herself repeating the following day when Farah, flushed with excitement, sat down among the women as the portions of glazed mutton were being served.

"Yes, a wife," she repeated. "It has all been arranged. The master only just told me!"

Zenobia was suddenly there too, her eyes flashing as she flung her hair onto her back with a toss of her chin. "It is not true! The master would not take you as wife before me. You are a fool, Farah, and, if you are lying, I will have you whipped!"

Zenobia was as menacing as a coiled snake and Farah retreated. "But you do not understand, Zenobia. I am not to be the master's wife. He is giving me to one of his headmen—a man I once saw below the harem windows." Farah raised her face ecstatically to the ceiling and wrapped her own arms around herself. "Ah! And he is so handsome. How I hunger to feel his touch." Then she looked back to the others blushing slightly. "The master is generous, no? In times past I have pleased him and now, when his interest has wandered far from me, he does not sell me as another man would. He gives me in marriage so I can bear sons to my honor and the honor of my husband," she said, caressing the word husband with her small rosy mouth. "And all of you are just as fortunate. The master told me he is going away for many months to the north and, before he goes, he will make us all wives." She turned to Juliette. "Even you, madame. The master says you are to be given the finest husband of all."

They all seemed overjoyed and Juliette realized only Zenobia and herself were stunned by the news as the rest of the girls giggled with excitement and began to speculate about exactly to whom each of them might be given.

Juliette felt turned to stone. He was getting rid of her. She knew too much and how much better—safer, to have her tucked away in the harem of another man where she could cause no trouble. It would be his ultimate revenge!

"*In sha'Allah*," Cassia began later, watching her mistress walking up and down the carpets of her private room as if to wear a path. "Let the will of Allah be done. A person's fate is written in the book of Allah during the fortieth day after his conception. Nothing can alter this." The girl paused and looked sidelong at her mistress, who did not answer as twice more she passed by, her red gauzy robe dragging the carpet. "It has been true forever," she continued. "All men want to be a woman's first lover, while all women wish to be a man's last. It is a battle that women many times lose. But I would not worry yet, madame. The master may change his mind, and I think he cares for you more than you think."

But for all Cassia's words, and even the tea Juliette later drank that was supposed "to help her sleep," she couldn't contain the wrenching in her stomach, or the horrible feeling that it was true—that Sharif was returning to Europe and giving her away. And to add to her anxiety, a series of weddings full of pomp and finery began during the days that followed. Farah's was first, and amid raised voices praising her beauty and wishing her happiness, Juliette watched the radiant Arab girl being lifted onto a pallet and carried from the palace to the house of her new husband.

Yes, fate—fate, *In sha'Allah*, Julliette said to herself. And what would be hers? When would her turn come? Certainly there were rumors if she cared to listen. One said she was to be given to the eldest son of the leader of the Assar, while another seemed certain it was to be a wealthy Ethiopian. But Juliette refused even to listen to the continuous speculation, and Sharif came no more either to confirm or deny anything.

He's torturing me, she thought, twisting her fingers in a
lock of shiny hair as if to choke it. But I won't let him. I
won't think of this now when all I can do is wait. But in
spite of her determination not to care, the time crawled by
unbearably slowly, more so with each day as she waited for
fate to fix itself upon her. And to complicate matters,
again Sharif was invading her dreams, caressing her silently, pressing his lips to her burning flesh before taking
her with slow intense strokes that made her awaken breathless and perspiring beneath the thin coverlet.

Yes, she was miserable, so miserable that, when one
night she awakened to an unfamiliar sound, she wondered
if she had finally been driven mad. Certainly she *must* be
seeing things, though there it was, and continued to be,
even when she rubbed her eyes—a little door near her bed.
She had never noticed it before, so well did it fit into the
wall. Only the flickering light from behind it outlined its
shape and revealed it to her now. And as she listened, it
seemed someone on the other side was groping for the bolt.

There was a tiny click, and the beam of illumination
widened to reveal a dwarf—no, a young boy of eight years
or so, tiptoeing closer and bringing a finger across his lips
to signal her silence before he said the impossible, "If madame pleases to escape, must follow me."

"Escape?" Juliette questioned in an outlet of astonished
breath. "Who are you? What do you mean escape?" Already she was scrambling up and throwing a robe around
her shoulders. "Who sent you—Cassia?"

The boy glanced over his shoulder and salaamed again
before whispering, "I Ramad, madame. White man send
me, a many rich one. Horses be at city gates. He come to
save madame."

"An Englishman?" Juliette asked, her eyes expanding
larger.

"Yes, madame. Many men. Guns."

Juliette's mind raced. Rodney? No. Rodney was dead—
wasn't he? Or was it possible that someone else had discovered her whereabouts and come to the rescue?

"Come, madame. Must hurry." The boy motioned her to
come.

Escape, Juliette thought. Once she had pledged never to give up trying, but did she dare try now?

On the other hand did she dare not to try? another voice within her asked. If she stayed here Sharif would marry her to one of his followers.

Before, unable to prevent anything Sharif wished to do she had avoided imagining such a future. But now with an alternative presented, her mind drew into focus an image of herself in the arms of a faceless man—a man even less civilized than Sharif, since few of his followers had any notion of Western customs. She would be the chattel of an Arab officer, bound by law and custom to serve his every whim and need, bearing his pleasure, his displeasure, and his children. And when she grew old, or if she should displease her husband, he could by law divorce her by simply saying he divorced her three times within her presence. Then her children would remain the property of her husband while she would be abandoned to the streets like a discarded toy.

It was a picture that made her insides crawl. If only she could be rescued and reach civilization again. Even being an outcast of her own society seemed heaven by comparison to what awaited her here.

She looked back to the boy. "Come, madame," he insisted. "It is dangerous for white friends to wait more. Must hurry." He handed her a burnoose of the common type worn in the street and watched as she flung it around her shoulders. Then crooking his finger for her to follow, he retraced his steps back through the doorway.

Even Juliette's whisper seemed to echo as they moved along the nearly airless tunnel. "Is this passage secret?" she asked.

The boy held the candle high as they went. "Not secret, madame. Many know." He waved a short arm left. "That corridor lead to master. This passage used many time. But more only a few know. Man give me this because I know and bring you." Ramad's white teeth glowed in the semi-light only less brilliantly than the diamond he displayed in his palm. "You surprised I know much. But think what surprise for sheik, eh?" He laughed childishly.

Juliette opened her mouth to answer but he put a finger to his lips to keep her from speaking. "No talk now, madame. Ears close."

So after that they were silent, though Juliette was burning to ask him a dozen questions. And later she would only remember a series of impressions—the dry airless smell of the low corridor, the ache in her bent back, the soft slapping of their feet upon the stone floor, the candle melting away the darkness and bobbing in rhythm with Ramad's steps and, at last, the crunching sound when Ramad pressed his hands to what appeared solid rock and it slid open to reveal yet another hallway where she could straighten up.

There was another doorway then, and the sweet smell of fresh air made her realize that this must be where it opened to the outside even before a heavy mat tied with acacia brush was pushed out of the doorway and she found herself looking out over the stretch of desert to the east where the moon perched just above the horizon against a lavender sky.

Coming toward her was a figure silhouetted against the moon and, she was just turning to ask Ramad who it was, when lightning struck.

With a blinding flash the world careened in a kaleidoscope of colors as her cheek struck the gritty sand.

There was a voice, and another, and then she felt a searing thrust in her side just after a shadow came near and then disappeared running. "Ramad," she heard herself say in a weak unrecognizable voice. But then the earth was sinking. She looked down to see a knife protruding from her ribs, a red stain spreading from it and dripping on the sand.

Breathless, she gasped, but now there were seemingly several knives all spinning in a blur as a mountain of darkness slid down over her.

Chapter 67

After that, the world became one of shadows and dark and vague shapeless colors moving in and out of her vision among voices, sometimes distinct and other times garbled.

"She is a fortunate young woman," one voice said swimming through milky fog. "The dagger missed both her lungs and kidneys. She's lost a terrible amount of blood, and I've put twenty stitches in her head, but she will live."

A familiar voice followed. "When will the worst be over?"

"She will have to be watched closely for a week at least, and she must not have any excitement for some time after that. If the wound is reopened, she could die. Obviously she has an extremely hard head to withstand such a blow."

A relieved laugh followed. "Indeed her hard head has been in evidence before this. I never thought I'd find myself grateful for that particular attribute, but under these circumstances. . . ."

Juliette wanted to respond, to open her eyes and speak, but clouds and spaces of timelessness prevented her until later when she was aware of longer periods of consciousness and at last the mist began clearing.

The first sounds she became aware of were those of chanting, the gentle voices of women raised together, "*La Ilaha Illa Allah, La Ilaha Illa Allah,*"—there is only one God. And feeling herself reviving little by little as the prayer continued, Juliette turned her hammering head, blinking against unaccustomed brightness as blurring colors and shapes slowly focused themselves into three knelling women and, beyond them, a series of arched windows that divided this room from a garden where a bird was singing as the last rosy light of day flooded the sky.

She sighed, her lips unconsciously forming the familiar phrases as they continued, "*La Ilaha Illa Allah,*" and slowly Juliette realized she was in a wide bed, a flimsy cover thrown over her.

To her right cheetah pelts were mounted on the walls and, on the left, a telescope poised on a tripod was pointing out an arched window.

The room reminded her of a castle keep, she thought. But then Cassia's face was swimming above her.

"Madame?" she questioned. "Are you awake? Can you hear me?"

Juliette's eyelids parted wider.

"Yes . . . yes, I'm awake. But where, where . . . how did I get here?"

"You are in the master's private rooms, madame. You have been hurt and very sick, but you are better now, the doctor has said so."

Juliette touched her forehead to find it bandaged. "Doctor? What doctor?" she asked.

"The master's doctor, a Spaniard. He lives in the palace and is one of the master's trusted friends. But now, madame, you must rest. Here," she produced a glass. "Drink this. It will make you feel better and you will sleep."

Cassia's arm slid around her back, supporting her head as, obediently, Juliette drank the creamy, slightly bitter, liquid. Then lying down again, she felt a slow drowsiness envelop her until Cassia's pleasantly chattering voice seemed far away, and she no longer listened, and the very next thing she knew, it was morning.

"Let me introduce myself," said the tall fatherly looking gentleman with a courteous incline of his head. "I am Dr. Santapalo."

Juliette felt better now. The room no longer wavered in mists, and she could see this man clearly. He reminded her of Roberto, only he was taller, heavier, more deeply tanned, and he carried the look of a man who had seen and experienced enough to accept life without unnecessary concern.

"As you might have been told, I've been taking care of you since you were attacked. You were unconscious for some time and gave us all a scare. How do you feel now?"

"I feel well . . . better certainly. But I don't understand. Who are you? I mean—how did you come here?"

The doctor smiled pleasantly, as if her question was slightly silly, before answering. "The sheik and I have been friends and business associates for nearly ten years—since I first traveled into the desert and, getting lost, discovered El Abadan quite by accident." The Spaniard's brown eyes shone. "I suppose you could say the city captured me, has taken me hostage in a way as it does romantics like myself. Being interested in the history of these desert tribes I found it fascinating. El Abadan is unique among desert cities. I think now it was originally built in the fourteen hundreds. Do you know they are still discovering passageways in the walls that have been hidden for centuries?" Impatiently then he waved his hand as if at himself. "But I won't bore you further with my idiosyncratic interests. Suffice it to say that I've found my studies here fulfilling and the desert a refuge from the complications of modern life. When I met Karim he had just become sheik. From that time until now we've found each other useful and also have become the sort of friends one makes only very few of in a lifetime. Now when, occasionally, I've returned to Spain, I've found life there drab beside the life the desert offers. This has become my home now, and I feel more Arab than Spanish. I hate the Hussar and the intrusion of European governments just as these Arabs do, so actually, I'm perfectly suited to be one of them."

"But you're not an Arab," Juliette said in a surprised tone.

"No, but I'm not English, either. I don't think Karim would have trusted me if I were."

Juliette turned away, toying absently with the ties of her gown. "Yes, he does hate the English. I already know."

Dr. Santapalo nodded, and something in his wan smile told Juliette he knew much more about many things than he ever told anyone. He nodded. "Yes, from what I've heard, Karim has made his hatred of the English clear to you. But tell me, do you care for him?"

The question, asked with blunt frankness, brought Juliette's regard snapping to his. "Care for him?" she asked startled. "That's a peculiar question, doctor. He's an Arab and he killed my father, as I'm sure you're aware."

The doctor nodded. "Yes, Karim did tell me that much."

A concerned frown crossed his face before he continued. "I mean to be direct, Miss Clayton, because I sense you are far too intelligent to be fooled by indirectness. And you still haven't answered me. Do you care for Karim?"

Suddenly Juliette found her eyes wavering under his serious look. "Well . . . no," she said surprised to realize she was no longer sure. But then she repeated. "No, I don't care for him." And then more firmly, "Actually, I detest him!"

Dr. Santapalo considered her for a moment more, his arms folded on his chest as Juliette wondered if he believed her, and why indeed she hardly believed herself.

"That is unfortunate," he said finally. "I was hoping you felt differently—that the desert may have taken you hostage too."

He leaned over her then, as if the subject were closed, and carefully began unwrapping the long bandage from around her skull before gently examining the wound.

Juliette flinched slightly beneath the pressure of his fingers against her healing flesh as she continued, unwilling to let the subject drop there. "I'm surprised to hear you say that. You seem to know something about my . . . my situation. I mean . . . surely you see what he has done to me. Do you think such behavior garners affection?"

"No," the doctor said flatly. "But it seems you were in love with him while you were both in Las Flores del Mar. There was some talk of marriage, was there not?"

"Sharif told you that?"

"No, but he did send a message from Las Flores some time ago delaying his arrival and notifying his household to make preparations for his bride. Then there was another cable a week later delaying his arrival with no mention of a bride." The doctor's expression became ironic. "Of course when he finally did arrive he had no bride but an obviously reluctant *you* instead. It wasn't difficult to surmise the rest." He peered at her closely. "I am right, aren't I? I've been curious and Karim offers few details. Tell me, Miss Clayton—or do you use Thorpe? What happened in Las

Flores? Was it that you realized he was an Arab and refused to marry him?"

"Well . . . yes, partly," Juliette admitted, wondering at
the ease with which this man pieced the situation together.
"And I use Thorpe, not Clayton, if that could possibly make
any difference now. But why are you asking all these questions? What does any of what happened or what I have to
say matter to you?"

The doctor straightened, raising his eyebrows. "I'm interested in everything about you—but perhaps I should explain since you seem unaware of some of the basic circumstances."

He sat down then, leaning an elbow on one knee as he
spoke with the casual familiarity of a man thoroughly
versed on his subject. "You see, all the sheiks of El Abadan
have been extremely important men in this part of the
world, and Karim al-Sharif is particularly so because, not
only does he control much of the economy of North Africa
through his dominance of the trade routes, but he is also
the only possible leader who can unite these desert tribes
between Egypt and Morocco against the Hussar and later
against the Europeans.

"He is perhaps the most powerful man in Africa today,
and when he planned to marry, I was surprised, if not astonished. I expected you to be an exceptional woman, and I
haven't been disappointed," he added with a smile and
slight bow. "The fact I find most difficult to credit is that
you are George Clayton's daughter. Yet here you are, and
somehow you've single-handedly managed to kill a mouflon which has made you a revered figure." The doctor
crossed his arms and leaned back in his chair. "How all of
this has taken place I'd like to hear. But, whatever the
explanation, you've become an important person in your
own right. You have had a great deal of influence over
Karim and therefore over all of North Africa and beyond.
These are crucial times, as you must already realize. Any
day war will come, and to answer your first question, I
believe that who you are, what you think and say, may
affect the lives of thousands and the events which are only
now beginning. As an adviser and friend to the sheik, it

behooves me to learn about you and, in short, I'm interested in anything you would like to tell me."

Juliette stared at him as if he had just announced that the moon was actually made of blue cheese and populated by leprechauns. Then she laughed, though it hurt her head and side and she stopped short with a croaking sound. "But you're mistaken, doctor," she said finally. "You began quite well, but some of your assumptions are not entirely accurate. If Sharif were willing to give you any details, you would soon learn that his feelings toward me now are quite different from ones he expressed in the past. Frankly, he hates me. So you see, your interest in me is misplaced. I have no influence over him now, nor will I in the future."

Dr. Santapalo's brow arched. "I see. Has Karim told you this in so many words? I mean, that he 'hates' you?"

"No, not in so many words. But his actions have left no doubt."

"And you regard him with equal dislike?"

"Yes!" Juliette lifted her chin. "And why shouldn't I?"

Santapalo nodded, studying her as he recalled the tormented expression on Karim's face during the previous days when he had leaned over her unconscious form. He had refused to leave her side. Yet, now that she was recovering, he had not been to see her. Dr. Santapalo's lips drew into a thin line. Well, time would give more of the answers, he thought, and said, "Indeed Karim makes his life far more complicated than need be. On the other hand, he usually has a good reason for what he does. But I can tell you, Miss Thorpe, that I don't believe he hates you—and with utmost respect, I also don't believe you hate him."

He smiled again and, giving her hand a reassuring pat, stood up to go. "And if I were you," he continued, "I would do my best to recover and not worry about anything for the moment. Situations often have a way of working themselves out."

He gave her another gentle look. "Now get some rest. I have a feeling you're going to need it."

Chapter 68

Was it possible? Juliette asked herself the following morning as Cassia helped her into Sharif's own bath, which was tiled completely in intricate silver and black mosaic and surrounded by mirrors that reflected her pale face from all angles above the foaming bubbles. Had Sharif's heart softened toward her? It was true, of course, that he had brought her to his own suite of rooms, when she might have been nursed in many other places. But why then hadn't he come to see her? According to Cassia, he had left the city and might be gone for days. And was that the way a man acted when he cared?

Juliette raised a hand to her temple where her head began to pulse again. Oh, what did it matter anyway? she wondered miserably. Why did she even try to think? She could never, no never, forgive him. So what difference did any of it make—except now, perhaps he would be merciful enough not to give her away.

Juliette was surprised when he finally did come that night, silently—unannounced, after her dinner tray had been carried away. Obviously he hadn't stayed away from the city long, she thought with a spark of something like hope. Yes, maybe there was a chance. . . . But then there was no more time to consider as he was standing beside her bed, his eyes with a hint of darkness beneath them as he looked down at her.

Instinctively Juliette pulled the silk cover up higher under her chin, putting another layer of gauzy material between them as he said, "So, you're still awake. Cassia tells me you're improving. Can you try to remember anything about who assaulted you—anything at all? What were they wearing on their heads, for instance? Anything might help."

His voice was cold, factual, polite, like a police chief questioning a recovering witness.

Something within Juliette dropped. How could Doctor Santapalo ever have thought she was important to this man? And why had she believed him, if only a little?

She managed to roll her head back and forth weakly against her pillows. "No . . . no, I didn't even see them, not really, only the boy—Ramad was his name."

"Yes, he warned us you had been hurt and where to find you. But now, unfortunately, even he has disappeared."

Sharif's jaw flexed with a hint of frustration due, Juliette told herself, to his present failure in avenging this attack on his property. "A man protects his property," he had once told her. And seeing his coldness now renewed her anger so she felt suddenly reckless.

"You can't blame me for trying to escape," she said angrily. "I'll never accept what you're trying to make me. You can't keep me from trying, no matter what you do or where you send me!"

She paused, wondering—hoping, he would deny he was planning to send her away and make her the wife of another man, and she was surprised when he replied without the usual sarcasm she had learned to expect in his tone. "No, I don't blame you," he said without emotion. "How could I, when I would do the same in your place. But by now you must admit you are safer with me than at the mercy of my enemies."

"I've told you before, anything is preferable to being here with you! I can only hope that the next time I am more successful!"

Juliette didn't have to look at him. She could feel his face harden.

"But, madame, there is not going to be a next time." His regard was not mocking but perfectly serious.

"What do you mean?"

"For now you will continue to rest," he said, ignoring her question. And that was all he would say other than a polite good night and an even more impersonal nod before leaving her alone to brood on his words.

* * *

From that moment on, they seemed to fall, oddly, and yet automatically, into the sort of relationship that reminded Juliette most of the polite veneer assumed by hostile relatives forced together by circumstances.

Ridiculous, she thought. Anyone could see that. Yet here she was, royally installed in Sharif's own rooms, with Sharif himself playing the polite, if distant, host. Ridiculous that he was suddenly being as nice as he had been during their brief romance in Las Flores, though his eyes no longer smoldered with a burning light and he always seemed serious and preoccupied with other matters.

So Juliette spent most of her days alone, her only contact with the world her maids and, from Cassia, she learned that the Hussar tribe under their leader Abu Hussar were forcing a confrontation. "Already his forces have attacked several tribes and taken them under his own control," Cassia said gravely. "It is war now. Now the tribes are forced to choose between accepting Hussar domination or joining the master."

For the next days then, Juliette stayed in her room resting on a divan placed below a window. From there she watched the steady stream of chieftains and emissaries who came and went every hour from the palace gates and also the men drilling on a sandy plateau beyond the city walls where they charged at a fierce gallop while firing at clay targets.

Looking on, Juliette found herself spotting men she knew, remembering how, not long ago, all these Arabs had seemed as dangerous to her as hungry wolves. Yet, having known many of them well, having fought at their side and tended their wounds, she realized their exuberance was infinitely more exciting than any of the dull properness of the English and, as the days passed, and the drills continued, she dolefully began to wonder which of these desert men would be dead when the fighting ended.

The nights Juliette spent alone too, aware that Sharif was meeting with the chiefs and emissaries and his own headmen, all housed now in the far wings of the palace. But sometimes Sharif did come and eat dinner with her, saying little, although often she felt his eyes on her and sometimes, glancing up, she would catch an enigmatic light in them that sent a strange shimmering up her spine.

As nights passed, he seemed more distant, more preoccupied than ever, though some evenings he lingered and read to her from one of his collection of books, sometimes translating Arabic poetry in a deep melodious voice that moved Juliette to tears.

"That's beautiful," she said one night brushing her cheek. "I had no idea Arabic poetry was actually . . ." She paused, realizing she couldn't say "good" as she had started to and thinking frantically of another way to complete the sentence. But he had already caught her meaning and, smiling, said with only a trace of condescension, "We are not *all* barbarians. We do have poets and scholars too."

At first, Juliette thought time would make a difference. Always before, even though he had hated her, he had still desired her. So, daily, she expected that hot light to reappear in his face. But when another week passed, and still he was the same, Juliette began to ask herself if indeed there was another woman who had taken his interest, a woman Sharif went to after leaving her with a brief, platonic pat to her cheek.

"Well, good!" she insisted to herself. But at the same time, there was a heaviness that weighed on her so she couldn't sleep soundly. And as the days passed, she grew silent and listless and only nibbled at the squab-stuffed pastries she had once eaten greedily.

In sha'Allah, In sha'Allah, she told herself more often. Maybe it was true what they said about fate. Certainly she felt helpless to change her situation or to understand Sharif. More and more time now he spent away from the city, and less and less often he came to see her. Yet he had never suggested that she vacate his rooms and return to her own, and wouldn't he if he really wanted to be rid of her?

So the days went by, still with no answers, while still she found herself dreaming of him, his hands, his lips, his hard driving body that aroused a fever even the briskness of the desert nights couldn't cool. And sometimes, awakening with a moan and feeling the tempestuous urges of her own body, Juliette knew that if only *he* was here, she would yield to him eagerly as never before.

Rising on one elbow then, she brushed damp locks from her flushed cheeks and, turning onto her stomach, lit a candle.

She thought of the night they had first returned to camp after she had shot the mouflon, when he had come to her, seeming to know she wanted him even before she knew it fully herself. But that night seemed an aeon ago. Now he would never come to her again, she thought, twisting for a more comfortable position. Now there were so many others to satisfy his needs. And it was then she noticed that the door at the far end of her room, the one leading to Sharif's private study, was slightly ajar so that a bar of light fell across the carpet.

Juliette felt her heartbeat quicken. So, he *had* returned while she was asleep. And not questioning why, but feeling suddenly compelled, Juliette slipped out of bed and into a light robe before going to the portal and nudging it slowly open.

Chapter 69

"You don't take Abu Hussar seriously enough, my friend. His ambitions are ruthless. He'll do anything to discredit you. And if he does have any proof—even something that could pass for proof, he could disrupt the entire alliance."

It was Doctor Santapalo speaking from one of the deep leather chairs. "You know better than I the emphasis Arabs place on blood lines and inheritance."

Sharif laughed briefly and harshly as he stood up to pour himself a cup of coffee from an urn on the heavy sideboard. Then standing opposite the doctor he said, "I take Abu Hussar seriously enough. It is his rumors that I find ridiculous. And now, even *you* are listening to this babble."

"It's not mere babble when it makes people question if you are in fact your father's son. If only there were some definite proof."

"Merde!" Sharif interrupted. "If you had known my mother you would see how ridiculous that allegation is. If I had been another man's child my mother would have been delighted to tell me. She hated my father until the day she died. Anyway, she was kept in the palace harem. What other man could have fathered me?"

Sharif paused to swallow the small cup of coffee in a single gulp. But as he reached to replace the cup on the table, his hand stopped in midair as he saw Juliette, most unexpectedly, framed in the doorway beyond Dr. Santapalo's shoulder.

Sensing the change in his friend, Dr. Santapalo turned to follow his gaze until Juliette found both men staring at her, the doctor's expression of surprise quickly masked and Sharif's, as usual, unreadable.

"Oh, pardon, Miss Thorpe," the doctor said getting up and bowing respectfully as if he were the intruder. "Karim was kind enough to have me here to discuss some business. I was just going." He bowed again. "You will excuse me?"

Juliette only nodded, suddenly embarrassed and without words. She had imagined Sharif would be alone at this hour, and what would the doctor think of her entering Sharif's private study with what must seem intimate familiarity.

Once they were alone, Juliette avoided Sharif's gaze. Butterflies whipped her stomach with a thousand fluttering wings. Oh, why had she come? Madness certainly—and worse, now that she was here, she could think of nothing to say and remained mute while the fragrant smoke from an incense burner curled to the ceiling behind him and time wound down to a standstill.

Juliette licked her dry lips. "I'm sorry," she said, finally starting to back out the door.

"No need to go," he said, abruptly taking her forearm and guiding her to the same chair he had just vacated. "You are welcome to keep me company."

He seemed stiff, more formal, and even more unreadable than usual. The corners of her mouth drew taut, and indicating his desk with a wave, she cleared her throat and said, "I see you're working," surprised to hear how normal she sounded.

He nodded once. "There is always something for me to do. Would you like coffee?"

"Yes, thank you," she answered feeling lost in the leather depths of his chair and watching nervously as he struck the bell and ordered another pot of coffee from the servant who answered it. There was silence again while they waited. He seemed preoccupied with some matter far apart from her and, by the time the coffee came and he poured himself a cup of the steaming brew, Juliette wondered if he had forgotten her.

She was not to know how keenly Sharif was aware of her—of her hair that seemed a rumpled halo, and of that languid, sensual air she had just after awakening, an attitude he would have considered intoxicating by itself, even if her lips hadn't been so red and full and parted in a shiny gleam. He didn't have to look at her. He knew exactly how she stood, that her gown was made of misty silk, clinging to her breasts and showing every detail of her firmed nipples.

With difficulty he withdrew the hand that reached out to give her the cup. But withdraw it he did, reminding himself of the oath he had made that night he had found Juliette unconscious, her life's blood nearly drained—that night he would never forget when, like a thunderbolt, the full measure of his love had burst upon him.

What a fool he had been. From the first moment he had seen her laughing at him from her bed in Las Flores, he had wanted her with a need that he could not quell. Then he had been dazzled as a schoolboy, ready to put his heart and all his earthly possessions at her feet. But in return, she had lied to him, gone back on her promise of marriage, and, when he found out she was none other than his enemy's daughter, he had lost all reason.

He had risked everything, discovery, capture, all he had worked so long to achieve. But he was determined to possess her, to hurt, to humble, and to hate her as he swore he would. And, for a time, it seemed he did. But when she had run away in Tripoli, just the thought of losing her had driven him to distraction. After that, he never again questioned her power over him though he constantly questioned the sanity of his obsession.

How she fascinated him, her radiant beauty, her enigmatic smiles, her silences, her defiance, and some unnameable, irresistible essence that only *she* contained.

So it had seemed there was only one solution. He must teach her to want him, he must awaken her passions and cravings as she had fired his. When he found her that night, drugged, sensual, he had made her a woman. And as they traveled toward El Abadan he had taught her to want him in spite of herself so that now there was no mistaking that he could seduce her. But suddenly he found himself wanting so much more. He didn't want just her desire, but rather her love, to feel she was truly his, to know everything she thought, what she felt, what secrets dwelled behind those wistful looks. Yet even as he longed to know, he searched from behind a mask of indifference. He must never let her suspect his weakness. He couldn't bear her rejection, or worse, to have her pity him. He should have seen from the beginning he could never make her happy— he, a man neither Arab nor French. A man between worlds.

Once he had imagined she had cared for him and could care again. He had hoped that night, after she had killed the mouflon and he had gone to her, to reach a new understanding. But while her passion had surrendered to his, the next morning she had been indifferent. Why hadn't he given up then? But still he had hoped. And when they reached El Abadan, he had begun to marry off his women because he wanted no one but her. But then, once again, she had risked death to escape him.

Inwardly now he shuddered. She had so nearly died. And when she had lain so still and white on his large bed, Santapalo feverishly working to close her wounds, he had prayed, not just forming the syllables, but with a new deep humility, swearing to send her back home if only she were spared. If she couldn't be happy with him, at least she might be able to pick up the pieces of her life again and go on. And now, gripping his coffee cup, he wondered if he had the courage to let her go. He wanted her now, more than ever, with a driving desperation that thundered for expression. Over and over he had told himself to forget her, had tried to force her from his mind, but always he had failed. What more was he to endure?

Beneath his probing eyes, Juliette stirred her coffee automatically, trying to keep her fingers from shaking. Holding the cup in her lap she tried to calm herself, catching hold of her thoughts as they charged like runaway horses.

Then, finally unable to bear the protracted silence, she glanced up at the stacks of papers on his desk and, clearing her throat, said, "I had no idea that you worked so . . . well . . . like anyone else."

Juliette noticed his face was tired though he smiled and she felt a sudden urge to take him in her arms and comfort him with soft words.

"Sheiks work, too," he said, unexpectedly bending to rest his hands on her chair's arms and bringing his face so close she could smell his shaving soap.

"Did you think all we Arabs do is dabble in our enemies' blood?" he teased.

His nearness, the sudden gleam in his eyes, the gentle, almost caressing note in his voice, played Juliette's heartstrings. She had only to raise her mouth to receive a kiss and, unable to prevent herself, she turned her face upward, closed her eyes, and waited.

But the anticipated feel of his mouth on hers was not forthcoming, and she felt him withdraw, abruptly shattering the magic by swiveling her chair to face a huge map of Africa in which several dozen black pegs marked places and red scrawls named them in Arabic.

"Why have you come at this late hour?" he questioned near her ear. "I thought you were asleep."

"It's nothing . . . I mean, I wasn't sleeping," Juliette finally got out, still trying to understand why he hadn't kissed her. It seemed he would and yet. . . . And if only she could think of something besides shrugging off her robe and giving herself to him as every fiber of her being urged her to do.

Willfully she dislodged her eyes from his bronzed hands that still rested on her chair's arms. She gestured toward the map. "What are those black pegs? I mean, what do they mean?"

His glance followed her gesture. "Those indicate the trade routes controlled by tribes already allied with me." A finger pointed toward a black peg. "El Abadan is here," he said. "And here is the pass through the mountains where the caravans travel north to south." He turned back to her. "They are in fact the reason the English government sent your father and many others here to try and dominate these trade arteries and thus control Africa's wealth.

"When they captured my father, Captain Clayton had him executed. I saw it with my own eyes and I've never been able to wipe out the memory or the hatred completely and, the next day when your father came to my cell, I had just time enough to use the dagger I had hidden and strike once.

"I escaped after that, and never knew I was responsible for his death until after I met you. When I found out who you really were I thought you must have known who I was all along. I thought you had been getting revenge of your own kind by toying with me. But when you were unconscious two weeks ago, you said things in your delirium that showed me I was wrong. I'm sorry I misjudged you."

Juliette shook her head as she looked up and saw the earnestness in his face, and something else, too, that she couldn't read. Why did he tell her this now? Suddenly she realized that she no longer felt the same way about the past. That dark space that always had clouded her heart with bitterness suddenly cleared away leaving behind only sorrow as tears filled her eyes again. "I'm sorry for what my father did to yours," she said. "When people don't understand each other, they do terrible things without ever understanding that they aren't really enemies after all."

There was silence as she waited for him to speak and again her eyes dropped to her lap as she felt him watching her and the tension grew, her heart bounding expectantly. Would he . . . would he . . . But then his attention returned to the map again and he seemed absorbed in his words as he continued.

"After my father was killed we destroyed those Englishmen remaining in the fort at Sevit though your father had already been sent back to the coast. It was years then before another expedition of Europeans threatened us again and, by that time, I was able to bargain with them. I had learned to speak their language and was able to strike profitable trade agreements which kept control of the routes in my hands. These agreements are still effective and, ironically, the gold they pay me is the very gold I will use to defeat them."

"You mean revolution!" Juliette said in a husky whisper.

"Revolution? No. A revolution is when a people revolt against their own government. But this government of puppets and foreigners is not ours, it is the Europeans' and run solely for their benefit. When I am in Europe as M. Phillips, they speak to me quite freely, assuming, of course, I'm on their side. And since only a handful of Europeans have ever seen the mysterious Sheik of El Abadan, none of them has ever realized the truth, and they won't know until it is too late. One day not only will this country be united, but after that perhaps all Islam can settle its differences and join together." His eyes shone with a deep glimmering light. "Then when all Moslem voices speak as one, the sound will shake the world."

Juliette looked from the map back to him, feeling the inspired determination in his words. He seemed capable of anything. Certainly he had carved an empire worth millions which held in it the seed of independence for his people. Some would call this man a renegade, a spy, a revolutionary. But now, as he stood before his desk, he seemed a most respectable businessman discussing his affairs with an interested listener.

His tone lightened as he continued. "Usually I spend the winter here, since it is the trading season," he was saying. "Then in summer I go back to Europe." He gave her a considering gaze as he finished, "Soon I'll be leaving again."

Juliette swallowed twice. And what did he intend to do with her? she asked herself. Would he really give her away? There was a strained quality about him tonight she had never seen before. Only a moment ago it seemed he would have kissed her, and then . . . her thoughts paused suddenly as another possibility occurred to her. Or perhaps he was trying to tell her something. The color drained from her face and the deep leather chairs and furniture seemed to sway before her eyes. Was that why he was explaining everything so carefully—talking about her father when it was a subject they had never discussed, and she had never dared mention.

The silence continued as Sharif studied Juliette's delicate profile, now so very pale. He had spoken hoping for a better understanding between them. Nothing could change the past or the present circumstances. He was what he was and the time would come when English blood would be shed. How could he ever expect her to understand or forgive?

His gaze slipped lower then, to where the tops of her creamy breasts were visible, and he gritted his teeth against an impulse to take her in his arms.

Since her illness he had slept in an adjoining room in a bed far too small for his large frame, cramped, sleepless, and thinking of her. Already now desire had crept into his loins, straining his reserves. How she bewitched him and, tonight, it was too much.

His mind made up then, he paused, feeling awkward with a woman for the first time in his life and, inwardly cursing his weakness, he cleared his throat and finally said, "It seems you have recovered."

"I am completely well again," came her answer.

"Yes, and . . . are you still comfortable in your . . . in my bed?" The expression on his face was one of a man starved, but Juliette's head had dropped and she didn't see it as tears flowed into her eyes.

She blinked them down. "Comfortable enough," she said in a voice barely audible.

Sharif unclasped his hands from the arms of the chair, moving away across the room to pour himself a drink and down it quickly. Their eyes met, and Juliette thought she had never seen his expression so opaque—like the desert sky on a starless night.

"Then I don't think it's necessary for me to sleep out of

my bed any longer," Sharif said quietly, as unconsciously his fingers tightened round the fine etched glass.

Something in Juliette fell, her heart squeezing into a small painful fist. It was all she could do not to burst into tears again. But she would never, never give him that satisfaction. The time for parting had come, just as she imagined it would. Her knuckles whitened as her fingers joined in her lap. She drew herself up stiffly, rising to her feet and facing him squarely. "Of course, there is no reason at all you should be inconvenienced anymore," she said. "I am quite strong again and would be relieved to return to my own room and . . . greater privacy."

There was a small tinkling and Juliette realized Sharif's glass had shattered in his hand. Calmly, he dropped the pieces onto the sideboard, his eyes still resting unreadably on her even as he struck the bell.

Juliette turned away as the servant arrived, unobtrusively clearing up the debris and disappearing again. Had her answer surprised him? Isn't this what he wanted?

But then he was speaking again, his voice quietly ominous.

"I'm sure it will be a relief," he said. "And you don't need to worry that I will trouble you anymore. Our time together has ended, Juliette. Soon I go to war with the Hussar and afterward will come the even more dangerous work of creating an independent nation. I won't risk your getting hurt, particularly if anything should go wrong."

Juliette felt turned to wood. "What do you mean?"

"I mean," he said, never seeming so coldly factual, "I've decided to send you back to England."

Chapter 70

The rest was like a bizarre play and Juliette felt herself a mechanical doll, so shocked that she could only nod her assent even as her guts rebelled.

No, no, he couldn't send her away, though he continued talking in a low factual voice, telling her she would have only a few days to prepare. "We won't see each other again," he said. "It is better this way. And if you should ever need anything, now or in the future—anything at all, you have only to contact my agents and it will be taken care of."

No, none of it seemed real, least of all the passionless lips that briefly brushed her brow before suddenly he was gone.

Was it possible? Juliette kept asking herself. Could it all end so abruptly? For months now they had struggled and fought between moments of desire and passionate hatred that had touched both the heights and depths of her being. And now, in an instant, it was all finished. "A chapter to leave behind her," was how he had put it. "You'll learn to start over. And don't worry about returning to England. Months ago I arranged Rodney's death to appear a suicide. As far as anyone knows, you have been on an extended, and very private, vacation to escape the scandal. Anyway, I think you'll find that when you're rich enough, people have a way of not asking too many embarrassing questions."

He had thought of everything—obviously had planned it from the beginning. Always he had been vague about just how long he would keep her. Certainly he had made no promises. So why now did she suddenly feel shocked—abandoned? Wasn't leaving him what she had wanted all along?

For the next few days, a bleak sense of hopelessness filled Juliette as a sandstorm stirred the desert's surface into waves of pelting sand that confined her aimless wanderings to within her room and also delayed her departure. And as she waited she couldn't help remembering the last sandstorm when the caravan had been pinned down. For those two days Sharif had been like a friend, and she had felt, or thought she felt, a bond forming between them. But the storm had not lasted long and, afterward, he had become just as he was before, as if those moments of intimacy had never been. Oh, why did remembering hurt so? she asked, tears clouding her sight. And why had she believed Dr. Santapalo, even a little bit, when it had all been lies?

Dejected, cooped up, Juliette became more and more restless, and finally, to occupy herself, she began exploring every inch of her new quarters for some hint of Sharif's mother.

What might she have been like? Had she been better suited to this life? Had she been happy? But after a methodical search, Juliette was disappointed when the most personal items she could find were several dried ink wells, a thick stack of writing paper, pens, and an intricately bound book of French poems by Alfred de Musset.

Settling down on a scattering of cushions, thinking of Sharif, Juliette flipped indifferently through the book. Suddenly, an idea struck her that left her breathless with hope.

Maybe if I told him I don't want to go . . . I've never told him how I really feel. I've given him no reason to want me to stay. I've said terrible things though, lately, he's been kind. What if I went to him now, just like this, and told him?

She stood with a rush of energy, dropping the book in her excitement. When she bent to retrieve it, she saw that a folded paper had fallen out from between its pages.

Actually, there were several sheets, discolored along their folded edges, as if they had been in the book for many years.

Impulsively she opened them, spreading them flat, her eyes jumping to read the scrawled feminine handwriting.

I am Anna Louise Phillips, a French citizen by birth and wife to Captain Brandon R. Phillips of Queen Victoria's army . . . it began.

Juliette's eyes widened incredulously. Karim's mother?— and this was *her* letter!

Juliette's eyes ran down the page, reading faster and faster as the letter continued telling the fantastic story of how Anna had been kidnapped and kept by Hamid al-Sharif. And Juliette felt herself struck immobile as it said, *Please forgive me, Brandon, my son, when I tell you the Sheik of El Abadan is not your father, but in fact the murderer of your real father, Captain Brandon Phillips, killed during the raid when I was taken captive. Little did I know at that time that I already carried you within me, the product of the true love and devotion which your father and I felt for one another.*

The scrawl began to shake. *I wanted so much to tell you this earlier, but fear prevented me. I always knew the sheik believed you were his son and that if he had discovered your real identity as the product of my husband, and by inheritance English, he would have murdered you as well.*

The letter continued then, telling of Anna's agony lest the secret be discovered—her devotion to her son, and her attempts to educate him along the lines of his civilized heritage. The last part of the letter grew more scrawled, *I am sick now, and while those around me say I will live, I think I will not.*

I wanted so much to tell you all this myself, my son—to explain. But though you are twenty, you are still impetuous. I couldn't risk the sheik discovering this secret, yet I cannot die without leaving you this and hoping it is discovered at a time when it will help rather than harm you . . .

I grow weaker. I fear I will not last this night. Yet now that finally I have unburdened my heart to you, I can accept death. Please take pity upon me, and try to understand the mother who loved you.

Anna Louise Phillips

Juliette's head whirled. Karim—English! And he didn't know! If he knew he were English himself, then he wouldn't—no, how could he hate me? He would reconsider . . . he would . . . Oh, how could she tell what he might do? And drawing a deep breath, she pulled back the curtain covering the doorway leading to his room and, to her sudden surprise, spotted a pair of ankles that kicked violently against cords that shackled them.

"Cassia!" she cried as she pulled the curtain back and saw the girl, lying bound and gagged on the floor. Cassia moaned a warning, but already it was too late. Juliette both felt and saw the huge arm that encircled her, pinning her own arms helplessly to her sides as a cloth was forced against her nose and mouth, smothering her cries.

Juliette refused to inhale the noxious fumes, jerking her head and kicking with all her strength. But it was useless, her lungs were almost at once ready to burst and waves of darkness swirled in her head as her oxygen ran out. And when she couldn't endure any more, she breathed deeply, from the bottom of her bursting lungs. The sickening odor permeated her brain and a blackness flooded her as in the flick of an eye, everything vanished.

PART XII

WOMAN WARRIOR

Chapter 71

Thick waves of nausea persisted as Juliette regained consciousness, aware first of a sour taste in her mouth, and then of the dank smells of dirty leather, rancid cooking oil, and sweat tainting the air. Then, sensing someone near, she opened her eyes and saw a heavy, white-robed Arab squatting on cushions a few feet away.

"Ah! So the *petite poule* is awake at last. You see what good drugs your countrymen bring us. Ether they call it. It makes everything so easy, does it not? No scratching or biting, and now here you are waking up again, magic, eh?"

"So, you are surprised I speak French," he continued before chuckling derisively. "But did you think your lover Karim al-Sharif was the only Arab with . . . how do you say . . . an education?"

He spoke with incongruous politeness, his thick thighs overhanging the sides of the soiled pillow where he sat cross-legged looking down at her.

Everything about him was thick, his arms, his lips, even his face was puffy and held small piggish eyes that watched with thinly veiled enmity, and as he smiled, an uneven row of rotting teeth came into view. "But don't be frightened, little pigeon. We are going to be friends, you and I—that is, if you cooperate. And what round eyes you have. I can never remember seeing any quite that color before . . . and your hair. Now I think it is true that five thousand pieces of gold were bid for you in Tripoli. Ah, yes, so lovely, and so fragile, eh? I will have Amin cut those bonds from your wrists. You will eat first and afterward, when we have gotten to know each other better, we will talk."

He waved a flabby arm and a boy of about nine appeared. At least he seemed like a boy, though his lips and face were painted like a harem girl's, and his dark brown hands held rings of gold and small jewels. He wore loose striped pants that drew tight at his knees and, as he came closer, flourishing a long dagger, the hostility in his movements was obvious even before he cut the ropes, purposely running the blade over her skin so a thin trace of blood appeared. Then, smiling like a young weasel, he retreated to sit on his haunches just behind his master.

"Amin, Amin," the Arab scolded as if to himself before saying to her, "Amin is so careless with a knife, mademoiselle. Please forgive him." He dabbed absently at her bloody wrists with a crumpled rag. "And please permit me to introduce myself. I am Abu Cassium Hussar. Perhaps Karim al-Sharif has spoken of me?"

He paused, peering at her, and apparently reading the startled look in her face, he continued, "Yes, I see my old friend has mentioned my name. But come, sit up! Our meal is being served."

His smile did not reach his close-set eyes as Juliette lifted herself from the dirty palm-mat floor and pulled the shredded ropes from her wrists before tearing at the bindings around her ankles. Hussar, Hussar, her mind echoed over the pounding in her head.

"But let me help you," came Hussar's silky voice as he thrust his own dagger forward, running it between her ankles to sever the ropes and then continuing in the same motion upward until the knife point pricked lightly beneath her chin.

Juliette swallowed hard, gathering her robes together across her breasts as his head jerked toward the cushion beside him. "Sit there. Amin will serve us."

Wordlessly, Juliette placed herself beside him. A wave of nausea traveled through her as she smelled his overpowering odor of sweat. So *this* was Abu Hussar, leader of Sharif's enemies. She must be calm, must think clearly. Oh, God, how he was going to enjoy killing her. Already she could see the lusty anticipation in his eyes. And to get away from his scrutiny, she looked around the tent, noticing a large chest, a hassock with dark stains on the cushions, and a tumble of saddles and blankets and assorted objects all tossed together in one corner.

Outside it was night. How far were they from El Abadan? How long ago had she been taken? Was it only hours,
or had she slept round the clock? And listening intently,
she tried to detect any stamp of a hoof that might indicate
a horse tied nearby.

Sardonically, Hussar laughed. "Don't look so worried,
mademoiselle. We are not so uncivilized. You will have a
chance to save yourself." His small eyes tapered nearly
closed. "But it will be on *my* terms, *comprends-tu?* And
don't expect your lover to rescue you. He won't know
where you are—that is, until he receives our message." He
smiled, pushing a plate in front of her with a fat hand that
lingered beside her arm, his voice cajoling, "Come. Let me
see you eat something. And when your little mouth has
satisfied you, then we will see how much pleasure it can
give me."

Juliette's eyes darted to his. What did he mean? Another
wave of nausea passed over her. He couldn't be thinking
that she . . . that she would. . . . Her eyes dropped, her
face blanching.

"How frightened you are, mademoiselle. Really, I think
you have overestimated me. I only have a few questions
for you, nothing difficult. And after you have told me
what I want, and after we have a little entertainment of
our own—also nothing too difficult for a *sharmûta* like
yourself, then you will be free to go."

Juliette stared blankly. Then, pinching a portion of rice
between her fingers in Arabic fashion, she began conveying
bite after bite to her mouth.

"There! Yes, that is better. My friend Karim has already
taught you to obey. He has a way with women, has he not?
You must tell me about him—and show me what he likes a
woman to do best."

He motioned to Amin who sullenly brought a basket full
of steaming pita bread.

Hussar took the liberty of setting one of the breads before
her. Then, to add to the mockery of the situation, and no
doubt to her terror, he began to talk about the desert and
himself, and the battles and mouflon hunts in the past, as
if she were a lady he was entertaining for an evening.

Juliette only half listened as he rambled on, thinking instead of some possible means of escape, and was recalled to him again only when he bent closer and said, "Tell me, little pigeon—is it true you killed a mouflon and the desert genies helped you?"

Juliette did not look up from her plate, pretending instead to concentrate on her food as she felt him peering at her.

"You don't answer when I ask you a question. Such a pity." He nodded to Amin, who was no longer sullen as he jumped forward, slapping her sharply across the face, his rings cutting her lips and sending her mouthful of rice across the palm mats.

Her own hand automatically rose to where a red stinging hand print remained.

"Oh, but look what Amin has done. I don't think he cares for you, mademoiselle, or any woman in fact." And then to Amin, "No, you must be more careful. I don't like to see her lovely mouth harmed. Her breasts perhaps, next time. Breasts don't appeal to me, not like her mouth."

Then he was looking at her again. "Come now, mademoiselle. You seem intelligent enough. We can make you speak if we want to. I would rather leave you . . . intact . . . shall we say. But you will answer."

Juliette's flashing eyes fixed on his face. "Very well," she said with stiff features. "I can tell you that I did shoot a mouflon, but it was no more than a lucky shot." Her eyes narrowed to a defiant slant. "But I don't think *that* is what you are really interested in and, I assure you, I know nothing about more *vital* matters."

Quick as a viper's tongue, Hussar's hand shot out, grabbing her forearm so tightly she thought it would break. "You will find it is useless to lie, little pigeon. We already know that you have a great deal of 'vital' information, as you call it." His fingers dug deeper into her bone until, in spite of herself, Juliette winced.

"Now you will begin by telling me how many men Karim al-Sharif has assembled at El Abadan, and when they will attack."

Juliette hesitated, wondering what information she could

fabricate that he would believe. His thumb pressed hard against her wrist bone as he leaned forward anticipating an answer.

With all her strength, Juliette jerked away, taking her wounded wrist in the other hand.

"I don't know how many men are in El Abadan," she said. "But any fool must realize he will not attack in the open when he can remain in a fortress."

A smile came to Hussar's lips. "Ha! So Karim al-Sharif *has* discussed his plan with you. And do not be so certain he will stay behind those walls where he cowers like a woman. Now that you are here with me, so very enticing, eh? perhaps that devil may find a reason to come to *me!*"

"He doesn't discuss anything with me, but with his chiefs instead," Juliette stated firmly. "It has not been my concern how many men he has or what his plan might be."

"No, little pigeon?" Hussar's close-set eyes slid down her frame. "A woman like you does not clutter her mind with such practicalities, does she?" His eyebrows jumped high, wrinkling his greasy forehead. "Oh, how insulted you look. Would you say I am wrong? But no—I am a man of experience. I can tell a passionate woman when I see one. But *that* I will take more time with later. For now you will tell me what I wish. It is known that lately you have stayed in the private rooms of Karim al-Sharif, and there is no reason for you to protect him, now is there?"

He pulled her closer on the pillow beside him before he sat back on his fat buttocks and looked at her sharply. "What anger is in your face, mademoiselle. But I think you know much more than you want me to believe. Shall I show you why?"

From inside his robe Hussar produced several creased sheets of paper—Juliette recognized the letter at once.

Her stomach protracted into a knot as he set it on the table and flicked it toward her with two fingers.

"You were in possession of this when you were brought here." His eyes scoffed. "Perhaps you thought to sell it to someone, eh? So why not tell me everything—you who know so little of 'vital' matters."

He laughed shortly as Juliette paled again. Naturally,

having found this letter, he must think she had searched Karim's most personal papers.

Hussar's face was drawn in ugly lines as he continued. "You see, little pigeon, you have provided just what I needed. Imagine how it has been for me, mademoiselle, to know all these years that Sharif was an imposter and never be able to prove it—to watch him growing always wealthier on a throne that rightly belongs to me. Can you even begin to know how much I hate him? Yes, I even hate his servants—and his women." Hussar's eyes took on the gleam of one possessed as he sneered. "Can you imagine—just knowing Sharif has touched you makes me hate you!"

Suddenly he had drawn his knife again and abruptly he stabbed her pillow just beneath her leg in a quick thrust that made Juliette spring up.

His laugh was chilling. "It pleases me to see you are frightened. It will make things easier. Although I think my men will be disappointed if you are not stubborn. You see, usually I let them have an incorrigible female for an hour or two. Afterward, well—women don't care what they tell afterward. But you, mademoiselle, I know you are smarter than that. Or would you like to see for yourself what they would do with a tender morsel like you?"

Juliette raised her chin. "I don't think that will be necessary. I have already said I will tell you what you want to know. But if I don't know something, how can you expect an answer?"

Hussar's chuckle was low as he came closer, and she felt his fat fingers close round her arm. "I think you flirt with me, mademoiselle—that you play little games perhaps." His second hand encircled her other arm. "Yes. You do have charm of a kind. Bewitching, I've heard it said. In fact, when I am Sheik of El Abadan, I will make you my favorite—that is, if you cooperate." He sneered with a kind of irony. "And wouldn't that be testament for the fates. Already the astrologers agree that you will be the woman who gives birth to the heir of El Abadan. And so it will be—*my* heir!"

His eyes roamed over her, his rotted teeth so close she felt sick from their foul odor. "And wouldn't now be a for-

tuitous time to conceive my son, when there is such violence between us. Wouldn't it make him all the more
fierce?" He pushed her backward, down onto the soiled
cushions, a sprinkling of sand falling off his sleeve and
into her eyes. "Now I will have my first little taste of you,
and you will not fight, or maybe you would like better to
be staked out on the floor of my tent?"

He drew her wrists together into one of his hands whose
short fingers were like a wrestler's. Then he had both arms
over her head, pinning her to the palm-mat floor as his
thick lips were covering hers, his tongue darting like a liz-
ard inside her mouth. She was going to be sick, oh, but she
must not. Then he was pulling away, withdrawing his knife
and slitting open her robe before replacing the weapon in a
carved sheath strapped to the center of his huge girth. His
hands crawled over her flesh, pulling at her breasts.

Her bravado crumbled under the assault. "Stop! Please!
I'll tell you what you want to know," she said, squirming
and frantically thinking of what she could make up that
he might believe. But it was useless and she felt his hands
going lower as he said, "Yes, of course, you will tell me, but
first . . ."

There was sudden confusion overhead before Juliette
saw the boy Amin throwing himself between them and
pleading with Hussar in a dialect Juliette couldn't understand.

Abruptly, Hussar released her wrists so she slid down on
the floor and she let herself roll until she reached the opposite side of the tent. Then, coming quickly to her feet, she
pulled her tattered robe tight across her breasts.

Amin had fallen to the floor, kissing Hussar's wide feet.
But now, whisking off his striped pants, he was presenting
his brown, upturned buttocks to his master as he continued
to plead.

A low growl emitted from Hussar's throat as he raised
his heavy fist. Amin was suddenly lying stunned on the
floor, blood dripping from his bruised mouth. Moaning, the
boy picked himself up and staggered from the room. Hussar turned back toward Juliette, smiling grotesquely.

Juliette's stomach contracted then. She could endure no

more and she was violently sick on the palm mats and cushions, helplessly wondering at the strange incongruity of Hussar's voice, suddenly polite again, as he held her head at the temples while she heaved.

"Poor Amin—so pretty, but so jealous. And how sensitive you are, little pigeon. But isn't it true that sometimes this European 'ether' has this effect of sickness from the stomach? Or have I scared you so?" Hussar's eyebrows arched, wrinkling his forehead in little bulging ridges. "But no. I will not have to rape you, little pigeon. After I am through with you, you will beg me to use you any way I please— and tell me, has Sharif ever taken you boy-fashion?"

Chapter 72

Juliette was sick until there was nothing else in her stomach and she retched and spasmed, rolling on the floor and wishing she would die. How easily they can break me, she thought. I'm so weak. But she realized now that, in her present condition at least, Hussar had declined to continue questioning her and had gone, leaving her tied up, her eyes swollen from the sand that rubbed them bleary red.

She slept then, or rather tossed and turned, dropping off in a stupor plagued by nightmares that aroused her for a time before she dropped off again.

At dawn she awoke and stayed awake, waiting. But to her surprise it wasn't Hussar's voice that she heard an hour later from the tent flap.

"Ah, so the little *sharmûta* is here. And she does not look so pretty this morning. Such a shame Karim cannot see you *now*."

No, it was quite impossible, Juliette thought as she rolled over to look. It was the damage the sand had done to her eyes, or maybe she was drugged. She stared until her clouded vision cleared.

"Zenobia!" her voice cracked before she could force strength into it.

"Yes—you remember me," Zenobia said bitterly as she

strolled closer and stood looking down. "What a shame my plan for you didn't work. But of course, if you were already dead, you would be of little use to Abu Hussar."

"So! It *was* you that tried to kill me—who sent Ramad," Juliette said.

"Did you ever doubt it? You should have bled to death that night but then Ramad was scared. He didn't realize we meant to kill you, so he went to the master and brought him to you. It was luck and that foolish boy that saved you. It only proves you are a she-devil yourself!"

Juliette's nostrils quivered, a new fury circulating in her veins. Her eyes became slits. "But what then of Cassia? Where is she?"

A disgusted sneer twisted Zenobia's lips. "The spirits work on your side, but they were of no help to your stupid little maid. She suspected it was I who paid the assassin. She was too clever, too quick to discover she was right. I couldn't let her ruin my plans. So when Hussar's men came to El Abadan to bring me here and to capture you, I had them bring her along." Zenobia laughed again, her gold encircled wrists bracing her hips. "Hussar gave her to his men last night. If there is anything left of her," Zenobia pointed a finger out the open tent flap, "it is out there."

Juliette couldn't prevent her voice from shaking. "And you dare call *me* she-devil!" she said in a seething tone. "What do you call yourself? Witch? Murderer?" Then overcome, Juliette spat at Zenobia's feet in a contemptuous Arab gesture.

Surprise crossed Zenobia's fine features for a moment and then a wicked smile. "So! You become an Arab while Karim is proved to be English. Ha! You see, I too know about the letter. It is amusing, don't you agree? And when they show Karim the letter written in his mother's own hand, how can he deny that he is an imposter?" Zenobia's eyes constricted to shining black slits. "He will be put to death as the law is written," she sneered, and leaning forward, Juliette felt the burning sting of the Arab girl's slaps as they rotated her chin from shoulder to shoulder.

"How I despise you! All of you whites who take and take and give nothing in return." Zenobia's eyes were abruptly wide. "But don't worry. When your lover comes to meet his death like a goat to slaughter, I will see that you don't miss it, and unless he wants you to die, he will bring the ransom alone into this camp where Hussar will be waiting. And he will come—very soon."

"No!" Juliette said, full of all the scornful bravado she could muster. "Hussar has planned very poorly if he is expecting Karim to ransom me! Didn't you know I had fallen from favor? Maybe no one told you, but the last time I saw Sharif he was planning to send me back to my home. Do you expect him to risk coming here for a woman he no longer desires?" Juliette stared into Zenobia's face, driving her point home and, seeing the girl's sudden hesitation, she sat back defiantly. "But of course even if Sharif comes and Hussar kills him, there is also a problem for you, is there not?" she continued in a smooth tone, her chin jutting forward.

Zenobia's forehead wrinkled into a tight network of ugly lines. "What do you mean?"

Juliette looked levelly at the girl. Zenobia was the only one who could possibly save Karim. Somehow she must make her help him. "I mean," she said at last, "that once Hussar has killed Karim, then what use will you be? Already you know too much." Juliette smirked. "Don't you think that after Karim is dead the tribes allied with him will suspect Hussar as his killer? And Hussar dares not risk turning them all against him. He wouldn't want anyone else alive who might tell of his treachery." Juliette's cut lips smiled. "Tell me, Zenobia, you know more about Hussar than I do. Tell me—do you think he is the type to concern himself with one murder more or less?" Juliette rubbed the hair out of her face with her bound wrists. "But who can know for sure," she said. "*In sha'Allah.* It is the Arab way, is it not, to accept the outcome in such matters as the will of Allah? And doesn't it say in your Koran that Allah protects the innocent while punishing the wrongdoers?" Juliette cocked her head. "If Allah is to determine this, then you must judge for yourself, Zenobia, what stains lie on your soul."

As Juliette hoped, the light of fear sprang into Zenobia's

eyes for a brief moment as the seed of doubt took root. She flushed then, red as her henna-stained fingernails. "But Allah does not help infidel dogs," she spat. "And after Hussar has finished with Karim al-Sharif, then I will begin on you."

Zenobia withdrew a small blade from inside her garments and passed its deadly stiletto point flashing beneath Juliette's nose.

"I'll make over that face of yours with my little knife so no one will even recognize you. And when I've finished, the camel drivers can have you. And when they've done what they will, I'll laugh as I watch you bleed to death," Zenobia finished with a sneer of chilling deadliness.

Juliette gritted her teeth. "You are poisoned with jealousy, Zenobia. You wish revenge against Karim for casting you aside, when he has not done so. You are still his favorite, yet you pretend to be so wronged. I do not think you ever really loved him."

Zenobia resheathed her knife in a single practiced movement. "I did love him!" she insisted. "More than you did! And yet it was *you* he chose!"

Juliette raised her eyebrows. "He chose to *reject* me. Do you not have ears to hear? He was sending me away. But how can you even speak of loving him when this love of yours turns so easily to treachery. And think, Zenobia. Karim doesn't know that he is English. He despises the English just as you do. He will use his power to drive them from the lands of your people. While Hussar . . ." Juliette shook her head skeptically. "With him as leader, what will prevent all of you from becoming slaves to the Europeans you hate?"

Zenobia's pointed breasts heaved with the deep breaths she was taking in an effort to control herself. "Karim al-Sharif wants power for himself! But already his downfall is near. I will have my own revenge, and there will be no one to stop Hussar from taking his rightful place as Sheik of El Abadan!" Zenobia flashed with a final piercing look. "Karim will come, and both of you will die!" Then turning in a whirl of raven hair, Zenobia stalked out of the tent without a backward look.

A low moan passed Juliette's lips. No, it couldn't be! Hussar and Zenobia were both insane. And anyway, both of them were wrong about Karim. He was an Arab, though not a drop of true Arab blood actually flowed in his veins. He would neither take such a foolish risk, nor surrender to Hussar tyranny. He would kill to possess a woman perhaps, but he would never die for one.

Juliette expelled a long breath. Hussar's torture would begin soon. He would want answers to all his questions. She wouldn't be able to save herself, from him or what would come afterward.

Oh, if I think about that I'll go mad right now, she told herself pulling again against the bindings around her wrists that were so tight she could no longer feel her hands. Then, finally giving up, she lay on her side, knowing within herself a depth of terror that made her shiver uncontrollably.

Hours passed and finally, exhausted, she slept in fitful bouts with Zenobia and Hussar and Karim all spinning about her head in feverish nightmares.

At dawn, a girl with a bruised face brought her a wooden bowl full of rice and dried meat and, looking at it, Juliette realized she would have considered the food inedible at any other time. But now hunger combined with a will to live overcame her sensitivities and she ate all her cramping stomach would allow before letting herself drop to the floor again.

How long would they wait before they killed her, she wondered, looking around the dingy tent through the gray blur that had formed over her eyes. Hussar had seemed ready to tear her to pieces last night. What delayed him now? Or was he just taking his time until fear turned her to a mass of quivering jelly?

A figure casting a long shadow from the doorway made her head swing round as Zenobia ducked under the flap and walked into the tent.

Immediately Juliette tried to read the girl's face for some sign, and seeing no triumph in the girl's eyes she said, "So, Karim has not come." She manufactured a confident smile. "You see, Zenobia, haven't I told you? You were so jealous of me. We women are all fools when it comes to

love. Men follow their brains, not their hearts. So it seems,
Zenobia, that both you and Hussar have gone to a great
deal of trouble for no purpose."

Zenobia glared poisonously. "You should be praying now
for him to come. Hussar is planning to send him one of
your fingers for every day he delays."

Juliette felt her guts twist though she made her face lazy
and contemptuous. "But no matter what happens, I still
die. Either way it is the same for me. It is *you* Zenobia,
who should be praying that Hussar doesn't decide to silence
those who might wag their tongues."

Zenobia bared her claws. "White bitch!" she spat starting
forward.

Juliette braced for her attack. Outside then there was a
shout as Zenobia slapped her across the face and both
turned toward the open tent flap as someone shouted a second time, "He comes!"

Running to the entrance, Zenobia stood silhouetted
against the blaze of sunlight as the camp began stirring
with new activity.

"He comes," Zenobia repeated suddenly out of breath.

Juliette struggled to her knees, her mouth bleeding. No,
he couldn't have. He couldn't, and yet the shout was repeated again and the rushing preparations outside told her
it must be true even as an inner voice repeated, *"He
comes! He comes!"*

For a moment her heart lifted with a thrill of soaring
joy. He was here! And if he had come for her—if he risked
so much, then he must really care. And in the same moment she gasped as something deep in her belly spasmed
and drew taut—he would die!

Zenobia spun away from the door, her black hair swinging out in an arch. "He is here for you!" she said through
clenched teeth—"You who are fated to bear his son. But this
time fate will not have its way." The Arab girl paused.
"Come, there is still time," she said, grabbing the lashings
round Juliette's wrists and jerking her to her feet. "And I
have arranged for you to see your lover meet his end. I
don't want you to miss any of the details!"

Chapter 73

Everything was happening too fast—the rush of warriors through camp—the hot glare of the sun—Zenobia's merciless fingers cutting into her flesh as she dragged her inside a tent on the outskirts of camp.

There was a tall thin-lipped Arab inside, too, holding a modern-looking rifle balanced on an upended crate so the long barrel pointed through the lifted tent flap.

Zenobia indicated him with her chin. "Mohab will not let your lover escape," she said with a cruel laugh as she forced a gag in Juliette's mouth and tied her legs and arms so tight Juliette felt the circulation in her hands cut off. Then, like a cat focused on its prey, the Arab girl settled herself to watch through the opening as Sharif topped the last dune outside camp and paused on the crest of a wave of sand, his burnoose billowing like a black sail in the wind.

The tightness of unshed tears, fear, and horror surged painfully through Juliette as she saw him. He had come and he would die.

The sun flashed bright against Fadjar now as the stallion snorted, nervously pawing the air, his black coat gleaming.

Juliette felt the separate hammering of her pulse at her throat and heart as her hands alternately ached and felt dead. Emotion overcame all reason then and, screaming, she jerked at the stake, though it didn't budge. If only he could hear her! But from behind the gag, her screams were barely audible.

Mohab paid no attention while Zenobia only glanced at her with sadistic satisfaction before turning back to watch Sharif. And finally, panting, Juliette stopped her useless struggles and, like the others, fixed her eyes on the horseman still paused on the summit of the dune.

Against the fierce sun, Karim al-Sharif's eyes narrowed as he scanned the stretch of dark tents below. There would be an ambush of course. He had never questioned that. How clever Hussar had been, even instructing him to enter the camp from the west so the sun would be in his eyes. Then squinting toward the group of mounted figures gathering at the center of the camp, Sharif scrutinized the three guards and Hussar as they rode toward him now, and particularly the veiled figure that should have been Juliette.

Carefully he searched the shrouded rider for a gesture he could recognize as hers. But, even if it wasn't Juliette, he told himself, he would have to play this hand out, even knowing Hussar held all the aces. If it was Juliette on that horse, he might have a better chance of bringing her out alive. If not. . . . And with a catch in his chest, he urged his horse forward. If she were dead, then it would make his own death easier, he thought. And again he cursed himself for his own self-deception. He could never have let her go, *never,* and if he had kept her with him this wouldn't have happened. What a hypocrite he had been, an idiot who deserved no more than the mess he found himself in now. If only she were still alive! And training his eyes back onto Abu Hussar with focused intensity, he promised himself that whatever happened, *that* Arab was a dead man.

Inside the tent, Juliette's large eyes suddenly froze in her graying face as Mohab's bony finger settled slowly round the trigger and he dropped his head over the weapon, bringing Karim into his sights.

Mohab licked his lips. Abu Hussar himself had ordered him to shoot if the sheik should retreat and, to his mind, Karim al-Sharif had already paused too long.

The knuckles of Mohab's left hand strained as they tightened around the barrel. He remembered hearing that the sheik's life was charmed, and that any who brought him harm would die a coward's death. But he had never imagined shooting the sheik himself. That hadn't been part of the plan. He was only to act as a "precaution," as Hussar had called it. But what could he do now before fate? If the sheik turned back now, he would fire.

Sweat surfaced in beads on Mohab's brow and Juliette stared at his profile as he squinted one eye into a fan of wrinkles while the other waited motionlessly trained down the rifle's spine.

Zenobia knelt, transfixed, her face white and taut, her hands raised in expectation, her eyes wide and unblinking as the tension reached the breaking point. Each of them held their breath. Then it all happened in a rush of blood and noise and confusion when a stiff burst of wind gusted at the figures coming toward Sharif, and the veils of the last rider were tossed in the air to expose not Juliette, but a youth with a pistol.

Immediately Hussar was shouting to his men to attack while, Karim was already wheeling his horse in the opposite direction.

Mohab took quick aim, squeezing the trigger. But in the same moment, Zenobia abruptly snapped out of her motionless trance, and drawing her dagger, leaped onto Mohab's back, knocking the rifle away and stabbing with full force between his shoulder blades.

Incredulous, Mohab tried to rise, Zenobia still clinging to his back, plunging the weapon in and out, slashing, stabbing, like a creature obsessed.

With his last strength, Mohab knocked Zenobia onto the floor, the knife skidding across the tent. Then turning, he pointed his rifle against her chest.

Zenobia's eyes bulged. "Please! Mohab—I love him . . ." But the rest of her words were blotted out by an explosion.

Juliette couldn't look at what was left of Zenobia, or the bleeding Mohab who fell unconscious across her body. She turned from them, and, crawling sideways to Zenobia's fallen knife, wet and sticky with blood, she manipulated the blade between her feet and rubbed the lashings against it until they split away from her wrists. Then, tearing the gag from her mouth and untying her ankles, she jumped to her feet, tottering on numb legs to the open flap.

Inexplicably, the camp was full of Sharif's men, a chaos of horses and gunfire and colliding men.

She dashed out, keeping her head down and running through a maze of thrashing swords and stray bullets.

One of Hussar's men charged after her, sword raised. But, ducking behind a tent, Juliette escaped his thrust just as a bullet knocked him from his horse.

She ran then, stumbling and rising until at last she reached Hussar's tent where a dead warrior lay across the entrance, a revolver still dangling from his stiffening fingers.

Bending, Juliette picked it up, bringing the weapon to full cock before stepping into the tent.

Hussar was there, leaning over a large open chest like a pirate, and hastily filling his robe pockets with gems and gold coins.

Out of the corner of his eye he must have caught her movement, since his head jerked up, his gaze shifting from her face to the cyclopean eye of her pistol that stared unblinking.

His fleshy tongue touched the corner of his mouth as he attempted a smile, his voice suddenly as wheedling as a small child's. "So the little pigeon has come to me." A hand indicated the chest of treasures. "All this could be yours. Don't shoot, little pigeon. I would have been kind . . ." But then, snatching a revolver from within the chest, he swung it toward her.

It was his last act of treachery. Juliette didn't hesitate as she aimed the pistol's blast directly into his heart.

Hussar gasped as he wordlessly tried to speak, his hands reaching to the wound before crumbling to the dirty floor. His body jumped convulsively, and then ceased.

Tossing the gun away, Juliette stepped over his bulk to rummage through the chest herself and then, more frantically, through the dead man's robes until her searching fingers halted and withdrew the four soiled pages of Anna Phillips's letter.

Deftly she unfolded it, smoothing it flat and staring at the black ink scratches before resolutely striking a match and touching the small flame to a corner.

The yellowed papers browned and curled and flared and she dropped it into a brass basin as the fire traveled quickly over the surface and then enveloped it in a brief burst of flame.

Juliette smiled slowly to herself. Now it was done. She had burned the secret she would never reveal and, without proof of it, the truth could never be more than a rumor. She would let no one hurt this man, let no one change him. He was a renegade, a product of two worlds, an adventurer, a revolutionary, the man she loved—just as he was—Karim al-Sharif, Sheik of El Abadan.

Outside now Juliette was aware of his voice calling her name, deep and unmistakable over the dying sounds of battle.

Rushing to the tent flap she answered, "Karim! Karim!" stretching her neck to see above the press of horses.

She was running then, ducking behind a collapsing tent as a sword struck just behind, "Karim! Karim!"

The sun was a blinding light as sprays of sand and swords and limbs thrashed past. Then she saw him, a path parting as he came.

It was the sound of other, closer, hooves that made her glance over her shoulder in the opposite direction to find three Hussar warriors, swords raised, charging toward Karim.

"Stay down!" Karim commanded as he engaged them, the horses spinning round in thick clouds of dust as the men tried to maneuver Sharif between them. But controlling his stallion with only his knees, Karim stayed out of their trap as he swung his sword at the men and Fadjar lashed out with teeth bared, foam dripping from his mouth.

Juliette screamed as one of the warrior's swords caught Sharif leaving a line of red across his chest.

Because he had concentrated too long on the other warrior, Sharif was taken from his blind side but, wheeling Fadjar, he brought the hilt of his sword under his assailant's chin, knocking him from his horse and under Fadjar's smashing hooves.

Rashid was suddenly there, too, taking his place at Karim's back and quickly dispatching the other warrior with a deft decapitation. Then once more Fadjar was galloping closer and closer, finally drawing alongside her. Then, as he reached down, she leapt up, so in a single sweep of his arm, she was brought to rest across the pommel of his saddle, and Fadjar's huge bounds were speeding them away.

He carried her out of camp before pulling the stallion to a halt with such suddenness Juliette was thrown against him in the manner she had once hated. But now she clung closer, seeing in his face a look she had one day hoped to see, a look free of pretense. His eyes held a penetrating light that saw into the depths of her soul and wanted her with all the power of his man's heart.

"Juliette." His whisper was deep and there was a catch in it for all his casual manner. "Here you are at last, my love."

Elation swept her, giving wings to her being. His touch was the thrill of soaring, the energy of life.

"I thought they would kill you," she began. "I didn't know before . . . not how much I . . ." Tears clouded her vision and emotion surged upward, closing her throat so words became impossible and instead she only buried her face against his bleeding chest in a gesture that said all her words and more.

It was a dream after that, Karim's arms, his kisses, his declarations of love. And later, when the victorious warriors gathered round them, and they headed toward El Abadan, it was a ride of perfect bliss, nestled in the arms of her beloved, the stallion carrying them powerfully over the sand, a warm breeze dancing in the desert twilight and caressing her face like a velvet glove.

Her heart sang. "He loves me! He loves me!" with growing belief and piercing happiness. And hours later, when they rode through the gates of El Abadan, the people were already gathered in the streets to greet them, smiling, cheering, waving as together they rode to the courtyard outside the palace.

EPILOGUE

*Life is made of two parts, that which is past—a dream;
and that which is to come—a wish.*
                                    —Old Arabic Proverb

A southern wind raced across the desert, swirling sand
about the walls and gardens and minarets of El Abadan,
blanketing the city in rippling white, and rising upward to
pelt the windows of its highest tower with the sound of a
thousand tinkling bells.

The tower of El Abadan was an ancient structure, its interior reached only by a spiraling stairway through its center
to a single circular room used for centuries to sight both
caravans and enemies miles beyond the city. But tonight no
guards stood watching at the arching windows, and instead
the room was hung in silk and ornaments of silver and gold
and scattered with pillows colored as brightly as jewels.
The air smelled lightly of perfume and, here and there,
around the bed, white wedding garments lay where they
had been discarded, one by one, in a timeless dance of love.

In a circle of amber lantern light, Juliette and Karim lay
entwined on silken sheets.

"Juliette, my love, my greatest treasure, my wife. How
long I've waited to hold you like this." A long finger traced
a line along her jaw before he pressed a kiss to her mouth,
savoring her petal-soft lips like a man long famished.

With the tips of her fingers, Juliette touched his forehead, the birthmark behind his ear, the crisp hair curling at
his neck, as the heart-shaped ruby ring sparkled on her
slender hand. "We've wasted so much time," she whispered. "How could I have ever thought that I hated you
when now I know I've always loved you. If only I had
married you that first night you asked me, we would have
never hurt one another the way we did."

Karim laughed softly. "But now all the past is behind us,
and tonight the seed of the future will take its life—a
child to stand astride two worlds and conquer them both."

Juliette smiled with joyous eyes. "But it might not be so simple. It might take nights and nights to create such a child."

Karim's eyes shone in the lantern light. "Indeed, nights and nights," he repeated, pulling her pale body tight to his bronzed one. Then, bending, he kissed her with a tender passion that erased any memory of time. And as the wind whirled clouds of sand around the tower of El Abadan, like a cocoon locking away a caterpillar to dream of becoming a butterfly, it was already easy to see that days would come and go before the storm would pass and the city would awaken again.